IT HAD TO BE YOU

It Had To Be You

Timothy James Beck

KENSINGTON BOOKS
http://www.kensingtonbooks.com

KENSINGTON BOOKS are published by

Kensington Publishing Corp.
850 Third Avenue
New York, NY 10022

All Kensington titles, imprints and distributed lines are available at special quantity discounts for bulk purchases for sales promotion, premiums, fund-raising, educational or institutional use.

Special book excerpts or customized printings can also be created to fit specific needs. For details, write or phone the office of the Kensington Special Sales Manager: Kensington Publishing Corp., 850 Third Avenue, New York, NY 10022, Attn. Special Sales Department. Phone: 1-800-221-2647.

Kensington and the K logo Reg. U.S. Pat. & TM Off.

Library of Congress Card Catalogue Number: 2001086910
ISBN 1-57566-889-0

First Printing: October 2001
10 9 8 7 6 5 4 3 2 1

Printed in the United States of America

To you . . . for focus and strength, love and understanding, laughter and fun, inspiration and creative energy, and most of all, for being there.

Acknowledgments

Thanks to Alison Picard for enthusiastically getting the manuscript to Kensington, John Scognamiglio for gifted editing, and Michael Vicencia for providing legal wisdom.

For loving support and encouragement, thanks to Timothy Brand, Michael Brimhall, Jean-Marc Chazy, Dorothy Cochrane, Steve Code, Victoria Harzer, James McCain Jr., Erin Swan, Bill Thomas, Ariel Wilsey-Gopp, and Tom Wocken.

Additional thanks to Dion Bell, the Carter family, Colin Chase, Caroline De La Rosa, Jonathan De Michael, Lynne Demarest, Mark Doty, Ghalib El-Khalidi, Erma and Harrison Forry, Michael Gangemi, the Garber family, Amy Ghiselin, Traci Lamarre, John and Nancy Lambert, the Miller family, Helen C. Morris, Riley Morris, Chad Pascarella, Lori Redfearn, Andy Schell, Terry and Allen Shull, Denece Thibodeaux, Steve Vargas, Ellen Ward, Carissa Williams, Sarena P. Williams, Lisa Yarbrough, Yojo, the boys in Tim's "living room" downstairs, and AOL.

In loving memory: Bill Cochrane, Jeff Crom, Max Gruber, Sarah Landis, John Munsell, Steve Rambo, Tim Rose, and Mary Schreiner.

For unconditional love and the use of your space, thanks Guinness, Lazlo, Margot, Mercutio, Pete, Stevie, and Striker.

ONE

When it was hot outside, I liked to sit on the chair in my garden and melt. The white, metal chair, though directly in the sunlight, felt surprisingly cool in the heat. I tilted my head back and relished the full force of the sun's warmth on my face. I enjoyed waiting to see how long it took before rivers of sweat ran down my forehead and dripped to the concrete under my chair. My friends and neighbors probably thought I was nuts to sit outside in the sunlight and humidity. But I loved my garden.

The garden was relatively small, tucked behind my apartment building on Forty-seventh Street and Eighth Avenue. I wasn't originally going to take the apartment because it seemed too cramped and old after the large two-bedroom I was leaving behind in Chelsea. But when I saw the garden, I knew the apartment was meant to be mine. The garden was just a bare concrete square, as big as my living room, but I knew its potential. I knew I could spend every day here and imagine I was out of the city and in the countryside. Well, a twenty-by-twenty-foot countryside.

The day after I moved in, I constructed planting boxes and schlepped flowerpots from Chelsea to my apartment. Most of my things stayed in moving boxes stacked in towers against the walls while I involved myself in creating my own version of Eden. My weekly manicure was all but forgotten as I grew used to seeing potting soil under my nails. While potting a Japanese maple, I broke a nail then realized I didn't need long nails anymore. I cut them off with the small scissors I used to snip the ends of my spider plant to regenerate growth.

The spider plant wasn't the only thing I hoped would regenerate. I understood that the new apartment, the sudden interest in gardening, sprang from my desire to start over, which had been building for months. Maybe it had been dread of my thirtieth birthday; maybe I just felt like my life was tired. I'd been a creature of the night for so long: the time of stale smells, hungry eyes, dark intentions. Though it had been my job to add sparkle and humor to the night, everything changed the night Diana, Princess of Wales, died in Paris.

There was simply no way I could continue to perform as Princess 2Di4, the Rapping Royal. I could work with bulimia, infidelity, bad in-laws, divorce, and tycoon hunting, but death . . . no. I was heedful of my friend Ken, whose Judy Garland impersonation still prompts occasional hate mail—and Judy's been dead nearly thirty years. Martin, who does a fab-u-lous Duchess of Windsor as a jewel-seeking ghost, agreed with me. Our audience tolerated the Ritas, Marilyns, and Graces only when the impersonations were all visual. For those of us with an act that went beyond looking glamorous and lip-synching, death could kill it.

Timing is everything, and my thirtieth birthday fell on the day of Princess Diana's funeral. My Aunt Jen, who is disdainful of everything royal but the Queen's yapping corgis, sent me a check with the words, "This should cover the basics for a year, Daniel. Toss the tiara and get a life."

So there I was in my garden, contemplating *getting a life* as I surrounded myself with it. I thought to myself, What the hell is that supposed to mean, anyway? *Get a life.*

It was a phrase I had heard most often from the bitchiest of queens who should have been focusing on their own lives instead of doling out their cheap advice to others. The first drop of sweat from my forehead hit the pavement as I considered this.

I was leaving behind the only thing I'd been able to depend on—my alter ego. Who was I expected to become? What was I supposed to do? The thought of not "doing Di," as I always liked to say, was foreign to me. She was such an integral part of me. Yet that need for change beckoned me. If only I could hear the direction from which it was calling.

I got up from the chair in my oasis and went into the apartment. Suddenly I was dying of thirst. As I passed the mirror next to the kitchen, I glanced at myself. Funny. In such a short period of time, was it possible I could have changed that much? There was a quality in my face that was generally reserved for others, something . . . wise. I scoffed at the thought. Me? Wise? Hardly. At thirty years of age and taking checks from Aunt Jen.

Well, maybe that was one of the wiser things I had done lately. I could take her cheap shots about *tossing the tiara.* I'd had worse things said to me. Besides, maybe she was right. It certainly wouldn't be the first time that I had taken her money or her advice.

As I opened the refrigerator, I thought about my high school graduation, when I'd been so desperate to escape from Eau Claire, Wisconsin. I'd felt as if my life were on hold; only my best friend and my older sister knew I was gay. I didn't even consider telling my parents, especially after they told me that the only way we could afford my tuition at the University of Wisconsin was if I lived at home. They wanted me to study business *(that's where the money is, son)* and were appalled when they found my brochures on theatre arts *(where's the future in that?).* The more paperwork I got from Wisconsin, the more trapped I felt. Then Aunt Jen intervened, sounding a bit like Elizabeth's father in *Pride and Prejudice.*

"You have an unpleasant choice to make, Daniel. If you accept your parents' money and go to school here to become some miserable accountant or loan officer, I will be *most* displeased. On the other hand, if you accept my more-than-generous graduation gift for a ticket out of here and your deposit and first month's rent on an apartment anywhere else, your parents will no doubt disown you. You can stay here and be comfortable. Or you can accept my gift with the understanding that it's a one-time offer. I won't underwrite your life elsewhere. It's up to you to make a living. But I will make an investment in your ability to take care of yourself and pursue your dreams."

I'd wasted no time heading for New York and the cheapest gay neighborhood I could find, settling in the East Thirties. My parents didn't disown me, but their disappointment shaded every interaction we'd endured over the past twelve years. When I'd come out to them in a letter only five years before, that disappointment became masked by politeness. They were anxious not to provoke me into discussions about my homosexuality. We painted a pretty picture over any unpleasant or controversial canvas in our home.

Over the years, my father seemed to have forgiven his sister, but my mother maintained a barely civil relationship with Aunt Jen. She'd always thought my aunt was outrageous; in time, she'd probably come to blame her not only for my defection but probably for my orientation. None of this daunted Aunt Jen in the slightest. Divorced three times from men who had made her increasingly wealthy, she exempted herself, and usually me, from anything conventional and certainly from anything boring.

My thoughts were interrupted by a voice from outside. I could barely hear the words, but right away I knew the voice. I poured iced tea into a tall glass salvaged days before from a box marked KITCHEN, then sauntered back out to the garden. The voice was coming from the alley. An iron gate opened from the garden into the alley, which then emptied onto the street.

"Diana! Get your royal ass out here!" Martin screamed.

"Oh, go away," I said, trying not to sound too bitchy. "I'm having a crisis. And don't call me Diana."

"My, my, aren't we sweet? Let me in."

Martin stood on the other side of the gate. His ring-laden fingers clanged against the metal. He didn't look like he was going to move, so I let him in. He strode into the garden with more drama than Bette Davis, sat on a metal chair, and crossed his legs. It was difficult not to notice his well-defined legs. Martin, never one to be shy or modest, wore his daisy dukes like a uniform. His tight blue shirt showed hints of his nipple rings.

"Please don't tell me you're still in mourning, Danny boy."

"More or less, but not for Diana, scorned princess of the House of Windsor."

"Let me guess. You're mourning 2Di4, tired queen of Club Chaos. Am I right?"

"Partially."

I refused to yield to Martin's prodding. He had been at Club Chaos on that night nearly a month before when I ran out after hearing the news of Diana's car crash. I realized everyone at the club must be wondering if I really meant to trade in my rhinestones for a different career. Maybe they'd even sent Martin to interrogate me. But I wasn't ready to voice just how uncertain I was about my future, to Martin or anyone else.

I turned toward the apartment.

"Pour an iced tea for me, would you, dear?" Martin asked.

I walked inside and was caught by the mirror again. I could see the garden behind my reflection in the mirror. The garden's double seemed brighter than the original. I glanced at Martin in the mirror as he lit a cigarette. Martin's left leg bounced on top of his right. I looked at my face again.

I was hardly the starry-eyed, eighteen-year-old boy who had originally moved to Manhattan from Eau Claire twelve years before. Those were the days! I could turn the heads of ten different men just walking down the block to get a paper at the deli. My skin was so smooth and my eyes so blue. Well, despite the few lines around my eyes and mouth, my moisturizer still afforded me smooth skin. And of course, my eyes would always be blue.

I had originally come to Manhattan to start an acting career. Who didn't? However, I thought I would be different. I would charm the pants off of every director and casting agent in the city; after I starred in nearly every production in my high school, everyone at Eau Claire Memorial High thought so, too.

We all thought wrong. Headshots, agents, and an apartment in Manhattan all required money. To have money, you needed a job. I soon got used to the joke: *Oh, you're an actor? Where are you waiting tables?* Eventually, I even got used to rejection as I heard over and over that I wasn't right for nearly every production for the first two years. Others would call those my Salad Days; however, salad cost money and I hardly had any. I called them my Free Meal Days after I bowed to the inevitable cliché and accepted the role of disgruntled waiter. I ate my one free meal from the restaurant and that was about it. Tips from tables were not footing the bill. I was starving. Starving for a good meal and starving for an identity.

I began to rely on my beauty to get me through life. I learned that being a pretty white boy might not win me a Tony, but would earn me a free meal, a night out, and a place in a man's bed. I applied this knowledge in the various bars around Christopher Street and Sheridan Square.

The West Village was a bevy of beautiful men at all hours of the day and night. I would usually stalk the streets after my shift at the restaurant or on my days off. Ignoring men my own age, I'd seek out significant glances from older men. Men who, although perhaps not successful in love, might be successful in their careers, and who would enjoy the company of an attractive young man for dinner or drinks. I needed food, a possible career boost, and most importantly, attention. I wasn't looking to receive money but would politely accept it if the situation arose—a little something for "the cab," or "breakfast, since I have to leave you," or "something expensive you won't buy yourself."

To assuage my guilt at prostituting myself, I pretended I was researching a character. I would even make up names and phony backgrounds when introducing myself to men. I met David, an art gallery owner who took me out to dinner, and told him I was "Mark," a boy from London. I faked an accent and charmed him into several dinner dates. A stockbroker who picked me up in a bar met "Charlie," a farm boy from Arkansas who was new to the city and wanted nothing more than to be shown a ritzy good time.

There were only a scant few occasions when I found myself in trouble. It never occurred to me that I wasn't the only one playing games. I met a man who claimed to be a casting agent for several Broadway shows and I foolishly believed him. He took me out to dinner. He liked my "look" and was interested in representing me. I went to his apartment with him to recite two monologues and found myself pinned down on his bed instead. I was taken by surprise but managed to snatch his clock radio off his nightstand and use it to beat my way free from him.

I called out sick from work the next day, as I was up all night berating myself for being so stupid. Although I was thankful that I hadn't been hurt, I realized how ignorant and green I still was when it came to city living. I'd thought I was the one holding the cards and winning. Although I was being fed, shown a good time, and getting twenty bucks here and there, I was still waiting tables and felt like I was getting nowhere close to being an actor. I knew this had not been what Aunt Jen meant when she urged me to pursue my dreams.

Although I sometimes felt like giving up and going back to Eau Claire, I always reminded myself why I'd left in the first place. There was nothing in Wisconsin for me. New York, with all its drawbacks, made me feel alive. Even when AIDS became a more haunting part of my consciousness, there was a sense that I was part of something bigger, more vital, than I could ever find in Eau Claire, where I'd always felt out of place and repressed. I was wearing Levi's and flannel on the outside, but inside I was just another Madonna wannabe. In Manhattan I was free to be whoever I imagined, because there were hundreds of people doing the same thing.

Which was another problem in and of itself. Not only were there thousands of gay men seeking refuge in a city where there was safety in numbers, it seemed there were just as many actors seeking center stage. I sometimes felt trapped in a vicious cycle, but my determination to succeed and not to disappoint Aunt Jen always won over retreating to the bleakness of life in Eau Claire.

A night came when I found myself in another bar accepting a free beer from a man I wasn't even attracted to. I nodded a thank-you to him and my throat constricted as I swallowed. This wasn't how it was supposed to be. I wanted friends, not strangers. I wanted a lover, not another one-night stand. I wanted to act, not act happy to serve blue plate specials. I diverted my gaze from the unhandsome stranger to a woman who was entering the bar.

She looked like a Tina Turner wannabe. Her black leather mini clung to her tiny hips and sat atop long, slender legs encased in fishnets. A wide-necked sweater exposed one bony cocoa shoulder. As she stepped toward the bar on high-heeled ankle boots, I noticed how tall she was. Was it her teased, shaggy hair that made her tower over everyone else? That seemed to be part of it, but she was really tall. Maybe taller than I was.

Do lesbians come to this bar, too, I wondered.

She stood at the bar, two stools away. She had on thick makeup, and I revised my opinion. She was more like the Pointer Sisters than Tina Turner. She turned and caught me staring while she took a silver cigarette case from her purse. I quickly looked away, not used to lesbians and not wanting a confrontation, but she walked over to me.

"Got a light for a girl with no flame?" she asked coyly. Her voice was kind of deep and scratchy.

"Uh, yeah." I took a book of matches from my jacket pocket.

It wasn't until I held the burning match to her cigarette that I got a look at her hands. They were quite large. I looked up into her eyes as she puffed the cigarette to life, and she winked at me.

"Thanks," she whispered in a breath of smoke. I tried not to gape at the wad of money she took from her purse and tucked into her bra. She turned to the bartender. "Tony, stash my purse?"

"Yeah," Tony said. He took it and stowed it behind the bar.

"What's your name?"

"Daniel," I answered, once I realized she was speaking to me again.

"Daniel. I like that name. I knew a boy named Daniel a long time ago. Knew him very well," she said with a laugh that dripped innuendo. "You new around here?"

"Kinda," I said.

"That won't last long. You look like a country boy on the outside, but I can see in your eyes you're becoming a New Yorker already. You've got that lost and lonely thing going on, but don't worry"—she raised one heavily drawn eyebrow and her red lips curled in a wicked smile—"the boys like that lost and lonely look. Don'tcha, Burt?"

She swung around and directed her booming voice to the man who'd bought me the beer. His face took on a disgusted look. He slugged back his beer and dropped some money on the bar.

"Oh come on, Burt," she laughed. "Isn't this child just divine? He's really pretty. And fresh. What's the matter?"

"Freak," Burt hissed as he walked by us. "You guys embarrass me. You give gays a bad name."

"Oh Burt! You don't mean that! Burt!" she called to him as he left the bar in a huff.

"Wanda, I've told you to leave Burt alone!" Tony scolded.

"Oh Tony, I'm just having some fun," Wanda replied as she contained her laughter. "Stoli on the rocks and"—she wrinkled her nose at my beer—"whatever young Daniel wants. By the by, I'm Wanda."

I shook her extended hand. First contact. Her eyes danced as she watched realization flood my face.

"You used to be a man," I sputtered.

"I'm still a man, honey," she said.

"You're a drag queen?" I asked, remembering all the warnings I'd ever heard in Eau Claire about the tragic fate of men who wanted to be women.

"I defy definition." She spun me on my stool until I faced the door. "Now there, young Daniel, there you see drag queens."

A line of women had come into the bar, holding on to each other as they swayed and shimmied their way around. They were an explosion of teased hair, Barbra Streisand nails, and a million sequins.

It was as if someone had flipped a switch. The lights dimmed and spotlights began hitting the mirrored disco balls on the ceiling. The room was awash in dark color and fragmented light. I realized boys were pouring into the bar and crowding the dance floor. The mood in the bar lifted to the sounds of Gloria Gaynor and the shouts of men trying to be heard by the people next to them. All the while, the drag queens moved to applause and whistles. They wore their confidence and beauty like they wore their falsies—right up front and going nowhere.

I stared in disbelief as Tony helped several of them onto the bar. They steadied themselves on their high heels and tucked everything in place before starting what appeared to be a well-choreographed dance. As they got used to the limited dimensions of the bar, their movements became more chaotic and frenzied.

"They're all *men*," I said stupidly and heard Wanda's throaty laugh.

"You *are* green," she commented, but her voice was a caress.

I turned to look at her and said, "I don't get it. Why would men want to look like women?"

She just laughed again and patted her stash of money.

I turned back to my beer and was startled by a pair of enormous acid green patent pumps kicking and stepping on the bar in front of me. My gaze traveled up legs encased in darker green fishnets. I grabbed my beer, fearful it would be kicked into my lap, then looked up into the eyes of the drag queen dancing in front of me.

She smiled at me and seemed to bask in the knowledge that one more person in the bar noticed her. She shook her groove thing even harder (*yeah yeah*) and showed us all how to do it now. I suddenly found myself grinning at her, swaying on my barstool along with the rhythm of old disco. For the first time, the power of the drag queen dawned on me—the tenacity involved, the sustained self-confidence they all carried. And to top it off, it was an act, one which, judging from the enthusiasm of the crowd, everyone loved.

An act . . . I glanced at Wanda's bra. An act that made money . . .

The next day I gave two weeks' notice to the restaurant and was promptly fired. Lesson learned. I found a job barbacking in a place where there were drag performers. Night after night I took every available opportunity to watch them and learn from their acts. They not only had to be good enough to make money for themselves, they had to make money for the bars. They either pumped up the energy level, making people drink more, or gave entertaining shows that brought in crowds. After a month of Drag 101, I decided I was ready to strike out on my own.

I bought cheap dresses, pumps, and wigs, made myself up as Penny Dime, and lip-synched to "Second Hand Rose" at every drag bar I could work. After a while they let me do more songs and a longer act. I moved to Pyramid and made more money as Go Go Drag Queen in better and flashier outfits. Eventually I worked my way through every club and bar in the East and West Village until I found myself a cult favorite as Princess 2Di4.

Unlike most of the vicious queens spinning their wheels in the great drag race to be seen and heard, I stayed true to my Midwestern upbringing. Most queens revised their value systems the moment their drag personas were born. They evolved into the razor-tongued, fighting divas they portrayed onstage. I was known for my big heart, open ear, and caring soul. Nearly everyone thought it was part of my act, but they were mistaken. I wasn't about to be walked over by four-inch stilettos and learned to hold my own in the den of queens, but I would not let it harden me and make me surrender to the concrete jungle.

As I stared now at the mirror, I brushed a lock of fine, blond hair from my forehead and looked right into my crystal blue eyes—Diana's eyes. I also had the same kind and delicate features as Diana, though more boyish on my part. Sometimes I didn't know where she ended and I began; over the years, young Daniel from Eau Claire became lost in an endless cycle of club life.

Until I walked out.

My garden became the perfect remedy, giving me time to separate myself from it all. It was like therapy, with Daniel from the days of yore leading the session. I was weeding out the repetitive falseness I'd acquired over the years and replanting the dreams I'd had when I arrived in Manhattan. I smiled wanly at myself in the mirror and wondered—

"Who's that pretty boy in the mirror there?" Martin's nagging song snapped me out of my reverie. "Shouldn't he be bringing me iced tea?"

"I gave up waiting tables years ago, Martin," I growled as I made my way into the kitchen. I took the pitcher of iced tea from the refrigerator and poured some into a champagne flute, the only other glass I'd unpacked since my big move. This time I ignored the mirror on my way out.

"Nice touch, Di–uh–Daniel," Martin said. "Why you ever moved into Hell's Kitchen is beyond me. I can't believe you left Chelsea for all . . . this," he added with a wave of his wrist and not an ounce of hidden disdain. He sounded like Aunt Jen. "And I would think a Nebraska boy—"

"Wisconsin," I interrupted.

"Whatever, would know not to plant in the fall. Fall is for harvesting. You're backwards."

It suddenly clicked for me what was wrong with Martin, why he resisted my efforts to change. He had taken his duchess beyond the grave, giving her the power and iron will of the woman who'd caused a king to forfeit his throne. If I let Princess 2Di4 die with Diana, it was a rejection of Martin's choice, maybe even a rejection of Martin. How could I explain that moving on—to a new career, a new apartment, a new life—did not negate all he held dear. Especially when I wasn't so sure it did not.

"What?" Martin asked suspiciously as I gave him a speculative look.

"Well, you tell me," I said. "What do I do with a lyric like 'I'm not anemic/I'm just bulimic/have you tasted our cuisine/fit for a queen/maybe, I guess/but it is not for this princess'? They're having fights in bars over Diana jokes. I'd be crucified now."

He rolled his eyes and said, "So you change your act, not your life. You *are* the one, are you not, who always says your act is *not* your life? Evolve, Daniel."

"Saved by the bell," I muttered as the phone rang.

"Oh god, you bought a cordless phone so you wouldn't have to leave your garden to talk?" Martin asked with an exasperated look. "Should I start calling you Chance?"

I answered the phone, ignoring his reference to an obscure Peter Sellers movie in which the actor played a mentally deficient gardener.

I had to hold the receiver away from my ear because of Andy's shrieking. Martin uncrossed his legs and stopped slouching as he recognized the voice of the owner of Club Chaos, one of the sleaziest men we knew.

"... so if you're really *determined* not to come back," Andy screamed, "I have the most *amazing* proposition."

Martin lit a cigarette and leered at me as I shuddered.

"Di raised all that money selling those gowns of hers . . . did you *hear* that some of them were a size fourteen? And so I thought, why not do the same for your tacky imitations here at the club? The *last* public appearance of Princess 2Di4, auctioning her frocks for some charity or other. God knows *everyone* is always demanding to use this place for some *dreary* benefit. What a *marvelous* way to raise money, give you a *spectacular* exit—"

"And free publicity for him," Martin muttered.

"Besides," Andy continued, "if you really *are* serious about not coming back, which *no one* believes for a second, darling . . . well, what*ever* are you going to do with those gowns? Lord *knows* you're not going to be *gardening* in them."

I'd had about all I could take from this idiot. I could tell Martin was getting somewhat anxious to see if this would be what pushed me over the edge. He was leaning forward, chin in hands, elbows on legs, just waiting for me to explode. He should have known better.

"Andy, darling," I replied calmly, " I have company. I'll have to get back to you."

I hung up the phone without waiting for a response.

"That's it?" Martin asked, with a slight edge to his voice. *"I'll have to get back to you?* That scumbag calls and has the audacity to ask you to auction your 'frocks' knowing the state of mind you must be in?"

I couldn't help but feel Martin was trying to goad me in much the same way Andy wanted to. The look in his eyes was sincere, yet there was something surreal about this whole afternoon. I was halfway expecting the phone to ring only to have Nancy Reagan invite me to tea with Leona Helmsley. I felt strangely detached from the whole situation, even from Martin at that moment.

Martin looked at me carefully and planted both feet firmly on the ground, as if to get up.

"Danny boy? Are you all right?" His eyes had a sudden look of concern, and it frightened me. I had never seen him look like that. Martin was generally so engrossed in his own life that to see him visibly concerned about another person only added to the surrealism of the day.

I looked back at him and my mouth opened but nothing came out.

How odd, I thought, that I have an audience of one with a man I've held so dear to my heart for so long, and I've forgotten all my lines.

I needed to work in my garden, my comfort zone. I wanted to touch the fresh living things around me as I tried to figure out how to go on. In my troubled daze, I wandered to the edge of my Eden, hardly noticing as Martin followed me to gracefully land on the concrete in a Betty Grable–like pose.

Wait, I suddenly thought. Martin, always fastidious, on the *ground?*

It was a combination of the bright sunlight and the shock of this stranger sitting in my garden. It was a realization as timely as any. At that moment I no longer had the urge to be derisive with Martin, which was always my natural reaction; he could be antagonistic toward an innocent school girl. Instead, just then, maybe it was the lighting, he looked like a brilliant answer. Energy that had been static, stagnant, welled up as he put his hand around my wrist and pulled me down beside him. His tenderness was new to me. I sat on the hot concrete, not minding. The warmth was comforting, as was his lap, where I put my head.

Martin was five years my junior, but told everyone he was twenty-two. He justified that number when I met him years before.

"See," he'd explained, "twenty-two is such a great age. It sounds more *adult* than twenty-one, but younger than twenty-three. Older men don't want to waste time on anyone under twenty-one, right?"

I, being an *older man*, had apprehensively agreed. Martin had remained twenty-two years old ever since.

I first met him when he sheepishly came into Club Chaos one rainy Saturday during rehearsal for a variety show the club was hosting. The event would debut the night before Gay Pride Day, and we were one week before show time. I was emceeing the opening night, of course, and Ken, as Judy, would host the remaining shows through the weekend. Princess 2Di4 was lending her talent at a number of clubs and bars all week.

Martin walked far enough into the club to be seen, but just enough off to the side to be in the shadows.

"Princess, *Princess,* I'm *so* sorry, but the dancers fucked up *again,"* Andy was shrieking. "Ken, would you lead them through their paces *once more?* And who the *fuck* are you?"

Andy whirled around and pointed a bony finger at Martin.

Martin's face took on the appearance of a doe in headlights as he looked carefully around him to see if someone else was being pointed at. Nobody was near him, however, so he put his hand on his chest in a *who me?* gesture.

"Yes, *you!"* barked an exasperated Andy. "This is a *closed* rehearsal. The club will open at *eight. Please* leave and come back later."

I suppressed a giggle, since it was unlike Andy to add "please" to any sentence.

"Um, well, I was actually hoping to audition for—are you the owner or manager of this place?" Martin asked.

"My child, I am *both.* And what do *you* think you can add to our little family?"

Those were the days when Andy was fond of referring to employees of Club Chaos as members of his *little family.* Little did he know that most of us called him the "Wicked Step-Monster," "Auntie Shame," "Miss Harridan," or even "Mother Miserable" behind his back.

"Play this tape and we'll see," Martin suggested.

After Andy plucked the tape from his hand and passed it to Bernie/Bernice, our sound man/woman (he was in the midst of "the change"), I checked out Martin as he took my place center stage. He was dressed casually in blue jeans and a color-blocked polo shirt. It was obvious he was from out of town, as no self-respecting gay boy from Manhattan would be caught dead in that outfit. I shuddered as his brown moccasins registered, and shot a meaningful look toward Ken, but Ken's own expression was intently focused on Martin as we waited for him to begin.

The song was Stevie Nicks's "Edge of Seventeen," and Martin lip-synched it with Stevie's own zeal. He whirled, twirled, and danced like a possessed ballerina.

By the middle of his audition, I had ducked backstage and returned bearing two large, lacy black shawls. I dashed to Martin, tying one around his waist and draping the other around his shoulders. As I raced back to the side of the stage, Ken passed me carrying a long, dirty blond wig, which he plopped on Martin's head. Now looking vaguely reminiscent of the Gypsy Diva herself, Martin gave the audition all that he had, not in the least nonplused by our interference.

As the last *oooh baby* faded away, Martin ended on pointe with his arms stretched out as if to soar away like the white-winged dove in the song.

We all erupted into applause, screams, and wolf whistles from backstage. Everyone poured onstage and shook Martin's hand, rubbed his shoulders, or patted his butt. Andy stood in the audience looking at Martin as if he were a pet brought home by a small child; part exasperation, part fascination.

"Can we keep him, Auntie Andy?" Ken begged, using one of the few names we called him to his face.

"Who *are* you?" Andy grimly asked.

"Martin," he answered, looking apprehensive but hopeful.

"Well," Andy said, "you need a *lot* of work, but you move *very* well and you're *good looking*. I haven't seen anyone who *looks good* walk in here since the day the *princess* strolled in pretending I wasn't being *set up.*"

He gave Ken a piercing look and Ken said, "I swear, I've never seen this one before!"

Martin looked confused so I introduced myself to him and explained that Ken had helped me get my start. Andy always suspected conspiracy when confronted with any act he himself hadn't "discovered."

"We'll use you in 'The Baths' number," Andy was saying. He gave Martin's clothes the once-over as Martin removed the shawls. "Do you even *know* Bette Midler?"

"Well, not really, but my friend Soph says I sound just like her," Martin said in a perfect Bette imitation.

"Then it's settled," Andy muttered. "Now, dancers, perhaps you can *rehearse* before I'm totally *ruined?*"

Ken and I befriended Martin and learned he was from Connecticut. He'd dropped out of the School of American Ballet a month earlier. His dismayed parents stopped his funds, certain they could force him to return home. Having been ejected from the dorms at Lincoln Center, Martin took up stripping at one of the seedy lounges in Times Square and moved to the Village. One of the other performers at the strip club told him about Club Chaos, so Martin donned his "Innocent School Boy" outfit (he wore it anytime he wanted to appear to be a hick and then impress the hell out of someone) and armed himself with his favorite Stevie Nicks song.

Martin's quick wit and ability to have fun endeared him to all of us. His Bette Midler impressions lured an audience that became regulars, so Andy was happy. A year later, Ken and I made up Martin as Wallis Warfield Simpson, the bejeweled Duchess of Windsor. This was meant to be a one-time appearance, with Martin playing an older, wiser royal outsider who could advise 2Di4. But she was such a hit that Andy gave Martin a slot before mine, as a lead-in for my act, and the Bette Midler torch was passed to the next talented newcomer.

Through the years, Martin's off-the-wall advice and knack for getting the story about anyone became a regular part of my life. He was forever ringing my doorbell, keeping me out for hours after our performances, or calling me with the latest gossip. Even though his excessiveness sometimes got on my nerves, I couldn't imagine life without him. He was his own brilliant invention and, to this day, vehemently denied ever owning a polo shirt and moccasins.

Now he was lulling me into the most comfortable sense of security as he stroked the back of my head, saying, "Danny, Danny, Danny. I never thought you had it in you."

His voice was soft but it still had the hint of a queen's razor tongue. I didn't think it was intentional; it was the result of years of training to be a diva. I looked up at him and he smiled down at me. I didn't understand where all of this emotion was coming from. In the garden, things were growing: Was Eden ever so fertile to allow an old friendship to grow new leaves? I was pleased by my poetic train of thought.

"What?" I asked. "Had what in me?"

"I just never thought you would have a blues act," Martin laughed and looked up at the sky. "I can see it now . . . Nina B. Moan. You'll get onstage with your nappy hair and a rumpled sequined gown with a vodka in your hand, singing 'I Won't Be Comin' to Your Door.' "

"Martin, that sounds more like Jeremy drama," I said.

He raised an eyebrow and looked at me inquisitively. I think he noted the slightly acidic tone in my voice.

"Are you still bitter about that two-timing, wilted, parasitic little slut?"

"No, of course not."

"Well, you have every right to be, but that isn't what this mood is about."

"Martin, I don't know what to do with my life. The act is old—dead, in fact."

I was feeling a bit better with my cheek against the warm skin of Martin's leg.

"Okay, Princess Diana is dead, the act may be dead, but you certainly aren't," Martin said. "You're hardly thirty and— 'But soft, what light through yonder window doth approacheth?' "

I didn't know if it were the sudden change in subjects or the badly quoted Shakespeare, but in my confusion, the urge to slap Martin returned. Things were getting back to normal. I sat up and followed Martin's lurid gaze across the garden and into the window of the building on the other side of the gate.

My handsome stud of a neighbor was home. I quickly looked at my watch.

"Five thirty-three," I mumbled.

He was undoing the knot of his tie and talking on the phone. Every day he returned from whatever job it was that drove him in a suit and tie from his apartment until this time each evening.

He looked like he was my age, short dark hair in the classic Ken doll cut, with a strong jaw and full lips. I couldn't see what color his eyes were or how tall he was, but I didn't have to. He was the sort of man whose upper half seen in a window is enough to go on . . . to know that if he took you in those strong arms, you'd never want him to let go. Unless, of course, he let go in order to unbutton his shirt.

"I never would've put down Hell's Kitchen if I'd known the scenery was this lovely," Martin purred. I almost expected rivers of drool to start sliding down his chin. "Why didn't you tell me about this . . . this . . . god who lives across the way?"

"I've never seen him before in my life," I lied.

I didn't want Martin to know that for the three weeks I'd lived here, I'd spent half my time planning and planting the garden and the other half learning this heavenly man's schedule.

I'd first noticed my neighbor while planting asparagus ferns in the boxes on either side of the gate. Just as I stopped to wipe the sweat from my brow, I happened to glance up and see the most gorgeous man leaning from a window. Like any good city boy, I quickly averted my eyes and resumed my planting. My heart was racing.

After counting to one hundred, I looked up again. He was standing in front of the window, removing his tie. He didn't seem to be looking my way so I let my gaze linger. I watched as he slowly unbuttoned and removed his shirt. He stayed in the window as he picked up the phone and began a conversation with some lucky person in his life. After a few minutes, he strolled deeper into the apartment, out of my view. I chose that moment to go inside my own apartment to take care of some urgent . . . urges.

This became my routine every weekday at five-thirty, but I had no intention of sharing that information with Martin. It wasn't that I didn't want him to think I was wasting my time pining for this man, or that I was some deranged stalker; it was more like I was a teenager caught coming home past curfew. Instinctive lying. It came out of my mouth before I knew I'd said it. Besides, if Martin did know the truth, that I was as fascinated and turned on by this stranger as he was, it would be all around the city on the Daniel News Network, with Martin at the anchor desk announcing the late breaking "facts."

"So, what were you saying about me not being dead yet?" I asked, trying to divert Martin's attention from my neighbor.

"I forget. You know I'm not good at all that spirit-lifting stuff," Martin said, never taking his eyes from the window. "That's your department. Just do what you think you'd advise me to do if I were in your shoes."

"You'd probably return them," I sighed.

"Yes, return them," he agreed, obviously having lost the thread of our conversation.

"Probably too tight for your size twelve feet anyway," I added softly, knowing Martin prided himself on squeezing his shapely nines into an eight and a half.

"Tight, yes, of course. The tighter the better."

His fascination drove my gaze back to the window, at which point I became as lost as Martin.

Five Thirty-three was still on the phone, but he'd unbuttoned his shirt and was absently running an ice cube from the hollow of his throat down that flawless valley between his pecs.

"Oh . . . my . . . god," Martin said. "Let me be his ice cube. Help me; I'm melting."

"Oh please, he's so obvious," I said, knowing my voice lacked all conviction.

Not that it mattered. I could have stripped naked and done an Ethel Merman medley without engaging Martin's interest.

"What does a man do," Martin mused, "to make himself look like that?"

The first part of his sentence shrieked through my mind like a siren. That was it. Of course. How had I missed such an obvious sign? I was looking for a new career. A minimal amount of friendly surveillance could lead me right into Five Thirty-three's territory. I might find my new career and my future boyfriend in the same place!

I had to keep the excitement from my face as I watched Five Thirty-three. In fact, I knew it would be best if I didn't look at Five Thirty-three. Martin could never know what I was up to; this was exactly the kind of furtive activity he would aid and abet until he abetted it to death. And my plans for Five Thirty-three had nothing to do with Martin.

TWO

I woke up early the next morning with a new outlook. A mission. But where to begin, I wondered. The prospect of a new beginning excited and frightened me. I had never been a member of the corporate club and really didn't know the rules of that game. Still, they couldn't be all that different from the rules of the game I'd spent the last years playing. Surely if I could climb to the top of a pile of lip-synching drag queens, it wouldn't be that much trouble finding a place as somebody's Miss Hathaway. I smirked as I pictured myself in the Jane Fonda role in *Nine to Five,* doing battle with the Xerox machine.

I rummaged through my closet. What does one wear to find a *real* job, I wondered. Certainly none of my costumes would be appropriate, yet I could hardly wear my gardening attire. It seemed obvious; my only real choice involved Barneys and a bit of Aunt Jen's money.

Hold it, Daniel; aren't you jumping the gun a little bit? my inner voice inquired. Shouldn't you find out where Five Thirty-three resides when not in his apartment?

How tough can it be to follow a guy to Wall Street? I answered the voice.

I jumped as the phone rang, startling me out of my fantasy of following Five Thirty-three, ducking behind buildings wearing a pair of oversized Liz Claiborne sunglasses. I walked to the phone and picked it up after waiting for the third ring. Old habit.

"Hello?"

"Good morning, princess."

I froze. Jeremy. His voice made my heart jump in my chest.

Stop it, Daniel, I commanded myself.

"Jeremy. To what do I owe the honor? You must need something."

"Oh, c'mon, princess. I can't pick up the phone and just say hello to my shining star?"

I rolled my eyes, wondering if Martin could have told him about the check from Aunt Jen.

"Well, yes, I suppose you could, but that really isn't your style now, is it, Jeremy?"

"Okay, princess. Point for you. But you'll never guess who I ran into last night."

"Depends. Were you driving?"

Jeremy laughed.

"No, darling. I saw Andy. He said you and he had come up with the most marvelous idea. You're doing a farewell auction of your gowns for some charity or other? I think it's wonderful. I think *you're* wonderful."

What a crock, I thought, as I rolled my eyes again.

"Jeremy. Why are you really calling me? What do you want?"

"Danny, you're being redundant." I was surprised he knew what that word meant. Jeremy remained silent long enough for me to escape to the garden. I grabbed my Yankees baseball cap on the way out to hide the mess of morning hair on the off chance that Five Thirty-three would be gazing from his window. "I want you to meet me. What time is it now?"

"It's nine-thirty in the morning, Jeremy."

"Okay, be here at eleven."

"Jeremy, I am *not* coming to your boyfriend's apartment. You have no sense of common decency, do you?"

"Not an ounce, dear. It's my apartment, too, but fine. Eleven o'-clock at The Big Cup."

"Shall I bring my checkbook?"

"Redundant," Jeremy said in a singsong voice.

"I'll see you at eleven. 'Bye Jeremy."

"See you later. Big kiss." He made a wretched kissing noise before hanging up, imagining he was Auntie Mame, no doubt.

Why I let Jeremy get to me was beyond my comprehension. Behind his shining, dimpled exterior lurked a scheming phantom. Jeremy could be smart; it was a mistake to be fooled by his blond hair and Spartacus body. I'd immediately recognized his potential for genius, which was why I was originally drawn to him. Or maybe it was only humiliated, squirming hindsight that persuaded me I hadn't been taken in by mere good looks. He was incredibly handsome . . .

In the months since our breakup, I'd viewed my relationship with Jeremy through a bitter lens. It was hard to keep the sour emotions at bay when I felt so hurt, especially because he was the first man I'd trusted enough to share a relationship that lasted more than two weeks. I had been in it for the long haul. Before Jeremy, I'd never wanted a committed relationship. I had friends for emotional support and never lacked for sex.

When Ken first introduced me to Jeremy on one of the nights Club Chaos was closed, I was immediately attracted by his good looks. He was charming and seemed almost innocent, untouched by the sometimes cruel dating world. I felt awkward in a good way; my jaws seemed to be frozen shut. I could barely utter a first word to him, my heart pounding. He made it easy for me by saying hello first. In an odd way, it was the fact that he took control of the situation that initially made me interested in more than just one night of sex, or one week of intense, but fleeting, emotions. In that first minute I imagined our relationship and what he was like or, more importantly, what he would be like within the relationship. What I imagined, of course, was far different from the eventual outcome.

Our first date began at the moment we met. Ken somehow disappeared from the picture. I don't think either Jeremy or I noticed when Ken left. We decided to go out to eat and later go dancing. Over dinner the conversation was easy. We discussed musicals and plays, finding we had similar tastes but different views, which kept things interesting. Jeremy seemed enthralled by the stories I told him about my adventures as the princess. I was equally entranced by his stories about his half-year-long, coast-to-coast trip. He surprised me. I hadn't pictured this rather dandy character as being the outdoor type, but he had gone mountain climbing on difficult terrain, hiked through deserts, and gone fishing in arctic climates.

We clicked. It was simple and easy. I never thought there would be a question of fidelity or secrets. We moved in together after only a few weeks. At first we had no problems. We even took a wonderful vacation to Oregon, where I think I really fell in love with him.

I thought I hurt so much now because I was still a little attached to Jeremy, even after all that had happened and the time that had passed. I resented the fact that I still felt this way; being bitter and spiteful were my ways of getting over it.

I still had the phone against my ear when I came out of my reverie. I saw a few weeds sprouting at the roots of my gardenias. I knelt on the concrete, which was just beginning to warm up beneath the rays of sun. I tugged on the soft shaft of an unwelcome dandelion which had not yet shown its yellow face. It pulled from the soil easily.

I glanced up and saw Five Thirty-three stretching at his window. I wondered why he wasn't at work. His arms were above his head, causing his white shirt to rise and open over his stomach.

"Good morning," I said aloud, as much to myself as to him.

Five Thirty-three lowered his arms and his face. He caught me.

There was no turning back. I did not avert my eyes. Neither did he. My heart thumped, my face flushed, and my cock, beyond all limits of control, became attentive and excited. Five Thirty-three smiled and turned away from his window.

I could still see his right arm. Someone in blue moved behind him. I couldn't tell if it was a man or a woman, but just knowing he wasn't alone discouraged me. I stood and made my way back into the apartment to shower and change. Since Five Thirty-three had a companion, I might as well meet Jeremy at The Big Cup, which he affectionately referred to as *the buffet*. I preferred the more scathing nickname: Big Slut.

The cab dropped me on the corner of Twenty-third Street. Ah yes, the boys were out and about in their wife-beaters and short-shorts. Eighth Avenue bubbled with sexual tension to the breaking point. The unspoken rule of Eighth Avenue was that you must surrender shyness and tact at the door. Sex was immediate and non-negotiable—it was everywhere, refusing to be silenced. I played the part well enough; living in Chelsea had taught me the rules of the game. Look hot and act cool—desirable, but untouchable.

My tight V-neck glimmered green in the sun, highlighting my chest and accentuating the roundness of my biceps. My shorts conformed to my hips and ass. I crossed the avenue aware of the eyes all around me; there was no pretense of minding one's own affairs. I locked gazes with young men every three feet and looked over my shoulder, before entering The Big Cup café, at a short bodybuilder talking on the phone. He smiled and raised his eyebrows then resumed his conversation.

I walked in and heads turned. Gregory, the "bartender," greeted me with a smile.

"Well, well, it looks like royalty is once again descending on her loyal subjects."

"Hello, Gregory." I leaned over the counter and pecked him on the cheeks. He was one of the few people I missed in Chelsea. "I'd like an iced mocha."

"For you, princess, anything."

Gregory turned to fix my drink and I saw Jeremy sitting on the pink sofa by the wall. A few boys milled around eyeing him but quickly walked away when they saw that Jeremy and I were gazing hard at one another. I felt a bit shaky but hid it with my natural grace. I took my mocha from the counter and walked across the café to where Jeremy sat.

My mind was racing with reasons why Jeremy would want to see me as I made my way through the occupied chairs and tables in the crowded café. I couldn't think of one credible reason and tried to mask my nervousness as I sank into the space on the couch he had reserved for me next to him.

"Welcome to my court, princess," Jeremy said. I rolled my eyes at his banal attempt at a joke. It seemed I would never shed the princess role I'd created for myself. For this moment, however, I would need it.

I calmly sipped at my iced mocha, taking in its cold bitterness and mingling it with my own.

Wait; was my hand shaking?

"So, what did you want to talk about? Did you find something of mine you didn't know you had? Or would you just sell it, like you did my CD collection?" I taunted.

"Oh my god, it was ten CDs and you told me years ago you were tired of them." He took a deep breath. "Dan," he continued, knowing I hated being called that, "can we dispense with the disparaging remarks and sarcasm? It's not going to solve anything."

Dispense? Disparaging? I didn't even think he knew how to spell those words, let alone use them in a complete sentence. Maybe he was finally up to the D section in the dictionary.

"I'll try," I said in my most placating tone of voice. "It would behoove us both to do so."

"What?"

"I thought so. Nothing." I smiled. "Go on, you were telling me why you wanted to see me."

"Well, as you know, I'm with Robert now. I've moved on and I'm concerned that you haven't done the same. So is Robert. He and I are in a production of *Anything Goes*, which opens next week. We were both wondering if you would like two tickets for opening night. You could bring someone, and maybe we could all go out together for drinks afterward, or something," he explained.

I almost spewed my iced mocha through my nose.

We had been a very good-looking couple. The actor and the drag princess. Jeremy was one of the few men who was neither turned off nor turned on by my dual life, merely accepting impersonation as the work I did. Most of our friends saw us as the ideal pair. Jeremy ruined all that by sleeping with Robert Orso after he joined the cast of *Guys and Dolls* the previous May.

Robert had replaced one of the gamblers, Nicely Nicely Johnson, and forged a friendship with Jeremy. They would meet to run lines and I would find myself helping, listening afterward when the conversation became real life and not just lines being fired back and forth. I was unaware how personal that friendship became as I, eager to support Jeremy in every way, also befriended Robert. Little did I know the only dance steps they rehearsed when I wasn't around were the old "Mattress Mambo." I was just as shocked by Robert, who I thought had become a real friend, as I was by Jeremy.

I was often with the two of them, since I joined Jeremy at Robert's apartment many nights after my club gig to watch them rehearse dance steps, songs, and lines together. I would find myself laughing along with them when they flubbed those same steps, songs, and lines. Although I had a successful career in nightclubs, I couldn't deny that spending time with Robert and Jeremy as they worked filled a void I felt for the theater. I would pretend I was a stage manager as they called for me to prompt their lines.

One afternoon Robert came by Club Chaos while I was rehearsing a song for my own act that Ken had written for me.

"Robert, hi," I said, surprised. "Hang on a second. I need water. Do you want any?"

"No. No. I'm fine," he said, tentatively following me into my dressing room and staring at the various flyers and photographs from my shows that adorned the walls.

"I've been practicing a new song that I'm doing tonight, so my pipes are rusty," I said. "Are you looking for Jeremy? I thought he was rehearsing with you at the theater today."

"No. I mean, yeah, he's at the theater, but they weren't doing any of my scenes, so I'm off today. I just came by to see if you wanted to go to a movie."

"Oh, that's sweet," I said, moving some dresses so Robert could sit on an ancient, overstuffed chair. I perched on a stool at my vanity table. "I'd love to, but I don't have time. And I have to eat."

"Surely one with a figure as lovely as yours does not eat!" a mock-shocked Robert gasped.

"Yes. One does," I said. "And stop calling me Shirley."

"You stole that from Jeremy."

"And he stole it from everyone else. Want to have dinner with me? I'm serving Mama Stephenson's Green Bean Casserole. Via the microwave."

"Made with cream of mushroom or cream of chicken?"

"Cream of chicken, of course."

"Then I accept," Robert said, rising from the couch and performing a courtly bow.

I served up the casserole and he served up the easiest conversation I'd had in a long time. He talked about a used bookstore that he'd found earlier that day in the East Village and the Mark Twain book he purchased. Which led us to a discussion of our favorite books. Then we talked about our favorite movies made from books. Robert never once brought up the theater or club life, which I found very refreshing as neither my nor Jeremy's friends talked about anything else.

It was the start of a friendship with Robert without the necessity of Jeremy's presence. Jeremy was a lead and Robert a supporting character, so he wasn't in rehearsals quite as much as Jeremy. He would often meet me for lunch or dinner before my shows, and sometimes we'd take in a movie. Robert was very easy to talk to and was also quite witty. Even Martin, who barely tolerated Jeremy, seemed to enjoy his chance encounters with Robert at Club Chaos.

From time to time I considered fixing them up, but as that rarely worked out when I tried it, I figured I'd let any possible relationship between them progress at its own pace without my assistance.

Once *Guys and Dolls* opened, Robert's visits slowed down as his schedule and Jeremy's became slaves to the demands of the theater. I had my own performances at Club Chaos and saw less and less of both of them.

During a time of the earth's rebirth from the frozen winter, it was the spring of my discontent. I heard from Ken that it was reported from Martin that Jeremy and Robert were seen kissing at the Duplex. Our entire crowd was abuzz with rumors: Was it true? Were we breaking up? Inquiring minds wanted to know. I gave Ken carte blanche to share the news as he saw fit: Yes, we were breaking up. I didn't even have to ask Jeremy if the rumors were true. I could smell Robert's signature scent, Eternity, in Jeremy's hair that night in June when he finally came to bed after a performance of *Guys and Dolls*. The next morning I interrogated him thoroughly and he did not deny their affair. He was not that good of an actor. A week later he left me for Robert.

It affected me more than I would admit. I was certainly guilty of taking Jeremy for granted on occasion, although I didn't have a patent on that. I supposed we weren't too different from other couples who had been together for a while, who start out doing everything for each other, living to do for the other. We'd been together just over two years, but it was apparently long enough for us to grow complacent. Still, I felt awful when it was done. I felt as empty when he was gone as I did when he was there and I realized what was happening between him and Robert. There were things about our relationship I had truly grown to rely on, things that I questioned whether anyone else would be able to provide, like the way he treated me as an equal personally, and professionally as a fellow performer, not some Victor-Victoria wannabe.

We'd started out thinking we'd be together forever. What couple doesn't? As time went on, we just went about our business, not even realizing when we began to drift apart. Our physical relationship had always been great. Though sometimes I felt Jeremy didn't challenge me enough mentally, I had friends who could fill that gap. However, emotionally, I'd apparently been blind.

When we finally did split, Ken and Martin tried their best to fill my time. What I really wanted and needed at that time was to be left alone. Since Martin usually avoided Jeremy, he was especially anxious to be with me, making up for what he perceived to be lost time. I mainly kept myself busy with work and with my potted garden in an apartment that suddenly seemed too big, too quiet, and too expensive without Jeremy. I guessed that, in some sort of strange way, gardening was a link to home that I couldn't have anymore. Sometimes as I planted new flowers, or whatever I happened to be working on at the time, I thought of my mother. It wouldn't have surprised me in the least to know that she was working on the same thing in her garden in Eau Claire. I tried to find new and exotic plants, or at least plants that would be considered exotic for New York. Because gardening felt so healing to me, I was thrilled when I finally found an apartment that would allow me to do it on a larger scale, knowing I could use the move into my new home, and my need to create my nest, to justify some solitude from my well-meaning friends.

Ken or Martin would come by and we'd work on a new act, busily putting steps to music or exchanging campy snippets for existing lyrics. Offers came in from other friends to spend time at Fire Island, or even to make a weekend trip to P-town. Although I feigned interest but just "couldn't make it," I really wasn't that interested. I appreciated that so many wanted to make sure I was okay, but what I really needed was just to be able to sort things out on my own. It was harder than anyone realized to put the pieces back together. That's all I really was trying to do.

And I was doing a pretty damn good job of it, until two months later when Diana died on the eve of my move into the new apartment. By walking out of Club Chaos, I'd isolated myself from nearly everyone but Ken and Martin, and my garden had become my entire focus. Though that had been less than a month before, I felt as if I were dealing with things in my own way, even if no one else agreed. Now that I was feeling a little stronger, here came Jeremy asking me to double-date with him and Robert.

"Yes, well," I began, in shock. "I'm not too sure that I would want to do this. Besides, I'm not—"

Wait. I didn't want him to know I wasn't seeing anyone. Maybe I could track Five Thirty-three down by next week and get him to go with me, throwing all that manly beauty in Jeremy's and Robert's faces. I felt like Lucy scheming to be in the show.

"I'm not seeing anyone in particular these days, but I think there is a certain someone I might want to bring," I casually said.

"Well, great," said Jeremy, standing up suddenly. "Maybe this could be a new beginning for all of us. Who knows, it might even be fun. I have to get myself to rehearsal now. The tickets will be at the box office under your name. You know how it goes. Leave a message on my machine when you get it worked out."

He looked like he wanted a hug or something. I hoped giving him one wouldn't bring back all the old feelings. I wasn't sure if it were him or me that I wanted to spare. I concluded that it was me. Why would it be Jeremy after all? He had Robert and was obviously very happy. He seemed fairly secure in his situation, secure enough to invite me to an evening of double trouble with him and Robert.

I suddenly had this vision of hugging him, feeling his arms around me and crumbling into a sobbing mess. He'd comfort me surely, rubbing my back with his strong hands. I could feel my arms around him once more. I missed the way that felt. I thought about all the times that I'd wake up in the middle of the night to find my arm draped casually over his chest, then would slide next to him, tightening my hold on his warm body. I missed the way he smelled. I thought about a shirt of his that I found in the closet after he'd moved out. I'd walked to the phone to call him and tell him to come and get it when I realized I could smell his scent on it. I dissolved into tears, holding the shirt to my face. When I was able to pull myself back together, I took the shirt back to the closet and hung it up. I never did tell him that I had it.

I wasn't sure whether this pending hug would undo all that I'd done to get a grip on myself over the last few months. His hugs were always so wonderful: firm, warm, and reassuring. I longed for that feeling from him now, even though it would be fleeting.

Oh my god . . . would he kiss me? My heart quickened at the thought. Oh boy, would that be a bad idea. I used to lose myself in his kisses. Even before I knew about him and Robert, but while it must have been going on, Jeremy and I could spend hours kissing and cuddling. I always recognized how rare that was, knowing how most couples lose that ability fairly quickly, at least the ones I knew. I could certainly get lost in his kiss right now, although I knew a tryst with Jeremy would be like lingering on the garden path to hell.

Bad idea, bad idea, bad idea, my inner voice chanted.

I wearily stood and gave him a hug. The smell of Eternity snapped me back to reality and we said an abrupt goodbye.

With Jeremy gone sooner than I'd expected, I looked at my watch. Maybe Five Thirty-three was spending the entire day at home.

"See you later, Gregory!" I called and dashed out to the curb of Eighth Avenue to hail a cab to my apartment.

I considered Jeremy's invitation all the way uptown, trying to think what it was he would get out of it. No matter how blind I'd been in the past, I now knew that Jeremy wasn't the sort of person who went out of his way just to be nice.

There must be an angle to this I'm missing, I decided.

Damn, he hadn't told me which theater the performance was in, either. Now I'd have to call him and talk to him to find out.

Oh please, my inner voice chided, you can get that information anywhere. Why don't you admit you like these little dramas with Jeremy?

If that were true, I wouldn't be racing to catch a glimpse of a stranger, I reassured myself.

The cab stopped on my corner and I paid the driver five dollars. The impending sight of Five Thirty-three made me indifferent about getting back the small change to make an average dollar tip. I raced through my apartment and into the back garden to look at Five Thirty-three's window.

The light of the midafternoon sun was reflecting off the window in a way that made it hard to see what was going on inside. I cursed the position of the sun. I had never had any reason before to try to see him at this time. He usually wasn't home during the day.

Just then the window slid open. I quickly dropped to the ground and began weeding. Glancing from the corner of my eye, I tried to look at him. Only he wasn't there. A beautiful young blond woman was leaning from the window taking in the fresh midday air. She saw me weeding and noticing her and gave me a pearly smile and energetic wave. I wanted to sink into the planter and die.

Visitor, I thought automatically.

In a white Marilyn Monroe robe, looking as if she were waving from the window at photographers?

Sister, I reassured myself. Sister, roommate, friend visiting from out of town, cousin—

Wife, girlfriend, lover, just up from a lazy morning in bed, my inner voice jeered.

I was beginning to tire of this inner voice. Once it had been my cheerleader: *You can do it, Daniel You go, girl. If anyone can pull off Princess 2Di4, you can. You've got the height, the bone structure, the naturally flushed cheeks and golden skin, the eyes that could entice any man to do your bidding.*

Or had that been . . . Jeremy's voice, back in the days when he watched me as if I were scattering the stars that brightened his cosmos. I'd spent months analyzing my entire relationship with Jeremy from beginning to end, trying to understand when we stopped speaking in one voice. Had we merely followed the natural progression of any relationship? From lust, then love, to comfort, then carelessness, and finally to indifference and betrayal?

I didn't want to believe all romantic relationships were doomed to go that route. Besides, the physical attraction between us had never really faded. But when had we stopped being each other's best friends?

Because we had been friends. When I had troubles at the club, Jeremy would rub my feet and hear me out. He didn't give me advice I didn't need. He just listened and let me vent. I'd done the same for him when he worried that he'd never get another part. We'd make a celebration out of any good news. He was always getting work as an extra on soaps, had gotten a couple of commercials with nonspeaking parts, and I'd treat him like an Oscar contender. So at what point did we open ourselves up to a temptation like Robert?

Robert, who had befriended me, talking excitedly about our shared tastes in music, books, theater, even architecture. Hours of mutual interests shaped into words that tumbled from us so quickly it was as if we thought our time was limited. Which it had been, of course, since Robert was only using me to get to Jeremy.

I squirmed at the memory of how they'd betrayed me. Neither Robert nor Jeremy had ever had the decency to really explain or apologize. Jeremy and I passed the few remaining hours of those final days we shared an apartment not speaking to each other, maintaining an icy, tense distance. I never saw Robert after Jeremy moved out. I'd been dismayed to realize that I missed him and the times we'd shared, constantly reminding myself of my humiliation at his hands.

I stared at my own hands, now covered with soil, feeling quick repugnance at the idea that took shape. But within seconds I had a lovely bunch of fall flowers and foliage arranged into a bouquet.

I haven't done anything wrong, I assured myself. Just because the memory of Robert making friends with me so he could steal Jeremy gave me the idea . . . I have *not* done anything wrong!

Yet.

No. This is just a way to get information. If she *is* his lover, if he *is* straight . . .

My quick movement caught her eye again and I held the bouquet toward her, making my face innocently friendly. She gave me another brilliant smile then shrugged, as if wondering how I'd get the flowers to her. Then she moved from the window, coming back with a piece of paper. I could read the black numbers clearly; would a New Yorker ever have given her apartment number so trustingly? She *had* to be a visitor.

I held up my hand to let her know I'd arrive with the flowers in five minutes and she nodded, her face bright with anticipation and another of her ready smiles.

I turned and sauntered casually back toward the apartment, in case she was watching. Once in private, I dropped the bouquet on the counter and raced to the shower.

OhmygodOhmygodOhmygod, are you out of your mind? the inner voice shrieked.

Shut up! I told it. I am perfectly in control of my faculties, thank you very much.

I stepped into the shower, paying no attention to the temperature of the water. I quickly ran the soap over my body, the water rinsing the lather down my legs and sending the soap swirling down the drain. I grabbed the bottle of Pantene and washed my hair in record time. I flipped off the water; its coldness had given me all that much more adrenaline, as if I needed it right now.

I toweled off and ran a comb straight back through my hair. I threw on a pair of jeans and a teal T-shirt with a pocket. I put the cap on again, as I didn't want to *look* like I had just showered, grabbed my keys, and slammed the door shut behind me. I was halfway down the hall when I realized I had forgotten the flowers.

Subtle, Daniel, I thought. I ran back to the apartment, grabbed the flowers from the counter, and hurried outside and down the stoop to the street below. I walked down the street toward Ninth

Avenue, forcing myself not to run. I was really anxious about meeting this woman and getting vital information about the man of my
wet dreams. I nearly got tangled in a web of leashes as I passed a
woman walking eight dogs while I wondered what questions I
should ask.

Where is he from? What is he to you? Does he drink decaf? Do
you sleep together? Is he good in bed?

There was no way I could ask any of those questions. Well,
maybe the one about decaf, I amended.

I turned left at the end of my street and walked down Ninth
Avenue. I warily kept my eye on a group of teenage boys hanging
out in front of a deli. One was on a pay phone, the others talking
and gesturing grandly as they spoke. They were half my age but still
evoked apprehension within me. They reminded me of the boys in
high school who used to taunt me for being different. I wasn't a
jock, nor was I a popular person or a druggie, so I was fair game for
harassment. I half expected the boys on the street to somehow pick
up on my past and start yelling names and throwing things at my
head.

Daniel, you moron, my inner voice chided, you're a grown man
now and most likely the last thing on the minds of those boys.
Besides, this is New York City; if they were going to attack you, it
would be with knives or a pistol.

How comforting, I thought. When had this become a part of
me?

City survival instincts must have crept up and settled within me a
long time before. It was all second nature. I had never seen or been
a part of the violent side of the city in the twelve years I'd lived in
Manhattan. However, I had friends who'd been mugged and gay-
bashed. And there was always the evening news to serve as a re-
minder that just because you made it through the day unscathed,
there was usually someone who had not.

Hell's Kitchen was a smorgasbord of actors, dancers, and singers
sharing a neighborhood with families who had inherited and held
on to their railroad apartments so they could continue paying fifty
dollars a month in rent. From block to block, old tenement buildings were juxtaposed with new restaurants, aging delis, Laundro-
mats, and hardware stores. Plants grew on fire escapes, evidence of
life still stirring within the walls of the aged buildings. Many of
those buildings were vacant and surrounded by scaffolding and

construction fencing so crews of workers could tear them down and erect offices or modern apartment housing.

Once a haven for prostitutes and crack dealers, Hell's Kitchen had been cleaned up by the police and made it a more attractive area to live or run a business. When I moved to my apartment on Forty-seventh Street, I was excited to be so close to Times Square, Lincoln Center, and the Theater District. Not to mention the scads of restaurants from which to order take-out.

But just because the mayor pronounced that crime was at a record low did not mean I should let down my guard. At heart, I was still a country boy in the big city. Not to mention a confusing hybrid of affluent Caucasian and gay minority. I would probably never stop looking over my shoulder.

As I pondered this, I realized I had reached the end of the block. I turned left again and made my way down Forty-sixth Street.

I found the building behind mine, an old tenement that had undergone a couple of facelifts over the years. Almost all of the buildings in this area were like that, including mine. I stood on the sidewalk, feeling queasy. I wasn't sure I'd ever been so nervous. I had forced myself to walk slowly and all I had prepared were a bouquet of slightly wilted flowers and *Does he drink decaf?* The hand holding the flowers unconsciously held my stomach as I rang the buzzer for the number the woman had shown me.

"Hello?" a faceless voice inquired, sounding like it was on one of those tiny transistor radios I'd had as a kid.

"Flowers," I replied.

Good one, Daniel. Very original.

The voice laughed.

"C'mon up!"

The door buzzed. I pulled it open and stepped into the dimly lit foyer. My stomach did a one and a half gainer with a twist, degree of difficulty, four point five. Executed perfectly.

I must have climbed the stairs to the apartment, although I don't really remember the journey. All I remember were the questions.

Who is this woman? Relative? Sister? Wife? Lover?

Oh my god.

Is he home? I only saw *her* in the window, but if he were going to work, surely I would not have seen him at all this morning. He must be home.

What do I say? was my last thought before the door opened.

"Hi! I'm Sheila Meyers."

A quick scan around the room suggested she was alone. The white robe was carelessly thrown over a chair by the window. She stood before me in nothing but a blue oxford dress shirt that appeared about two thousand sizes too large.

That's a lot of shirt for a lot of man, I thought enviously.

Her long, bare legs were a stark contrast to the naiveté of her guileless blue eyes.

"Are you okay?" she asked.

"Yeah. Fine." I snapped out of it. "These are for you. I'm Daniel, and you have the most beautiful eyes I have ever seen. That's not a come-on. I mean, sometimes I just say things as they come into my head. I mean, I wouldn't come on to you, because . . . Sorry. I didn't mean to embarrass you. Did I tell you my name? I'm Daniel."

I felt a blush rise to my cheeks.

Very smooth.

Sheila laughed.

"Thanks, Daniel. They're lovely. Won't you come in and sit down?"

Her voice was very calming, and I detected a note of an accent, but I couldn't say from where.

I took a deep breath and entered the apartment.

"Sit down, Daniel. Would you like some iced tea? Or hey, I just made a pot of coffee; how 'bout that?"

I sat in a large overstuffed chair with Ralph Lauren paisley print upholstery.

"Iced tea sounds great, thanks, Sheila."

I heard a noise in the kitchen behind where Sheila was standing. My heart leapt in my chest.

He's *heeeeeeerrrrre*, my inner voice whispered.

"Dexter? Is that you? We have a visitor. Come on out." Sheila turned her head while she was pouring the iced tea and didn't notice that the glass was about to overflow.

"Sheila, the tea!"

"Oh my!"

The tea overflowed and spilled onto the counter then to the floor. Sheila giggled and poured some of the excess tea into the sink before handing me the glass. A black and brown mottled cat strutted around the corner and went straight for the puddle of tea on the floor.

"Dexter loves his iced tea, doesn't he? Oh, yes, yes he does."

Sheila knelt to pet the cat and I got a better view of her Victoria's Secret–clad ass than I ever wanted. There were footsteps coming from outside the apartment. My heart began its adrenaline-fueled dance once again.

The footsteps ceased and the jingling of keys was loud outside the door. Sheila was busy behind the counter petting Dexter and wiping up the remains of the spilled iced tea with a paper towel. The key turned in the lock and the door opened.

"My god, the line at the market was so long. What business do people have shopping at one in the afternoon on a Thursday?"

It was Five Thirty-three. He had not yet turned in my direction. He walked to the counter and put the grocery bags down.

"Sheila? Where did these flowers come from?"

Sheila stood up from behind the counter.

"They're from my secret admirer." She looked at me and winked.

Five Thirty-three turned around. His eyes—oh, god, so green—widened and his face flushed. The keys dropped from his hand. He turned back to Sheila.

"You let a complete stranger into my apartment? This is New York, not Wisconsin."

"Oh get over it, Blaine, he's nice. And cute too." Sheila smiled at me, grabbed the groceries from the counter, and began putting them away.

I gathered my strength and stood. I knew my voice would be shaky, not to mention my hands and legs, which felt like foam.

"Hi, I'm Daniel. I live across the alley. I saw Sheila in the window and offered her the flowers. I didn't think it would be . . . did you say Wisconsin?"

Blaine seemed to relax a little and held out his hand.

God, I thought, could it be that I'm about to touch this man? Even though it's only his hand, I'll know from the moment I touch it whether or not he's the one for me. The man who'll take away all my worries, all the speculation, all the past years of unfulfilled love.

I shook his hand.

"Hello, I'm Blaine Dunhill. I've seen you somewhere before.

Your face is very familiar. I'm sorry I reacted the way I did just now. You know how it is, New York and all."

"I know what you mean."

His hand felt very soft against mine. I wanted the handshake to linger but I pulled my hand away.

"So, Daniel. You are one in a long line of Sheila's admirers. Ever since I've known her, men, and women," he added as if this would be a surprise, "have offered her kingdoms for an hour of her time."

"But you were the one who won out?" I prompted.

"Well"—Blaine looked down at the floor—"I wouldn't quite say that. No one wins with Sheila."

"Blaine!" Sheila screamed from behind the refrigerator door. "You make me sound impossible. I'm just . . . challenging."

"So, what are you doing in New York, Sheila?" I asked.

"Well, I just knew I had to get out of Eau Claire."

"Well, didn't we all?" I said, too amazed to finish.

"You are *not* from Eau Claire, too?" she gasped, touching a hand to her mouth after she asked.

"Um, yeah," I said, startled by the untrusting and indignant look on Blaine's face. "I'm new to this area of the neighborhood, too, but I moved to New York, gosh, about twelve years ago."

"Excuse me," Blaine said to me and went down a small hall to one of the back rooms in the apartment.

I turned back to Sheila; her face was lit up by her wide grin. She began to bombard me with questions about Eau Claire, her eyes warming by the minute. It was obvious she was finding me a bit too attractive. As I wondered how the hell to put her off without telling her the truth—that I was gay—my answers became shorter. Though Sheila seemed up to managing whatever cards she was dealt, as long as Blaine played close to the vest I wasn't willing to tip my hand. She picked up on my reticence and her smile faded a bit.

"I guess I'm being way too nosy, huh?" she asked. "It's okay. Everyone tells me that."

"I just don't want you to know how dull I am, even after all these years in New York," I said. "Maybe we could start a support group for recovering Midwesterners."

Her face relaxed into another smile, then we laughed together. I was relieved, feeling I had almost lost my only link to Blaine's world.

"Sheila," Blaine's voice boomed from behind us. We both jumped, having been unaware that while we were laughing, he'd reappeared. He'd changed from blue jeans into black pants and shiny wingtips. Correction, he was in the middle of changing, because he was bare chested and holding his crisp white shirt still on the hanger. "We have to get moving if we're going to make that appointment tonight."

Window, walls, plants, paintings—must direct my eyes somewhere other than Blaine's chest, I told myself.

He wasn't looking at me; he was unbuttoning his shirt on the hanger.

Did you see those abs? my inner voice screamed.

His abs were as ribbed as the old washboard my mother had comically hung on the wall in our laundry room when I was growing up. Firm, rippled, hard, and tan. I wanted to run my hand over them. Forget my hand. I wanted to run my tongue over them.

"Oh, shit!" exclaimed Sheila. It seemed impossible such a word could pass the lips of this porcelain doll from Eau Claire. "Blaine, I'm sorry. I completely forgot. What time is it?"

"Almost two; we have to catch the train at three," Blaine said. "Sorry, Daniel, I don't mean to be rude or anything, but we have an appointment we can't miss."

"That's okay," I said as nonchalantly as possible. "I actually have an audition to get to."

The lie didn't even surprise me. Though I had never thought of myself as duplicitous before, I seemed to be adapting quite well.

"You're an actor?" Sheila asked.

"Um, yeah. You could say that," I laughed.

"Sorry we don't have longer to get to know each other," Sheila said. She half led and half followed me to the door. "Maybe we can get together sometime for lunch or dinner. Something?"

"Sure," I said, opening the door.

"What's your last name?" Sheila asked. I could see Blaine buttoning the shirt over the expanse of his firm pectorals.

"Stephenson," I stated, wondering when the last time someone had bothered to ask that question was. "But I'm not listed, if that's why you're wondering."

I didn't want to give her one of my cards, which had *Princess 2Di4* emblazoned across the front in silver script with my answering service's number at the bottom. Dotting the *i* in princess was a little tiara. I didn't want that as my calling card anymore, and I felt an inward shudder at the thought of Blaine seeing it. I worried that even if Blaine were gay, he would not be as comfortable with my princess persona as Jeremy had been. I'd suffered through too many occasions when men who looked like Blaine had regarded my drag attire with disgust. It was a sad reality that some of my worst detractors were other gay men. Men with gym bodies like Blaine often desired only carbon copies of what they'd built themselves into. I'd spent years in Chelsea seeing Blaines shop and walk and eat with other Blaines. Martin called them bookends who wouldn't have our biographies on their shelves. Maybe I was judging Blaine as unfairly as I feared he'd judge me, but as long as he was giving off no signals, I had only his appearance to go on.

"Well, how can I get in touch with you, then?" Sheila asked, that charming smile spreading across her face. "And Blaine says *I'm* impossible!"

"*I'm not bad, I'm just drawn that way!*" I said, doing my Jessica Rabbit impersonation, sending Sheila into a fit of giggles. "Sorry, I couldn't resist." Over her shoulder I saw Blaine look my way and raise his eyebrows, a half-smile creeping over his face. "Tell you what, I'm apartment 1RS over on Forty-seventh Street. Ring me any time you wish."

"Okay, but watch out," Sheila said. "I just may take you up on that offer!"

"Any time," I repeated. "Have fun, whatever you guys are doing."

"Oh sure," Sheila sighed, surprising me with a hug and a quick kiss on the cheek. "I'm going with him to some merger/dinner/meeting thing. I'm not really sure what it is. I just smile and nod and try to be charming," she whispered, then released me and gave me an example of her "charming" laugh.

I couldn't help but laugh, too.

"Nice to meet you, Blaine!" I called past Sheila.

He walked over, finishing the knot on a plain, black tie. He held his hand past the doorway and I took it, giving it a firm shake.

"You, too, Daniel. Again, I'm sorry we couldn't have more time to get to know each other. Maybe there'll be more opportunity for that in the future."

I scanned his face for double meanings, certain that his eyes held mine just a fraction of a second longer than necessary.

"I'm sure there will," I said, trying not to purr.

I'm not certain how I made it back to my apartment without being run over. I felt as if I were floating miles above mundane activities like walking and unlocking doors and . . .

He had touched my hand twice and could not have failed to notice the charge between us. His eyes were greener than any eyes had a right to be. His face, that chest, that reluctant little smile. Oh, one day I'd make him smile, I'd make him . . .

I came back to earth with a thud as I surveyed my apartment. The half-unpacked boxes, the prints stacked against the walls, unwashed coffee cups everywhere.

What self-respecting fag would ever live this way, I wondered. What had I been doing, thinking my home was contained within the perimeters of my beautiful garden?

It was time to build my nest. The job could wait. Sheila was a contact who could provide all the answers that would help me get close to Five Thirty—

Blaine, I reminded myself. Blaine Dunhill.

I could visualize it on the outside of an envelope. Mssrs. Blaine Dunhill and Daniel Stephenson. *Mmmmmmmm.* The Dunhill-Stephensons cordially invite you to . . .

I reached for the nearest box to begin unpacking.

THREE

Three days later I returned from shopping, overburdened and exhausted, to find I'd left the alley gate unlocked. Paradise was lost.

"Well, if it's not Adam, Yves, and the snake," I muttered as Jeremy and Andy gave me big smiles and air kisses. Robert lurked in the background with the grace to look ashamed. Apparently he was the only one who would acknowledge having heard my remark.

"You never called to make arrangements about the tickets," Jeremy said, taking the sack I thrust at him so I could unlock my door.

Had I gone through the front entrance, I might have been able to hide inside until they went away. Instead I'd made a habit of going in and out the back, hoping for a glimpse of the mysteriously missing Blaine and Sheila.

"This garden is incredible," Robert said, taking my bundle of laundered clothes without being asked. "Really amazing, Daniel, what you've done back here. I had no idea—"

"Yes, yes, he's a *wonder*, we're all just tickled to *death* by Little Abner, but meanwhile, *when* do you plan to help me organize this *auction*?" Andy interrupted, doing some kind of Suzanne Sommers flounce into the apartment ahead of the rest of us.

"I assume you do still want tickets, plural, for *Anything Goes*," Jeremy said. "Really, Daniel, we're all sorry that the world's last two princesses are, er, defunct, but you can't—"

"Defunct," I repeated incredulously.

"Well, that was your choice," Jeremy said.

Before I could express my shock that Jeremy knew the meaning of "defunct," Robert spoke.

"This apartment is . . . extraordinary, Daniel. I had no idea—"

"That's right, you were never in *our* apartment, were you?" I asked. "We seem to have always been at yours until Jeremy decided he liked it so much he moved in."

This was followed by one of those nasty little silences so rare among a group as sharp-tongued as this one. I turned away from the injured look in Robert's eyes and took the sack from Jeremy, heading for the kitchen.

"Put the laundry down anywhere, Robert. And yes," I added over my shoulder, "I need two tickets."

"Should I leave them in your name or his?" Jeremy asked.

"Mine. But he is a she."

The silence after this remark had a whole new tension to it.

"She?" Jeremy asked blankly. "Oh, you're bringing Gretchen?"

"Good lord," Andy snapped. "I can't imagine a place in the world you'd be *less* likely to see Gretchen than *Anything Goes.* This whole garden *spell* Daniel is under is undoubtedly the influence of her communal farming *frenzy* at Lesbian Lake, or whatever it's called. And we have more important things to discuss—"

"It isn't Gretchen," I said. "Her name is Sheila. And she is . . . well, she certainly is no lesbian."

My attempt at some heterosexual smirk was met with stares that were a mixture of disbelief, horror, and bewilderment. The silence was deafening. I turned to let it all soak in while Andy and Jeremy stood gaping at each other. I began to put the groceries away, and Robert poked his head sheepishly into the kitchen.

"Can I do anything to help?" he asked, innocently enough. He reached for the six-pack of Diet Coke and I casually took it from his hands and deposited it inside the refrigerator in one fluid motion. Robert stood and blinked at me like a drugged cocker spaniel.

"I think I can handle this much, Robert. But it seems your friends need oxygen."

Jeremy's and Andy's mouths snapped shut in unison, like a couple of puppets.

"Well, princess, *do* tell!" Andy taunted.

"Nothing to tell, darling. Besides, if it were all that newsworthy, surely it would have made *USA Today* already, right?"

Jeremy eyed me suspiciously.

"Stop calling her Shirley," he said dryly, using one of our old favorite jokes. I chose not to acknowledge it. Jeremy decided to let me off the hook for the moment. "Well, I hope we get to meet this Sheila, Daniel. If she's a friend of yours, she's a friend of ours, right, Robert?"

Ours . . . I heard that loud and clear, just as I was sure Jeremy intended.

"Huh? Oh, right. Absolutely!" Robert was a bit overenthusiastic in his reply. "Daniel? Where is the . . . uh—"

"Down the hall, first door you come to."

Robert left the kitchen. Andy decided to revisit his favorite topic of the minute.

"Well, Daniel, you never *did* answer. When *are* you going to help me with this auction? You know, if you didn't help me, I would simply *die!*" Andy dragged the last word out dramatically.

The implication of his emphasis on the word "die" was not lost on me. I felt like taking one of my Chanel scarves and strangling him with it.

"Andy, darling, you know what I love about you?" I asked sweetly.

"No, princess. What?" he asked, taking the bait.

"I don't know, either. I was hoping you could help me figure something out."

Andy straightened his spine and glared at me.

"Now, girls," Jeremy interrupted.

"Look, princess, you aren't doing *me* any favors by doing this. You just walk out, leaving everyone's tongues *wagging* about what could *possibly* be wrong with you, and I have done *nothing* but try to help you out of this whole mess as *gracefully* as could be allowed, but if you don't want—"

"Help me?" I was incredulous. "The only reason you'd ever help anyone is if it serves some objective of yours. I can't believe you would have the audacity to—"

"How *dare* you! When I have done nothing but break my *back* trying to help you from day *one.*"

"Break your back? The only way you'd break your back is if you slipped off of whatever social ladder you were climbing, you self-serving—"

"Self-serving?" Andy sputtered.

The temperature in the room was increasing exponentially by the minute.

"Daniel," Jeremy warned.

"What, Jeremy? What?" I turned my temper on him. "What is it you want from me, anyway? Out of the blue I get a phone call from you and the next thing I know, I'm being invited to see you and Mr. Right Now in *Anything Goes*. However appropriate the title of your current production may be, I'm still left wondering what on earth you want from me? You said you were concerned that I haven't moved on, but you seem to be doing everything in your power to keep me from doing just that."

From the corner of my eye I could see Andy raise one eyebrow at Jeremy, making mental notes for future reference.

"Okay, Dan. Evidently I didn't check the calendar closely enough to notice you would start your period today. I'll leave the tickets for you and whoever—Sheila—whatever, in your name at will call."

He turned and Andy followed him out the door toward the alley gate.

I leaned against the counter and put my head in my hands. God, I hated it that he knew just the buttons to push to make me lose my composure. And then, of course, there was that little fucker Andy. Damn Jeremy anyway. Honestly, if he ever gave any thought to anyone other than himself I just wouldn't—

"I love your bathroom, Daniel. I had no idea—" Robert's sentence broke suddenly as he realized his partners in crime had left him high and dry.

That was the *third* time he'd said that and I snapped.

"You're right, you don't have any idea. I think you'd better leave, Robert."

Robert slowly closed his mouth and skulked to the door. He paused in the doorway and turned.

"Daniel." He looked at me and took a deep breath. "You may not want to hear this, and maybe you won't believe it, but Jeremy cares for you very much. He knows he hurt you and he feels like shit about it. He would never admit it to you, of course, but I think he feels like he's made a big mistake. I feel that way, too."

I turned myself to stone at these words, placing my arms defensively across my chest as if I could deflect bullets. I wasn't sure if Robert meant the mistake was his or Jeremy's.

"I don't care, Robert. What's done is done. You have Jeremy. Go. Be happy. Just don't be surprised if you wake up one morning to a stranger in your bed."

I had to admire my ability to sound coldly sure of myself when I was anything but.

Robert backed out of the door. He looked like he wanted to say more but didn't know where to begin. I, on the other hand, had said as much as I wanted and more than I'd intended.

I slowly started toward Robert, with the intention of following him into the garden to lock the gate against any other stray animals. I was within a foot of him when he turned to face me and flung his arms around me.

A second passed in which I couldn't believe his lips were on mine and his tongue was trying desperately to force my lips apart. I threw myself and Robert back against the edge of the doorway. Robert made a gasping sound as the wind was knocked from his lungs. His arms were off of me and he was sinking slowly to the ground, a cinematic death scene. I backed away from him, incredulous.

"Slut! Jeremy's not enough? You have to have me, too?" I dropped my voice to a hiss, aware that Jeremy and Andy had to be somewhere close by. "What the fuck's the matter with you?"

"All I wanted from the start was you," Robert snapped back, his voice as desperately low as mine. "Were you so blind you couldn't see that? You were too busy building resentment and disdain for Jeremy to see that it was you and I who were meant for each other. Daniel, we have to face this for what it is. I know you want me, too. We'd be a great team. Please, can't you just give me a chance?"

I noticed the tears in his eyes. I couldn't help but feel numb. Any respect I'd had for Robert diminished; any inkling of desire I'd had—there had been desire, I *had* wanted Robert, I could admit that to myself—was now tantamount to a grain of sand in the Sahara. In spite of my earlier desire, he was not someone I wanted to be on the same "team" with. Hell, we weren't even in the same league.

He looked especially pathetic as Jeremy called from the alley.

"Sweetie, c'mon! We'll be tardy for rehearsal."

"And that's another thing," I whispered in the same furious undertone. "Is one of the games you play in bed with Jeremy called 'Increase Your Word Power'?"

Robert's face froze into some kind of agonized expression as he backed away. I hesitated, allowing him to speak before closing the door.

"Daniel, I need to talk to you. There's so much left unsaid. There's no one I can talk to about Jeremy who won't eventually run to him with every one of my words hyperbolized to the point of malevolence. There's so much you don't know."

"Robert, I don't care. Tell Jeremy I'll see the show. Tell Andy I'll talk to him about the fucking auction. As for you, it would be best if we didn't speak at all."

I slammed the door and fell against it. I couldn't breathe. I could hear Robert's sobs as I gulped big swallows of air. Finally I heard him hobble to the alley. I wondered if I was having a heart attack. I put my hand on my chest and let out a large breath of air.

No, my heart was pounding away. Actually, quite hard.

I didn't know what to think, much less what to do. I wiped my mouth on the back of my hand, hoping to get rid of Robert's kiss, trying to erase it from existence.

Once I knew they were gone, as if they would have been able to read my thoughts while still close by, I tried to figure out how Robert's kiss made me feel. I had wanted Robert to kiss me a long time ago but had refrained out of respect for Jeremy. Had I known then what I knew now, I might not have been so quick to rein myself in. But at this point, after knowing what Robert's lips had been doing behind my back to god knows what parts of Jeremy while we were supposedly a monogamous couple in love . . . I wanted to spit. My stomach lurched and I almost ran to the bathroom. I heaved in another gulp of fresh air, realizing that I had stopped breathing and that my face was probably pulsing bright red from anger.

Composure, I thought. I have to regain my composure.

But it had happened. It wasn't going away.

Did Robert think so little of me that he thought I'd welcome his attention now? That I'd want him to kiss me? I'd just admitted to myself that there had been a time I'd desired him, had even wanted him to kiss me. Had I sent him signals to that effect?

I tried to remember all the times we'd spent together over meals or seeing movies. Hadn't I always made it clear that I was completely committed to Jeremy? I'd had many opportunities to cheat on him. At Club Chaos it was understood that I was in a relationship, but I did appearances everywhere and met all kinds of men. I'd had my share of offers. A lot of them were appealing; sometimes even the idea of someone new was tantalizing. Plus it was flattering to be desired. But I'd think of what I had at home, of all the connections Jeremy and I shared, of the life we'd built, and it never occurred to me that a quick thrill with some other guy would be worth what I might lose. Besides, Jeremy trusted me and I thought that meant something. It *had* meant something to me. If I'd flirted with Robert, it was never done consciously. And even if I had, did he think I would just brush off his betrayal of our friendship?

Robert was bright enough to understand my relationship with Jeremy and what it meant to me. If Jeremy had somehow given him the impression it was an open relationship, certainly the fact that it ended when Robert crossed the boundary into our bedroom should have enlightened him otherwise.

Of course, Robert and I had never discussed any of this. But if that's what he wanted to do, to somehow clear the air, it was sure as hell not a conversation that was going to start with a kiss.

I jumped as the buzzer shrieked from the front of the apartment, announcing someone's determination to be let in.

"What the hell is it now?" I grumbled, making my way to the front door. "It can only be Death trying to take me, too. Little does he know I'd go willingly at this point. Take me now!"

I hit the "talk" button.

"Um, welcome wagon!" a distorted voice said.

"Great, ask for Death and you get Jehovah's Witnesses." I sighed as I hit the "talk" button again. "Sheila, is that you?"

Who else would use such a Midwestern expression as "welcome wagon"?

"Open up, I know you're in there," I heard her say.

Though still shaken up and reluctant to have more visitors, I was nonetheless intrigued by the opportunity to gain information about Blaine. I hit the "open" button and buzzed her in. I heard the front doors creak open and slam, then her clicking heels as she made her way down the hall to my door.

I opened the door to see her holding a covered dish in her hands.

"I brought my grandmother's beef Stroganoff with me as a

housewarming gift. Well, it's not my grandmother's, actually, I made an extra one last night to bring to you as an excuse to say 'Hi!' But I expect you to make something for me when you return the dish. You know, to welcome *me* to the neighborhood, since I just got here, too."

I stood there, slack-jawed and silent, as she chattered on. It was the only natural response, since I had lived in seventeen different apartments during my twelve years in Manhattan and nobody had ever once baked me a casserole. It was so . . . Eau Claire of her.

"I hope you like it," she went on, pushing past me to make her way into the kitchen.

I couldn't tell if she knew that I was upset or shaken. If she did, she pretended really well not to notice.

"Shit, you're not a vegetarian, are you? The thought never crossed my mind until now. I mean, you look really healthy and all, like you eat sensibly and might be a vegetarian. Actually, your body is almost as good as mine. You're kind of slim that way. Are you?"

"Am I what?" I asked, a little confused. Still dazed, really.

"Vegetarian," she sighed and may just as well have added *stupid* to the end of her explanation, because it was in her tone of voice. Not in a mean way, just a silly and sarcastic way, like a young girl who is asking her friend if she ever kissed a boy.

"No, I'm not," I said. I almost said, *No, I've kissed a boy. He just left, as a matter of fact.*

"Good," she said, rolling her eyes and giggling. "Oh wait, I was going to heat this up now. But I bet you eat later, don't you? I'm used to eating around six, but I've come to learn that a lot of New Yorkers eat later."

"Um, yeah, it's five-thirty now," I said, looking at my watch and thinking, five-thirty? Three minutes until Blaine would get home . . . "I usually eat around eight or so. But thanks so much for the dinner."

"Daniel, are you okay?"

She'd said it. I was hoping she wouldn't. I was hoping she'd keep on with her bright and refreshing, noncatty chattering, cleansing the room of its bitter queeniness with her giggles and babbling.

I sighed and fell onto a bar stool on the other side of the kitchen counter.

"No, I'm not all right," I said.

"Is there anything I can do?" Sheila asked thoughtfully. "If you need me to leave, I will."

"No, that's okay," I smiled. "But won't Blaine be expecting to find you at home?"

"Blaine's away," she said. "Business trip. He'll be in and out of town the next few weeks. Really, Daniel, if you want to be alone—"

"I like having you around." This elicited another of those dazzling smiles and I groaned inwardly. There was simply no way I could be as treacherous as Robert and Jeremy. It was time to come clean. "My ex-lover and his flavor-of-the-month just left. Seconds before you buzzed, actually. Oh, and that bastard Andy!"

She didn't even blink. Maybe I had underestimated her. Or maybe I hadn't made the gender clear enough.

"Andy?" Sheila made her way around the counter to the vacant bar stool next to me. "Is that the ex-boyfriend or the new guy?"

I relaxed; she did understand.

"Neither," I said, rolling my eyes. "Andy is the owner of Club Chaos. In the Village on Christopher Street."

She shook her head blankly. She'd never heard of it. That made me so glad.

"Andy wants something from me. So does Jeremy; I have no idea what. As for Robert, I thought we knew our places in our separate corners, but it turns out . . ."

I was waving my hands around and getting bitter, but as I tried to figure out Robert, I calmed down.

"I don't know what the deal with Robert is."

"Okay, Jeremy is your ex?" Sheila asked patiently.

"Yes."

"Andy is just an asshole?"

"Good!" I giggled.

"And Robert probably just kissed you," Sheila very matter-of-factly said.

"How did you know that?" I asked, in awe of her psychic abilities.

"It's happened to me before," she said. "Well, reverse some roles and make a couple of people straight and it has."

I was still confused and made a face to show it.

"Well," she laughed, running a hand through her hair. "I broke up with this guy 'cause he was cheating on me. He stayed with that tramp and she tried to be my friend. Actually, she *was* my friend, so she tried to continue being my friend. Anyway, she wanted to know how to keep him, 'cause, well, you know, once a cheater, always a cheater. She didn't want it to happen to her and she knew it would, 'cause he was already losing interest in her. So, she tried to get close to me to learn how to keep him. As if that made sense, when I hadn't been able to keep him myself!"

"So you mean—"

"Robert could be trying to get close to you to learn more about Jeremy so he can keep his interest," Sheila said, with a smug, Angela Lansbury grin on her face.

"Thank you for shedding new light on this," I said, massaging my temples. "I would've obsessed on it all night."

"Sure," Sheila said, reaching over and rubbing my arm. "The hardest part is staying friends with the guy."

"You stayed friends with him?" I asked, amazed at her apparent power of forgiveness.

"Um, yeah," Sheila said, suddenly a little uncomfortable. "I don't know why, but I always stay friends with my ex-boyfriends. Especially if we break up over something stupid. You know what I mean?"

"Enlighten me," I smiled. "This is an area I probably could stand to work on."

"Well . . ." Sheila thought a minute before answering.

I suddenly liked that about her.

"The same guy I was just talking about, for instance. He cheated on me. In my mind that makes everything over between us, as far as pursuing a romantic relationship goes. It's just not something I can continue with. You know? I can forgive him for that, but I can't keep seeing him. But there's no reason why we can't be friends, since I did forgive him. It's a matter of drawing a line and not crossing it."

"Wow."

I thought about that for a minute. I wondered if I could do that with Jeremy.

"Do you want to stay friends with Jeremy?" she asked, reading my mind.

"I have no idea what I want."

"Tell me about him."

"He's an actor."

"Is that how you met him?"

God, I wondered, is there no end to deception once it's started?

"Sort of," I said. "There was an instant attraction, though I was a little wary of him. When someone seems too good to be true, especially when he's an actor . . . But one thing led to another . . . Anyway, we took this trip to Oregon together. Once we were out of Manhattan, away from our friends, I thought I saw the real Jeremy, no illusions, no acts. There seemed to be so much more to him than his looks. But as it turned out, Jeremy is a chess master and I was a pawn in his game. I didn't figure that out until he left me for Robert."

I still remembered Oregon as a magical time for Jeremy and me. We'd been together about a year then, and Jeremy wanted to take a vacation. On his travels a few years before, he'd fallen in love with the Oregon coast. He'd been on his own and had dreamed of returning there some day with the man he loved. As he talked about it, I caught his enthusiasm. I hadn't taken a real vacation for a long time.

Our friends had been full of dire predictions, warning us that traveling with a lover tests all the weaker parts of a relationship. But Ken, who was proprietary about our romance because he'd introduced us, forced Andy to give me the two weeks off. We planned to fly into Portland then rent a car and return to some of the places Jeremy remembered. We got into the habit of poring over maps and travel guides as he retraced his other trip for me.

The divas at the club rolled their eyes, warning me that two weeks without glamour would really test my nature. I just laughed at them. If Brooklyn-born-and-raised Jeremy could handle it, I knew that I could. I hadn't grown up in a city. Anyway, our trip was not about roughing it, even if we were planning a visit to the Klamath Mountains in the southern part of the state for some day hiking.

I could still recall Martin's horror the evening Jeremy showed up at Club Chaos with hiking boots. He'd found some he thought would be perfect for the light walking we'd be doing and bought us each a pair. He wanted me to start wearing them immediately, to get them broken in, and Martin had mocked him.

"You can take the princess out of the kingdom, but you'll never turn your little Bobbsey twin into a Camp Fire Girl!"

"Don't worry, Martin," another of the naysayers spoke, "they'll never get to that part of the trip. They'll kill each other before they park the car at their first Motel 6. When Danny makes Jeremy take a wrong turn, or when he realizes Jeremy forgot to pack the loofah sponge, it'll all be over."

In a way, they'd been right. We experienced all the little disasters a couple can endure when traveling. Driving too many hours looking for decent lodging . . . blisters on our feet after hiking . . . weariness at not being in our own bed . . . not being able to order takeout from our favorite restaurants . . . using up our film too quickly so that when we saw a perfect photo opportunity we couldn't capture it . . . spending too many hours in each other's company . . . arguing over what music to listen to in the car. And we'd had the time of our lives; our honeymoon, we called it later. Our bickering always ended in laughter at how stupid we sounded, and we spent each night in our comforting spooning position, sure that no one else in the world was as happy as we were.

Jeremy—ugh, I didn't want to think about him or apply Sheila's philosophies to him just yet.

"New topic," I announced.

"Okay, I understand. What do you want to talk about?"

"What the hell is the story with you and Blaine?" I asked, getting up from my stool with huge *Oh my god* eyes. I went in the kitchen to pour a drink.

"Oh my god, you're blunt." Sheila laughed.

"It's really quite endearing, once you get to know me." I smiled. "Do you want a drink?"

"Yes!" Sheila rasped. "I thought you'd never ask! Gin and tonic, please."

"Bartender, make that two."

I took the gin from the cabinet and two glasses from the drying rack. I had finally put my kitchen together and washed all the newsprint off the dishes.

"You were saying?"

"Me and Blaine," Sheila pondered. "Blaine is my brother Jake's best friend. We all grew up together, only they're four years older than me. So, umm, let's just say Blaine is like another brother to me. He came to New York to do something more with his MBA than Wisconsin offered."

"And what are you doing here?" I asked politely. I hated to get her off the topic of Blaine, but I thought it would be rude to ask only about him.

"Well, I ran away from home, sort of," Sheila said. She took the sweating glass of gin and tonic from me and sipped it with a look of relief. I couldn't tell if she was glad to change the topic from Blaine, or if the drink hit the spot. "I graduated from college and didn't know what to do with myself. I have a liberal arts degree, but the only thing I was ever good at was winning pageant titles. I didn't want to go to graduate school; there was nothing happening for me in Wisconsin; so I came here. Blaine said I could stay with him 'til I got something going."

"And what *have* you got going?" I wondered aloud, sipping my drink.

"Daniel, I just got here last week!" Sheila giggled. "You sound like my mother."

I put down my drink and threw up my hands.

"Heavens no! Anything but *that!*"

Sheila almost lost the sip of gin and tonic she'd just taken. When she recovered, she said, "Actually, I used to model for local businesses in Eau Claire. My manager sent photos and letters to his contacts here. So I have appointments at a couple of agencies. I'm just not sure about it yet."

"Girl, do it! You don't just say no to all that glamour and money! I'd do it if I thought that I . . ."

I trailed off, lost in thought.

Maybe I could model. In drag. Should I become Blaine's assistant/love slave or a drag supermodel, I wondered.

Must be the gin, I decided.

"Would you like another?" I asked, suppressing a hiccup after I downed my drink.

"Again, I thought you'd never ask," Sheila said with her signature grin before finishing her drink, too.

I paused in the act of making fresh drinks, struck by the way Sheila's blond beauty seemed very familiar.

Eau Claire, I realized, and all of us Scandinavian descendants. Spending time with Sheila seemed so natural to me, as if she were another of my many cousins. I could tell already I'd always feel comfortable with her.

"Why are you staring at me?" she asked.

"I feel like I've always known you," I admitted.

"We escaped the same place," she said, as if she'd read my mind again. "Pale food, pale landscapes, pale people! But I sure never knew there were any gay men in Eau Claire!"

"Oh, there aren't, now. I was their first and last. I had to sign a document swearing I'd never return. In fact, I violated Clause Six just mentioning it to you," I joked.

Sheila's face fell like a child's whose helium balloon had just floated away.

"I'm sorry," she said. "I didn't mean to offend you. I just never knew any gay people before."

"Oh my god, no, you didn't offend me," I said, touching her arm. "I was only joking around."

"You sure? I'd really like for us to be friends."

"Feeling a little homesick?" I asked.

"A little," she admitted. "Meeting you—well, I feel like I've always known you, too. Is there anything about Eau Claire you miss?"

I wanted to take her question as seriously as she'd asked it. I'd found my place in Manhattan, but I'd been here for more than a decade. I reminded myself that it was all new to Sheila. When I'd been younger than her, overwhelmed and alone in the city, had there been things about Eau Claire that I missed? I'd never been an adult there, only a kid. I pondered why that kid had been so desperate to escape.

In high school, I was always the outsider looking in. I'd had a handful of friends from junior high, but they all slowly detached themselves from me once it became apparent that I was "different." High school was a world where the caste system never died and your acceptance and popularity stood between you and a table all alone in the lunchroom.

I never excelled at sports. At the end of gym class I was always nursing bruises from the red rubber dodge ball that was constantly winged at me with the velocity of a speeding bullet fired from the hands of the more popular and stronger jocks.

Dodge ball. It was almost always played on rainy days when we couldn't go outside to one of the playing fields. If I woke up and found it raining outside, I would start rehearsing an Oscar-winning performance as a headache sufferer or stroke victim because I knew I had forty-five minutes of dodge ball to look forward to.

Early in my dodge ball career, I'd tried to win the acceptance of the brutal jocks by staying in the game as long as I could, but by the end of the first semester I found it easier and less painful just to get hit by that damn ball as soon as possible.

The purpose of the game changed from the development of

speed and agility into a sort of lottery system whereby the least popular students were weeded out first, usually in the most humiliating fashion. The jocks would aim for my shoulders, but generally would nail me in the head. I'd wear the red mark where the ball connected with my cheek or forehead like a scarlet letter for the next few periods.

Shop class was slightly better, thanks to years of helping my father with little projects, though that usually meant nothing more than holding pieces of wood for him or passing nails. Still, having watched him use jigsaws or power drills, I fared well with my shop projects and passed the course. I did these things alone, however, as most of the guys in shop were in my gym class and spread the word of my less-than-manly abilities at dodge ball, football, and even floor hockey.

To make matters worse, I loved art. Drawing was therapeutic and calming after a morning of fearing for my life in the gym. I was creative and had "vision," according to several of the school's art teachers. I understood line and shadows. It was no wonder. Between class periods, I had a mapped-out plan of how to get from class to class without crossing the lines of the popular students. I stuck to the shadows. When I did cross the lines and was seen, they'd torture me with loud comments so everyone in the halls could hear. Sometimes they'd even throw things at me. I felt I was always dodging people, verbal assaults, small objects, and red rubber balls.

I could never understand why I didn't fit in during my first year of high school, why I had become the class scapegoat. My parents were not unaware of the situation. The school sent letters and my teachers would talk to them during parent-teacher workshops. My parents would ask me what I thought was the problem. I knew what they wanted to hear, so I would say, "Nothing. They're the problem. I'm fine. Really."

And I was. I hadn't suddenly changed at fifteen. I'd never been into sports and "manly" activities and my friends from junior high seemed indifferent about that. But as they entered high school, kids developed a kind of radar. They knew how to pick out the "different" kids and followed society's message that different is not acceptable.

Apparently the kids in my high school also had "gaydar." It went into overdrive with me, and it wasn't long before I had no friends at

all. I walked through school like a zombie. Art was my only salvation in a society of peers that placed me as an "undesirable" in its
caste system. I added chorus to my roster of unacceptable activities.
In the hallways I received new labels added to the verbal assaults:
"chorus geek" and "art fag."

A new student was always a momentous occasion in high school.
For the popular kids higher up in the caste system, the new kid rep-
resented either a new victim or a new ally. For the less popular,
there was the opposite potential—a new tormentor.

In my sophomore year, I was introduced to Bill Hamilton in gym
class. It was a hated rainy day and I was huddled among the mass of
students in the center of the gym, awaiting my destined meeting
with the red rubber ball. The new kid (he would wear that moniker
until his place in the caste was decided) was on the sidelines holding the weapon. Coach Mike introduced him to us and announced
that Bill would have first throw, which was evidently regarded as
some kind of honor.

Bill spotted me just standing in front of everyone else. I'm sure
he could tell that I was a favorite target. Even the pimple-faced
geeks weren't talking to me as Coach Mike told us about Bill moving to Eau Claire from San Jose. They ran behind me as the game
started, knowing that I would stand there so I could be hit and go
sit in the corner. I gave Bill a defiant look, daring him to wallop me
with the loathsome red rubber ball. He gave me a smile and
mouthed the word *move,* trying to stir up the spirit in me to stay in
the game and win. Little did he know that the jocks and popular
kids had broken my spirit long ago. I stood my ground.

Bill shrugged and threw the ball into the crowd, but pointedly far
enough away to avoid hitting me. At that moment, Bill told me all I
needed to know about him. He wasn't going to give me an easy way
out. Nor did he have anything to prove. Bill didn't need to demonstrate his strength to the others by catapulting the ball at me and
basking in the sound of its hollow thunk as it rebounded off my skull.

I was amazed that he didn't throw the ball at me and stood staring at him with a puzzled look on my face. He smirked at me
briefly, but then called, "Look out!"

I'm sure I said, "Huh?" but didn't get far as the ball suddenly
smacked me in the back of my head. I sighed and left the mass of
people still in the game. Instead of heading for the corner, I went
over to Bill and introduced myself to him.

"I'm Daniel," I said.

"I'm Bill."

"Yeah, I know," I said to the floor. "Thanks for not killing me with that thing."

"Well, I knew some other guy would take care of that for me. I didn't think it would happen so soon though."

"Yeah, okay, see ya."

I thought he was saying that I was a wimp and he was trying to make it easy for me. I went to my usual corner to pray that the game would last until the end of the period so I wouldn't have to be humiliated again.

It did, and I didn't see Bill again until school was out. He was on my bus.

Riding the bus to and from school was the only part of my day that I hated as much as gym class. I lived in a rural section of Eau Claire; unfortunately, so did a lot of our school's redneck and more criminally minded students. To avoid them, I would race from the school as soon as the last bell sounded so I could get the seat right behind the driver. I was it of the first ones on the bus so getting the seat in the morning was usually not a problem. However, it also meant that I was one of the last ones off, and the potential for abuse increased exponentially.

My seat behind the driver didn't mean I was in neutral territory. Sure, the driver was a force to be reckoned with, and the bus was "school grounds," so he could hand out detention slips like the teachers. But his eyes were on the road most of the time, so I was still open to flying objects and verbal torture.

I was in the front seat of the bus, slouched down and crouched against the wall, when Bill dropped down beside me.

"Hey," he said, "you're on my bus."

"No, you're on *my* bus," I said.

He threw back his head and laughed. I was afraid he'd call attention to us, but he didn't seem to care at all.

"That's funny. Hey, tell me, are you on the track team?"

"No."

I almost laughed out loud at that one.

"Oh," he said. "I ran track at my old school in San Jose. I was hoping to do it here, too. You should join up with me."

"I don't think so," I sighed.

"Suit yourself." There was a moment of silence as he looked

ahead. "I hear the drama club is doing *Rebel Without a Cause.* You'd be a good Jim Stark. You've got that quiet and troubled youth sort of . . . you know. Are you auditioning?"

I gave one of my patented derisive snorts.

"No, that's all I need. It's bad enough that I sing."

"What do you mean?" he asked.

I honestly believed he didn't know and I gave him a bewildered stare. It was like I had walked the world with stigmata for the last two years and everyone knew it. I wasn't used to someone my age who wasn't throwing something at me.

"I mean, I like art. They call me 'art fag.' You're in danger of guilt by association just sitting with me. You'd better change seats."

He laughed again.

"Do you think I care what *they* think?" he asked. "I don't. I think I need a friend here as much as you do, so stop trying to blow it, okay?"

We both sat in silence as the bus drove us ever forward. I thought about it. Maybe he was right. Maybe I was the one who made everyone think they had a right to pick on me. Maybe I could change my fate and be accepted.

"You're right," I said softly. "I do need a friend."

He lived close to me and we hung out a lot after school. He would go running and I would join him for the hell of it. In one of those mysteries that punctuate adolescence, popular, jock, and geek alike bestowed approval on Bill. He covered all the categories the caste system allowed by acting in plays, singing with me in the tenor section of the chorus, and becoming a track and field legend at our school. He helped me get through those years by encouraging me to participate in everything with him. He got the James Dean role in *Rebel,* but I surprised everyone in my role as Plato, pure typecasting because I was nothing if not Bill's devoted admirer and sidekick. In time, as his best friend, I gained grudging acceptance from our classmates. Occasionally I even managed to slip out of his shadow and get some of the starring roles in our high school plays.

Bill's weaknesses were math and science. I tutored him at night after our runs. Bill always said if it weren't for me, he wouldn't have graduated. The self-degrading side of me would think that if I hadn't tutored Bill, some other geek would've been more than happy to gain acceptance and do the job. But my fragile and slow-growing self-confidence acknowledged that without the connection Bill and I had, someone else's efforts might have been fruitless.

It was partially because of Bill that I'd had the nerve to take Aunt Jen's offer of escape. Because he'd kept up with his coaches from his San Jose high school, Bill was being actively recruited for track and field or cross-country programs in several California universities. His excitement about graduation seemed directly proportional to my anxiety over my own unpromising future.

One night during a long run he slowed down until I caught up with him. He told me we needed to talk and I could tell by his expression it was going to be serious.

We climbed a fence and sank to the grass in somebody's pasture. My stomach was clenched as I tried to anticipate what he was going to say. After all, for years I'd been keeping a secret from him. Now that we were coming down to the wire, I knew I'd rather have Bill move far away than abandon me as a friend.

"You've decided which college you're going to, haven't you?" I asked, hoping this talk would be about him and not me.

"Nope," he said. "Lately, I've been thinking more about your plans than mine."

"Oh well, you know, I'll just go to college and end up teaching high school English and take over the drama department or something," I said with a nervous laugh.

"You know I think you're a really talented actor, Daniel. I'd hate to see you waste it. But no matter what you do, I think you should seriously consider moving away from Eau Claire. In the long run, most of this high school stuff won't matter. Coach Wilson"—this was his coach in San Jose—"has a hundred stories about jocks whose last moment of glory comes in high school."

"So you think I'll be a late bloomer?"

"I think you'll come into your own when you find a place where you feel you fit in. Not Eau Claire. Don't you get tired of pretending to be somebody you're not?"

I was grateful for the darkness when my face got hot even though the rest of me felt like ice.

"Yeah," I finally said. "I do."

"You never had to pretend with me, you know. It doesn't matter. It never did."

I felt like I counted to a million before taking a deep breath to say the one word that scared me more than any other.

"You always knew I was gay?"

"I didn't *know* it because you didn't tell me. But I figured you were, yeah."

"So what, you hung out with me because you felt sorry for me?"

He gave a startled laugh and said, "I hung out with you because you're the best friend I ever had. You know how to make stuff funny, the way you look at things. Look, I'm going to go be a brilliant college athlete and have a bunch of dusty trophies on my bookshelf when it's all over and I'm just a regular guy. And you may not be the next James Dean. But you can be happy. And we'll always be friends."

Bill had been right. We still kept in touch occasionally, and he was a regular guy now, with a wife and a kid. And I hadn't become James Dean, but I had been happy in Manhattan in a way I never would have been in Wisconsin. Now Sheila had followed the same path. Maybe there'd been no Bill on the start of her trip to encourage her. And maybe Blaine wasn't doing the job on this end.

"I've been gone a long time," I reminded her. "Even though I was joking, because Eau Claire does have a big gay community, I was never part of that. When I graduated from high school, my best friend went west and I came east. I never really looked back. I guess I do miss my sisters though. They spoiled me rotten."

"Don't you have any girlfriends here to spoil you as only girls can?"

I let out a snort as I thought of Gretchen.

"My best female friend is a lesbian who would howl at the idea of spoiling me. She's this wildly aggressive businesswoman who's accustomed to girls waiting on *her* hand and foot. As a matter of fact, the last time I saw her . . ."

"What?" Sheila asked as I stopped.

"Well, she and some partners invested in land in upstate New York. This group of antiestablishment types are building some kind of retreat for affluent women who want to escape the city. I went with her to check it out. The next thing I knew she was thrusting a hammer at me in some misguided attempt to make me do manual labor."

Sheila giggled and I realized she couldn't possibly understand how the sight of that hammer clutched within my red nails like some kind of scene straight out of *The Women* had terrified me.

Princesses wrote checks for Habitat for Humanity; they didn't lay floors or talk about lumber quality. I shuddered at the memory.

"So you and Blaine," I said, determined to change the subject before I found myself spilling out every detail of my life to her. "Is that, you know—"

"What?"

"Are the two of you, um, together?"

"There are two bedrooms in our apartment," she reminded me.

"Uh-huh."

"One is his and one is mine."

"Uh-huh. But—"

"Nothing is going on," she said.

Because he's *gay?* I wanted to scream, but only asked, "Why is that?"

"That's the way I want it," she said. "What about you? Anyone since Jeremy?"

"No."

I had obviously come across someone as adroit at changing the subject as I was. A stray thought crossed my mind. I slapped my forehead.

"Shit! I forgot to ask what theater, *again!*"

"Come again?" Sheila asked, bewildered.

"Want to see a musical next week?" I sighed.

Sheila's face lit up.

"Sure! I'd love to!" she gleefully replied. "Which one?"

"Anything Goes," I said. "And I'm sure it will."

FOUR

The following days were relatively calm. I'd had Martin call and make the arrangements for "theater night," extending Jeremy's invitation to him and a date, knowing Jeremy would acquiesce if for no other reason than to avoid dealing with me. The plan was for my party to meet early enough to get sufficiently cocktailed before proceeding to the theater.

When the buzzer sounded, I took one last look in the mirror and grinned. Not bad. The days in my garden had been more worthwhile than visits to the tanning salon. I would definitely be a suitable escort for the stunning Sheila.

My host smile grew genuine as I opened the door to find Ken with Martin.

"Judy!" I gasped, grabbing Ken's hands. "Whatever made you lower your standards to this?"

Martin made a face before giving me a quick kiss on the cheek.

"I wouldn't miss tonight for anything," Ken said. "Jeremy's chance to redeem himself!"

We all rolled our eyes, remembering Jeremy's worst theatrical adventure. A friend of a friend had written and directed a disaster of a play that had blessedly closed immediately in some hole-in-the-wall theater. Unfortunately, Jeremy and I had invited everyone we knew to opening night to ensure a full house. The play itself would have provided weeks' worth of vicious dish, but Jeremy had been woefully miscast and whole lines of his dialogue were incorporated into our friends' drag vocabulary, painful reminders of his humiliation. Jeremy's ego had been so fragile afterward that he'd barely mentioned getting a part in *Guys and Dolls,* desperate not to risk another agonizing public failure.

"I'd have thought your history was enough to make you avoid Jeremy," Martin said. "But Ken figured Jeremy hounded you to do this so he could finally have some success in your eyes."

"Why would he care what I think?" I asked blankly.

Ken smiled, taking the drink I offered, and said, "He's always needed your approval, Daniel. He measures himself against your success."

"But I never made it into *any* play," I argued. "I don't get it."

"Sweetie, 2Di4 is a legend. Okay, maybe the world isn't knocking at your door. But in *our* world—"

"The only one that matters!" Martin interjected.

"—you are a huge success. Believe me, since you left Club Chaos, the audiences have been dismal."

This was not what I wanted to hear at all. I'd been racking my brain for weeks, wondering if adjusting to the real world was the right thing to do. Now Ken was saying things were hard for him as a result of my actions, which made me feel terrible.

Ken had always been my guardian angel, watching over me and helping me out of one sticky situation after another. I first met him in an East Village club long forgotten, where drag queens were welcome, but at a small price. The bartenders, cocktail servers, and performers were all drag queens. All drag, all the time.

The owner, Sal Delbruccio, was as straight as a ruler, but had a penchant for very tall women. He was a leg man, after all. His wife, Sylvia, was a Rockette until she was fired when she toppled the kick line as a result of her drinking. Sal had opened a bar in Brooklyn, much to Sylvia's delight, then moved it into the East Village. While Sylvia was pleased, she didn't like to ride the train and Sal found he had more time to harass his waitresses. One night Sylvia decided to surprise Sal in the city (it was rumored she was out of cash and wanted to drink for free), but was surprised instead to find the bar closed and Sal with his pants down and two of his leggy employees giving new meaning to "slow" gin fizz.

The bar stayed closed for two weeks while Sal's black eyes healed and a new staff was selected by Sylvia, who appointed herself manager of the bar. Sylvia's decision to hire a staff made up entirely of drag queens worked out quite well. Not only did it provide jobs for many out-of-work queens, but it brought a little lost glamour back to Sylvia's life. Not to mention that it provided Sal with a lot of leg to safely ogle. The drag queens certainly didn't mind Sal's salaciousness. The attention was fun in a creepy way, and Sylvia was always close at hand just in case.

I had been playing the part of a judge in an awful drag show called *Marilyn Monroe Versus Wade* in the meat-packing district. I had been looking for a way to get out of it and heard about Sal's bar from a juror in the show. Sylvia was holding auditions for new acts, as she had just bought out the space next door and expanded the bar to create a performance space.

I was frantic the day of the audition, trying to decide what to do for an act. I had been so many different characters in so many months that my apartment looked like the costume room of a variety show. I was about to give up, chicken out, and settle for my rather disgusting role as a judge who performed "Baby with the Bathwater" when I was suddenly inspired to make my misery work for me.

I showed up for the audition at Sal's bar in perfect Marilyn Monroe attire. I was given ten minutes to impress Sylvia with my act. I watched her as I waited for my turn. She was sitting at a table right in front of the stage. The only thing separating her and the person auditioning was a rum and Coke. If she didn't like the act, the drink would be significantly emptied and replaced, much like the auditioner. If she liked the act, she would be too engrossed to drink. Sylvia seemed pretty toasted to me, so I figured I had a good shot.

I resituated my long white gown, adjusted my breasts, draped my white stole over my shoulders, and strode onto the stage. I whipped the stole off my shoulders in one fluid motion and dropped it onto the stage, the cue for "Diamonds Are a Girl's Best Friend" to start playing. I impersonated Marilyn to the hilt, which was easy for me as I'd seen every movie of hers on tape. I vamped, I pouted, I thrust hips in ways hips shouldn't be thrust.

At the five-minute mark of my audition, I noticed Sylvia hadn't touched her rum and Coke. At that moment, the music, played from a tape I had made a mere hour earlier, segued into "Diamonds" by Herb Alpert, a song which had just hit the Top 40.

It was jazzy, upbeat, and featured vocals by Janet Jackson. It also was a fun juxtaposition with the Marilyn Monroe number, as both songs said that love has its price.

When I finished, Sylvia sat in silence for a few seconds. I stood at center stage, not knowing quite what to do, until Sylvia said, "Not bad, toots. Not bad. Sal! What do you think?"

I hadn't noticed Sal sitting in the back of the room making notes in a ledger. He looked me up and down briefly and said, "Nice gams."

"Shut up, Sal. You're hired. You go on tonight."

"But I'm in a—"

"You go on tonight. Did I stuttah?" Sylvia said, glaring at me and then downing her rum and Coke.

I played at Sal's bar for two months. The downside of the rather sleazy joint was the clientele, mainly straight men who liked to come to heckle the performers. It was like working for a circus side show. At most drag establishments it was frowned upon to harass the performers, and there would be someone large and imposing to show you to the door if you didn't comply. At Sal's, it was the opposite. And we weren't allowed to dish back the insults and rude behavior. We were supposed to shut up, keep on with our act, and take it like a man.

It was hard. After the first month I was beginning to wonder why I wanted to work there in the first place. I had been tuning into the grapevine to find another job, but there just weren't any openings anywhere, so I stuck it out.

Sylvia demanded that I work as Marilyn, she was so taken with my audition. Her instincts were right. I closed every night's show with the rowdiest, bawdiest hoots and hollers. I got excellent tips, but I also got pinched, groped, and was asked to sit on many a face.

One night I decided to deviate from the norm of simply lip-synching to Marilyn. I developed a split personality for her: Marilyn Mundane. She was bored. She was tragic. She was suicidal. It wasn't that far from the real Marilyn, and it was fun to bring that side onto the stage. I performed tragic torch songs, which actually caught the attention of the boozehounds and kept them at bay. I ended it with a Marilyn does Marlene Dietrich number and watched the guys drool. When it was over, the boys went wild with applause and whistles. It was almost nice.

We would often work the room after our acts to collect tips, which was a grab bag of sorts. You never knew if you'd be tipped or grabbed. After my performance that night, I mingled with the patrons and was surprised at the modicum of respect that I received along with a generous number of tips.

A young man was in the middle of passing me ten dollars and squeezing my ass when I was tapped on the shoulder by one of the cocktail servers.

"There's a man at the bar who'd like to buy you a drink," he said.

"Oh really? This should be fun. Is he scary?"

"No! Actually, he's really nice. Very polite. He's the attractive one who looks like he's read a book without pictures."

The description wasn't needed. Not only was the man attractive and smiling at me as I walked across the room, he also wasn't sporting coveralls, gold chains, or greased-back hair.

"Hello. My name is Kenneth Bruckner," he said as he stood up and shook my hand.

"Hi, Kenneth. I'm Daniel."

"Please, call me Ken and sit down with me for a moment. What would you like?"

I was about to say that my drinks were comped, but I caught Sylvia in my peripheral vision as she was lurking around the bar. She didn't know that we often drank for free, "free" not being a word in her vocabulary.

"I'll have a martini. Sharon knows how I like them."

"I sure do, honey," Sharon, a tall drag queen in an even taller red wig, butted in. "You were unbelievable tonight, by the way. Want a kill stick?"

Sharon passed me a Marlboro Light, lit it for me, then set off to make my martini.

"I'm sorry," I said, exhaling away from Ken, "do you mind if I smoke?"

"I almost expect you to cross your arms with smoke pouring from your body like Morticia Addams," Ken said. "I mind, but it's your body. Go ahead. I wanted to talk to you about your act. It was fantastic."

"Thank you," I said, enjoying the praise. I stubbed out my cigarette, worried that I was smoking all over him before I realized that the entire bar was filled with smoke.

"I kind of have an ulterior motive in buying you a drink, I'm afraid. I—"

"Oh. Listen," I interrupted, "that's really sweet and you're really nice. And very handsome, but I'm not looking for anything like that right now. And you're not really my type. I—"

"Please stop. I'm not trying to pick you up," Ken said, laughing. "And you've shot me down enough. No need to continue."

"I'm sorry. It's just that with the guys in this bar, you have to nip that stuff in the bud right away. Not that I think you're like any of the guys in here."

"Smooth, baby," Sharon said to me as she set my martini down. "Real smooth."

"Look. Let me start over," Ken said. "I work at a place called Club Chaos in the West Village."

"I've heard of it," I said.

"We're looking for—"

"Keep it down. The owner's wife is afoot and I think I know where you're going with this," I implored.

"I need your help," Ken said, leaning in and speaking in low tones. "One of our headliners did something a bit stupid and can't perform tomorrow night. We don't want him to get fired, so I need someone to fill in for him. It might be a couple of nights, actually. I'm not sure. But you'd be perfect. I want you to do it."

"That's really great, but I'm not allowed to perform anywhere else or I'll get canned. As much as I hate it, I need this job."

"We can disguise you," Ken said. "That's really not a problem. Could you get at least two nights off?"

"I'm off tomorrow night, anyway. And I could probably get the next, too, I guess."

"That's great," Ken exclaimed, even though I hadn't really committed.

"What did this guy do anyway? The one I'm filling in for?"

"For an act?"

"No."

"Oh," Ken said. "He fell asleep in a tanning booth and is too fried to get into a dress."

The next night I met Ken backstage at Club Chaos. I was in awe of the posh surroundings and theatrical presence of the old building. It was exactly where I wanted to be, not only in the heart of gay Mecca, but in a place where I could be admired and my talents appreciated.

"Okay," Ken said, ushering me into the dressing room. "This is what's going to happen. I close the show as Judy every night."

"Garland?"

"No, Judy Tenuta," Ken said, swatting the back of my head. "Judy Garland is my hero. Anyway, you'll be going on before me as Tina Yothers."

"Whaaaat?" I shrieked, as Ken laughed at my surprise.

"No, really. The spot is called The Tina Yothers Comeback Special. I just wrote it last night."

"But 'Family Ties' is still on the air," I said, rather confused.

"Perfect! That's your first line! Trust me, it'll be hilarious. Besides, you won't have to look glamorous, so nobody will recognize you. Not that anyone from Sal's bar ever comes here. Plus, the band refuses to play with Tina, so it's all simple a cappella songs. Or you could play a guitar."

"I don't play guitar."

"That could actually work," Ken pondered. "It's all comedy. Just read the script over and you'll get it. Now follow me."

I followed Ken to the wings of the stage. He motioned for me to be quiet and we crept along the edge of the scrim that hid the backstage from the audience's view. There was a rehearsal in progress being led by an older man who was barking at the actors for missing their steps.

"That's Andy," Ken whispered to me. "He owns this place. He doesn't know yet that Oliver is out tonight because of excessive tanning. If he did, he'd freak out and fire him."

"Well, won't he figure it out when Oliver doesn't show?"

"It's possible. But I believe one of two things will happen. Andy will think he didn't get the revisions to the set list. To save face, he'll just go with the flow of the evening and pretend he knew all about it."

"But won't he wonder who I am and why I'm performing?"

"Which is the other thing that might happen," Ken explained. "The act is hysterical and might be such a success that he'll pretend he knew about it all along—"

"—to save face," I finished.

Which is exactly what happened. The Tina Yothers Comeback Special was such a hit that a rather caught-off-guard Andy announced its permanent spot at Club Chaos that night. I was introduced to him and he hired me on the spot, though eyeing Ken suspiciously.

I learned that Ken had been watching me at Sal's for quite some time. He figured that if I could hold my own in that den of lions, Club Chaos would be a walk in the park for me.

It was difficult for me to think that my split-second decision to leave Club Chaos could have disastrous repercussions on the very place where Ken had offered me salvation so many years before. I stared at him, wondering what to say. If I apologized for how bad things were at the club, it would sound like I was taking all the credit for the successes of the past. I sincerely felt that Ken's creative vision was the real reason Club Chaos thrived. I knew how hard he worked to pull things together, often having to fight Andy even as he tweaked his ego. I had never meant to make things even harder for him.

"However," Ken continued, reading me like a book as always, "I don't hold that against you. Not in the least. As I told Martin on the way over"—here he cast a stern glance Martin's way—"turning thirty is a good time for you to regroup. I did the same thing. I'm happy with the choices I made. Those of us who love you, and we are many, want you to be happy, too."

I was flooded with gratitude. As long as I'd known Ken, he'd always made things sound so reasonable and sane. Even Martin's usual flakiness became something endearing in Ken's presence. And Ken's explanation of Jeremy's insistence that I subject myself to this evening finally solved that mystery. Still, I was not totally convinced that Jeremy didn't have some more sinister motive yet to reveal itself. I made a mental note to discuss Jeremy and the current state of Club Chaos with Ken at a more appropriate time.

The buzzer sounded and I hastily said, "There is something I was hoping. I'll explain later, but I haven't really told my friend about the 2Di4 gig. She thinks I'm an actor."

Ken's face took on a look of mild concern and Martin gawked at me as I went to let Sheila in.

We heard a flurry of steps outside; I opened the door before she could knock and the three of us gaped at Sheila as she made her entrance. She could only be described as breathtaking.

"My friend Sheila Meyers from Eau Claire," I said, noting her slight frown as I gave the impression we'd known each other from there. It was immediately replaced by one of her brilliant smiles and I felt myself relax. "Sheila, my best friends Ken Bruckner and Martin Blount."

"Hello, Martin. Hello, Ken. How nice to meet you both," Sheila beamed.

"Nice to meet you," Martin said.

"The pleasure is entirely mine," Ken answered.

Everyone stood admiring each other for a moment, until all eyes turned to Sheila. Well, more to Sheila's dress, actually. I swear I could see a trickle of saliva at the corner of Martin's mouth.

"Your dress is fabulous, Sheila," I said.

"Thank you," she said and handed me her black satin wrap. The dress was also black satin with spaghetti straps that tied behind the back of her neck. The fabric clung to her lithe frame and left very little to the imagination. The back of the dress was open all the way to the small of her back; the hem reached the floor but was slit on the side to the middle of her thigh.

"I hope you don't get cold," Ken said. "It might be cool out tonight."

"Well, I have the wrap. And that's why I wore boots," Sheila explained, thrusting a foot forward and propelling a long, curvy leg out of the slit in her dress. Her feet were clad in high-heeled, black fabric boots.

"Someone went shopping," I observed.

"I had nothing to wear. Everything that I had was so boring. It all screamed, 'I'm a hick from the Midwest!' so I asked Blaine where I should go shopping for tonight."

"And where is this fabulous ensemble from?" Ken asked.

"Barneys," Sheila answered. "They were nice enough to open an account for me."

"Ahhh," Ken, Martin, and I said in unison.

We stood another few moments staring at her in admiration. Martin was scanning her up and down, and I could tell he was looking for a flaw. I felt as if I had proprietary rights to Sheila and must protect her from him. Almost as if she hadn't existed until I found her.

"Sheila, that dress ties behind the neck, right?" Martin asked, edging toward her. I suddenly tensed up, wondering what he was going to do.

"Yes," Sheila said, raising a hand self-consciously to her neck.

Martin eased his way behind her and gathered up her hair.

"You should wear your hair up to show off how it ties around your swanlike neck," Martin insisted.

I nearly exhaled in audible relief. Martin, usually scathing to newcomers, would be playing nice that evening. He walked her to the mirror, holding her honey-and-wheat-colored hair in a twist on her head to show her.

"That is better," Sheila agreed. "You're right."

"I know," Martin said. "Daniel, do you have any bobby pins?"

"In the bedroom," I said and he dashed off to get them.

"Drink, darling?" I quickly asked Sheila, in case she got curious about why I had bobby pins.

"The usual, Daniel, please."

I liked that Sheila felt comfortable enough to have already claimed gin and tonic as her usual.

"So," Martin chimed in, as he returned with a fist full of bobby pins and proceeded to create the ultimate updo on Sheila, "how long have you and Daniel known each other?"

"Not long. I guess, well, what has it been, Daniel? About a week?"

"Umm . . . something like that," I replied.

Damn; she'd just blown the whole *We've known each other for ages from Eau Claire* setup.

"Oh? I thought you knew each other from Wyoming?" Martin pressed on.

"Wisconsin," Sheila and I both interjected.

I glared at Martin as I handed Sheila her drink, then took Ken's and Martin's glasses to make them another. I tossed the rest of mine back in one gulp.

"Oh, no," Sheila continued innocently. "I've only been in New York a couple of weeks. Daniel brought me flowers one afternoon. I live around the block. Across the alley, actually. In fact, you can see the apartment window from Daniel's garden."

"Say it's not so," Martin gasped with faux surprise. He looked at me with a sly smile and a raised eyebrow as I gave him his drink.

"Why don't we go out to the garden? It's such a lovely evening," I suggested in a feeble attempt to change the subject.

As he went through the doorway to the garden, Ken, seeming to sense my discomfort, asked, "Have you ever seen *Anything Goes*, Sheila?"

"No, I haven't. In fact, this will be my first New York show."

"Well, you will love it, dear."

Their voices became fainter as they walked farther from the open door.

Martin hung back to speak to me.

"Okay, Danny boy, you want to let me in on what this is all about?"

"What are you talking about?"

"Who is this Sheila? What exactly *is* her relationship to Mr. IBM across the way? I mean, she does live with him, does she not? I can't possibly think of a window more worthy of looking into across the street. By the way, giving her flowers was a nice touch."

"Oh, Martin. You're incorrigible. She's just a friend. One can never have too many allies in the city, can one?"

Martin drew a breath to say something but the phone rang.

Boy, I thought, that thing has a way of doing that to him; saved again. However much the phone company makes off me, it's not enough.

"Hello?" I inquired after the third ring.

"Hello, dear heart."

"Aunt Jen! What a surprise!" I exclaimed for Martin's benefit. He gave a sour look to express his disinterest in my dear old aunt then left to join Sheila and Ken in the garden.

"Daniel, have you found a respectable career yet?"

Her raspy voice jabbed at me from the phone. I heard her inhale from a cigarette, Benson & Hedges Menthol held delicately in a foot-long holder, no doubt. Aunt Jen envisioned herself as a forties film star beauty. Too much time and money had allowed her to live in a delusional fantasy world which no one else could share. She liked to make sure everyone around her lived a "normal" life of which she was the dictator.

"Oh, I've had a few interviews. Mainly at advertising firms," I lied, not in the mood for a sermon.

I caught Sheila's gaze as she eavesdropped on my conversation from the doorway to the garden. She was holding her empty glass, obviously returning for a refill, but found my phone call more interesting. Her eyebrows lifted and she smirked as if she were plotting something.

"Good boy. You've always been my favorite, you know. Which is why I'm coming to visit you. I haven't decided when. It may be sooner than you think, but I'll be sure to let you know."

This I knew was pure fiction. Aunt Jen loved nothing more than descending on family members without warning, as if hoping to catch them in some decadent or scandalous activity. More often than not, she was merely bored by their ready hospitality and ordinary lives. Poor Jen had been born into the wrong family; I provided her only diversion from its all-American wholesomeness.

"Okay, Auntie." She loved when I called her this. "I'm going to a show with some friends so I have to run. We'll talk later, okay?"

"Yes, my dear. Ciao." She hung up before I could say goodbye.

"Advertising?" Sheila piped. "I guess your audition didn't work out. You know, Blaine's firm is looking for an administrative assistant. Someone to make appointments, handle clients. I'm sure with your charm, you'd be great."

"Really?" I tried to suppress my sudden excitement.

The flowers for Sheila were going to pay off after all. I had visions of late nights in the office with Blaine, his tie loosened—

"Yes, but we can talk business later," Sheila said, interrupting my fantasy.

We shared a cab to the theater. Sheila's eyes were glowing. I knew that look. It was the face of someone new to New York. She looked like glitter had been sprinkled over her body. Her mouth was slightly open as she gazed up at the one-story television billboards of Times Square. Coca-Cola never looked so appealing as when the bottle was as tall as a house in the country. I still felt like I could squeeze myself into one of those giant bubbles and remain suspended over the twinkling electric stars above Broadway.

The cab turned down Forty-fifth Street and dropped us off in front of the theater. A long line of people waited for tickets, hoping someone would cancel or one seat would open just in time. Luckily we did not have that hassle to worry over. We flounced—well, they flounced, I glided, as becomes royalty—up the steps and went inside the theater. Men in tuxedos and women in all their end-of-summer finery were posed next to columns, sipping champagne and acting rich. Heads turned toward Sheila as she slipped her arm through mine. I was proud to be on the arm of such a dazzling woman, though I must admit that I was a bit jealous of all the attention. That was one thing I would miss about being the princess. I almost wished Martin, Ken, and I had dressed in drag.

Martin went to the box office to retrieve the tickets. Sheila turned to me and gave me an excited smile.

"This is like a movie. Like everything I came to New York for.

The glamorous people, the lights." She stopped her little mono-
logue and her eyes grew to the size of saucers. "Oh my god, is that
Cindy Crawford and Robert Redford?"

I looked in the direction she was gazing.

"Why yes, that is Cindy."

"She's just like her pictures. I think I will do it. I will be a model."

"Good for you," I said, although I still felt jealous. I remembered
my own early struggles and could not stop myself from comparing
them to Sheila's nonchalant *choice* of opportunities in New York.
"What made you suddenly decide?" I queried.

Sheila was still gazing enrapt at Cindy, mentally dissecting her
and taking notes, I imagined. She suddenly swung her head in my
direction.

"Because I'm better looking than she is," she commented.

A giggle belied her serious expression and made me laugh,
which made Sheila giggle again. I noticed Cindy sneak a sidelong
glance at us as if worried we might be laughing at her.

Martin returned with our tickets and we walked toward our
seats. My stomach had begun to ache a little. It was fifteen minutes
until curtain and the gin was finally beginning to catch up with me.

"Should I throw something at the stage when the little slut walks
out?" Martin asked with an evil glint in his eye.

"If you do, I'll say I don't know who you are when the ushers
drag you out, scratching and screaming," Ken said in his low, fa-
therly tone.

"You always ruin my fun," Martin scowled, mock-pouting.

"Daniel," Sheila said, turning to me and putting her hand on my
upper arm. "Thank you again for inviting me."

"Don't thank me just yet," I said as we took our seats in the center orchestra section. "Just because this show's on Broadway doesn't
mean it won't bomb."

"I don't care if it is a bomb. This is the most glamorous and fun
night I've had in ages," Sheila gushed, sitting next to me.

"Honey, obviously you've never seen Jeremy act," Martin
sneered. Ken promptly smacked him on the head with his program.

The whole house fell quiet as the theater lights dimmed and the
orchestra welled up into the lively Cole Porter overture. I scanned
the *Playbill* program and found Jeremy's small theatrical biography.

It listed his B.A. in Theater/Performing Arts from Juilliard, numerous commercials and small parts in experimental theater, his dedication of this performance to me—

His *what???*

I almost dropped the *Playbill*. I looked up, mouth agape, to find Sheila, Martin, and Ken looking at me with their eyebrows raised. They had just read the same dedication I had.

"Girl," Martin drawled, but that's all he could say (thank god) because the lights went out and the show started.

Anything Goes was a relatively easy performance to stage, since the whole production took place on a boat. The set was pretty and creative, with each character's small cabin either folding out of the main set or turning in from the revolving stage. Jeremy played a rather handsome Billy and his voice had never sounded better. I was quite impressed and a little surprised by how much his voice had improved. Maybe it was all that *rehearsing* with Robert.

Robert, who had dedicated his performance to his mother and not me (again, thank god), played a hilarious Sir Evelyn Oakleigh. I was amazed at his British accent and impeccable comedic timing. His facial expressions were rather overexaggerated but seemed perfect for the role.

I found myself laughing and being swept up in the romance of the production. I didn't know who I would rather be: Hope, the innocent girl running into a long, lost romance, or the bawdy nightclub singer finding romance, once again, with a spoken-for man, wondering if it was all worthwhile.

"The nightclub singer. Definitely," we all agreed, sipping champagne in the lobby during intermission.

"Or else that ditzy blonde with all the fabulous costumes," Martin interjected.

"You would want to be the gun moll," I chided.

"I just love that number she did," Martin said.

" 'Heaven Hop'?" Sheila asked.

"Yeah, it's cute," Martin said. "Like me."

"That's open for debate." I laughed. "What are we doing after the show?"

"Well, if this were six months ago," Ken pondered, "you'd head backstage to either congratulate our star or have a nice bitch and claw session."

Sheila wore a somewhat puzzled expression.

"Ken's right," I said to her. "But I don't know if that's allowed anymore. Not the fighting, but backstage rights."

"Well," Martin said carelessly, "did he ever go backstage after any of your—"

"Any of *my* shows?" I interrupted with a nervous laugh. "Don't be ridiculous."

"Oh, Daniel, what shows have you done? I never did ask you," Sheila inquired.

The lobby lights started blinking, signaling the end of intermission. Saved by lights.

"Gee, we'd better get to our seats," I said, hurrying my companions along.

We headed back into the theater and found our row. I was thankful we had hurried; I hated having to hurdle those people who sit on the aisle, almost always some old woman who refuses to move her knees aside to let you by.

As I was about to follow the others, I was tapped on the shoulder by one of the ushers.

"Excuse me, sir."

"Yes?" I detested being called *sir,* especially after having been called *princess, your highness,* and *your worship* for so long.

"Are you Mr. Stephenson, sir?"

"Yeah," I slowly answered. Though I never revealed my last name to any of my fans in the drag bars and clubs, I was suddenly afraid this young usher was one of my former loyal subjects who had flocked weekly to my shows and would now blow my cover to Sheila.

And no, I don't have an overactive imagination and not everything is all about *me me me,* I told that oddly silent inner voice.

"Jeremy Caprellian requests that you and your party join him backstage after the performance," the usher explained. "Just show this pass at the backstage door and you'll be allowed through."

"Thank you," I said blankly, taking the laminated white pass with the show's logo on it.

"What was that all about?" interrogated Martin as I took my seat.

"It would appear our plans have been made for us," I said, brandishing the pass as an explanation.

The rest of the show was sheer perfection as Billy (Jeremy) won back Hope's heart, along with the hearts of everyone in the audience, judging from the cheers and applause he received. Robert had us all in stitches as he stammered and bumbled his way around Reno Sweeny's advances and finally into her arms at the end of their big duet, "Let's Misbehave." I found myself forgetting it was Robert onstage, laughing at his clever lines, hoping they'd get together, even though I knew the whole plot of the musical beforehand. It was a brilliant production and would obviously be on Broadway for a long time to come.

After the final curtain call, we made our way through the packed aisles and lobby. True to form, a crowd had gathered outside the stage door of the theater. A makeshift aisle from the door to the street to allow the actors to get to their waiting cars was sectioned off from the onlookers with velvet ropes.

Chanting *Excuse me* like Buddhist monks and holding the pass in front of us like a deity, we made our way through the crowd and found ourselves at the stage door. A rather large man was guarding the door with his barrel chest and *Kill first ask questions later* demeanor.

"Hi, my name is Daniel Stephenson and these are my friends. This pass is from Jeremy Cap—"

"Yeah, yeah," he said, eyeing the pass. "Inside."

He opened the door and swept us in while holding back the crowd with a stare that would freeze molten lava.

The atmosphere was electric with the feeling that came only from a hit. We wound our way through droves of people, Sheila's face ecstatic as she took it all in, Ken quietly getting directions on where to find Jeremy, even Martin dropping his usual above-it-all expression. I felt as if I were being swept along by some tide stronger than my will to control all the separate compartments of my life.

Finally we were inside a dressing room where hordes of people laughing and talking left me feeling dazed. Then, in one of those moments possible only in movies, the crowd parted and there seemed to be a hush as Jeremy and I stood watching each other, he flushed with success, his eyes boring into me.

My heart pounded as I waited for him to make this moment totally his, to find some way to demean me all over again with his faithless, reckless disregard of years of my loyalty. I felt dizzy as I was bombarded with a montage of memories . . . our first kiss after being caught in Central Park in a sudden rainstorm, running for cover, giggling, breathless, and then finally that riveting moment of skin on skin, lips on lips . . . long nights of laughing and eating and making love all over the apartment . . . staring at the ocean from the Oregon shore, wrapped in each other's arms . . . endless mundane activities made meaningful when they were shared, like shopping, learning to cook new things, doing laundry, refinishing the antique bookcases that now held someone else's books.

I could remember all the things that were right about our relationship. I just couldn't figure out what went wrong or when it happened. Blaming Robert was taking the easy way out. Apparently our life simply became too small to hold Jeremy. He grew bored, restless, and the hit his career took caused the final fracture that leveled a crumbling relationship.

I'd tried to be as supportive as I could during that time after the play folded; it was truly Jeremy at his worst. There was no laughing him out of it, no making him put things in perspective. He was convinced his career was over; nothing I could say helped. Maybe Ken was right. Even though my career was played out on a much smaller stage, it was possible the minor celebrity I enjoyed made Jeremy a little bitter. Especially since his own dismal failure came at a time when my act was going better than ever.

Things were certainly different now. I no longer had a career and Jeremy was celebrating a triumph. Even as I felt sincerely happy for him, I became aware of a new feeling: detachment. None of it seemed to have anything to do with me. More than anything in the world, I wanted to enjoy an evening with Ken, Martin, and Sheila, and plot my way into Blaine's office and, with any luck, his arms.

I felt a little stunned. Was I really, finally, over Jeremy? Was I actually ready to risk my heart again? Something inside of me felt tentative and fragile, but also determined. I thought of the times I'd grown flowers from seeds. Each time I saw the first tiny, green shoots, I'd wonder how anything that delicate could survive. When my planters and pots grew heavy with flowers, every time seemed like a miracle that never failed to excite me.

In some ways, I knew I never stopped being a naïve kid from Eau Claire. Though I had not been innocent when I met Jeremy, I had been dumb about love. He'd been the first guy who got past my barriers and made me want to believe in love. I'd learned so much with him. Maybe my last lesson was to let go, to trust that I could experience all of this again with someone else.

Just as Jeremy had. I realized his moment had arrived, and somewhere in this crowd of people would be Robert waiting to share it with him.

The pressure in the room made me feel like my heart was being squeezed out of me as Jeremy slowly made his way to stand in front of me.

"Congratulations," I said. "You were better than flawless. You were spectacular."

"Daniel, I . . ."

He trailed off. I could feel Ken and Martin tense behind me as they anticipated one more emotional swing taken at me. I felt my chin lift a little, regal to the core of my being. No matter what he did, no one would ever know he could still hurt me. It had taken a long time, but I knew that, however uncertain my future might be, Jeremy was my past. In some strange way, his success had ended our association in a way his failure never could have.

I watched as he took a deep breath and finished, "I want to come home."

My brow furrowed. I could not possibly have heard what I thought I heard. Jeremy looked at me and let out a sigh so deep it could well have included oxygen from his first breath of life. Evidently, this was quite a load off of his mind. Martin, Ken, and Sheila glanced at each other uncomfortably. Jeremy and I stared at each other. The ball was clearly in my court. I decided I'd better return it fast, before Robert showed up as another of the spectators.

"Well," I laughed, "it seems you are home. The audience loved you."

"Don't make this more difficult for me than it needs to be. The audience may have loved me, but I love you. I want to come home."

"Jeremy, believe me, I am not trying to make this difficult, but . . ." The sentence faded into nothingness.

"Daniel, please. What is it you want me to do? Do you want me to beg? I'll beg."

He moved as if to get on both knees in front of me.

"Jeremy, stop it. You're embarrassing me," I said, feeling my face flush.

"I'm serious, Danny. I'm begging you. I'll do anything. I made the biggest mistake of my life leaving you. If I could turn back the clock, I would in a second. But please, don't deny me the chance to do it right this time. Please, let me come home."

"Robert," I reminded Jeremy, glancing around anxiously. Jeremy seemed less concerned than I was. But Robert was nowhere in sight, no doubt the center of his own crowd of friends and well-wishers.

"Robert has known this was coming for a long time. He already confronted me about it, but I denied it. Not because it wasn't what I wanted, but because I didn't want this to affect his performance tonight."

Jeremy taking someone else's feelings into consideration? Who was this man in front of me, and what had he done with Jeremy?

"I really don't know what to say."

"Just say yes. Say yes and that you love me, too. I know you still do. Please, Danny, let me come home where I belong."

Martin's, Ken's, and Sheila's gazes went back and forth as if they were watching a tennis match. They obviously were torn between not wanting to eavesdrop and wanting to be supportive of me, should I need them. It wasn't as if Jeremy and I were going to be able to obtain any privacy in this backstage circus anyway.

Everyone appeared to be waiting for my response, but I didn't have one to give. I looked pleadingly at Ken, hoping somehow he could telepathically send me an answer to this unexpected riddle. I saw in his eyes that he felt awful about the predicament I was in, but could offer no assistance.

"Jeremy, I need some time to think this through. This is all very sudden for me, and I honestly don't know what to say. I'll call you soon. I promise."

I turned to walk away through a crowd that parted like the Red Sea. Sheila, Martin, and Ken followed.

"Do you want to talk about this?" Ken asked with a sympathetic cushion beneath his voice.

I was so distracted that I could barely reply, "I think I need to be alone."

I wandered through the crowd on the sidewalk outside the theater. Past memories of Jeremy lodged themselves between my thoughts and reality.

It was a perfect sunset, the kind that cowboys ride into with their fair maids behind them on the saddle, the kind of sunset that fulfilled a day. The old house stood stately and proud on the cliff overlooking the Pacific Ocean. The world was quiet except for the ringing of pure love in my ear, quietly overlaid with the perfect singing of sirens on the rocks below, dipping their hair into the ocean. That is what I imagined; that is how it all seemed, so unreal that it could only be happening.

I sat on the verandah beside Jeremy, his soft hand in mine, and I thought, Yes, yes, god, this is it. This is the one love that authors write about. This is the love the entire world strives for. This is emotion untouched by the tainted tongues of pedantic philosophers. After two weeks in Oregon, now on this cliff, in a rented house—

—a borrowed dream.

I took a cab by myself, grateful to have escaped the concern in my friends' eyes. I was stunned that Jeremy had tried to make our reconciliation as public as our breakup. I thought maybe it was his attempt to atone for the humiliation I'd endured; part of me was grateful for such a gesture. But Ken and Martin would never understand any softening of my attitude toward Jeremy. Even their scents were warning signals, their energy flooded with disapproval and fear that I might make a decision too quickly.

The drive was short. I could have walked.

I was about to go down the alleyway to the garden but I decided I needed something to distract me. I began walking to the deli on the next block.

"Daniel." Jeremy had a serious look on his face, but tender and vulnerable, too. "I see the world more clearly when I'm with you. I believe in myself, in you, in us. I believe we are an answer to suffering." His words had meaning to me. Jeremy cradled me as he looked out to sea at the slowly darkening sky above the Oregon coast. Spires of rock thrust out of the sea with the command of bravery beneath them. This was the land of strong people who forged lives out of loss.

I had felt strength like nowhere else for those two weeks in Oregon. Not only from the love that I felt for Jeremy, but because of a positive energy that seemed to be generated by the very soil around me. I could have moved there, would have willingly dropped the princess act to feel like that for the rest of my life. I was sure then that Jeremy would always be there, a part of it, part of the cause for that feeling.

So why can he not be now? I asked myself.

I slipped into the brightly lit deli and waved at the man behind the counter, who was accustomed to seeing my face late at night when I got strange cravings for chemically baked pastries. I picked up a pack of Twinkies, then a Coke from the cooler, and walked to the counter. Beside the counter was a rack of romance novels. I felt the ache of insomnia building behind my eyes and knew that something would have to occupy the late hours. I picked up a novel and set it on the counter beside the Twinkies. The deli man looked at me.

"You don't look so happy tonight, sir."

"Oh, I'm fine."

"You look like a man with a dire decision to make."

I was a little shocked that the deli man could read me so well. Then again, day in and day out, he had to deal with people. There could be few others who witnessed more of the varied manifestations of human nature than one who worked in a deli.

"Let's just say love has thrown me a hard curve."

I was trying not to open up to the deli man. Had I wanted a psychotherapist I would have talked to Ken, who would serve that purpose better than almost anyone.

"Let me say, my young friend, that history has taught us very little about man's ability to love; that we often misunderstand love until it becomes an unrecognizable mutant. Love is the simplest thing in the world; to love is to stop resisting."

I would have sworn I looked at the deli man with crossed eyes as I hesitantly slid my brown paper bag from the counter and backed out of the door. My heart was pounding in my chest like a child pounding against a closet door. As soon as I felt the cool night air on the back of my neck, I turned and bolted down the street. I ran into the alley, tears streaming down my face, and hastily unlocked the garden gate. I ran into the garden and dropped the brown bag. I felt like screaming as I picked up the potted gardenia. I held it over my head for a second.

I've never watched an entire sunset before, Daniel, I've never been able to sit so still . . .

The muscles in my arms worked and I released the pot, sending it sailing through the air.

We woke to the sun on our naked bodies. We slept the entire night beneath the stars. We fell asleep to the sound of dreams singing at the base of the cliff.

Sirens screamed on the street; someone in the city was dying. The pot slammed against the side of the building, sending dirt in every direction. I picked up the hammer I'd left with the gardening tools.

Jeremy held my hand proudly as we walked through the small ocean-side town, as if we were back in the city, where no one stared oddly at two men in love. We kissed on the deck of an outdoor café; the salt in the air was a perfect accent to the taste of him.

The Japanese maple fell over as the hammer struck the side of the huge red clay pot. Its roots, out of the soil, looked like rheumatic fingers clutching at the cement trying to find stability. I lost interest in the hammer and found power in my fists clenched around the necks of flowers. The siren screamed, but faded. Maybe someone's life would be saved tonight.

Jeremy, I simply love you.

I held the demented bouquet of mangled flowers in my hand and returned to reality long enough to hear the muffled end of a message on my answering machine. I clawed for my house keys, ripping out my pocket, and ran into the apartment. I didn't know who I wanted it to be. My fingers fumbled, becoming clumsy when they needed to be nimble. The door finally opened, but the machine had already started rewinding. Whoever it had been had hung up. When the tape stopped, I hit the play button. The machine buzzed for a moment then began to play back the message.

"Daniel, it's Blaine. I know this may seem strange, but I took your number from Sheila's address book before I left. I'm coming back into town next week and I was wondering"—he paused, his voice getting shakier as he progressed—"if you would like to meet for dinner? Just don't tell Sheila, she doesn't know I—"

The machine cut him off before he could finish.

The world spun so fast I couldn't keep up. Time faded and the next thing I knew, the sky was gray and I was covered in dirt with bunches of flowers beneath my head like a pillow.

I want to come home.

Was that real? Was it?

FIVE

I awoke the next day tangled in my sheets and still wearing my best suit. My feet were swollen in my Fenestrier dress shoes. I sat up and rubbed my aching head. Little particles of potting soil rained down onto the bed from my hair. I looked at my hands. They were gray from dirt. My nails were black tipped from the soil embedded under them.

"Nice," I sighed. I tried to piece together the night before.

Jeremy wants to be back in my life. I went on a bender and killed my garden. Blaine left that bizarre message.

I stumbled into the kitchen and took a carton of orange juice from the refrigerator. Not bothering with a glass, I opened it and drank straight from the carton. It was then that I noticed the empty Absolut bottle on the counter. That explained the headache.

I put back the orange juice, went through the living room, and opened the door to the garden. I knew I'd trashed it, but I was hardly prepared for the carnage that lay before me.

Potting soil and chips of red clay pots lay everywhere. Petals of every hue were scattered like confetti after a New Year's Eve party. The Japanese maple lay on its side, as if it should be in a chalk outline with yellow police tape blocking off the scene of the crime. I stepped into the middle of the disaster area and heaved a big sigh.

I looked through the iron fence to the building across the alley.

I thought I saw Sheila suddenly back away from Blaine's window. My overactive psychosis might have been playing tricks on me.

Was I psychotic? I thought I must be if I could do this to my garden.

I heard the sound of the phone ringing through the open door. I took another look around then went back inside. I didn't hurry this time, letting the machine pick up the call.

Beep! "Daniel? It's Ken. If you're there, would you please pick up?" I was treated to a polite moment of silence as Ken waited for me to pick up. I nervously bit a hang nail off of my right index finger. "Daniel, pick up the damn phone right now!"

Are there cameras in here, I wondered. I immediately picked it up.

"Oh my god, Ken, what?"

"Daniel, I know you better than anyone. I know you're hung over. I know you were probably staring at the machine and biting your nails. And I know you'll just sit in that apartment all day, afraid to go outside because you don't want to deal with whatever trauma might happen to you next. But that's no way to live your life and you know it."

"If I needed Maria von Trapp to come in and turn my life around, I'd have phoned the nunnery weeks ago. Okay?" I replied, very sarcastic and very unlike myself.

I could practically hear Ken count to ten before he said, "I'm only trying to help you."

"I know," I sighed. "And I appreciate it. But if you know me so well, then you also know I don't like unsolicited advice. If I need help, I'll ask for it."

"So until then you're going to sit around that apartment, drink heavily, and stare at the walls?"

"For god's sake, Ken, it's—" I searched for the clock. What time was it, anyway? "It's only two in the afternoon!"

"Yes, well, it may be only two in the afternoon for you," said Ken in his best parental tone, "but for some of us it's the start of a brand new day. By that, I mean this; in your old life—"

"As 2Di4?" I interrupted.

"Yes. In your old life, you'd be looking forward to another day as the queen of the night."

"That life is over," I reminded Ken.

"I know," Ken simply stated. "But there are some traditions that still carry on. In your old life, as in this one you're going on with, you meet me for brunch every goddamned Sunday as if it were high mass."

I forgot brunch with Ken! Was it really Sunday? I nervously ran a hand through my hair as I considered the ramifications of this.

"Oh my god, Ken," I stammered. "I'm sorry. I'm so sorry. I forgot."

"Obviously," Ken said. "I've waited at the Screening Room for *hours*. They were so kind as to let me use their phone, since we're here *every* Sunday."

I sat in silence, like a little boy being reprimanded by the principal for pushing a girl on the playground.

"Since I know you're having some troubles lately, I'll excuse you this time. And since you don't want my advice, or help, I'm going to hang up now. If you need me, you know where I'll be. That is, if you can recall enough of your old life to remember where Club Chaos is. Or what time I perform on Sundays," Ken said, really emphasizing the *ifs* in his sentences.

In true "A Ken Scorned" fashion, he quietly hung up instead of saying goodbye. I set down the phone and wondered if I could sink into the floor and die. Then some residual anger flared up. I almost called him back before he could get away from the Screening Room, to demand that he wait there for me so we could work this out now. Ken *did* know me better than anyone else did. He should understand how confused and upset I'd be after last night's scene with Jeremy.

Then I remembered what he'd said about things being harder at the club now that I was gone. He'd always been supportive of me. In return, I'd been thoughtless, self-absorbed, and inconsiderate. In fact, for months everything had been about me and my worries: Jeremy moving into Robert's apartment, Diana's post-divorce problems, Andy canceling my performance slot on Thursday nights, Diana's death, and my move to Hell's Kitchen, leaving my life as a drag performer behind.

Every crisis sent me running to Ken for comfort. It wasn't just the fourteen-year difference in our ages that made his counsel seem so wise. It was his way of delivering wisdom with humor. No one could tell me things I didn't want to hear the way Ken could. That had certainly been proven this past spring, when he'd invited

Jeremy and me to dinner on a night that left an all-too-vivid memory . . .

Jeremy had been in one of his playful moods, sliding through
our apartment in his socks, doing his Tom Cruise routine, but without the underwear, making up his own words to "Old Time Rock
and Roll." He'd just heard he'd gotten his part in the limited run
of *Guys and Dolls*. He was doing a really lame Bob Seger impression,
wailing something about taking those old actors off the shelf. Of
course, that was when I still found him adorable, and we'd ended
up late to Ken's, expecting a small group to make rude comments
about the delay. But it was only Ken. He'd picked up on our mood.
We skewered a few friends' eccentricities along with our swordfish
shish kebabs and the evening had us all in giggles.

Later when we were helping him clean up, Ken dropped a glass
that shattered the night. He burst into tears and I stared, a little
dumbstruck, while Jeremy wrapped his arms around Ken.

"It's only a glass, babe, we'll clean it up," Jeremy crooned, giving
me a bewildered look over Ken's shoulder.

"You guys, I have to tell you something," Ken said. "And I don't
know how. I didn't want a lot of drama and here I am weeping."

I followed as Jeremy led Ken to the living room couch.

"On the plus side," Ken finally said, "at least I'm not in makeup."

"Yeah, mascara can be a bitch," I said.

"Then again, I could have done a marvelous Tammy Faye," Ken
said. "Okay, here it is. I haven't been feeling so great lately. I suspected it was menopause. But of course, they did the test."

There was no reason to ask him what test. I shot Jeremy a
stricken look and he motioned for me to join them on the couch,
which I did, taking Ken's hand.

"There's nothing right to say, is there?" I asked. "Except that we
love you. I love you. And if it had to happen, at least it's happening
when we've got all these new drugs."

"Absolutely," Jeremy added. "You're in good health. The drugs
can keep your viral load down, your T-cells up, and you'll outlive all
of us."

"At least this doesn't mean a hysterectomy," Ken said, deliber-
ately steering us back to lightheartedness.

We'd ended up staying at his house that night, making a slumber party of it. The three of us lay in his oversized bed, sometimes
watching, sometimes talking over, a Grace Kelly film festival. Ken

explained that he'd wanted us both to know because he needed someone to be honest with. He needed friends he could trust not to treat him like he was condemned and to keep his private life just that, but who could also handle it if he had days when he didn't feel like being cheerful or pretending everything was great. He didn't want our other friends told because he fully intended to remain in good health and hated the thought of being subjected to the gloom-and-doom-attitude queens. I ended up feeling like Ken was comforting us rather than the other way around.

But that's how it always seemed to be with Ken. Nothing kept him down for long. If I didn't have that night to remember, I would never have guessed that he had any reason to worry more about himself than his friends and their problems.

These days, I felt like he should be grateful not to see me and endure my dramas on a daily basis. The previous night was supposed to have been pleasant, followed by a witty postmortem at today's brunch. Instead, I'd allowed Jeremy's startling change of heart to drive me into yet another tailspin. But really, how much could a princess take?

The phone rang again; this time I picked it up.

"Ken, you're right and I'm so sorry," I began.

"Daniel, is that you?" asked the not-Ken voice on the other end.

"Um, yeah," I slowly said. "And this is?"

"It's Blaine. Listen, I left a message and got cut off last night. By your machine, I mean. Anyway, I called Sheila later, and she said everyone went to some bar after you dropped her off. I guess you were too tired to return my call?"

After a few moments it dawned on me that I wasn't answering. Instead I was seriously thinking about moving to a remote island. As his words penetrated, I realized Sheila must not have told him anything that had happened the night before. Sheila was a goddess.

"You got cut off," I reminded him. "There was no number to wherever you are."

"Oh yeah." Blaine laughed. "That's right. I'm in Philadelphia on business. I've been in meetings since I got here. I guess I'm pretty out of it."

"Me, too," I said under my breath.

"What?"

"Nothing," I answered quickly. "You mentioned something in your message about getting together?"

There was nothing like being blunt at a time like this. I had to move fast to be prepared for Jeremy's next onslaught.

"Yeah, I did. I'll be back next Thursday. I was wondering if Friday night you'd like to join me for dinner and discuss your job," Blaine explained.

"My job?" I asked, heart sinking.

Martin must have told Sheila about 2Di4 and Sheila had told Blaine. Sheila was a bitch.

"Yeah," Blaine said. "Sheila said you'd like to be my assistant. I make my own coffee, don't worry."

Assistant? Oh, Sheila *was* a goddess!

"Daniel, that was a joke," Blaine explained.

"Oh yeah, funny," I feebly chuckled. I could work on his sense of humor at the office. "When do I start?"

"Well, gee, I haven't even asked if you can type. That's why I wanted to meet you for dinner," he said. "Consider it an informal interview. Sheila seems to like you a lot, so I thought maybe I could get to know you, too. Any friend of hers should be a friend of mine."

This guy was too much.

"Okay, Blaine," I said. "I'll see you next Friday night. Have a safe flight back and don't work too hard."

"I'll let you know where and what time. See you soon," he said.

I hung up the phone, amazed that in such a short time, from the tragedy of offending Ken, my life was taking an upward turn. All I had to do was avoid Jeremy for a while.

Screw Jeremy, I thought. It's time to resume work on my Blaine project.

And speaking of projects . . .

I went outside to take another look at the disaster area formerly known as my garden. I uprighted the maple and examined it. All I had to do was prune the broken branches. Surveying the rest of the damage, I ascertained that more than half of my plants could be re-potted and saved. It was a good thing that in my obsessive spending of Aunt Jen's money, I had bought way too many pots. I could get the garden back in shape before the first frost wiped it out again. I began to feel better, more in control than I had since Jeremy's surprising behavior the night before.

I thought about the afternoon Robert kissed me in the garden. Maybe Jeremy only wanted to come back because he and Robert weren't working out. But it was over. It had been over months ago, even if I admitted I still had feelings for him.

Once you love someone, you don't just stop, Ken had once explained to me. That was after Jeremy decided to move into Robert's apartment, whereupon I took a drink at every bar on the way to the Christopher Street Pier on Gay Pride Day.

It was a working weekend for me. As usual, my Pride weekend was jam-packed with appearances at various events around the Village. Andy wanted me to ride on the Club Chaos float down Fifth Avenue and across the West Village, but due to my strained home life with Jeremy, I graciously bowed out. Much to Andy's chagrin, of course, as it was the second year in a row I didn't participate in the parade. As easy as it was to escape my emotions about Jeremy and Robert by throwing myself into my work, I wanted one day to myself to stand on the sidelines. Even if it was just a half-day, since I was hosting a post-parade, midday tea dance and then kicking off the Pier Dance that evening. But having the morning to watch the parade and not having to perform or be glamorous was a relief.

I donned a pair of sunglasses, shorts, a tank top, and sandals, and watched the parade from the streets. Float after float of hunky boys, dykes on bikes, gay police officers, political factions, ethnic support groups, and marching bands all passed me by. It took hours. The parade would creep along, come to a halt to let crosstown traffic pass through, then creep along again.

I walked downtown on the sidewalks, following the parade route, until I arrived at Sheridan Square Park. The sidewalks were jammed with people watching the parade. I was lucky to find a spot close to the street to watch the rest of the parade, stable as long as I clung to a tree.

The Club Chaos float eventually passed by, thumping and bumping with dozens of drag queens dancing to music specially mixed by a local club deejay. Ken, in his Judy costume, was standing on a platform above the heads of the rest of the queens with his wig in curlers, à la Judy arriving at Carnegie Hall many years ago. The parade came to a stop again, and the Club Chaos float magically halted outside of the Stonewall bar. The crowd, seeing Judy and Stonewall as one on Gay Pride Day, started cheering. Although I knew the moment was a planned part of the parade, it still got to me, and I forgot all about the bad feelings I had carried with me as I walked down the parade route from my apartment.

Martin and the drag queens on the float got to their knees and started bowing in a "we're not worthy" gesture before Ken/Judy. The club music died down, and Ken gave a performance of "Over the Rainbow," to everyone's delight. The crowd noise died to a hush as everyone watched Ken with awe, admiration, and respect. He spotted me in the crowd, clinging to the tree, and gave me a pointed wink. I smiled at him and he returned it, knowing I wasn't happy, as if to say, *It'll be okay*.

The parade did have to go on, however, and the float started moving again during the song, but the crowd remained quiet until the float reached the end of the block, then they erupted in cheers and waved until Ken was out of sight.

After that, the rest of the parade seemed rather anticlimactic for me, and all I could think of was Jeremy. I remembered how Jeremy and I had watched the parade together the year before. We stood together the whole time and held on to each other even though it was beastly hot out and we were sweating all over each other.

My emotions got the better of me, and I got angry thinking how, instead of Jeremy, all I had to hold on to was a tree. He and Robert were probably holding each other somewhere in the massive crowd, just as we did the year before. My mind went into all sorts of scenarios about what Jeremy could be up to, and it got to be too much for me. I crossed the square and ducked into the Monster, since they were having a two-for-one special. The alcohol relaxed my nerves and was comforting. I didn't know anybody there, which was a relief, as I wasn't in the mood to talk to anyone.

I decided to watch the parade again, but the crowds were very intense. I grew tired of fighting my way through all the hot, sweaty strangers. Instead, I ducked into another bar and had another drink. I kept repeating the pattern; duck in, drink, duck out, all the way down Christopher Street until I was quite inebriated and forgot what I was upset about in the first place. When I reached Washington Street, a hand grabbed my shoulder and pulled me to the side, out of the pedestrians' way.

"Daniel, what on earth—"

"Judy!" I shrieked. "You were so great in the parade."

Ken looked me up and down in one quick assessment.

"You are drunk."

"You are right," I said and dissolved into a giggle fit.

"Daniel, it's so easy to get plastered when you're upset, but it's only temporary," Ken sighed.

"Say 'plastered' again," I giggled.

"Plastered," Ken grumbled and couldn't help but laugh at me.

"Look, I know, okay? I know. I know what you're saying, Ken, I know," I stuttered. "Just let me do what I need to do right now and I'll be okay, okay?"

"Right," Ken said. "You do that, hon. I'm appearing at Stonewall at eight tonight and then hosting a party at . . . uh . . . some other club. You know how I don't keep up with the club scene these days. Anyway, I'll be home by midnight."

"Okay," I said.

Ken grabbed my shoulders and looked me in the eyes.

"Call me if you need me," he said emphatically.

I stopped by my apartment to change and transform into 2Di4. The apartment seemed empty and tomblike to me. I didn't slow down long enough to let my eyes settle on anything. Instead, I headed to the bathroom to shower and put on my makeup. After the dress, wig, and high heels were in place, I dashed through the apartment and, despite the heat, opened all the windows to air out a bad feeling.

Once I was in my heels, I was in working mode again. Although I was wobbling a little bit, I felt a lot better. At the tea dance I said a little speech about "royal pride" and how we were all royalty on Gay Pride Day. It didn't make a lot of sense, but half the boys on the dance floor were on drugs of some sort, so it didn't really matter. I danced on a platform for a few hours and had a few more drinks to keep my spirits up until I had to dash off to the Christopher Street Piers.

At the Pier Dance, I changed into another dress that I had in my handbag. It was an imitation Issy Miyake, long, dark, lightweight fabric and intentionally wrinkled, so it traveled well and was perfect for the occasion. The boys were already dancing, and the party was in full swing, so I had another drink and made my way to a small makeshift stage where the deejay was spinning and the special guests performed.

I was introduced and gave another tumultuous speech about gay pride.

"Thank you. Tonight it is with great, well, pride that I stand before you as your ambassador of, uh, again, pride."

Everyone was laughing, and I grew a bit uncomfortable, not knowing if they were laughing with me or at me. I felt like I was lying. I wasn't in character. I felt like Daniel in 2Di4 drag. I absentmindedly tugged at my elbow-length gloves and tried to think of what to say.

"I must say that I'm quite sad. Yes, sad. I'm sad that, in this day and age, we still have oppression. We still have judgmental people, and we still have to fight for our rights as human beings on this earth. Today I saw my dear friend Judy sing 'Over The Rainbow' on a float outside of Stonewall, and it reminded me that, although we are celebrating the voices of yesterday, we still have to shout out for the voices of tomorrow. Today I also saw a mother marching in the parade all alone. In the mother's hands was a sign that said, 'I love my gay son.' Somewhere out there in the universe is a very lucky boy."

The crowd started cheering, and I felt a little bit more like 2Di4.

"Am I making any sense?" I shouted and the crowd cheered even louder.

"Oh good," I continued when they quieted down again, "because your highness is quite drunk."

They laughed again, but this time I knew they were laughing with me.

"That woman was your mother, too, today. She was my mother. I hope that today as you celebrate your pride, you remember your mother. Remember your family and everyone's family. Because they are the reason you're the beautiful people you are today."

The crowd began applauding again, and a tear rolled down my cheek as I thought of Jeremy's family, who was so good to me, and how much I would miss them.

"I'm sure you've heard by now that I have had a divorce." I stifled a feeling of nausea, reminding myself I was speaking as Diana, not Daniel. "It's been a very trying time for me, and I wanted to thank you for your support and understanding. One thing I've learned that I also want to share is that whether or not your family accepts you, you must accept who you are. That's the only way you're going to make it in this world. So, to sum up, let's just spread a little love today, okay?"

The crowd started cheering and I gave a little royal wave and a demure smile. Then I grabbed the microphone again.

"Oh, by the way," I said, "I have a message from Fergie. She told me to tell you to *party on babe!*"

The music started pumping again, the boys began dancing, and I made my way down some steps behind the stage to the pier.

"Great job, your highness," one of the event coordinators said.

"Thanks; where can I get a drink?"

"Over there," he said and pointed to a makeshift bar set up for VIPs. I wobbled over and asked for a gin and tonic.

"They really loved you," a voice behind me said into my ear. I turned and looked into the eyes of a handsome, Italian-looking man.

"No, they didn't love me. They liked me. They really liked me," I deadpanned and he laughed, his green eyes twinkling.

"You're really beautiful," he said. I looked up and down his gym-toned body. He was the beautiful one. I felt like a cartoon character in his presence.

"Thank you," I murmured and finished my drink.

"I bet you're incredibly handsome, too," he said. "Can I buy you another drink?"

"No, I've had way too many," I said. "Besides, they're free."

"Can I take you to my place?" he asked.

"Yes."

"My name is—"

"I don't care," I said. "Just take me home."

It was Gay Pride Day, but I'd had no pride that night.

I glanced inside at the clock as the phone rang again, and had to laugh. Right on schedule. If it wasn't one past haunting me, it was another.

I didn't even say hello, just picked up the phone with, "Hi, Mom."

"Danny, how did you know it was me?"

"Lucky guess," I said.

My sisters and I had long ago given up waiting for our parents to do or say a single unpredictable thing. I only half listened as I began working in my garden, easily anticipating each topic. The visit to Grandma in the nursing home . . . How she and Dad were going to the Great Lakes next summer (every trip took months of logistics and planning that would be the envy of NASA) . . . The weather, always the weather, and when it would snow or how much it had snowed or when the snow might melt . . . A series of mind-numbing stories about people from work, people from church, a lot of names I couldn't put faces with . . . The terrible ordeal of Mary Kate's third pregnancy, with far more gynecological information than anyone should know about his sister . . .

The last time we'd talked, my mother got me so worked up and scared that I called Mary Kate, whose response had been a most unladylike snort and an *I'm not dead yet, squirt, you know Mom is an alarmist* . . .

As kids, because only two years separated us, Mary Kate and I had mostly pretended the other didn't exist. But my older sister had been the first person in my family I told I was gay. She wasn't surprised, as she'd watched me lust after her boyfriends for years. She and her husband, Ray, had chosen "Daniel" as their oldest son's middle name. Of course, he'd turned out to be an evil little hellion who might more appropriately be named Damien, but I appreciated their gesture of love and support.

From Mary Kate, my mother went to Gwendy, who was three years younger than I was and such an object of my childhood and adolescent terrorism that I wasn't sure how she'd managed to survive to adulthood. She was now in her last year of law school. I liked to credit myself for making her tough. She was fond of telling me her revenge was becoming the successful son our parents had always wanted.

For as long as I could, I kept the phone pressed to my right ear and endured listening to my mother's secret hopes that Gwendy would marry a nice man and make more grandchildren. Then I changed the phone to my left ear and the subject by asking about Lydia.

As the baby, Lydia was everyone's pet. She'd been a surprise, coming six years after Gwendy. She was only nine when I left Wisconsin, but for some reason she was my favorite. She was in college at Stevens Point, but she came home whenever I visited, for which I was always grateful. She was the only reason I didn't lose my mind after a few hours in Eau Claire.

The last time I'd been there, right after Jeremy and I broke up, Lydia had come into the house with a wicked gleam in her eye and kept breaking into inexplicable laughter. Finally she'd untucked and unbuttoned her tidy denim shirt, flashing me with her T-shirt, which said, "I'm not gay but my brother is." The rest of that day we'd dissolved into giggles as various relatives made the usual stupid comments about my many girlfriends in New York, all the more unpleasant because I was miserable about Jeremy. The next day my mother had neatly folded Lydia's laundry without a word, the T-shirt tucked in with her other clothes.

Sometimes I wondered what would happen if I just sat my parents down and forced them to talk to me. In retrospect, I realized all the mistakes I'd made in coming out to them. Everyone said not to do it in a letter or on a holiday. I had sent off my bomb in December of 1992, just after the separation of Diana and Charles was announced. For some reason the royal scandals that year seemed to speak directly to the lies and evasions I gave my family. At the time it had all made sense—especially after a night of heavy drinking—but as soon as I mailed the letter, I wished I could take it back. I awaited their response with dread. Would they send a scathing reply? Demand that my sisters stop talking to me? Ask me to return my Christmas presents?

Instead, the weekly calls continued, with no mention made at all of my letter. For a long time I'd been relieved, thinking it was no big deal to them. But eventually, especially when I visited Eau Claire and was treated with the polite deference they'd give to any stranger in their home, I came to despise the invisible barriers between us. I just didn't know how to tear them down.

It was like being a teenager again. As long as I pretended like everything was okay, they were more than happy to accept my act. I gradually learned to suspend my true self when I went there, rarely mentioning my friends, and never my job, to my parents. Only my sisters gave me any relief. They were frankly curious about my 2Di4 act. For years, Gwendy had kept an eight-by-ten glossy of 2Di4 on the back of my bedroom door, occasionally hitting it with a dart just for fun. Whenever we went home, this was the first thing she and I looked for, certain it would still be there. Taking it down would be my mother's admission that it even existed. Lydia loved to hear stories about my fellow performers and friends. She was delighted when I told her about falling in love with Jeremy, as was Mary Kate, who hoped I'd find the domestic bliss she had. Both of them had offered ready sympathy a few months before when I told them we were no longer a couple.

In person, my mother talked about the same things she did on the phone. My father, who was a supervisor at a steel fabrication plant, liked to tell me which of my classmates worked for him or were moving up at the plant. I knew he'd once envisioned me there, or at any of Eau Claire's industries, going to work in a suit and tie and making decisions that would benefit the community. My parents were hardworking, decent people, generous and thoughtful toward their neighbors—and they drove me out of my mind.

My father had been better prepared than my mother for a disreputable family member. Aunt Jen had kept the Stephensons reeling for years with her exploits. Maybe if one of his daughters had followed in her footsteps, Dad could have handled it. But to have his only son not only move away, but work in satin and sequins and give him no hope of seeing the Stephenson family name passed on, must have been a huge disappointment to him. I knew I should be grateful that the worst I got from my parents was silence. But that silence made going home an ordeal.

Going home, of course, was the reason my mother had called.

"Danny, I was wondering about Thanksgiving and Christmas this year," she said.

"Mom, I was just there in July."

"I know, dear, but you weren't yourself. I think all these years living in that city have changed you."

The subtext was *I think that city made you gay,* but of course, those words would never be spoken.

I took a deep breath and said, "I know definitely not Thanksgiving. I have too much going on."

I considered telling her that a new job might not allow me enough time off for a trip to Wisconsin. But that might lead to uncomfortable questions and fuel her fervent hope that giving up drag might mean I was becoming straight.

"What about Christmas?"

"I don't know, Mom. I'll have to tell you later."

I closed my eyes, knowing what was coming next.

"Are you well, dear? Doing okay?"

This was her way of dancing around AIDS. Things would be so much easier if she would just ask and I could reassure her that I always tested negative. Instead, she tormented herself with worry, not even allowing the girls to relieve her anxiety.

"I'm great. Hey, Aunt Jen called me last night. She said she might be coming to see me."

"That's nice," she said, her voice flat.

I'd known that would stop the conversation dead, as my mother was still annoyed by my birthday check. It was just one more in a long line of grievances she had against my aunt. The friction between them began in my childhood and came to a head with the graduation gift that allowed my escape from the Midwest. Mom always felt that Jen overindulged me. Of course, she was right, but what were aunts for?

I didn't know why my aunt had picked me from among my sisters and cousins to lavish her attention and money on. Maybe from the beginning she could tell I was as different as she was. Had I lisped out a rendition of "Mame" from my high chair and endeared myself to her? Shown an unusual interest in her heels and jewels? Or had my adoration of her flamboyant style and appreciation of her acerbic wit simply affirmed for her that she was the best show our family had ever produced?

Regardless, I treated her as the grande dame she aspired to be. She rewarded me accordingly, bestowing on me the closest thing to maternal lunacy she was capable of feeling, though that didn't always exempt me from her sharp tongue or brutally honest criticism. She could change in a moment from Rosalind Russell to Joan Crawford. Perhaps my mother thought Jen was trying to supplant her, or even that it was Jen's fault I was gay.

"Well, I don't want to run up the bill, honey, so I better go," Mom interrupted my thoughts. "Please let me know about Christmas. And it would mean so much to everyone if you could be here Thanksgiving, too."

I reminded myself again that I was lucky as we said our goodbyes. A lot of my friends had families who wouldn't even speak to them. Though my parents ignored who I was, at least they hadn't disowned me. But it was a far cry from the easy relationships Jeremy had with his family. In fact, the Caprellians had always given me the same mixture of love and torment any of their noisy, quarrelsome brood received. My family was so . . . Eau Claire by comparison.

I remembered the first time Jeremy insisted that I join him at a Caprellian event. I kept trying to talk him out of it, thinking of my own family. If I took Jeremy to Eau Claire, he'd be treated with a sort of kind but detached pity, much as if I'd brought a wounded deer into their midst. *It's nice that you want to help it, dear, but it doesn't really belong here, does it? Better if you leave it in the woods and let nature run its course.* And if we dared to blur the line between friendship and romance, we'd be met with strained silence and a quick change of subject—not to mention a screaming lack of invitations for a repeat visit.

I simply couldn't understand why Jeremy would subject me to that kind of disapprobation at his sister Adele's wedding. He kept swearing it wouldn't be the way I feared, just one huge party from start to finish, and I'd have a great time.

He'd been right. No one even blinked when Jeremy introduced me as his boyfriend. In fact, his sister Reva even licked her lips and said, "Yum, Jer, does he have a brother?" It didn't matter that his family was caught up in the day's events; I was immediately absorbed into them. His mother insisted I listen to all the awful things about Jeremy that I should beware of—too much bathroom time, too selfish to share his toys with his sisters, and a tendency to throw tantrums if he didn't get his way—and his father grunted a hello to me and tried to get me drunk on wine: *I paid for it, dammit, every drop's gonna be drunk today, hand me your glass again, son.* Jeremy had the honor of leading his grandmother to the floor for her first dance. They exchanged a few words, she slapped at him with her lacy handkerchief, and the next thing I knew he was pulling me into his arms as the band crooned a Tony Bennett song. It was *The Godfather* gets *Moonstruck.* The earth didn't swallow us and the relatives didn't do a slow death scene, although various nieces and nephews nearly mowed us down getting to the cake table. If I'd had any doubts about whether or not I was falling in love with Jeremy, they ended that day. I wanted him, I wanted his *family,* for the rest of my life.

I sighed, wondering if my thoughts would ever stop leading me back to Jeremy.

Though my own family would never be the Caprellians, I'd ceased having unrealistic expectations of them when I'd begun to understand that a family is not necessarily those who are related by blood. During my many jobs leading to Club Chaos, I got close to my coworkers and relied on them for friendship. I'd bond with certain individuals in much the same way one would with a brother, sister, or parent.

Wanda, my first real friend in the drag scene, became like a parent to me. Later Ken did, too. They both had a way of making me feel protected and cared for. They also had a way of making me learn from my behavior with patient guidance, without provoking my defenses. This was something my "real" parents had never learned to do.

The coterie of drag queens at Club Chaos had been my family for many years. It was easy for me to relate to them, and they could care for me with an understanding I'd never have found back in Wisconsin. My sexuality kept me at a distance from my biological family; many of my friends had experienced those same feelings of isolation until we made our own family in New York. In an age when nearly every family in the United States was deemed "dysfunctional" in one way or another, the family of drag queens at Club Chaos was certainly no different. We fought, pulled each other apart, protected each other, stole each other's clothes, boyfriends, and other prized possessions when backs were turned, and nurtured, loved, and leaned on each other. I did much of my growing within that family. I blossomed under the warmth and light on the stage. I wondered if I was really ready to risk losing my New York family by giving up 2Di4. Other than Ken and Martin, if I stopped performing, stopped being who they wanted me to be, would my friends turn their backs on me? Did *all* families, even the ones we created, demand that we meet their expectations and not break old patterns for a new life? Did I dare take that chance again?

I looked at the overturned Japanese maple and reminded myself that plants and trees often thrived as a result of being transplanted. Their roots had more room to spread and take hold, which created luxuriant growth and more resilient blossoms. Or a taller, stronger tree.

It took me a couple of hours to do paradise regained. Though the vibrations I picked up made me feel the plants no longer regarded me so trustingly, a stranger—maybe even my friends— probably could not detect the physical remnants of my destructive behavior. I managed never to glance at Blaine's window. If Sheila was there, she might feel a bit reassured by watching my return to sanity. But I didn't want to talk to her—to anyone—until I could make things right with Ken. That, more than anything, would make life normal again.

I sat on one metal chair and propped my feet on the other while I surveyed my handiwork. I had a sudden, clear memory of Martin's comment the first time he saw my garden: *Oh, look, Scarlett, you've come home to Tara. But you'll think about that tomorrow.*

Of course in some ways he was right. Working in the garden was my way to avoid things that didn't bear thinking about. Anxiety about friends and family, Jeremy, Robert, my dead career, my uncertain future, and Ken.

Ken . . . what I was really afraid of was loss. I'd lost my sense of rightful place in my own family. I'd lost the Caprellians in the divorce from Jeremy. I'd lost Jeremy and the friend I thought I had in Robert. For all I knew, I'd lost the rest of my Club Chaos family. I'd lost the royal icon who'd been the guiding force of my career for nearly a decade and thus lost my career. But having lost other friends to AIDS, I knew that everything paled in comparison to the idea of being without Ken as a part of my daily life. To love him and be loved by him was the greatest gift I'd ever received. I could hope that the love and time we shared would go on forever, but life had certainly taught me there was no guarantee of that. Though Ken, always looking at things in the best possible way, might regard a missed brunch as evidence that life was as normal as ever. He didn't want to be treated as if he were going to suddenly drop dead. He probably even liked being taken a little for granted. But I still didn't want to squander any of my chances to enjoy time with my best friend.

I knew what I had to do next. Ken always went onstage just before midnight at Club Chaos. Judy would lip-synch her heart out to those poor souls facing another week of drudgery at their jobs. Soon I'd be one of those poor souls.

I decided to go to Club Chaos that night and learn how it felt to say, *Just one more and I'm outta here. I've gotta work tomorrow.*

More importantly, I had to atone to Ken for breaking Sunday tradition. And I had to face my demons at Club Chaos. The last night I'd performed there, after the accident in Paris was announced on the television backstage, I simply walked out and never looked back. I never said goodbye or returned for my final paycheck. I was too much in shock.

I wondered if my silver beaded MiuMiu clutch was still backstage.

A long bath, the best manicure I could manage, a little fussing with my hair, only an hour to discard a dozen ensembles before I made up my mind, and I was on my way. I'd decided on a pair of deep blue Calvin Klein jeans and a white 2xist T-shirt under a burgundy button-down twill shirt. I finished off the outfit with a pair of trendy sandals I'd found on sale at Barneys.

The streets were unusually quiet. The crowds from Times Square had dwindled slightly since the hostile takeover of Disney that closed down the *Girls! Girls! Girls!* quarter-operated video stalls. I could still hear the shouts of drunken frat boys from Long Island and Connecticut whooping it up on their night in the big city, but the energy, sometimes schizophrenic and unnerving, was a little subdued, as if some kind of bomb were about to drop.

I rounded the corner of Fiftieth Street and walked down the newly renovated stairs to the E train. The subways had become much cleaner over the past five years. I had perfect timing as the train squealed into the station. The car was nearly empty and smelled sterile. It was only a few jerky stops until I reached West Fourth Street, which let out very close to Club Chaos. I came out of the subway stop and met the hustle and bustle of the weekend crowds, including the white-cap jocks from NYU with their made-up girlfriends. Mixed in with the mostly homogenous crowd were the ever-present practitioners of the love that dare not speak its name. It was an automatic reaction to look appealing to them, knowing that sex and desire are, inarguably, written on the body. I managed to remain regal as endless eyes observed, judged, and approved me as I continued up Fourth to Club Chaos on Christopher Street. It was surprisingly cool for early October. I knew the night air was coloring my cheeks in the most becoming way.

A hard right took me to the back of the building before I was spotted by the patrons waiting out front. Though the name "Club Chaos" called to mind thousands of people on ecstasy gyrating to transient house music until four in the morning, in reality it was more like the musical *Cabaret.* Andy had taken over a midsized theater many years before and made Club Chaos what it was today, a large bar/performance house. I'd always been gratified to see a line outside, knowing it meant 2Di4 would play to an enthusiastic crowd.

I slipped through the back door to the sights and smells of a dozen divas doing their best to mask testosterone.

"Ah, the princess enters," Bette—Midler, not Davis—sighed. "Daniel, I'd give my right arm to have your figure."

"You'd have to give a lot more than that," the Duchess of Windsor said, brows raised.

I met Martin's gaze until I saw him break out of his duchess attitude, the flicker of approval in his eyes acknowledging that I was not all distraught about Jeremy.

Andy, hurrying through, glanced over and said, "What *are* you doing dressed like *that*, Di?"

"He sure didn't dress out of *your* closet," Bette snapped.

"This is *silk*," Andy said, holding up one silk-clad arm.

"Yes, they're making it so affordable these days," I answered absently, searching the crowd for Ken.

"Andy has always depended on the blindness of strangers," Martin drawled in his best Blanche DuBois voice.

"Where *is* Ken?" I finally asked.

"Change in schedule," Martin answered. "Ken is on now."

The shocked stare I gave him made the others wander away in uncomfortable silence. Andy looked like a raccoon caught pilfering from the trash can.

"But Judy has the best slot—"

"This is what happens when you run away from home," Martin said sourly, his expression exactly like the divorced American duchess cheated out of her chance to be queen of England. "Andy made some changes."

"You're telling me Ken has been bumped from my slot?" I demanded incredulously.

"Correct."

"For whom?" I asked. "Who among these faded blooms could fill that time better than Judy? Other than England's rose, of course."

I followed the direction of Martin's gaze as a door—the door to the dressing room that had once been the domain of 2Di4—opened. My eyes widened as the figure before me turned to face me after shutting the dressing room door. My disbelieving stare shot from Andy to Martin and back to Andy as my mouth gaped like a fish out of water.

"Excuse me, Butch," she spoke softly as she rested her hand on my arm in an effort to squeeze past me toward the stage. I took her arm in my free hand, perhaps more firmly than I intended, and she turned to face me with a raised eyebrow as if to inquire, *Yes?*

It was astounding, yet at the same time horrifying. It was like looking into a mirror. At least it was like looking into a mirror at show time. Or more accurately, it was like looking into a funhouse mirror that distorts proportion and truth. The new Di didn't maintain all that I held dear about our departed Princess of Wales. She had none of the sophistication, glamour, or gentility I had tried to capture in my interpretation. Instead, she exuded the same bitchiness that the other queens did. I was furious that this impostor had no respect for my creation.

The spurious princess gave me a look that said, *Do you mind?* as the second eyebrow was raised to match the first.

I held her arm and spun the pseudo-princess around to meet the stare of Andy. A smile upturned the corners of Martin's lips ever so slightly.

When I found my voice, all I could muster to say to Andy was, "This?"

Knowing full well what I meant, and seeing the fury rise in my eyes, Andy instinctively took a step backward. I realized I couldn't move forward into my new life knowing my creation went on without me. I had to end it tonight.

"Well, *darling,* just because Lady Di, God rest her soul, has left us and so have *you,* doesn't mean I don't have an obligation to give our audience what they *want* does it?"

"*This?*" I hissed in retort.

The nameless pseudo-Di said, "If you don't mind, I really have to—"

"I mind," I growled through a clenched jaw. Her mouth snapped shut. I wheeled back to Andy. "How could you? How dare you! How fucking *dare* you!"

"Daniel, darling, do I have to remind you that we have a *show* going on out there? Would you keep it *down?*"

"*She's wearing my fucking dress!*"

Though I didn't care as much about the dress as I did about this impostor's audacity in assuming my role of nine years, this was all I could say through my anger. I stamped my foot on the floor like a child, desperately needing an outlet for my rage. Martin sat back on his throne, taking a reprieve from putting on his makeup to watch the fireworks, his tiny smile now a broad grin.

"You go, girl," said a faceless voice behind me; it could only have been Tommy's.

"Daniel, please, hold it down," Andy cooed to me, his voice uncharacteristically low. "I tried to get you to come in and do something about the frocks, but prying you out of that garden has been like pulling teeth. You wouldn't help me organize the auction, and well, when Marc showed up and did the audition for me, I couldn't help but notice that he *does* wear your size—"

"—and evidently he *does* wear my jewelry as well," I finished for him.

"Well, darling, I didn't see any harm in giving him a little push into the spotlight to lend a hand. You know, if it weren't for me, you'd still be singing 'Second Hand Rose' at Pyramid."

My blood boiled. Andy's attempt to take credit for the hard work, lessons learned, and courage I'd cultivated from my life's friends, teachers, and legends—my *family*—was just what I needed to propel me over the edge.

"Well, as long as we are giving Marc a little *push*, let me do all I can to help."

I released the arm of the pseudo-Di with much more force than I had intended. She let out the hurt yelp of a dog rudely awakened from a nap when his paw was stepped on.

"Daniel!" Andy shrieked. Even Martin's grin faltered a bit at the slow motion scene that followed.

Marc lost his balance on the heels that were obviously too high for him to manage. I had a fleeting moment of satisfaction that my own height had allowed me to wear the lower-heeled shoes so beloved of our late princess. Marc's arms pinwheeled madly as he tried to regain his footing. As he began to topple, Andy tried to reach him before he landed, shoving me out of the way, but it was too late. The only thing for Marc to grab was the silver-sequined curtain that separated front stage from stage left. The curtain, the rod to which it was attached, Andy, and Marc all came crashing to the stage just as Ken mimed for us to "Get Happy." The religious overtone of the lyrics, combined with Ken's horrified expression, morphed Judy into a deranged evangelist witnessing an appearance by Lucifer, stage left.

An audible gasp rose from the audience, and somewhere in the bar, a startled waiter dropped a tray of cocktails. Only the recording of Judy Garland continued to break the silence.

Marc sat stunned for a moment, then looked at me and cried, "You bitch!"

He scrambled to his feet, kicking off the heels in one motion, and dove for me. Andy rolled out of the way, covering his face, sure that Marc meant him.

I attempted to dive to one side but Marc caught me by the collar of my shirt and maintained a pit bull clamp as I dragged him onto the stage. When his grip finally broke, I crashed to the stage with a thud, feeling something in my arm snap. The pain was tremendous but I was too stunned to feel the full impact. As I rolled onto my back, Marc leapt on top of me like a cat. I reached up with my one good arm and snatched the wig—*my* wig—off of his head.

The crowd by now had broken its silence and divided. Some gathered in a circle to get a front row seat at the live performance of Alexis and Krystle, while others tried to break apart the barroom brawl. I had a dim impression that Ken was fending off people who tried to clamber onstage and join the fray. The "straight" guys and husbands scurried from the bar like roaches scattering for the cupboards when the kitchen light is flicked on.

I heard sirens blaring over the shouting voices in the bar. The last thing I remember seeing, as Marc's fist crashed into my cheek, was the wig, with attached tiara, flying across the floor like some kind of royal rodent.

SIX

had no idea how much time passed as I drifted in and out of awareness. When I was finally fully alert again, I found myself lying on the floor of a holding cell, my arm in a sling. The pain in my arm shot through my entire body as I managed a sitting position. My head was not faring well either. A dull ache pulsed as I tried to focus my eyes on the grayness around me. I heard the jingling of keys and footsteps coming my way.

"Daniel Stephenson? No charges were pressed. We can release you now that someone's here to take you to the hospital."

"Who?" This single word sent a thunderous bolt through my head. My teeth rattled like the windows of the century-old Eau Claire house in which I'd grown up.

"Some dame out here. She doesn't look very happy."

I thought it could be Sheila or Gretchen, though it seemed inconceivable that they would know where I was. I went through a mental Rolodex of my various drag friends but could think of none who would tear themselves from the glitz and faux-glamour long enough to rescue me. Except for Ken. Of course, it must be Ken, still in his Judy drag. He was always so convincing.

I stood with great effort and followed the officer down the long corridor of the holding tank. A buzzer rang; the large metal door at the end of the hall swung open and we passed through. The bursar returned my jewelry and wallet. The policeman escorted me down another hall and at the end, in a waiting room, my worst nightmare awaited me: Aunt Jen.

She turned her head slowly and smiled a pearly smile that could only have been practiced in front of the mirror, the smile of Yvonne DeCarlo modeling denture cream.

"Daniel. My precious angel, what did those monsters do to you?"

Aunt Jen pushed the officer aside and tenderly touched the side of my face. Her own visage became serious. Her lips made a slight pucker and her eyes squinted until only a sliver of blue showed through.

"I can't lie, Daniel; I am very disappointed in you." This was the last thing I wanted to hear with my head so rotten. "But we'll save that for later. Right now we are getting you to a proper hospital. Aunt Jen is here to take care of you."

I woke up in the hospital with that afterglow feeling of heavy barbiturates. Aunt Jen was asleep on the couch next to my bed. There were flowers all around me. The sun was shining; I could hear birds and the low murmurs of other patients and staff in the hall. The door opened and a nurse walked in with another vase of flowers. I had words in my head but it was a challenge to get my mouth to form them.

"Who are all of these from?"

"Oh, just your adoring fans apparently." The nurse sounded like Angela Lansbury but looked like Kathy Bates. For a second I was very frightened, still half in a dream world.

"Let me see." The nurse began reading the cards to me. Many said, "For the real 2Di4, may the dream live on," or "No one compares to you, Daniel." It felt good to know I was getting support.

Aunt Jen awoke and sat up, gracefully placing her silk-clad feet on the floor.

"I never imagined I'd spend my trip to New York in a jail and then a hospital. Charming, Daniel."

You could have warned me that you were coming, I thought, but decided it would be best not to offend her.

"How did you know where I was?"

"When I couldn't reach you at home, I spoke to your former employer. He told me about your brawl and where I could find you. He also suggested that I pay for damages. But I was sure you'd want to take responsibility for that."

I rolled my eyes and let my head sink back into the pillow. The events of the night before seemed very distant to me. I could barely suppress a chuckle as I thought of "Diana's" wig skittering across the floor.

The nurse looked at my chart then addressed me.

"Good news. No concussion. No more broken bones. You're scheduled to check out at three today. You have three hours. Would you like something to eat?"

"Yes, please," I wheezed.

The nurse stepped into the hallway and Aunt Jen stood to stretch.

"So, when do I get to see your apartment, Daniel? I think I deserve to see it after all I've done for you."

"Of course, Aunt Jen."

The following hours were spent with Aunt Jen making the most of my invalid status to dissect the rest of my family, pronouncing various criticisms and judgments of their many flaws as determined by her. Sadly, I gave her wholehearted encouragement, thrilled that anyone else was getting the treatment I'd expected for myself.

I had always thought the routine of wheeling the patient to the curb was simply diva drama served up by television and movies. I was very pleased to discover that this was, in fact, a real hospital rule and thoroughly enjoyed the exit scene it provided. As the studly orderly wheeled me down the hall from my room, I wrapped the Hermes scarf that I'd received as a gift from Ken last Christmas around my head and tied it under my chin. I completed the look with a large pair of black Chanel sunglasses.

"Get those things off your head," Aunt Jen snapped. "You look like Greta Garbo."

"I was thinking more like Jackie O, but that's okay," I laughed. I brought my fingers to the side of my temple, as if I were trying to shield my face from flashbulbs, while we made our way through the sliding glass doors of the emergency entrance to Roosevelt Hospital.

It was a short ride down Ninth Avenue to my apartment. After Aunt Jen, the obedient tourist, carefully scrutinized the photograph and name on our cab driver's permit, she began her lecture about the horrific neighborhood we were entering.

I found myself staring at the permit to avoid her tone and the reflection in the rearview mirror of the driver's amused eyes.

"Just look at all this trash," she said, clucking her tongue. "This is hardly the New York I'm accustomed to. And those delis! Why must the store fronts be cluttered with all those cigarette advertisements?"

"Perhaps they sell a lot of cigarettes and make money that way?" I suggested.

"Don't take that tone with me, young man."

"Yes, Aunt Jen. Please, just pull over here," I said to Samir Singh, the cab driver. "Far corner."

After crossing the street from the near corner, which was, of course, where we were let out, I showed Aunt Jen my building in the middle of the block.

"It sure doesn't look like much," Aunt Jen commented.

"It's everything to me," I sighed. "Why must you belittle my whole life?"

"Why, Daniel!" Aunt Jen gasped. The hand once holding the rail on the steps now fluttered to her chest. "I am not belittling anything that has to do with you. I would never do that. You know you've always been my favorite nephew."

I held the first door open for her after I had unlocked it then went to work on the second.

"Please," I sarcastically begged, "you've done nothing but criticize me, everyone who is related to me, and my tiny piece of New York since I first came back to consciousness."

We made our way through the second door and, after I checked my mail, down the hall beyond the staircase to my door.

"Daniel," Aunt Jen began, "I'm just tired after my trip. And quite frankly, a bit shocked to come to town to visit my nephew only to find him in jail for starting a nasty brawl at some bar."

We stepped into my apartment and I locked the door behind us.

"I'm sorry if I snapped at you," I repented.

"Daniel," Aunt Jen said, taking in the view of my apartment, "this is hardly the hovel I anticipated. It's . . . quite quaint. What's out there?"

She pointed toward the door to my garden and made her way to it. Not waiting for my reply, she opened the door.

"Oh, Daniel. It's lovely!"

I followed her outside and pointed out the begonias, salvias, and my small rosebush. She "oohed" and "ahhed" and I was happy I'd taken the time to repair the damage done by the combined forces of my temper and sadness.

"Well, you've certainly inherited your mother's green thumb," praised Aunt Jen, which gave me pause. I remembered thinking about my mother when I'd been working on my plants in the old apartment. By creating my new Eden here, had I escaped most men's haunting fear of turning into their father by turning into my mother?

I remembered the vegetable garden behind our house in Eau Claire. I used to hate having to move slowly down the rows, helping to pull the tiny weeds from between the plants under the hot summer sun. I would think of how I'd rather be swimming in a lake with the other kids, or riding my bike somewhere down the road. Anything but kneeling in the dirt of that garden.

I also remembered the fragrant blooms that my mother planted around the trees in the front yard. Tulips? No, irises. And little pansies. The tulips lined the walk from the driveway to the front door. Around the house were pots of begonias. I wondered, now, how my mother had had the time to perform her job as a dental hygienist, help my father with the vegetable garden, and keep up her flowers in the front yard. Not to mention feed and look after me and my sisters. But my mother never went on a vodka bender or pillaged her plants, whereas I couldn't even manage an ex-lover and an ex-job without doing so.

"Well, you be sure to rest up tonight and watch that arm of yours," prescribed Aunt Jen. "I'm going back to my room at the St. Regis for the night."

"Um, how long will you be staying, Aunt Jen?" I asked.

"As long as it takes." I couldn't decide if her smile was ominous or kind. She led me to the couch and made me lie down. After kissing my forehead, she collected her purse from the kitchen counter and let herself out.

My eyes weren't closed five minutes before the phone rang. I groaned and let the machine pick it up.

"Daniel, this is Martin. Girl, are you okay? You should see how Marc looks, honey. She'll be holed up in her room nursing raw steak on her eyes for a week! Call me when you get this, 'bye!"

I laughed to myself, thinking about how Martin must be in the S section of his calling list with the news of the brawl at Club Chaos.

I got up and checked my machine. There were three more messages. I hit the play button and sank back into the couch.

Beep! "Daniel, this is Ken. Are you okay? You'll be getting home from the hospital soon—hope you got the things I sent over—and I want you to know I'm sorry I got bitchy with you about missing brunch on Sunday. It seems so petty compared to what you've been going through with Jeremy. I hope you're doing okay. Not only after the fight, but with your feelings and all. Call me if you need anything, okay? 'Bye." Click.

Beep! "Daniel, it's Sheila. I haven't talked to you in a few days and I was wondering if everything is okay with you. Maybe we don't know each other well enough for me to talk about this, but I hope you're okay after that scene with Jeremy backstage. I know what happened to the garden, but I hoped since you cleaned it up . . . Anyway, I wanted to let you know that Blaine called and I told him that you might want to work at his agency. He's probably already called you, so this message might be pointless. No, it's not, 'cause I wanted to let you know I'm thinking about you and that I hope you're all right. Oh, and I didn't tell Blaine anything that might've been too . . . um . . . private. Come over sometime, okay?" Click.

Beep! "Daniel, it's me." Ugh. Jeremy. "I wanted to wait a few days before calling you, but I'm afraid I didn't last too long. The show's going great! But you probably don't care about that. I'm sorry if I embarrassed you the other night in front of your friends. It's just that seeing you after the show brought this rush of emotions to the surface that I've been ignoring for a long time. I hope you took me seriously, because I did mean everything I said. Do you remember how in Oregon—uh, I have to go. Please call me." Click.

It sounded like Robert had come home at the tail end of that message. I snatched back my hand as it reached for the phone. I'd told Jeremy I would call him after I had time to think; so far I'd managed to avoid thinking by getting drunk or thrown in jail. He would have to be patient a bit longer . . . like maybe until I sent him a Christmas card or something.

As Martin's message played through a second time, I opened the low, rectangular trunk that served as my coffee table to take out a quilt, then sank back into the couch. Burying myself in its comfort, I again grew nostalgic. If I were home and feeling unwell, my mother would be tucking the quilt around me, and my sisters would wait on me hand and foot. It was no wonder I'd blossomed into a princess; I'd been given royal treatment much of my life.

I pushed the quilt off my arm and stared at the cast, managing a few tears of self-pity. How could everyone leave me alone at a time like this? What were the chances of Blaine hiring me now—although, frankly, this would provide an excuse about the whole typing thing. I hadn't touched a typewriter since high school and I knew nothing about computers.

I lost myself in a highly improbable fantasy of Blaine nursing me back to health after an injury sustained in some more valiant endeavor than thwarting the career of a wannabe female impersonator. Of all the scenarios, I most liked the one in which I rescued Dexter from the path of an oncoming cab, thereby endearing myself to Blaine for eternity.

I finally fell asleep to the image of Blaine showering me with passionate kisses after spoon-feeding me chicken soup.

By the following Thursday, I was worn and frazzled by Aunt Jen's company, although she had provided the perfect excuse for avoiding my friends and their lust for gossip about Club Chaos. All of them understood the trauma of visiting relatives ("house pests," Martin had called them; I didn't bother to tell him Aunt Jen was staying at the St. Regis), and none of them were encouraged by my admittedly exaggerated grim tone to ask to meet Aunt Jen.

This all changed, however, when Aunt Jen showed up to take me out to brunch.

"Daniel," she said as I took my place next to her in the back of the service's Lincoln Town Car, "I thought we'd go to Le Cirque for brunch today."

"Le Cirque? For brunch? Are you mad?" I joked, trying to imitate one of her socialite friends.

"You're right. Where's my head? Driver," she said, leaning toward the front of the car, "change your course to the Four Seasons, please."

I rolled my eyes, annoyed that we were going somewhere so refined. I felt like I should slap a Gucci logo on my cast.

The car wound its way back up to Fifty-seventh Street and deposited us in front of the towering monstrosity known as the Four Seasons Hotel. Aunt Jen was concentrating so hard on her grand entrance that she missed the wink the doorman gave me.

After we were seated in the sleekest, most modern restaurant I'd ever been in, Aunt Jen began her crusade.

"Now that we've ordered, I was wondering if I could discuss something with you," she said.

"Um, sure, what's on your mind?"

"Well, for starters, you deposited my check."

"Yeah," I drawled slowly, not sure where she was headed or if I wanted to go there with her.

"Well, I thought that must mean you heeded my advice and gave up that ludicrous . . . *performing* job to get on with your life in a more normal fashion," Aunt Jen said, waving her hands like someone on an airline runway as she spoke. "But instead, I find you in jail with your arm broken as a result of that—that—hedonistic place."

Instead of shouting words about those things she found offensive, Aunt Jen stage-whispered them.

"I did give up performing at Club Chaos," I explained as the waiter set down French bread garnished with fruit. "I was there visiting my friends. That's all. I can't leave my friends behind."

"I don't expect you to abandon your friends," Aunt Jen said. "I'm not a monster."

"Auntie, I don't think you are. I just hope you don't think giving up my performing career is going to automatically make me straight," I gently answered.

Aunt Jen stopped chewing her bite of melon. She set down her fork, finished chewing, swallowed, and said, "I see it's not a monster you take me for, but a complete ninny."

I was aghast.

"Aunt Jen, no!"

"Keep your voice down," she whispered. "You know for a fact that I don't care that you're a homosexual. That's your mother's trepidation, not mine. I just want you to make a name for yourself."

"I have, darling."

"I mean," she tried to explain, "I want you to leave a mark on this earth. I want you to make a name for yourself in a way that everyone, including your parents, can be proud of."

I pondered this in silence for a bit. Aunt Jen was the one person in my family who was entirely honest with me. One of my earliest memories of her involved a time, when I was only five, that Mary Kate had enlightened me about the existence of Santa Claus. I brooded a few days, sure my sister had the information wrong, but unwilling to take a chance by asking my parents. Like any Virgo, I had to process and consider all the ramifications of a fact. Did an absence of belief lead to a decline in presents? This was not a risk I was willing to take. Aunt Jen noticed my furrowed brow as I watched *Miracle on 34th Street* and quizzed me until I confided my dilemma. I could still remember her response.

"Of course there is a Santa Claus," she pronounced. "Oh, not that jolly old fat man dished out by Hollywood. Santa Claus is a concept, Daniel. Do you know what a concept is?"

I did not and she frowned.

"Santa Claus is like being hungry. You don't know what it looks like, but you know when you feel it. When you eat, it goes away. But does that mean it wasn't real?"

Her view of Santa seemed a lot better than the one Mary Kate was asking me to discard. Let other kids be satisfied with their once-a-year fling. I didn't care if he was fat or slender, jolly or solemn. It was apparent that if I placed a daily faith in this *concept,* it could only mean more gifts for me.

In a way it meant exactly that, as my acceptance of Jen's explanation, which she mistook for comprehension, forged a bond between us. From then on, I was her favorite and she was my source for all information. And lots of presents.

Perhaps the greatest gift she ever gave me came on my tenth birthday, when she actually made a special visit two weeks early just to discuss it with me.

"To be on this earth a decade is a momentous occasion, Daniel. We must celebrate it properly. Tell me somewhere you'd like to go, anywhere, and we'll do it."

"Craig Shroeder had his birthday at McDonald's," I said.

"Craig Shroeder is not my nephew."

"Is there a zoo in St. Paul?"

She muttered something like, "I could give him Africa . . ."

I blinked. She blinked back.

"Daniel, learn to think *large,*" she commanded.

"Then I'd like to go on a Boeing 747."

She tapped her nails on the table then smiled and said, "Outstanding."

To this day I could only imagine the effort it took to convince my parents. Our trip—on a Boeing 747, as requested—not only provided my first and only glimpse of the city I would years later make my home, it unfolded another world for me. I sat mesmerized at the original Broadway production of *Annie*. My mother was wrong. Aunt Jen didn't make me gay, she just taught me how to enjoy it. She certainly encouraged my love of theater and made every effort to see all of my high school productions, never betraying by a single expression or remark how tedious she must have found them.

After I moved, she requested no accounts or explanations of my activities. As long as I never complained or bored her, she would listen to whatever tales I chose to divulge. She had never gone along with my parents' "don't ask don't tell" policy. Nor did she accept the blissful ignorance of my extended family, who regarded me merely as an eccentric actor living in New York City. She did not always applaud me, or even always approve, but she always heard me out. From time to time she felt compelled to tell me what she thought of me, then to give me several supporting arguments to back up her case. I valued her candor highly and returned the favor often. This seemed like one of those moments.

"Aunt Jen," I began carefully, "you say you accept me for what I am, right?"

"Yes, my dear, I've told you that so often," she sighed.

"Well, saying I should make a name for myself in a way that will make everyone proud of me implies you think there's something wrong with what I've been doing."

Aunt Jen looked around at the Four Seasons' dining room. The tables were placed far enough from each other to allow semiprivate discussion. When she realized the immediate tables were vacant, she relaxed a little.

"Daniel, I am proud of you. From what you've told me about what you do—"

"Did," I interrupted.

"Yes, did," she agreed, "it would seem you cornered the market on female impersonation."

"Well, I probably could've gone further," I laughed.

"You forget, dear," she smiled, "Arthur and I used to attend parties when he was wasting his money on those dismal films. We often ran into Milton Berle. *He* cornered the market and look where it got him. Such a horse's ass."

I was surprised at her language, but she was often blunter with me than she was with other people.

"Auntie, I don't think you quite understand what it was I did."

"Really?" she asked.

"Ever heard of RuPaul?" I asked.

"Is that in the south of France?" she queried.

"No," I giggled.

"Well, if it's significant to what you've been doing for the past decade, then maybe I don't understand," she conceded.

I took a deep breath and said, "I'm a lot like you."

"I beg your pardon?"

"You haven't exactly lived the most sedate life," I said.

She gave me her "off limits" look.

"You've done your share of flouting convention," I persisted. "You've always lived outside the box, Aunt Jen. We're not so different."

Her movements were deliberate and practiced as she removed a cigarette from its case, putting it into the holder that, for as long as I could remember, had seemed like an extension of her jeweled hands.

Our waiter stopped midstride to say, "I'm afraid this is no smoking."

"Do you see smoke, young man?" Her chin jutted out. "I suggest you bring us both more coffee. As a matter of fact, bring us a carafe because we don't want to be interrupted."

"Yes, madam," he answered meekly, then vanished.

"You've had three husbands—"

"I fail to see what my husbands have to do with anything. It's not as if I killed them, even if one or two of them deserved it from time to time."

I decided to try a different approach.

"Your exploits are legendary, Jen. You insisted on coming east to school when none of the girls in the family had ever done such a thing. Then you proceeded to get expelled how many times?"

"The accounts of my misdeeds have been greatly exaggerated."

If she was going to play hard, I could play harder.

"You were expelled the first time when you were caught in a car full of boys with a trunk full of liquor. You were expelled from the second school when your diaphragm rolled out of your purse to land at the feet of the dean of women students. You were expelled from the third school when you and a bevy of beauties were caught dancing onstage at a nightclub in Harlem. Shall I go on?"

"This is supposed to make me sympathetic?"

"If you'd been a girl in the twenties, you'd have been a flapper,"

I said. "If you'd been a girl during the Second World War, you probably would have gone to Europe and been an ambulance driver. If you'd been in college in the sixties, no doubt you would have been smoking pot and getting arrested in demonstrations. All I'm saying is that you refused to be a 'good girl.' Instead, you became a person. Well, I couldn't stay in Wisconsin and be a good boy. I'm sure there are lots of guys who are satisfied to marry and have men on the side. Some of them are probably even in our family. But I'm like you. I did what I wanted no matter what they thought. I couldn't give up me, who I am, just to make things easy for them, any more than you could."

"I have never suggested you live a lie, Daniel. Though the rest of the family, perhaps even your parents, might have wished for that, it would have been a bitter disappointment to me if you had. But explain to me, please, how living your life as a woman is not also living a lie?"

"Good god!" I exploded.

The waiter dropped our check on the table as if it were hissing and coiling and made a rapid retreat.

After several deep breaths, I tried again.

"I do *not* live my life as a woman. I had a job impersonating a woman. It was not only a lucrative job, I used it to give something back to a community that befriended me during the loneliest time of my life."

We stared at each other a minute. I realized by the agitated tapping of her cigarette holder that I needed to bring the tension down a bit.

"Aunt Jen, there are all kinds of men who do drag. Did you know most cross dressers are straight men who just enjoy wearing women's clothes? Some transvestites are gay. Some of them feel they were born in the wrong bodies. Some of them even have surgery to change their gender."

"Daniel," Aunt Jen interrupted, "I'm afraid I'm even more confused. I certainly don't need to hear about operations in the middle of the Four Seasons. You don't mean to suggest that you're going to have an operation?"

"Don't be absurd," I said, then gently added, "Just listen, okay?"

She raised her eyebrows dramatically, fanning out her hands to suggest she would say no more and that I had the stage. I suppressed a grin and continued.

"There are drag queens on the pageant circuit who compete for titles, money, and prizes. There are drag queens who invent personas, like RuPaul, and some of them may dress in drag day and night, but most don't. There are drag queens who impersonate famous performers like Judy Garland or Cher. I sort of combined the last two. I impersonated Diana, but I created a separate persona. Sometimes I did lip-synching acts, and sometimes I used original music or did spoken performances, even rap, that I wrote with the help of friends. But 2Di4 was an *act*. I've used her to emcee drag pageants, to entertain, to raise money for AIDS or other things that matter to me. I'm either paid for what I do or I do it to raise money and awareness. I don't want to be a woman. I love being a man, and I love other men. Being gay didn't make me do drag. Doing drag didn't make me gay. One was what I did. The other is who I am. Can you understand that?"

She retrieved her platinum card from our waiter. "I have an idea. Tonight we'll go to your Chaotic Club and I'll see what it is you've been doing all this time."

Oh god, the inner voice moaned, now you've done it.

After her car dropped me off, I debated whether to warn Ken and the others about what would transpire, then realized there was no reason why my aunt had to meet them. We could see the show and make our exit like any other Club Chaos patrons. I was sure to be recognized by the staff, of course, but with Aunt Jen on my arm I knew we wouldn't be hassled.

I wanted to take a shower but didn't have the energy to find a way to keep my cast dry. I seemed to be out of garbage bags. Instead, I went to the sofa and put up my feet. I was bored. There was nothing on television, and I didn't even feel like tending to my garden. It would live for a day without me hovering over it.

I stared at my feet and was struck with an idea. I wondered if I should share some of my memorabilia with my aunt, if seeing my many scrapbooks would help her understand my life in Manhattan. I opened my coffee table trunk and began pulling them out, willing to experience a bittersweet nostalgia for the first time since I'd walked out on my career.

I settled back with four scrapbooks beside me. I opened one and a picture fell into my lap. It was a photo of Ken and me backstage at Club Chaos. He was in his Judy costume with his hand on my shoulder. I, as Liza, was on bended knee at his feet. Both of us were wearing top hats, tails, and broad grins. It must've been taken right before we went onstage the night Ken rescued me from a career crisis.

I hadn't settled into any particular act. I was a walking variety show, doing different characters each night. An homage to the new pop diva on the *Billboard* charts, Madonna, on Friday nights. Octavia Thunderpussy, who sang the theme songs from James Bond movies, on Sunday nights. Or even Rose Bloomensnatch, a sort of takeoff on Bette Midler's character from *The Rose,* during the week.

After a few weeks of my Sybil-like performances, Ken loaned me a wig one night when my Madonna hair got caught in the subway doors and went traveling on to Brooklyn without me. He laughed and calmed me down from my near hysteria, telling me I should create a character and stick with it.

"You're doing really well as it is," Ken said, "but you could be more. You're a brilliant performer."

"I'm a washed-up actor and I didn't even get started," I sulked.

"You don't think what you're doing out there is acting?" Ken asked.

I sat in silence, finding it easier to be hard on myself than to believe I had talent.

"I'm not going to waste my time on you if that's what you think," Ken said. "Or my wig, for that matter. If you think what we do isn't acting, if you can't see how it entertains and touches people, then forget it. Not only aren't you believing in yourself, you're not believing in me. I'm not lending my wig to someone who doesn't believe in me."

With that, he snatched his wig off of my head and marched in his character heels to his makeup table to apply Judy's alcohol-induced rosy glow on his cheeks.

"I'm sorry," I said, getting up. I moved my stool to where Ken sat at the makeup table. "I'm just . . . I don't know . . . a little worn out, I guess. Scared."

Ken put down his huge blush brush and turned to face me.

"We're all scared, Daniel. We're all afraid that at the end of the night we don't matter, but we do. I was taught that a long time ago when I was young, closeted, and all alone. We matter. What we do on that stage matters. Not only to us but to those people getting drunk and trying to figure out what they want out of life. Where they fit in. Everyone is looking for a place to belong. We can help them find it. Daniel, we can inspire them! That's pretty fucking powerful, isn't it?"

I nodded in agreement. When I'd come to New York, there'd been no one to guide me gracefully into gay life. I had to figure it all out for myself and tell myself there was no shame in what I was. The closest gay idol I had was Boy George, and at that time, even he wasn't admitting anything.

"No wonder you're tired," Ken went on. "You go from character to character like Carol Burnett on a bender. That would be a good lyric . . . Anyway! What you need to do is settle into a persona. Find a woman you admire and respect. Someone you want to emulate. Then stick with it. Bring her power out there with you and watch them adore you. It'll do a lot for your self-esteem problems, let me tell you."

"Is that why you do Judy all the time?" I asked.

"Yes," Ken sighed. "That is why I do Judy all the time. She had such determination. Such performance skills. And even when she was nearly washed up, she refused to believe she was finished. She was a diva to the end. Hey, I've got an idea."

"What?"

"You need a wig, and I'll be damned if I let you go out there and roll around in a wedding dress like that pop tart wannabe virgin woman," Ken declared, getting up and going to the shelf where his wigs perched on Styrofoam heads. He plucked a short, black wig from the group and brought it to me. As I stretched on a wigcap and fastened on the wig, Ken outfitted me in tails, hose, and heels that matched his own from the costumes on the rolling racks outside his dressing room.

"Tonight you're gonna be Liza. Just for me. Tomorrow we'll work on finding you someone to emulate. I'm telling you, it'll do wonders for your career. You'll see."

He was right. We brought down the house with our Judy and Liza number, and Andy wanted me to join Ken's act. But I refused, insisting I didn't want to muscle in on Ken's territory. Ken graciously agreed, maybe a little worried that I might get all Diana Ross on him and steal the spotlight.

The next day Ken came to my apartment and we looked through my record collection. We thought maybe the perfect diva would be lurking in the milk crates holding my albums. With such treasures as Cyndi Lauper, Led Zeppelin, and Janis Joplin, there was little hope. We lay on the mattress on the floor and tried to recall great divas of yore who'd affected my life. I couldn't think of one. At least not one with the endurance of Judy. Ken thought I should do Barbra Streisand, but I put my foot down. It was too predictable. I thought that might hurt Ken's feelings, but he understood and added that not everyone liked Barbra, especially after the crackpot movie roles she'd been doing.

I was skeptical about Ken's advice to settle into one particular role. The idea seemed to go against what I had already learned as a drag performer. I was afraid of growing tired of repetition. The possibility of audiences not liking the character also lurked in my mind. But I was willing to try something new, since my erratic characterizations were exhausting me. Perhaps Ken was right; creating a single character might bring me the stability I needed to take my career down a new path.

The more I thought about it, the more the concept grew on me. I realized Ken's idea might also bring me back to my acting roots. I could apply character development and improvisational technique to bring one drag character to life; in fact, I would make her larger than life. People change and so could my character.

I made a vow to give this a chance and accept Ken's help. I was never good at taking aid from others, probably because of the years that I was desperate enough to seek out kindness from strangers. Then again, there had been times when swallowing my pride had served me well. Aunt Jen had taught me that altruism and wise advice were nothing to shun. Especially when they came from Ken, who got me my job at Club Chaos in the first place, and whose motives had never been selfish.

After I got the mail, I had a revelation. Among the past due notices and my weekly greeting from Ed McMahon was my latest issue of *Good Housekeeping*.

"Ken, look!" I exclaimed, holding up the magazine.

"Oh my god, I can't believe you pay money to get that in the mail. But then again, its ideas have done wonders for this place," he chided. He did a Vanna White impression and showed off my lovely, one-room Barbie Dream Hole.

"First of all," I explained, laughing as he hummed the "Wheel of Fortune" theme song, "my mother got this back home and I subscribe for that 'home' feeling it gives me. Second, I meant look at the cover!"

Diana, Princess of Wales, was on the cover yet again. It was another of the many stories that every magazine in America churned out about her. I loved her and thought she was one of the most beautiful and poised women who had been in the media in a long time. I enjoyed reading about her and felt that, although she was royalty, she was one of the little people, too.

"That's perfect," Ken whispered.

Princess 2Di4 was born.

Ken helped me hone my act and come up with ideas that would whip the crowd into a frenzy. As my cult status grew, I eventually surpassed him. There had been many Judys, but only one 2Di4. Andy gave me Ken's time slot and my own dressing room. If Ken minded, he never showed it, choosing instead to be supportive and proud of me. He became my best friend and most important teacher. He helped me see drag as a unique way to reach people. I could express myself and say something about modern culture at the same time. As the years went by, the money didn't matter. It wasn't the be-all, end-all that it was in the beginning.

I had to smile at myself. It was a lot easier to dismiss the importance of money now that I had some.

I carefully tucked the photograph of Ken and me back into the scrapbook, then thought better of it and removed it to frame later. I paged through the old album and found an eight-by-ten glossy print of Wanda, Ken's predecessor.

In one of my first jobs as a fledgling drag queen, I worked at a club in the East Village. I had wanted a job performing, but there were no slots open, so the club gave me the next best thing: bartending. Shortly after my interview, I was introduced to the other bartenders, all of whom were beefcake boys who refused to wear shirts. I frowned at this, having no bulging biceps or rippling abs of my own, and wondered how I could compete.

"Country boy!" I heard from behind me.

I spun around and saw a tall, thin black man. He was dressed in jeans, boots, and a turtleneck. Nothing about him was familiar, so I just smiled and said, "Hi."

"Don't tell me you don't know me?"

I wracked my brain trying to conjure up a name, an event, something, to link this person to. Nothing.

"I'm sorry, no. I don't."

He threw back his head and laughed, throwing his hand forward and grasping my shoulder.

"It's all right, country boy," he said, looking right into my eyes. "I guess you haven't seen me in drag before."

"Wanda? Is that you?"

"Child, it's Roland," he said, pulling me into a hug. "I stopped by early today to get paid. But someone else canceled for tonight, so the owner's done the ol' guilt trip–kiss ass combo on me and now I'm going on tonight. You are a sight for sore eyes. I'm so glad to see you."

"I can't believe it's you. The last time I saw you was in that tacky bar on Christopher Street."

"Oooh, child. Don't remind me. That Tony turned out to be bad news!" Roland wrinkled his nose in disgust and shuddered.

"You mean, you and Tony were—"

"Oh yeah, but that's old news and old times. I'm on to bigger and better men now."

The sight of Roland in "drag," as he called it, was hard for me to take in. He was an effeminate man, and every time he spoke, I'd conjure up the image of him as Wanda. He didn't have to tell me that, when he walked the streets during the daylight hours in these clothes, he felt uncomfortable and unnatural. Just the way he pulled at the collar of his turtleneck and kept moving his hands in and out of the pockets of his jeans told the story. I surmised that he was quite relieved to be "coerced" into performing that night.

"Aren't you going to ask what I'm doing here?"

"Child, you are not mysterious. So don't even try it. I know what you're doing here."

"What? How do you know what I'm doing here?" I laughed in disbelief, sure that he was pulling my leg.

"Honey, I'm the whole reason you have this bartending job," he smiled as he explained. "I'm dating the owner of this place. I saw you pathetically trying to get a job performing in here."

"I was not pathetic!" I huffed.

Roland put a hand on one hip and swung his head to one side, glaring at me like a mother who has had enough of her disobedient child.

"In that very same office where you showed up looking like Dolly Parton in her coat of many colors is a big ol' mirror! Now do you suppose that mirror could be one of them two-way mirrors? And who do you think was on the other side of that mirror?"

"You?" I ventured.

"That's right. And when Mr. Thomas left you in that office alone, who do you think he was asking if you had what it takes to work here? Do you think that man knows shit about performing? No. I screen the talent here. If I'd thought you have what it takes, you'd be filling in tonight, not me."

I didn't know what to think. Not more than a minute ago I was thrilled to see Wanda again. Now here was Roland telling me that all my efforts to become a drag queen weren't good enough. Not even Penny Dime, my most successful creation, could charm him.

"Oh, don't go lookin' like a kicked puppy now," Roland smiled. "You're cute. I'll give you that. You've still got that country look. That's why I suggested you work the bar. You can start out small and work your way up to that stage."

"But I've been onstage. I've performed in lots of bars and—"

"But"—Roland silenced me by the mere motion of a raised hand—"you haven't performed here. I've turned out some of the best queens in my time. This place isn't the tops, but it's not one of those tired little bars that you've performed in, either. This is the House of Wanda now and I'll send you out a true diva, baby. It takes time and work. You have to learn attitude. You have to learn self-esteem. And you'll learn it here."

I was reminded of the opening montage of the television show "Fame," where Debbie Allen thumped the floor with a big stick and told her dancers that fame costs with pain and sweat.

I showed up for my first night of work in thigh-high black patent boots, a black sequined miniskirt, a tank top, and a leather biker jacket. My wig resembled Priscilla Presley's hair in the sixties, when Elvis made her dye it black and tease it high.

"What the hell?" one of the beefy bar boys said.

"I'm sorry, do you have a problem?" I asked.

"I'm just not sure you're in the right place," he answered, stepping up into my face.

I took a cigarette out of an ashtray on the bar, inhaled, and exhaled in his face.

"Oh, I think I'm right where I belong," I whispered. "If you have a problem with me, just say so, and I'll make sure your life is problem-free from then on. Know what I mean?"

The guy could've punched me out and made me crumple to the floor like a rag doll. We all knew it. Instead, he smiled and kissed me on my lips. The whole bar broke out in cheers and cat calls at our performance. I broke the kiss and pretended to slap him across the cheek. He mimed extreme pain and cowered in mock fear.

"All right! Show's over! Next performance will be the next time someone tries to fuck with me! Anyone wanna try for now? Good! What'll it be, Jack?"

I was Rizzo, Joan Jett, and Cher rolled into one. It had been Wanda's idea that I work the bar in drag. We both knew I would never make the same tips as the boys, since I didn't have the body type. But Wanda wanted to try something new behind the bar anyway and my kitten with a whip act was just what she had in mind. The patrons of the club loved me and I made more tips than the boys every night. It was also great training for one-liners and over-the-top banter. It wasn't long before Wanda decided that I was ready to take my bar act onto the stage. Of course, in true Wanda fashion, she didn't tell me so much as order me.

"That was Chevette Harlette! Give her a hand!" Wanda announced from the stage one night as a diva made her exit.

I was behind the bar, mixing a Tequila Sunrise with one boot up on the bar. The man I was making the drink for was licking my boot as punishment for interrupting me during a story with his drink order.

"Ladies and gentlemen," Wanda continued, "we have, working for us, one of the most fabulous bartenders in the East Village. You all know the lovely Marissa Mayday?"

She gestured to me and the club burst into cheers and whistles as I raised my hands and waved.

"Now, now, we don't want her getting a swelled head. So to speak," Wanda went on. "Tonight we give you the honor of Marissa's debut in our little club. On that note, I give you Marissa!"

All my control as Marissa the bitch drained away as a spotlight swung on me and the crowd went wild again with anticipation of my performance. Two of the bartenders passed me over the bar to two bouncers on the other side, who lifted me onto their shoulders and carried me to the stage. The crowds parted for our procession and I waved with all the bravado I could muster as I wondered what song I'd perform to and if I could get through this. I was deposited onstage with Wanda as the crowd still cheered.

"This is a test, country boy," Wanda said through her stage smile. She gestured grandly to me and exited stage left. I was left all alone wondering what was next.

"Thank you," was all I got out before the opening of "Bang-Bang," a Cher song written by Sonny Bono, wiped away all applause. The lights dimmed and I took a few deep breaths before Cher's vocals began.

Thank god Wanda picked a song I know, I thought as I brought forth every gut-wrenching emotion conjured up by Cher in the song.

At the end of the song, amid the wild applause, the guitar lines of an early demo of Madonna's began (she had given them out everywhere in those days), and I realized my performance was far from over. The song was called "Laugh to Keep from Crying" and it fit perfectly with how I was feeling. Far from the pop princess who blossomed on the radio, the song was more like the darker Chrissie Hynde. Which Wanda must have taken into consideration, because the music segued into "Brass in Pocket." I pranced around onstage singing about how special I was.

The mike was off, so it wouldn't have mattered that I was singing along even if the crowd hadn't been as loud as it was. I reached down into the audience, teasing the boys in the front row. Two of the bartenders joined me onstage and allowed me to run my fingers down their chests, playing along with all my coy movements.

This time when the song ended, Wanda returned to the stage, holding up my hand, and announced that I'd be on again next week and was not to be missed.

I looked through a few more pages of pictures of some of the acts Wanda had put together for me. She allowed and encouraged me out of the role of Marissa Mayday. She was of the school that it wasn't good to get locked into one particular role. She was tough as nails, my drag Svengali, but underneath she was a kind and loving teacher.

After I went on to Club Chaos and Ken's guidance, Wanda and I lost touch. I didn't see her again until she lay in bed at Mr. Thomas's loft in Chelsea. She was very sick and wanted Mr. Thomas to find me so she could give me a present.

"I wanted you to have this," she murmured, pressing an unlabeled tape into my hand.

"What is it?" I asked, feeling the impending doom creeping in.

"The first side is a copy of the music I chose for your first performance for me," she whispered. I could tell every word was an effort for her. "The other is a copy of Madonna's demo tape. They're hard to come by. I know you like her. I caught that show you did at Club Chaos, when you performed as her. You're good, ya know."

"I have good teachers," I whispered, trying not to cry.

"Child, you've got spirit. It's deep within you. You just needed help learning to fly," Wanda smiled.

That night at Club Chaos, I performed as Fraudonna for the last time, using the tape Wanda gave me. The last song on the four-track demo was the original version of "Stay," by Madonna and Steven Bray. The ethereal keyboards provided a dreamlike feeling and I performed the song while standing in place in front of a microphone stand. The whole performance came off reminiscent of an old movie from the forties, but there was no orchestra behind me. I was crying by the end and the audience must've thought I was quite the chanteuse.

Wanda was my first teacher. She was also my first friend to die of AIDS.

I set aside those memories with the same tenderness I used to turn the last page on Wanda.

I paged through clippings from old *Village Voice* ads of benefits I had hosted, some announcements of New Year's Eve parties, and found an absurd question-and-answer session I did in *Interview* with Tammy Wynette in their *Ones to Watch* section: "The Queen of Crossover Talks to the Princess of Crossdressing." Tammy was in the throes of yet another comeback due to KLF's club hit and I was becoming well known in New York City as Princess 2Di4. The interview was done by phone; Tammy had never seen me, but I was thrilled all the same. Andy was ecstatic and even gave me a raise, which was totally out of his nature, but all the press I was getting increased the number of Club Chaos patrons and allowed him to expand and redecorate.

A picture of Jeremy caught my eye in the next scrapbook. It was taken outside of Nell's. We were standing side by side; I was out of drag. We both had the shy smiles of two people who didn't really know each other but were thrown together for a photograph by a group of mutual friends. I knew that scrapbook was a montage of "The Jeremy Years" and firmly set it aside.

I flipped through the other two scrapbooks and gathered strength and joy from all the pictures of friends who had come and gone. My life wasn't so bad. And it certainly wasn't over. I was in yet another transitional period. The scrapbooks revealed to me that I'd had as many, if not more, transitions as Shirley MacLaine and each one was a success in different ways.

For the first time in weeks I was completely clearheaded. It really was time to move forward, whether or not Blaine gave me a job.

Maybe tonight would even give me the opportunity to show my friends that I wasn't the mess of indecision they thought I was. I might not know exactly what to do about Jeremy; I might not know what my next job would be. But my years as a diva hadn't been wasted. I was a survivor.

I put in a Gloria Gaynor CD and headed for the shower with renewed confidence and energy, suddenly excited about the evening ahead.

SEVEN

Aunt Jen arrived promptly with her Lincoln, her imperturbable driver, and her newfound enthusiasm for understanding her favorite nephew. She was resplendent in a regal, black Dior cocktail dress and let me choose from several short-sleeved shirts she'd purchased that would accommodate my cast in a fashionable way.

Joey, the doorman, waved us through the velvet ropes.

"We don't have to pay?" Aunt Jen asked.

"Lady, the princess here don't ever have to pay at this joint," Joey explained.

I winced at the use of my "title" in front of Aunt Jen.

"How marvelous," was all she said.

I didn't know if she was talking about the fact that we were comped or if she was referring to the bar. She gazed at the red velvet walls and the multitude of pictures cataloguing Club Chaos events over the years. A whole section of the wall between the two doorways that led to house left and right was enshrined in Princess 2Di4's honor, but I doubted Aunt Jen would recognize me in costume. I was surprised that Andy hadn't taken them down. Perhaps he still relied on the legend of 2Di4. Or maybe he was still hoping for my return.

"This place looks like a burlesque house," Aunt Jen whispered.

"It kind of is," I whispered back.

The barroom itself was huge and took up a large portion of the front of the building. Most places have one bar, but Club Chaos had two bars running down either side of the large, dark room. Thursday was seventies night, so Anita Ward implored us to ring her bell at a very loud volume.

"Daniel, is there more to this place, or must I be subjected to this vile music?" beseeched Aunt Jen.

We left just as two drag queens came out selling cigarettes and candy from large cases suspended from straps around their necks.

I led Aunt Jen into the performance hall, where she marveled appreciatively.

"It looks like a cross between the theater where the Follies played and the Rainbow Room," she mused.

There were tables set up all around the house (the floor had been leveled), with a large square left vacant for dancing. Before I could object, Luis seated us at the tony table in front of center stage. Although Andy himself might not be thrilled to see me, it was apparent the rest of the Club Chaos staff was in no way dismayed by my little brawl a few nights before.

I ordered my usual Brandy Manhattan and a Tanqueray martini for Aunt Jen. As Luis disappeared, Andy took the stage to introduce the next act.

"Ladies and gentlemen," he began. I saw him flinch as he noticed me in the audience, but knew he would never call attention to me when I wasn't in drag. "Our next performer— uh"—again he looked at me, then continued—"our next . . . excuse me, please," he stammered and vanished backstage.

"What was that all about?" Aunt Jen asked.

"I haven't a clue," I said innocently, certain Andy had been terrified of a repeat performance between me and his fake princess.

"He looked startled to see you," she commented.

"It would appear so, wouldn't it?"

Andy returned.

"I'm sorry, folks," he chuckled nervously, "it seems our next performer is *ill*. *But* we have someone to take her place, of *course*. Someone who needs *no* introduction, but I will anyway. Say hello to Judy!"

The music swelled and Ken came out in full Judy regalia, a glittering black dress, stockings, high heels, full makeup, and a short, black wig. And he looked mad as hell.

"Ladiesh and gentlllmen," Judy slurred, "I'd like to shing a shong that I hold dear to my heart." On the word "heart," Ken put his hand on his head. The audience laughed. Ken/Judy looked confused. "Uh, to my heart," he said again and this time put his hand on his stomach. More laughter. "It's a shong about a man, as mosht shongs are. It'sh about that one shpeshial man. You know the one, don't you? The kind that getsh you all worked up, hot and running? Then one day you turn around and he'sh gone. He'sh the one that always sheemsh to dishappear when you want him to shtick around the mosht."

Then Ken performed his special Judy miracle, transforming her from an object of ridicule to a tortured, vulnerable star as he lip-synched to the "Man Medley" he'd created of Judy singing "Can't Help Lovin' That Man of Mine," "My Man," and "The Man That Got Away."

He finished to thunderous applause and left the stage. I glanced at my aunt and saw she'd been completely charmed by his performance.

"Come on," I said. "I want you to meet Ken."

I led the way to the dressing room backstage. Ken was seated at the makeup table in his costume. He was drinking bottled water and looking pensive.

"Knock, knock," I intoned.

"Daniel," Ken said warmly, getting up from his chair.

"This is my Aunt Jen," I said. "Jen, this is Ken Bruckner."

"How do you do?" Ken asked, smiling at Aunt Jen and taking her hand.

"I'm fine, thank you," Aunt Jen pleasantly answered. "That was such a marvelous little show you put on out there. I'm quite impressed. I saw Judy Garland so *many* times in my day and you captured her essence completely."

Ken gave me a quick aside look that implied *I thought you said she was a battle-ax* and beamed at Aunt Jen.

"Why, thank you so much. What a sweet thing to say. Would you like a seat? Can I get you anything?"

"No, dear, I'm fine," Aunt Jen assured him.

Martin chose that moment to burst onto the scene in a flurry of frumpiness.

"I can't believe that fucking prick!"

"Martin!" Ken and I yelled together.

"Martin," Ken repeated, taking hold of Martin's shoulders, "I'd like you to meet Daniel's Aunt Jen."

"Hi, what's shaking?"

"I—" Aunt Jen was at a loss for words.

I was trying my best not to dissolve into nervous giggles. Martin was in his Bette Midler costume, red curls tumbling down his shoulders over a padded black dress.

"That bitch Andy is in rare form," Martin ranted. He plopped down in the chair Ken had vacated. "He's making me do Bette tonight."

"Is that bad?" Aunt Jen timidly asked, and I did a double take. Could it be that she was actually intimidated by Martin? Maybe it was the huge red hair?

"Well, no, but Bette never closes the show," Martin fumed. Ken stood behind him and massaged his shoulders, which must have been difficult through the shoulder pads.

"I was going to ask about that," I said. "Why would he put Judy before Bette?"

"Because I was the only one in costume and ready to go on," Ken frowned.

"Darling, he had to put someone on," Martin said, putting a hand on one hip in true Bette fashion. "He saw *you* in the audience and panicked."

"I don't understand," Aunt Jen said.

"Andy found a substitute 2Di4," Ken explained, "who was about to go on. That is, until he saw Daniel in the house. Andy was afraid Daniel might ruin the show again, so he put me on in her place."

"How about them apples?" Martin smirked, shimmying his fake breasts.

"Is that what your brawl was about, Daniel? Someone impersonating *you* impersonating *Diana?*" Aunt Jen asked. I nodded and was rewarded with a grim smile before she said, "Well. It's almost like *All About Eve,* isn't it?"

"Oh, Bette *Davis* is here, too," Martin said. "Wanna meet her?"

"Dying to," Aunt Jen answered, linking her arm in Martin's as he stood.

They maneuvered through the crowded backstage area, meeting such notables as Bette Davis, Joan Crawford, and Cher.

"Do you think she'll be safe with Martin?" I asked Ken.

"Are you kidding? I think it's a match made in heaven. They're both very capable girls," Ken answered.

Would I ever tire of Ken being right? Martin was like a younger version of Aunt Jen. Or perhaps what she had been like when she was Martin's age.

"Ken, I'm sorry about—rather, I want to thank you for—"

"Daniel," Ken began as he turned away from the mirror to face me directly, "you don't owe me an apology or thanks. I was a little hurt when you missed brunch, but I got over it. The intent of my call really was to help. You have a lot of decisions to make. I just want to be available to you when you need me. But you already know that."

Ken was always there for me when I needed him. He'd gotten me out of that terrible bar in the East Village and into Club Chaos; helped me create Princess 2Di4; listened to hours and hours of Jeremy drama recounted and repeated; he'd even introduced me to Gretchen, my financial advisor. Suddenly I felt guilty about all that, too.

"There's just so much going on right now," I blurted, tired of myself the moment I opened my mouth. "I know that's pretty lame, but you know how I get when I'm juggling too much."

Ken sighed, swinging around with cold cream on his face.

"What did I just say? I know you. I also know how hard it is to start over. Start something new, whatever. I've been there. We all have. Don't worry about me; I'm fine. You will be too," he added, dismissing the subject with a wave of his hand and reaching for tissues. "Now tell me what's keeping you so busy."

I sighed deeply, unsure where to begin.

"Well, it seems there's this—"

"Daniel, *darling!*" Andy's voice and rapid approach made my mouth snap shut before I could tell Ken anything about Blaine or the upcoming "interview."

"How is your *arm?* You poor *thing!* Imagine how surprised and delighted I was to look into the audience tonight and see you there? When*ever* are we going to sit and discuss this auction? What a *lovely* blouse you have on!"

I looked from Andy to Ken, wondering which of the questions or comments I was supposed to address first.

"Andy, it's nice to see you, too."

He smiled demurely, which frightened me a little. It was as if he were attempting to channel June Cleaver but came up with Faye Dunaway in *Mommie Dearest*. I glanced at Ken's reflection in the mirror. He had his hand over his mouth, most likely trying not to laugh.

"I was actually thinking about this auction idea of yours," I continued. "Why don't you tell me a little more about it?"

"Be still, my *heart!* Do you mean to say you're actually *willing* to hear me out? I'd better talk *fast!* As you know, I was thinking of using the auction for charity. You *need* to get rid of those dresses *any*way, don't you? Well, I thought we could have a little function *here* at the club to benefit AmFAR! You could emcee the event and give a final appearance as 2Di4 at the *same time*. Wouldn't it be *fabulous?*" Andy squealed with such excitement I felt sure he would wet his pants.

I glanced again at Ken, who was now moisturizing. He gave me a look that showed he approved. But did I?

"Andy, I'm not sure I *want* to get rid of them. Besides, 2Di4 is done. Over. I swore I wouldn't resurrect her for anything. I agree the fundraising aspect is a good idea. But I'm uncomfortable about doing 2Di4. I don't think it would be in good taste. What if someone thinks we're making fun of Diana's dress auction? I'm just not sure."

"*Da*rling, *Dan*iel! Not at *all!* Why, I'm sure Diana her*self* would look down from heaven with approval. *Especially* considering the charity we have in mind! You don't need *me* to tell you that AIDS research was one of her pet projects. Besides, Daniel, you *know* how committed I am to this. I've been asking you about it for *ages!*" His voice dropped several decibels, always a bad sign, as he continued, "I'm sure I don't have to remind you that even though you aren't performing currently, you are still under contract to Club Chaos."

He put his hands on his hips as if to demonstrate his firm stance on the subject. Ken raised a freshly moisturized eyebrow and glanced from Andy to me, waiting to see my reaction before he interjected anything. He bit his lower lip to illustrate his self-control.

I hadn't thought about my obligation to Club Chaos. During my hasty departure and potential transition into Blaine's world, my contract was the last thing on my mind. I tried to conjure up the fine print and what it said about termination of contract, dismissal, and resignation. However, I couldn't understand it when it was in front of me, much less remember all that legal jargon under this kind of pressure.

"Andy, I'd hate to have to bring lawyers into this," I said, carefully choosing my words. "Let's agree to this verbally and shake hands, okay?"

"Agreed," Andy replied.

"You go ahead and organize the auction. I'll donate some of my 2Di4 dresses. I'll think of some way to host this thing and hold on to my scruples. I only have one demand. I want Ken to handle the production end."

"I'm fine with that," Ken said, brushing out his hair after removing his wigcap.

"Fabulous!" Andy squealed again, this time shaking his fists excitedly in front of his shoulders. *"Oh,* could you just *die?"* His mouth snapped shut as he comprehended the double meaning of his words. "I mean . . . well . . . it's just . . ."

He closed his mouth again, turned, and disappeared into the dimly lit backstage area.

"Are you sure you want to do this?" Ken asked. He'd finished removing Judy and stood to put on a robe.

"Ken, he had me against the wall with my contract. I'm not even sure what it says about me quitting. Besides, if you produce the auction, I'm at least assured it won't be a tacky affair. I mean, what can Andy do to ruin me or Diana's image by making a few phone calls and sending out some invites?"

Ken tied the sash on his robe and folded his arms.

"Do you really want me to answer that?"

I stared blankly at him, knowing full well that I didn't.

"Ken," I begged, "humor me for a little bit, okay? At least let me pretend this isn't going to be a disaster that I'll regret forever."

"Humor you? Why, of course, dear."

Ken took my chin in his hand and kissed me on the cheek just as Martin and Aunt Jen returned.

"How positively charming," Aunt Jen said. "What a delightful evening, Daniel. Why don't we all go for a cocktail? I'm absolutely parched."

"I'm afraid Martin and I will have to decline," Ken politely said to Aunt Jen. "We have to plan an event."

"We do?" Martin asked, still linked to Aunt Jen's arm.

It was apparent that he had been completely charmed by Aunt Jen and was disappointed not to show her a night on the town. Or perhaps he was trying to get written into her will. I could never tell with Martin.

"Yes, we do. Andy's already planned the auction, Daniel. It's been ready to go for weeks. He's just been trying to get you to do it. It might've happened with or without you. Need I remind you about Marc?"

"No, you needn't," I frowned.

"Daniel, that was bait to lure you into the whole auction thing," Martin jumped in, finally clued in to what we were talking about. "If you didn't agree to the auction, Andy would have used Marc. Ever since you've left, he's been trying to get back the attention you took away."

"So this is all about publicity?" I was outraged.

"Daniel, this is Andy. Sure he's a bit of a curmudgeon, but he does have his good side. Besides, it's a worthwhile cause and he's sympathetic to that. We all, Andy included, know people who could use the money we'll raise."

Ken bit his lip and raised his eyebrows again. I didn't need any codes to agree to anything he said.

"Okay, I'm in. So you won't come out with us?"

"I'm pretty tired; no. Besides, need I remind you that you never shook hands on the deal with Andy?"

"Oh shit!"

"Don't worry. You two go and I'll deal with Andy," Ken said. He and Martin ushered us out of the dressing room and to the back-stage door. "You can count on us to make this go smoothly. We'll talk to you soon."

"It was a pleasure to meet you," Martin said to Aunt Jen and kissed her cheek. Ken agreed with him and did the same, all to Aunt Jen's delight.

Later, as the Lincoln sped up Eighth Avenue to drop me off, Aunt Jen said, "I think I have a better view of what you did now. I'm still glad you've put it behind you to pursue a more respectable career."

I groaned at the word *respectable*.

"Now, now," she said, wagging her finger at me, "don't get impertinent."

"Auntie," I sighed, "do you understand why I ended my performing career?"

"I would hope at my suggestion, but I'm sure that wasn't the case. What was it, then?"

"My character was based on Princess Diana," I said patiently.

"Daniel, I'm not entirely without intelligence."

"I didn't think it would be in good taste to continue with that persona."

"I don't think it was in good taste to mock those inbred British wastrels to begin with, but what do I know?" Aunt Jen said, folding her arms and resuming her patrician facade.

I smiled at her.

"It probably wasn't. But I didn't exactly mock Diana—it doesn't matter. Everyone loved it. However, with Diana dead, especially the way she died, I was left with nowhere to go. Anyway, I met this man who might need a personal assistant. It seemed to go along with your 'toss the tiara and get a life' advice, so I took it as a sign."

"My dear nephew," Aunt Jen said, placing her hand on my arm. "I hope you didn't take that the wrong way. All I meant is that it's unwise to put all your eggs in one basket. Your whole life was the character you were portraying. It sounded to me as if you didn't know where she ended and you began. You wrote me on 'From the Desk of Her Highness' stationary and signed it 'Love, Di.' I was concerned."

I nearly cried as I heard Aunt Jen say everything I had been worrying about over the last few months. She understood more than I gave her credit for.

"I must admit, Daniel," she said, placing a hand on my arm, "I am a bit worried about you resuming this I'dDi4U role again for this thing you boys are planning."

"As long as Ken and Martin are helping me, I'll be fine. I just hope I can pull off the auction and also start working for Blaine."

"This man—is he handsome?" she asked.

"Aunt Jen!" I exclaimed in mock disbelief. "Surely you don't think I'd become a personal assistant to catch a man?"

"Why not?" she asked with a small smile. "We did it in my day."

"Not you," I flattered her. "They pursued *you*."

"Oh, go on," she said with a small but entirely gratified smile.

I had worried that our night at Club Chaos might make her even more determined to understand my New York life, but the next morning she arrived at my apartment to tell me about a call from Wisconsin. Some second cousin had managed to get herself pregnant and a wedding was being hastily planned. Aunt Jen was convinced the entire event would be the last word in tastelessness. I wasn't sure if her eagerness to go home was to prevent this or relish it.

I managed to get her into a cab headed for the airport in plenty of time to prepare for my dinner with Blaine. With Jen's lectures on frugality ringing in my ears (ironic, since the finger she pointed at me was heavily weighed down by diamonds), I took the subway to Union Square, managing to arrive at the Blue Water Grill well before Blaine.

It was not a place I would have chosen and reinforced my conviction that if Blaine were, in fact, gay, he had acquired none of the more festive qualities of being so in New York and must be closeted. I tried not to wrinkle my nose in distaste, knowing I could somehow use that to my advantage. The important thing was to get him in bed. I was certain he would need no instruction there, and afterward I'd have all the time in the world to educate him in other areas.

When he arrived, he looked as exhausted as I felt. He barely sat down before ordering a martini, forgoing any type of greeting. This made me happy, as I was keeping my cumbersome, casted arm well out of sight. When his drink arrived, he immediately asked for another, and I suppressed a smile.

"Brutal week?" I asked sympathetically.

"You don't know the half of it," he said, launching without preamble into the single most boring account of corporate life I had ever heard.

My ears picked up a common theme in his diatribe that gave birth to a blindingly brilliant idea. Apparently, his business trip had been forced on him by the firing of some underling. He was highly insulted that he had been expected to take up the slack in a way he considered so horribly beneath him.

I murmured little words of support and understanding at appropriate intervals, and after we'd ordered, I began my careful campaign.

"Well, considering everything, I'm afraid I'm wasting your time," I said. "They'll never allow you to hire me."

"Allow me?" he asked, brows raised over those incredible green eyes.

"Blaine, I'm an—" I stopped myself from saying actor, knowing it might come back to haunt me later. "I'm a performer. I have absolutely no office experience of any kind. I can't even type. And if I could"—I finally brought my arm up to the table— "I had a little accident. I'm out of commission. I can't imagine why Sheila thought this was a good idea," I finished, throwing her to the wolves without a twinge of guilt.

"If you've been supporting yourself so well as an actor—"

"Oh, I've had to do other things, make sacrifices for my art," I said. "You know, I've been a waiter, worked retail, whatever. I don't mind doing other things. But I know nothing about working in an office for someone as important as you, and of course they will want you to have the best. So they'll never let you hire me."

"I can hire who I damn well please," he muttered, finishing his fourth drink. "You'd be working only for me. Anyone in the secretarial pool can do my typing. You know nothing about advertising?"

"Not a thing," I answered cheerily.

"Ever used a computer?"

"Never."

He was silent as our plates were set in front of us. I hoped he was thinking about me, but suspected he was just feeling the effects of the alcohol.

"What I really need," he finally said, "is someone with the loyalty and protectiveness of a rottweiler. Someone who can handle infighting, competitiveness, vindictiveness—"

"In that respect," I assured him, thinking of the performers at Club Chaos, "I'm your man."

"You think so?" he asked, green eyes seeming to pin me down like a particularly interesting specimen of butterfly.

"So how long have you and Sheila been together?" I asked nervously.

"Sheila and I are not together," he said. I waited for his confession, my stomach doing odd flips while other parts of my body reacted predictably to that unwavering stare. "She's like a sister to me. And she's only a kid."

"Oh? That's funny. I don't know why, but I sensed a certain intimacy between you two. Was I imagining that?"

"What was it you observed that gave you that idea?" Blaine's eyes continued to bore into me.

"I was thinking about the evening we met. When you and she were attending some business function? I can't exactly tell you when I felt it, but it was like listening to a husband and wife bicker in those last moments of getting ready before leaving."

Blaine smirked.

"What's funny?" I laughed nervously. "Did I say something wrong?"

"No. I just find your 'husband and wife' remark interesting."

"Interesting?" I asked.

"Well," Blaine continued, "interesting and somewhat amusing."

A slight smile danced on his oh-so-luscious lips.

"How so?"

"Because I always sort of pictured that last-minute bickering taking place with someone a little more . . . masculine." His eyes met mine, emeralds piercing into sapphires. A long pause followed. "You think you're man enough for the job?"

"Umm. Are you referring to the position under you professionally speaking, or the position under you on a more personal level?" I asked, plunging in headfirst.

His eyes sparkled in the dim light of the restaurant.

"Take your pick," he replied.

My face flushed. I flashed my best grin.

"Waiter?" Blaine lifted his chin as he caught the eye of the waiter. "Check, please?"

I let him handle the logistics of the cab, noticing he gave my address rather than his. He walked into the apartment ahead of me as I took the keys from the lock. I entered and shut the door behind me. As I turned, I drew a quick breath, surprised to find Blaine's strong, handsome face inches from mine, those emerald eyes piercing me. As he had surprised me in midturn, I lost my balance and leaned against the door, hearing it click shut behind me. Almost immediately his hands were pressed against the door on either side of my shoulders. I swear the light in the hall where we stood grew dimmer as he closed his eyes, tilted his head slightly, and moved his lips closer to mine. I inclined my head, parted my lips, and my good hand instinctively rose to his ribcage, slipping around his back as I felt his lips press mine.

My heart beat wildly and my breath quickened through my nose as he slipped his tongue into my mouth. As if doing some kind of push-up, his elbows bent, bringing the weight of his body onto mine, pinning me against the door more firmly.

I was burning from the inside out; his kisses were all I had imagined, passionate and hot. My left hand slid down his back and clutched his firm ass and for a moment I forgot my right forearm was in a cast. I swung the arm up and whacked Blaine in the back. His grunt was muffled by our kiss. Then he let out a half groan as he pulled away from me. He placed both hands on the collar of my shirt and ripped it off as if it were paper. He yanked it down and the right sleeve caught on my cast. My left hand, freed from the prison of the dress shirt, reached down and unbuckled Blaine's belt. Blaine finally ripped the shirt from my cast. He grabbed me by my belt and pulled me across the apartment. We neared the door leading to the garden.

Perfect; the garden, I thought, the new and improved Adam and Eve.

We stepped into the warm, fragrant air. Blaine frantically pulled me toward him again and unzipped his own pants. I reached for him as his hand found the zipper of my pants. The hand on the back of my head pulled me toward his face; as we kissed, I opened my eyes and saw a light come on in his apartment. Sheila's silhouetted form appeared. I gasped. Blaine turned and looked at the apartment window.

"Oh my god," he moaned.

He pushed me back into the apartment. I tried opening my mouth to speak, but Blaine shoved his tongue into me and lowered me to the floor. As we tumbled and fumbled with the task of removing our pants, all the while ignoring my bulky cast, I fell in and out of reality, caught between the desire to do this and fear that it would lead nowhere.

My nakedness suddenly felt childlike, and Blaine's arms were suffocating.

"Wait," I interrupted. "Should we be doing this?"

"I've wanted to since the moment I first started watching you in your garden."

Blaine continued running his tongue down my chest. He teased my hipbones, half tickling me, half arousing me even more. I was already sweating and raising my hips. Part of me wanted to recreate *9 ½ Weeks* with Blaine, but another part of me was void of anything, distant and removed, as if my emotions had been amputated.

Blaine's words caught up with me.

"Watching me?" I asked.

"Yes, I used to watch you in the garden. Did you think that all that time you went unnoticed? Now shut up."

Blaine ferociously took me into his mouth and I could not suppress the long-awaited passionate groan.

"Wait!" I screamed.

Blaine looked up at me. His eyebrow lifted in annoyance, and his nostrils flared. He released my arms and sat up straight, perching on his legs.

"Christ, Daniel! What do you want? You don't want this? What?"

"I don't know. I've just given it up so easily so many times. I want this to be different."

"I'll give you a choice. This happens now, and you've got an honest job, or this doesn't happen and you can go back to being a two-bit whore in a dimestore dress."

Whoa! How the hell did he know about 2Di4? And what made him think I'd rather be *his* whore than a two-bit whore?

"Wait a second, buster," I said in complete shock.

"Blaine," he corrected, rolling his eyes and losing his balance. At that moment, I realized just how drunk he was. I pushed him backward and awkwardly scrambled to a sitting position.

"I am no whore and those dresses cost more than that JC Penney special you've got on!"

Blaine looked down at his suit and I realized it was an Armani. No matter. I needed to gain control of the situation. I opted for silence as the best defense and stared at Blaine with the coolest gaze I could muster after such a heated embrace.

"Well, what's it going to be?" he asked, running his hand through his hair. Most people would chalk it up to vanity, but I interpreted it as a nervous gesture.

"What are you talking about?" I asked.

Play to the alcohol, I told myself. Make him tell you what you want to know.

What do I want to know, I wondered. What do I want?

That detached part of me, sounding frighteningly like Aunt Jen, said, You can have whatever you want. And you can just as easily use your mind as your body to get it.

"Are we gonna have some fun tonight, or am I leaving you to dance in a dress for dollars?" Blaine sneered.

Obviously this man knew nothing of the lifestyle to which I was accustomed. Sure, people would tuck tips into my purse when I performed as 2Di4, but I gave that money to charity. The real money was in making appearances. Andy was an obnoxious and conniving bitch, but he paid me well. I had a contract with Club Chaos, and Ken got his lawyer to add a clause so that, although I was contracted to Club Chaos, my performing there was not exclusive. I was paid at any bar, club, or event where I made special appearances, and they were more than glad to have me.

I was even discussing an appearance at next year's Wigstock with the Lady Bunny herself just before the fatal car wreck that changed everyone's lives. I'd bowed out of performing at this year's Wigstock festivities because RuPaul had been the big headliner the year before. I wasn't about to have people think I was riding on her frocktails or something like—

"Daniel!" Blaine was waving his hands in front of my face. "I'm waiting."

Oh yeah.

"Listen," I said, getting to my feet and heading to the bar in the kitchen. "I don't know what you're talking about. Dresses? Dancing for dollars? Was that how you put it?"

Blaine was staring at me blankly, his mouth hanging open. I found a bottle of gin and prepared a pitcher of my meanest martinis.

"Whatever," I said, dismissing his accusations with a wave of my hand. "I'm just glad to know what you expect of me now, before I start working for you. I'm not the type of boy who likes to be chased around a desk. You just saved yourself one sexual harassment case, buster. Oh, excuse me, Blaine."

I plopped an olive in each glass and stared at Blaine. He sat on the floor trying to follow what I was saying, trying to figure out if he was still going to get lucky tonight. I found it a shame that such a handsome man turned out to be nothing more than a typical male. It was his bad luck that he had just come across one very typical drag queen with all the necessary survival skills intact.

Although, I rationalized, relenting a bit, he *was* drunk. Also, it sounded like he was having a rough time at work. Maybe his boorishness was a passing, overemotional reaction to all of that. If it was, I should be able to empathize. I'd had enough experience in that area lately.

I'd figure it all out later. My plan was to get him to an ever higher level of drunkenness, mess with his mind, then figure out what to do with him.

Right now we're aiming for a level known as *stupor,* I decided.

I sipped from one glass and held the other toward him. He clumsily took it from me, nearly spilling the contents as he moved it toward his mouth. I neatly plucked the olive from my drink, raised my glass to him, downed its contents, and plopped the olive in my mouth. I gave him my most adorable smile as I slowly chewed the olive.

Blaine was still trying to figure me out but wasn't about to be outdone. He sniffed at the strong martini and looked at me. I raised my eyebrows and smiled, egging him on. He took a breath and knocked back the martini. His eyes bulged as he swallowed it in a single gulp. After a brief coughing fit he regained his rather addled senses, raising his glass as he gave me his most cavalier smile.

I plucked his glass from his weak grip and headed to the counter for the pitcher.

"Now, Blaine," I said, discreetly pouring another club soda for myself and another double martini for him, "what's all this nonsense about me in dresses?"

"Well," Blaine began, trying to get control of his tongue, "when I first moved here, I would go out to bars and clubs downtown. At one of them, I forget which one, they had this sort of stage. At ten or eleven they had this show and you'd never believe what it was."

He paused and waited. I realized he was expecting some sort of response from me. As if I, who'd lived in New York City for over twelve years, would be shocked by his story. I suppose I might have been startled to hear him say that every night at eleven this bar had a choir singing hymns until the patrons repented of their wicked ways and went home to their loved ones, completely absolved of their sins. Ah, but that was *Guys and Dolls,* not *Anything Goes.*

As it was, I simply asked, "What?"

He took the fresh martini I offered him.

"They had this show. It was a bunch of men dressed up as women. Not just any women, but famous women. They looked good, too. They all pretended to be singing other people's songs. You know, like those two guys?"

He was really slurring now and I suppressed an automatic disclaimer that my fellow divas and I were anything like Milli Vanilli.

"Lip-synching?" I inquired.

"Yeah, that's it," he said. He took a big swig of the martini. "So, this guy pretending to be that dead Dorothy in Oz woman lip—synched—sunk?—some song about not getting a kick from champagne and cocaine and for some reason it was all hilarious to everyone there. I didn't get it."

"Oh. The song is 'I Get a Kick Out of You,' I believe," I said, laughing to myself. I had forgotten Ken did that song from *Anything Goes* in his act once. "See, Judy Garland died of an overdose of alcohol and prescription drugs. It sounds like the performer did a play on that." His eyes showed no comprehension, so I tried again. "The song talks of her preferring her man to champagne, drugs, or a plane ride, which would all bore her. It's ironic."

Blaine slugged back the rest of his martini and stared at me.

"Anyway," he said, shaking his head without understanding, "they also had this guy pretending to be that dead princess. Whatshername."

"Grace?" I asked, determined to be difficult because I was truly annoyed by his cultural ignorance. What kind of gay man was he?

"Nuh-uh. Dinah? Diane? Diana? You know, the one that bought the farm in a car a couple of months ago?"

"Yes," I winced. Had he no respect for the dead?

"He was beautiful, too. Looked just like her. She—I mean, he—did. I mean, he didn't even lip—um—sing—synch? all of her—his—songs. She—he—did some of his own songs and then lip—pretended to sing some song. What song was it? Oh yeah, he did a bunch of them. He was last and I guess he was the big finale or something. He did 'Try' and 'Save Up All Your Tears' and it was funny to think of Janis Joplin's and Cher's voices coming out of that prim and proper woman."

I smiled wanly at the knowledge that my show hadn't gone completely over Blaine's empty little head.

"Then she—he—whatever, finished with 'I Will Survive' and the place went nuts."

Blaine looked at me. It seemed like he was looking through me, or where 'I Am Princess 2Di4' must've been written on my forehead. After a long silence he apparently caught up with himself and said, "And she, uh, he looked like you. I mean, you look a lot like Princess Diana and, like, you could have been up there dressed like her, or something."

I took Blaine's glass and went to refill it, suppressing a smile at what could easily have been the most convoluted conversation I'd ever endured. Had I not known what he was talking about, I'd have been hopelessly confused.

"Nope," I said. "It wasn't me. You'd never find me doing anything silly like that. That's not acting. That's mockery. I was doing a show in a real theater not far from here around then."

"Really?" Blaine asked, without the presence of mind to question how I knew when he'd seen the show.

"Yup," I lied. I nervously eyed my coffee table trunk which, in addition to my quilt and scrapbooks, held at least one or two wigs. It was not more than five feet from where he sat.

I handed him another martini. The guy should've been floundering in his own vomit by now; what was going on?

I sat on the floor and held up my club soda in a toast.

"To misconceptions," I laughed.

"To great beauty," Blaine said, attempting to wink at me, but only blinking in the process.

We downed our drinks and Blaine ended up falling forward in a coughing fit. I smiled and patted his broad back.

"There, there, sailor," I said. "Take it easy."

I brought his head up and raised his arms in the air so he could breathe better. After a couple of deep breaths, his coughs subsided. I let go of his arms and they fell like dead weights on either side of his body. Blaine fell forward as well, giggling at the whole series of events.

That's better, I thought.

"So, Blaine," I began, uprighting him again, "do you believe me when I tell you it wasn't me you saw onstage?"

"Yeah," he giggled. "Now, Daniel, do you believe me when I tell you that I want you?"

"Sure, big boy," I said. "I believe you. They all want me. Trouble is, I think you're too drunk to do anything about it."

"No, no," he stammered. "I'm not drunk."

He tried to stand and fell over his own feet.

"No, not at all," I sighed, standing and taking our glasses to the kitchen. "Congratulations, Daniel. Very nicely done."

I deposited the glasses in the sink and tried to think of what to do with Blaine. I didn't think he could return home in this condition. Nor did I want to carry him over there myself, much less explain or make up a story for Sheila. I decided he'd have to stay the night. That would give me a chance to further mess with his head in the morning.

I went over and straddled him, attempting to hoist him to his feet. Much easier said than done, since he must've weighed a little over two hundred pounds.

"My god, you must work out a lot," I grunted.

"Wha—?" Blaine mumbled.

"Come on, big boy, we're going to bed," I said, dragging him to a position where he could lean on me. I maneuvered him down the hall to my room and deposited him on the bed.

I was glad he was already undressed and I didn't have to get him out of his clothes. It wasn't too often that I found myself thinking *that* way. I gazed at his firm, hard body lying limply across my bed.

"Why did you have to be such a jerk?" I asked out loud.

When he only snored in reply, I slid next to him, pulling the covers over us.

I was disturbed from any attempts at slumber by the phone ringing. Ignoring the extension on the table by my bed, I decided to screen the call. Blaine didn't move at the sound, or in response to my leaving the bed. I hurried to the living room to listen to the machine.

Beep! "Daniel? This is Sheila. Sorry to be calling so late, but Blaine didn't come home and I knew you two were meeting for dinner tonight. Anyway, um, I thought I saw him earlier in your garden. Not that I was spying on you! But I happened to glance out the window and . . . well, anyway, if you get in and get this, could you call me? Thanks."

She gave the number again, just in case I didn't have it, then hung up.

Something in Sheila's voice created my first twinge of remorse and I picked up the phone. She answered on the first ring.

"Hi, sweetie," I said. "It's Daniel."

"Uh-huh."

Her tone spoke volumes.

"You know what?" I asked. "Blaine had a really, really shitty day and drank way too much at dinner. His behavior has been . . . extraordinary. Anyway, he's passed out and I figured the best thing is to just let him sleep it off."

"Uh-huh."

"So he's snoring in my bed and I'm just about to hit the couch with a good book."

"Uh-huh." Long silence, then in a tiny voice, "Did you get the job?"

"Well, I figured tonight was not the best time for him to make decisions, you know? Maybe he'll feel like discussing it in the morning."

I turned on the lamp next to the couch in case she could see my light from her window.

"Hmm," she said.

"What about you?" I asked. "You're the one who has all those great opportunities. Made any decisions?"

"I think I may go back to Eau Claire," she said, her voice flat. Now I really felt like shit.

"Don't do that," I quickly spoke. "There's nothing there for a woman like you."

"What is there for me here?"

"You never know," I said. "Besides, I'm selfish. I don't want to lose a new friend."

"Really, Daniel? You think of me as a friend?"

"Of course I do!"

She sighed and said, "Well, I'll think about it. Anyway, it's late. You're really sweet to take such good care of Blaine. Maybe I'll see you soon, huh?"

"Count on it," I promised.

We hung up and I crawled on the couch, some shred of honor making me live up to what I'd said to Sheila.

Surreal dreams of the adventures of yuppies in drag at the Blue Water Grill woke me early. Blaine showed no signs of life as I made coffee and showered. I finally took the cordless phone to the garden and called my friend Gretchen, launching without preamble into questions.

"How much does a secretary make in Manhattan?"

"Nice to talk to you, too, Daniel. Depends on his or her experience. And they are not secretaries. They're administrative assistants or word processors, based on their skills."

"Whatever, how much?"

"Mine makes forty. She's good and worth a lot more, though of course I'd never tell her that. But they usually start in the upper twenties and go up, geez, as high as the sixties, I think. Depends on what kind of firm they work for, what they do, you know. You can't afford one, and if you're sleeping with one, he can't afford you."

"I was thinking of being one," I said.

She let out a roar of laughter and said, "You? Is this for some company I own stock in? I may need to sell now."

"How rude," I commented and changed the subject, gossiping about our mutual friends and asking about her latest love interest. I brought the conversation to a quick close as I heard sounds of life from the apartment.

Blaine stumbled out, his clothes askew, but even in disarray and the pitiless sunlight, I had to admire his beauty.

"God," he said. "Coffee."

I poured him a cup from the carafe and watched as he tried to pull himself together.

"I talked with Sheila last night," I said. "I told her you had a bit too much to drink and had to sleep it off here."

He grunted then turned those green eyes on me.

"Exactly what did happen here last night?" he asked.

I gave him a smug smile and said, "What time should I be in your office on Monday?"

The fleeting fear in his eyes was quickly replaced with determination.

"I *do* remember that you have no skills," he said.

"*No* skills?" I smiled again. "I believe the salary we agreed on was forty."

He choked on his coffee and said, "Daniel, my last girl—"

"Yes, where *is* your last girl?"

"But you can't even type!"

"So you lied to me? About being able to hire whoever you want?"

"Thirty," he said desperately.

"Thirty-five."

"Jesus. Fine. Nine o'clock. Go to Human Resources. I won't be in until later. But you should be prompt."

"You can count on it," I said. "I am always where I should be when I should be."

"I have no doubt," he commented acidly, staring at his coffee as if it were a prisoner's last meal.

I had no idea why I was so determined to get a job for which I had no qualifications and in which I had no interest, but my instincts had never failed me yet. Nor would my savings hold out forever. I was not finished with Blaine Dunhill. No doubt destiny was taking me where it should.

After discussing a few more specifics, Blaine left, and I spent the rest of the day going through my wardrobe to assess what I had and what I would need for appropriate work attire. I found it a little exciting, as if I were preparing a whole new drag persona. Which, when I thought about it, was exactly the case. Even though my new look might be subdued compared to my costumes, I had no intention of being drab. I had to find a look somewhere between the Eau Claire business getups of my father's bosses and the far too expensive and conservative clothes Blaine wore. After all, I was his assistant. I wasn't running the agency—yet.

I woke up Sunday morning with a pleasurable feeling of anticipation. This was always one of my favorite times of the week. It was the special time that Ken and I reserved for each other, different from spending time backstage preparing for a show or even going out shopping. We got together each Sunday at the Screening Room in the early afternoon. We called it brunch. Even though the brunch time as set by tradition was gone by noon, Ken and I adhered to a different clock. Our work schedules demanded it. Getting home after two in the morning and requiring beauty sleep mandated that we always met at a later hour.

I was eager to get my Ken-fix. I walked into the restaurant to find him already sitting at our table, a Bloody Mary in front of him, chewing on the edge of the celery stalk before placing it back in the glass prior to my sitting down.

"You know," he began as I sat down after giving him a peck on the cheek, "it's not going to be as easy as you think, giving up those dresses."

I snickered and said, "I've thought about that. You're right; I will miss them. One could hardly help but feel pretty in some of those gowns. But it is for a good cause, and I certainly won't be needing them."

"Oh? You sound like you have a definite plan in mind."

"Me? No. I just, you know, think it's time to cut loose that part of me. Besides, I'm going to be starting a new job."

"Uh-huh. I have an idea. Let's start at the beginning, shall we?"

I grinned.

"I met a guy."

"Uh-huh."

"Actually, he's the guy I'm going to be working for."

"Uh-huh."

"No, it's nothing like that. We haven't done the deed. We had dinner."

"Uh-huh."

"Oh, Ken, please. Enough with the 'Uh-huhs.' This guy lives in the apartment across the way from me. I noticed him. Who wouldn't? He's stunning. His name is Blaine Dunhill. As it turns out, I became acquainted with his roommate, Sheila, whom you know. He's also from Eau Claire. Sheila introduced me to him, and he and I had dinner the other night. When all was said and done, and no, not *all* was *done*, I had agreed to go to work for him. It's that simple, really."

"And you've thought, I'm guessing, of the possible ramifications of working for the man you're dating? You wouldn't be the first that backfired on, you know."

"I know. Trust me, if either the dating or the job doesn't work, I'll be the first to admit it and bail out. Anyway, about the dresses. I need room in my closet. Maybe it's all for the best. I've been working hard to move on, to let destiny take me where it's going to. Now here I am entering a whole new field, one that I certainly never thought I'd be in. I'm going to be his assistant at Breslin Evans Fox and Dean, a big advertising firm. I can hardly show up at my new office in a classic Chanel, can I? Actually, now that I think about it, I could. I'd probably look better than some of those office gargoyles. Lord only knows what they wear to work."

Ken clicked his tongue to show his disapproval, rolling his eyes at the poor taste of my new prospective colleagues.

"So it's time for a new wardrobe. I feel like I've spent so much time shopping for Diana dresses that I haven't bought anything new for myself. Maybe it's about time? What do you say? Let's do some shopping after brunch."

"Would love to, darling, but I can't today. I'm just putting the wraps on a new number at the club. But speaking of putting the wraps on a new number, I don't believe you've given me sufficient dish on this new guy of yours. I know his name, and where he works, since it's where you work now, but apart from that—"

"He's incredibly attractive; intense green eyes, Olympic-class body, well endowed—"

"You just had *dinner?*" Ken asked pointedly.

I told him about Friday night and how I'd left the naked Blaine lying in my bed so I wouldn't feel guilty about Sheila.

"And that's how I know the more intimate details of his anatomy," I finished, miming ecstasy.

"Well, I'd love *that* part."

"Oh, hush. You asked. Anyway, I've given him the impression it's to be all business between us. In fact, right now it has to be. Even if he was drunk when he talked about his foray to the club, his total lack of understanding of our performances gives me the impression 2Di4 might be a barrier between us. You know how some guys can be. After the auction is over and my princess is laid to rest, we'll see what happens when we're off the clock."

"Uh-huh. What time does your walking Ken doll actually leave the office?"

I looked at him, wide-eyed, and said, "Oh my god. I thought he looked like a Ken doll when I first saw him. I can't believe you just said that."

"Answer the question, Mary."

"He's generally home around five-thirty. I'm not sure what he does in the evenings. I mean, we're not quite married, Ken."

"Would you like to be?"

"Huh?"

"Do you think he's Mr. Right?"

"I haven't really thought about it."

"Oh yes you have."

"I have?"

"Daniel, please." Ken sighed with exasperation. "I'm one of your oldest and dearest friends—"

I opened my mouth to make a wisecrack.

"Don't interrupt."

I closed my mouth with a smirk.

"I know you as well as you know yourself. Better, sometimes. It's been ten years we've known each other. I saw you fall in love with Jeremy. I've seen you smitten with a few others besides. I know that when you're sizing someone up, one of the first things your analytical Virgo mind does is run through about twenty-seven preset pictures of how your life will be with him. Don't sit there and tell me you haven't asked whether he's Mr. Right. You forgot who you were talking to." He bobbed his head exaggeratedly from side to side as he said the last sentence.

My smirk turned into a grin. He was right, of course. Sure I'd wondered. Had I answered it to myself? I could honestly answer no. Had I run through those pictures in my mind? Maybe.

"Well?"

"I don't know, Ken. Yes, I've thought about it, but I can't tell you what conclusions I've come to. I haven't come to any, really."

"How do you feel when you're with him?"

"Confused. I don't have him entirely figured out yet. But . . . nice."

"Adds to your happiness, huh?"

This was one of Ken's trademark questions. He was a firm believer in not asking something like *Does he make you happy?* because he didn't believe one could make another person happy, that one could only add to another's happiness. I agreed with him, but still smiled at how he worded the question.

"Yeah. He adds to my happiness."

"Good," he concluded, while signaling for another round of drinks. The bartender nodded in acknowledgment as the waiter came over to take our orders. This was superfluous, since we always ordered the same thing from the same waiter. But we relied on the consistency of these mornings. We'd had enough separation anxiety from not working together anymore. Old habits were comforting.

"So I'm assuming your aunt is gone?" When I nodded, he said, "Martin adored her."

"He must have gotten a look at her jewelry," I said, buttering some bread.

"You're too hard on him."

Something serious about his tone made me look up.

"I'm only joking. Martin can be a little shallow, but I know his heart's in the right place."

"It is," Ken agreed. "I'm sure it's been hard on you to endure his unending criticism of Jeremy. But he's young. He thinks by slamming your ex, he's showing loyalty to you."

"It's also insulting. To me and the years I had with Jeremy. Even if Martin never liked Jeremy, we did have something special, and I don't like to hear it dismissed as nothing."

Ken raised his eyebrows and said, "Wow, that almost makes it sound like you've gained some perspective, Daniel."

"Miracles do happen," I said. "I'm still bitter about him and Robert. And I'm sure not ready to deal with his confession after *Anything Goes*. I just want to move on, I guess. I've wasted enough time wallowing."

"Mourning something you've lost is never a waste of time," Ken defended me to myself. "I know you did a few things you're not proud of, but I admire you for not falling into a bunch of self-destructive patterns to avoid dealing with your situation."

"Daniel grows up," I commented.

"Seriously, it means a lot to me to know that you try to take good care of yourself after you suffer a big loss."

I suddenly had a difficult time swallowing my food.

"Ken . . ."

He shook his head and said, "I'm not throwing in the towel, darling. You'll have me around for a long, long time."

"I'm counting on it."

His smile was reassuringly uncomplicated.

"Now, for more important things," he said. "Let's do a little brainstorming about the auction."

We settled in to do what we could do so well together, create a hit show, and all other topics were put aside for the afternoon.

EIGHT

If my purpose in going to work at Breslin Evans Fox and Dean was to pursue office dalliances with Blaine, by the end of my second day I had to admit defeat. I hadn't even caught a glimpse of the man.

Day one was all about orientation. I was led around by a mousy woman from Human Resources who never even told me her name as we made our way through a bewildering labyrinth of cubicles, offices, departments, and people. So many people, none of whose names stuck with me. All the men wore the same suit and most of the women did, too. Four other new employees and I were herded into various conference rooms to learn the history and purpose of the company (*We must keep our clients happy and sell their products!*), our benefits package (the wonderful world of 401k, health insurance, and a bonus plan, all of which required stacks of paper for us to read later), and the rules. I dozed through most of the rules since they came after a catered lunch of five pasta dishes and three versions of cheesecake. Finally we were ushered off for our drug tests (for a secretarial position?) and the day was over.

I was as limp as those pasta noodles by the time I made it home through rush hour crowds. I knew I should be thinking about the auction. I had to choose which ensembles to donate and decide what role I wanted to play in Andy's project. But I had never felt so tired in my life. I lay for hours in front of the television until I stumbled to bed.

It was amazing how shrill an alarm could sound before noon. I jumped about a foot off of the mattress as the clock clamored, announcing that 6 A.M. had indeed arrived yet again. I blindly reached from under the covers and hit the snooze button.

My inner voice spoke sternly: Daniel Stephenson, you know you'll be late if you start this drill.

I groaned, shut off the alarm, and stumbled into the bathroom. It was impossible to believe that most of America woke up this early. My internal clock would never adjust to this new schedule.

I showered, shaved, and primped myself in a stupor. I may not have been conscious, but I'd be damned if I'd go into the office looking like I got ready that way.

I threw on some "working girl" wardrobe staples: black slacks, white dress shirt, and a clever black blazer. I slugged down the rest of my coffee and walked to the front door.

The cool October air hit my face immediately upon leaving the building. It felt good because I knew it was only the beginning of the season. The fall clothes would soon be collecting dust in their drawers, and out would come the thicker sweaters, scarves, and heavy coats. One of the few perks of being up this early was seeing well-groomed men in their business drag. I could definitely appreciate a man in a becomingly cut coat, so unlike the heavy parkas in colors not found in nature that the men in Eau Claire would be wearing this time of year.

In Times Square I descended the stairs to the subway. I fed a token into the turnstile and followed the masses to wait for the NR train. The train was ten minutes late, and after I had squeezed myself into an overcrowded car, I wondered if I would be on time.

I read the advertisements around the edge of the ceiling and wondered if Breslin Evans Fox and Dean had handled the accounts. I brought my eyes back down to the armpit of the person in front of me and caught a woman staring at me. She averted her eyes quickly and I smiled to myself.

The train stopped at Twenty-third Street, so I turned to follow a throng of commuters out. A man in a long, black top coat stared at me this time. I wondered if I had dried toothpaste on my chin and ran my fingers over my face to check as we ran like lemmings out of the dingy subway station and up to the daylight.

I arrived at the office building on Fifth Avenue with time to spare and pushed myself through the heavy brass and glass revolving door, careful not to meet the eyes of anyone else.

Such a strange practice, I thought. In a city with so many people, you would think a slight acknowledgment could do no harm. Nobody appeared to see anyone else, but I knew people were watching all the time. I was always catching the wondering glances of elderly women, the critical stares of teenagers, and the appraising eyes of other men on the street. Martin called this "eye tag." He would blatantly stare, always hoping to be "it."

I hurried onto the elevator with what seemed like five dozen other people and pushed the button for my floor before I was jostled to the back of the car. Everyone stood and gazed like zombies at the ascending numbers, some managing to propel their way out of the elevator each time the doors noiselessly slid open. When we finally reached the thirty-second floor, there were maybe only a dozen people still in the car with me, which made it significantly easier to find my way to the opening.

Day two involved some kind of basic training on the electronic mail and calendar systems. Then I was taken on another tour. The word processing group took care of Blaine's correspondence and other documents. The graphics group took Blaine's work from ideas into tangible images. There were various other departments that nurtured his projects from conception to delivery, which was fine with me. I didn't want to have the man's children. But it might be nice to see him now and then.

As I understood it, my role was to handle his calls, making sure his clients always felt he was available to them while never, in fact, wasting his time with anything or anyone not desperately important. But my most vital function was to manage his calendar. This was no mere appointment book he kept on his desk. He had some kind of electronic gadget that plugged into his computer and downloaded the information that I was to keep current on the system so it would be available to him or any other person in the company.

Finally I was introduced to my own desk and computer. I sat down and gave it a blank look. It looked blankly back. I couldn't even find an "on" switch. I did manage to find the coffee maker, the electric pencil sharpener, and a couple of hot guys who worked in the mail room and wouldn't meet my eye. Evidently an executive assistant was too high in the pecking system for flirting with office drones. Blaine was out for the afternoon, so I spent my last two hours self-training on how to answer calls, transfer calls, make conference calls, send calls to voice mail, lose calls, forget calls, and perform acts of posthumous voodoo vengeance against Alexander Graham Bell.

That night I armed myself with videos. Fast-forwarding through my favorite parts of *Nine to Five* got me in the mood. *Baby Boom* was about a high-powered New York ad executive who gives it up for the good life. I fell asleep during that one, dreaming of watching Blaine chop wood in Vermont, until Andy made a guest appearance and woke me. *Working Girl* distracted me with its big hair. And something called *The Temp* scared the hell out of me.

On day three, it was a chastened boy who powered on his computer while he pondered what he'd gotten himself into.

I was saved by Mindy, who brought me a cup of coffee and a brownie.

"Hon, we never come straight to our desks," she said. "That's for the riffraff. You are an assistant. Which is all about attitude. You don't start work until they feel like you're doing them a favor!"

She left and someone named Teresa came by to say, "Oh good. You're at your desk. We were beginning to think you didn't really exist. It's important that you get here early because Blaine's phone is busy in the mornings!"

Next it was Cathy.

"Do you know how to use a dictaphone?" she asked.

"Uh, no."

"Good!"

She grabbed mine and vanished. Within minutes, another woman popped up.

"Hi, I'm Lisa. Where's your dictaphone? I knew it! Cathy got here first, didn't she? Damn!"

She hurried away without giving me a chance to say anything. I stared at the computer screen, which was demanding a password. I stared at the phone, which didn't ring. I closed my eyes, hoping that when I opened them, I'd find myself in the middle of a number on the stage of Club Chaos.

Instead I opened them to Blaine's dazzling and—dared I hope?—sympathetic smile.

"You don't have a clue, do you?" he asked.

"Nope."

He reached for my phone and punched in a number.

"Sharon? Blaine. My assistant Daniel needs real training on the computer, not that crap they do in orientation. Can you help? I promise I'll make it worth your while."

"Thank you," I rasped when he hung up.

"I have no doubt by next week you'll own Boardwalk."

"Monopoly was never my game," I said.

"So what is your game?"

"Trivial Pursuit?"

"Watch out for those sports questions," he advised with another grin.

Then he winked and disappeared into his office. For the first time in three days I felt like I could breathe.

My feeling of well-being vanished as yet another perky woman appeared.

"Hi, Daniel, I'm Sharon."

"Hi, Sharon, I'm confused. Have you come to save me?"

She smiled and said, "Yes, but don't get attached to me. I'm only a temp."

I shivered involuntarily and said, "Well, at least you don't look like Lara Flynn Boyle."

She laughed and said, "Don't worry. I don't want your job. Believe it or not, I'm getting married next week and leaving this marvelous place behind. Besides, you'll be fine. Blaine is like the Murphy Brown of the agency, but you're the first assistant he's ever requested help for. That must mean he wants to keep you. Now ask me whatever you want to know. After all, I'll be out of here soon and you can pretend you did it all on your own."

"Well, to start with, who are Breslin Evans Fox and Dean?"

"Nobody can answer that question," she giggled. "Their offices are on some higher floors but I don't think they've actually been seen for years. I worked for Blaine for a little while. I may still have a list of his key clients and the people in the office it's important for you to know. I'll give it to you later."

My computer screen went black and I gave a little yelp. She looked from me to the computer, then back at me.

"It's just gone to sleep," she said.

"Good, perhaps if we tiptoe away quietly, it won't wake up," I grinned and beckoned for her to follow me.

"Have you ever—"

"No. No computer experience at all."

She shrugged and said, "It's no big deal, I promise. I'll teach you what you need to know, and if anyone thinks you're slow, you can blame it on that broken arm. Ready?"

"Uh-huh."

By lunch time, in spite of numerous phone interruptions, the computer and Sharon were my new best friends. Blaine emerged from his office with an offer to take us to lunch. Sharon declined, saying she had wedding errands to run. She promised to return after lunch with the sacred list, then left me to Blaine.

"You don't have to buy my lunch," I said to Blaine, figuring he'd asked mainly to reward Sharon for her help.

"It'll give us a chance to talk," Blaine said.

My heart gave a little skip and I stood, wondering why he was still so appealing after his oafish behavior in my apartment the week before.

"Yeah, I'd like that," I said.

"Good," Blaine answered crisply. "You need to know exactly what I expect of you here."

It's all business with him, my inner voice warned. Cut out the Doris Day–you're so wonderful act or you'll be in the mail room with the other boys.

"Can you be ready to leave in about five minutes?" Blaine asked.

"You're the boss. I guess I can be ready anytime you need me to be."

"Good," Blaine said again and disappeared into his office for what I assumed would be the next five minutes.

I proceeded to make some requested adjustments to Blaine's calendar, returned some files to their rightful place, and cleared my desk of miscellaneous papers just as Blaine came out of his office. He was slipping into a three-quarter-length black wool coat.

Incredible, I thought.

"Pardon?" Blaine asked, a puzzled look on his face.

Did I say that out loud?

"It's incredible how hungry I am," I attempted to cover lamely.

"Good. Me, too. Let's go. I know just the place."

Blaine flashed a smile, his brilliant white teeth matching his starched white shirt. I trailed behind him to the elevator so I could admire the way his coat emphasized his broad shoulders.

We arrived at Aureole and were promptly seated. This was a minor miracle, considering there were a number of people waiting for a table and the place was packed.

"How did you do that?" I asked.

"How did I do what?"

"How did you get us seated like that? This place is a zoo!"

"I called ahead. I entertain clients here pretty frequently. They know me," Blaine shrugged.

I looked around. As crowded as the place was, it was extremely subdued. I observed the people around us. It seemed to be a very power-lunch crowd. Tables of just men, just women, or a mixture of men and women all seemed to be holding intense conversations. I couldn't hear anything that sounded like an intelligible word. It reminded me of some of the theater productions I had done where, in crowd scenes, a group of cast members would murmur, "Peas and carrots, peas and carrots, peas and carrots."

I turned my eyes back to Blaine to find him sitting with his elbows on the arms of the chair, his hands folded loosely in front of him, and a slight smile dancing on his lips. His eyes sparkled. The appeal I had noticed earlier had returned yet again. While his behavior after our previous dinner was not quite what I had in mind for that particular evening, I found that I was still drawn to him. In fact, each time he looked at me like that, the obnoxious, drunken Blaine became a more distant memory.

The waiter arrived to take our order shortly after the busboy supplied us with goblets of water, a fresh lemon slice waltzing with the ice cubes.

"I'll have the Caesar salad and an iced tea," I said, folding my menu shut.

"Same here," Blaine said when the waiter turned to him with a raised eyebrow.

"Thank you, gentlemen," the waiter said as he turned to glide through the maze of tables toward the kitchen.

"You seem to be picking things up quickly," Blaine began.

"Thanks. I couldn't begin to fathom some of it without Sharon's help. She's marvelous."

Blaine grunted in response. I suddenly remembered she was one in a long line of executive assistants to Mr. Dunhill.

"She's been a great help to me, anyway," I offered.

"Well, whoever is responsible, I checked my calendar earlier and it's finally right. For the first time in a long time, I feel like things will be more organized. I have complete faith in you."

"Thanks. So, you were going to fill me in on what else you expect of me?"

The waiter set down beautifully prepared Caesar salads in front of us.

"Can I bring you anything else?" he asked.

"More iced tea," Blaine answered, tapping the rim of his glass. The waiter glided away again. "Actually," he continued as he returned his gaze to me, "it's not so much what I 'expect' of you. It's really more of a request."

His emerald green eyes locked on mine, and I felt my heart jump again.

"Oh?"

Blaine took a deep breath before continuing, "Daniel, I feel like an idiot about the night we went to dinner. I don't remember a lot of what happened after dinner, but I feel pretty confident that I could have handled things very differently. I was hoping maybe you would give me the chance to make that right? Would you let me take you out to dinner? I promise to behave."

He flashed the smile that I knew must have won at least a couple of accounts over to Breslin Evans Fox and Dean.

"Blaine," I started, then pursed my lips for a moment, gathering my thoughts before continuing.

The waiter returned with two fresh iced teas then disappeared again, buying me a little time. This was a potentially treacherous moment. I could say yes and possibly make my position as Mr. Dunhill's executive assistant all that much more secure. Something warned me that this would not be among the smarter things I could do. But what if I said no? Would that mean my job? Did that really happen to people? Surely it must. Stranger things had happened, after all.

"I don't think that's a good idea. Things are pretty complex right now. I have a lot going on. There's the . . ." I almost said "auction" and stopped myself in the nick of time. "There's the possibility that my aunt is coming to town, and I'll have plenty to take care of while she is here, and—"

"And the dog ate my homework. I know," Blaine finished for me, nodding his head and looking a bit sad. "I blew it that bad, huh?"

"No, that's not it at all. I just don't know how wise it would be for us to attempt to add that dimension to the start of a good working relationship."

"Okay," he sighed disappointedly. "Well, then, here's to a 'good working relationship.' "

He reached for his tea and knocked it over, spilling the full glass across the table and into my lap. As the cold liquid hit me, I instinctively leapt to my feet, bumping the table with my thighs. The force with which I hit the table not only toppled my glass of tea but dumped the remainder of Blaine's salad onto his lap. His reflexes forced him to shift his chair back so quickly that it overturned, and he landed flat on his back in the middle of the restaurant.

The only sound following this acrobatic display was the single clink of a fork being set down on a china plate.

"Blaine! Oh my god, are you okay?" I exclaimed in horror as I rushed around the table to where he lay. He was still seated in the chair, albeit horizontally on the floor and not upright.

"I'm fine. I think I'll just lie here for a minute, if that's okay," he said calmly.

"Uh, sure," I said, hoping he really was okay and that I still had a job.

I noticed the iced tea stain running from the crotch of my pants down my left leg. Thankfully I had stuck with Manhattan black and it wasn't too noticeable.

The waiter came back with his pitcher of iced tea. He glanced at Blaine on the floor, my wet crotch, the overturned glasses on the table, the salad, which was scattered like confetti, and the patrons who stared at us as if they were watching bad kabuki theater.

"I'm guessing your glasses need refilling?" he asked in a bored tone.

The people sitting around us began tittering and snorting like elementary students during a sex education class. I was appalled, embarrassed, and horrified, until I looked down and saw Blaine laughing, too. I glanced around at the aftermath, let go of a little tension, and joined in. Blaine looked up at me and raised his hand, which I took and hoisted him into his proper upright position. The waiter left to fetch another salad and clean glasses. The tablecloth was flawlessly whisked away and replaced by a tag team of busboys with the speed and efficiency of a racetrack pit crew.

"Are you really okay?" I meekly asked.

"Yeah, I'm fine. I just had the wind knocked out of me," Blaine said, smoothing his hair into place. He looked so handsome to me then, even while picking croutons and lettuce out of his hair. Plus I had to give him style points for handling the situation with calm humor. I shuddered to think of the scene someone like Martin might have made.

"I knocked over your glass," Blaine continued in an apologetic tone. "Are you quite damp?"

"I'll dry. Would it be okay if I didn't go back to the office today, Mr. Dunhill? It appears I had an accident during lunch."

"Yes, I believe that would be okay. Besides, I'll get my money's worth out of Sharon that way. There's no sense in wasting a perfectly good temp."

"Um, can I ask you a question?" I ventured.

"Sure."

"You seem pretty easygoing. Why is it you can't keep an assistant?"

"I'm not always easygoing," Blaine said. He appeared to deliberate a minute before continuing. "I did really well at my agency in Eau Claire. As a matter of fact, I performed so well on one of our cosmetics accounts that when the client decided to defect to Breslin Evans Fox and Dean, he requested that they hire me. There's some resentment in the office about that. They think I'm too young and don't have enough experience. So I'm under a lot of pressure to prove myself, which means I can be really hard on the people who support me."

"Uh-huh," I said.

"I'm sure you realize I'm not out at work," he said. "They keep hiring these inexperienced girls who get crushes on me. I don't mean to sound conceited, but it's been a problem. Sharon worked out pretty well, because she's all wrapped up in her fiancé and their wedding plans. But she doesn't want a permanent job. So . . . Needless to say, Human Resources thinks it's a plus for me to have a male assistant."

"Are you saying you don't want people at work to know I'm gay?"

"No, not at all. Do what you want to about that. Just respect my privacy and it won't be a problem. Can you do that?"

I nodded, stifling my reservations. It was, after all, Blaine's life and none of my business. But it made it even clearer that, in the office at least, Blaine expected me to be professional. That was further incentive to move slowly about getting involved with him privately. I'd been living a dual existence for a decade and I was tired of it.

We spent the rest of our lunch going over the clients he was meeting tomorrow, what files he would need, and the cast of support staff who would be attending each meeting. He then presented me with an attaché from Coach with a laptop inside for me to use for any business I'd have to take home. As we said our goodbyes, I hoped my expressions of surprised gratitude adequately masked my terror. I felt as if someone had just shoved a pit bull at me and said, *Here, make friends.*

I decided Sixty-first and Madison was close enough to walk home, enjoying the midday sun and the brisk air in my lungs. The brisk air on my damp crotch and pant leg was another story, but that had dried by the time I reached my block. I had the notion I might take a nap and catch Oprah, already enjoying playing hooky like a seasoned jaded working stiff.

Of course, as soon as I was in the door, the phone rang. I figured it was okay to screen, since normally I wouldn't have been home anyway. Besides, it might be Jeremy, and I was still avoiding him.

Beep! "Daniel, this is Ken. You've got to get some dresses down here fast. The ones you keep at the club just won't do. Andy is being relentless. The *Village Voice* was going to do a blurb about the auction, but when they found out 2Di4 is hosting, they decided to do a whole article about the benefit and your last performance. You told me at Sunday brunch that you don't want Blaine to find out about this—by the way, I hope your new job is working out—but there won't be any publicity about your private life. That's not their angle. They just need to get photos of some of the dresses for the article in next week's issue. It's gonna be big. Andy's in a frenzy and wants dresses now."

"Now, Daniel!" I heard a scream.

Then Ken's voice said, "Andy! I told him. Anyway, call me as soon as you get this, or just come down with some gowns. Oooh, good lyric. *Down with some gowns.* 'Bye."

So much for Oprah, I thought.

I went down the hall to my bedroom. After I had changed clothes, I opened the larger closet, which was a warehouse for the clothes I'd once worn at night. I pawed through gowns, sheaths, and various replicas of dresses in which the Princess of Wales had made appearances. I gathered from Ken's message that I didn't have to bring down the whole collection of dresses to be auctioned, perhaps just a selection of more notable frocks that would fetch a pretty penny and generate interest. I could take the rest of the dresses to the club later.

I laid out on the bed ten dresses that I thought might arouse interest, among them a replica of the simple blue dress from the *Good Housekeeping* cover that originally gave me the idea for Princess 2Di4. I had worn it in my first performance as my alter ego. I chose it now in homage to simpler times, for both Diana and 2Di4.

The next dress I selected was a copy of the purple dress Diana wore to a Chicago function earlier in the year. In my version of the dress, I'd performed a song Ken and I wrote entitled, "Free at Last to Dance with You (and You and You and You)."

The next few were luxurious gowns featured in numbers about royal scandals, bitter divorce, humorous takes on eating disorders ("How to be a Princess and Retain Your Girlish Figure in Three Easy Lessons"), and marital infidelity.

I pulled out my favorite costume and smiled. It was the sort of dress a princess would wear during the Elizabethan period. It was enormous, high-collared, and required me to be cinched into a corset. As a result, the act I performed was pure lip-synch; I could barely draw enough breath to speak. I performed "Can't Help Loving That Man," "Control," by Janet Jackson, and Bette Midler's "Hustler." The entire time, a chorus of pageboys with overly exaggerated codpieces danced around me. It was one of my biggest crowd pleasers.

From the back of the closet, I withdrew a scaled-down version of Diana's wedding gown. Even so it was enormous, billowy and as white and delicate as new snow. In it, I looked like a huge pile of quivering tissues. One of the Club Chaos divas had rudely suggested I enter it as a float in the Pride parade.

As I ran my hands over the fabric, I recalled the only time I'd ever worn it. When the royal separation was announced, we'd thrown a huge Diana support party that drew a packed house. In memory of happier times, we chose to reenact the hours before the wedding took place. That was for the best, since no one wanted to play stuffy Prince Charles. At the time, everyone was blaming him for the breakup.

The curtain went up with me, as 2Di4, in my chamber awaiting the call to depart for St. Paul's Cathedral in my replica of the wedding gown. The audience went wild as I sat there nervously wringing my hands. I performed a song that Ken and I penned called "Too Much for One Girl," then a parody of Madonna's "This Used to Be My Playground" called "I Used to Be a School-marm." When Martin burst in as Diana's sister Sarah, we segued into "A Boy Like That" from *West Side Story*, to the audience's delight. Instead of moving into "I Have a Love," I had Peter, our sound technician, cut to "Like a Virgin." I proceeded to reenact Madonna's performance at the MTV Awards in 1985, where she rolled around on the floor at the end. Martin, as Sarah, stared aghast at my display, ran offstage, and came back with Tommy dressed as the Honourable Frances Shand Kydd, Diana's mother. Peter cut to Bette Midler's "Going to the Chapel" and we brought the house down.

I realized I couldn't reminisce about each dress. It would take too long and make it harder to give them up. I folded the garment bags with the dresses and gowns into a case with a shoulder strap. The various hats and accessories I placed into a duffel bag, hoping they wouldn't get crushed in the trip downtown. I put the bags by the door just as the phone rang again. I answered it this time.

"Yes?"

"Daniel, it's Ken. Did you just get home from work?"

"No, I got off early today," I replied.

"Oh, did you now?" Ken giggled. "Are we being chased around a desk already?"

"Ken, come on. You know I—"

"Okay, okay! We don't have time for witty banter. Did you get my message?"

"Yes, and I have a small selection of my best frocks ready to be photographed. I must say, I'm not sure I want to part with them. There's a lot of baggage in my baggage, Ken."

I looked at the bags that contained so many memories of good times gone by. Why did I feel so attached, even though I was supposedly moving on?

"You know it's for a good cause, Daniel. Just think of that and we'll worry about moving on later, okay?"

"Okay," I agreed. "Oh, hey, do I have to model these for the photographs?"

"Actually, that's kind of why I called. Andy's decided to send a car for you. I thought it would be good to arrive in 2Di4 drag. Just in case the photographers take pictures. You might not want to take any chances."

"What about my cast?"

"We'll work around it."

I sighed audibly, annoyed at the prospect of transforming myself into . . . what? The thought of putting together 2Di4 suddenly made me uneasy.

An hour later, I clipped on the diamond earrings that Diana was wearing on the cover of an issue of *People* that I kept next to my vanity. I looked in the mirror and noticed the exact same expression. On the cover, she was smiling and glancing off to the right, but her eyes belied that beautiful smile. There always seemed to be something troubled in her face, as if she wanted to escape.

I felt myself pulling away from the face that looked back at me in the mirror. I felt like Daniel more than Diana. The trouble was, I didn't seem to know Daniel as well as I knew Diana. Or did I mean 2Di4?

A funny possibility interrupted my serious train of thought. What would happen if I went to work dressed like this? I laughed out loud just as the phone rang. I picked it up and remembered, before I spoke, to use the Diana voice I'd worked so long to perfect: soft-spoken, its English accent tweaked by a bit of Welsh and Yorkshire. It was the driver calling. He was waiting outside to take me to, hopefully, my second-to-last appearance as the departed princess.

I picked up all of the garment bags and made my way to the black Lincoln. The driver opened the door for me. I forgot for a second that I was Diana, until the driver called me "ma'am."

Huh, I thought as I settled into the seat. That's different. I used to *become* 2Di4. Now it's more like I'm just dressed as her.

I leaned forward and asked, "What address do you have?"

When he gave me the address for the front entrance, I changed it to the back. It was still too early for any significant crowd at the club, but I was taking no chances. I stepped out into the cool air as the driver opened the door for me before he took out the garment bags. When we went through the back door, I reached into my Gucci clutch, but he said, "No, I'm supposed to wait. I've been assigned to you for the night."

How unusual for Andy to be so extravagant, I thought, but merely nodded.

When Tommy waved hello, the rest of the performers turned around and waved or called my name. Martin and Andy were nowhere in sight, but I saw Ken near the stage helping several strangers who were obviously setting up for the photographer. He came over as soon as he realized I was there.

"Your royal highness, I'm so glad you're here."

"It's good to see you, Ken. Thanks for doing all this for me."

Ken took the bags from the driver. I followed him to the rolling racks and a few of the others walked over to help us hang the dresses.

"Diana, it is *so* good to see you," Tommy said, giving me a hug.

I smiled, knowing my eyes were troubled as they met Ken's over Tommy's shoulder. I felt the knots twisting ever tighter in my gut. I didn't want to do it. I didn't want to model my dresses. I felt that the entourage of drag queens here could model the dresses for the photographers as well as I could.

"Ken, do you mind if I leave?"

"No, Daniel. You want me to handle this?"

"Please."

It was odd for Ken to call me Daniel while I was wearing the mask of the princess. Perhaps to him, too, it was obvious that I was not 2Di4 anymore than Marc had been the night of the brawl. Clothes could not make the drag queen.

I tried to hide my shiver with a regal, "I trust that you will pick the right dresses and the right people to wear them."

"You know I've always had an eye for this kind of thing. Look at you!"

I smiled, for real this time, partly out of relief.

He doesn't know, I thought. For once, he's not attuned to me. If I can just maintain the illusion through the auction, it will be finished. Then I'll be free.

NINE

Less than a week and this anxiety over the auction will end, I reminded myself as I walked through the glass doors of the agency.

I was preoccupied by my job as well as by the auction. I finally was getting to use my brain, now that I'd figured out how to do more with the computer than turn it on and stare blankly at it. Blaine had asked me to do research on a new fashion house based in New York. He seemed to think it might become really big and he wanted a report on it to see if it was worth pursuing as an account.

I stood by the receptionist's desk and waited for Blaine's and my mail as I flipped through the Lillith Parker Designs profile. I didn't look up but heard the crack of someone chewing gum very quickly, open-mouthed.

"Oh, Daniel, sorry, I was just reading this article. Here's your mail."

"Anything good?" I asked, talking about the mail.

"Yeah," Mitzi, the receptionist, said in her nasal voice. "It's about an auction for these dresses. The dresses look okay but there is something about the women that's a little—"

"Those were some of my best dresses," I said absently, looking at an envelope with a law firm's return address.

"Huh?" Mitzi asked.

It took me a minute to realize what I'd said.

"I was talking about this return address. It's from a law firm."

"Oh. I forwarded all of Blaine's calls to your voice mail. It's gonna be a busy day!"

I hurried down the corridor toward my desk. As I whirled around a corner, I ran headlong into Evelyn, who, unfortunately, was carrying a huge stack of collated photocopies. They became uncollated very quickly as they flew into the air and fell around Evelyn and me like oversized snowflakes.

"Just because you are Mr. Dunhill's pet doesn't mean you can go whipping through the office like you actually have somewhere to be," she barked.

"Oh, Ev," I said in a slightly sarcastic voice, knowing how she hated this name, "I *am* sorry. Please forgive me, just this once."

I heard her make a noise that sounded something like a growl and decided it was time to run again. After filling my Charlie's Angels mug with coffee, I sat down at my desk. I jiggled the mouse to wake up the computer and decided to search the Internet for information on Lillith Parker.

I was engrossed in the *New York Times* web site when a shadow fell over my desk. I looked up slowly and saw a figure with its back turned to me wearing a black wool cape.

Batman? I thought and stifled a chuckle.

"Yes?" I said to the figure. It whipped around. It was Gretchen! Before I could go around the desk to hug her, the phone rang.

"Good morning. Mr. Dunhill's office." I lowered my voice to be inaudible to the person on the phone. "Hey! How are you, sweetie?"

"I beg your pardon?" the voice on the phone returned.

Gretchen's face broke into a large grin.

"Hey, handsome. Aren't we looking mainstream today?"

"Just a little something I threw on." I giggled. "How are you, darling?"

"I'm sorry to be interrupting, but if Mr. Dunhill is not in, could I please leave a message?" the voice in my ear persisted.

"Fabulous, thanks. I have a meeting this morning with a client on the thirty-fifth floor, and I couldn't be so close and not check in to see how things are going for you. Is it everything you dreamed it would be and less?" she teased.

I held up one finger, signaling to Gretchen that the person buzzing in my ear was becoming too impatient to listen to our reunion much longer. I placated the caller by forwarding her to Blaine's voice mail then put my phone on DO NOT DISTURB.

"Oh my god, Gretchen, you look wonderful," I said as she removed her cape. "You've lost weight!"

Gretchen turned to the side to model her new profile for me. Rather than her usual concealing black or brown dresses, she wore a fitted gray dress suit. Her brown eyes twinkled vivaciously as she did a little twirl on her now slender and shapely legs. I could also tell she'd recently had her hair done. It was now short, with a wild look, her natural chestnut color streaked with white. Her face had a slightly rounded shape that gave her a cute look, belying her aggressive nature. I looked her up and down again, amazed by the transformation.

"Forty-seven pounds and counting, sweetie."

"Oooooh, girlfriend, have I got a gown for *that* new figure."

"Oh, Daniel, puhleeze. The last time I wore a gown was my senior prom, and that was only because Mary Singer said she'd be embarrassed to go with me if I wore tails!" We both doubled over laughing at the thought of this. Gretchen continued, "I was hoping we could go to lunch when I'm done with my meeting. My treat. I should be through about eleven-thirty. Is that too early?"

"Sounds perfect. Where do you want to meet?"

Blaine breezed around the corner, a startled look on his face as he stopped just short of slamming into Gretchen. He looked from Gretchen to me, then back to Gretchen.

"Pardon me," he mumbled and proceeded into his office, shutting the door.

Gretchen raised an eyebrow at me.

"Nice looking, Daniel. Not much in the personality department, but quite the stud. I won't ask what you did to land this job."

"Just never you mind," I smirked. "I'll tell you the story at lunch. You'll love it."

"Okay, sweetie. Meet me at Gramercy Tavern around eleven-thirty."

Gretchen disappeared into a swirl of black wool as her cape trailed behind her.

I finished sorting Blaine's mail then walked into his office, not bothering to knock. His back was to me as he stared through the window at the Manhattan skyline.

"Do *not* come to my office," he was saying. "My schedule's too full today. I'll have to meet you later . . . Anywhere, I don't care. But not here."

He whirled around as I dropped the mail on top of his already-packed "in" tray. His eyes held panic and his face flushed crimson as I gave him a bewildered look. Until that moment, I'd thought nothing of his call, assuming it was business. Its tone took on an entirely new meaning if the call was personal.

I fought against a surge of jealousy. So far ours had been a pleasant working relationship. Even though Blaine was my boss, I still felt as if I had the upper hand because I knew he was open to being more than that. But if he was seeing someone and didn't want me to know . . .

"What?" Blaine snapped. "No, not *you*, just a minute. I'm talking to my assistant."

"I'll catch up with you later," I murmured, backing out.

"Yes, please do . . . No, not *you,*" he said again, even more exasperated.

I shut the door, my mind racing. If Blaine *was* seeing someone, he didn't sound too happy with him. I flipped through the carbon pages of my message book, but other than an occasional call from Sheila, everything seemed business-related.

I returned to the reception area.

"Mitzi, have you taken any messages for Blaine?"

"I *told* you I sent them to your voice mail," Mitzi said, obviously annoyed that I was yet again interrupting her reading. "I *said* these models looked funny. They're not girls!"

"I don't mean this morning," I persisted. "In the past couple of days."

She rolled her eyes and shoved her message pad at me, saying, "This might be a hoot. Although I don't usually go to *that* part of the city."

And that part of the city thanks you, I thought, flipping through the pages. But the only ones for Blaine seemed as innocent as my own messages. Suddenly it dawned on me what Mitzi had said.

"Oh, god, no, you have to be careful where you go. It could be dangerous!"

"Probably not for a girl," she giggled. "I'll have to see if any of my friends want to go."

"Go where? What is it?" I asked.

"This show at a place called Club Chaos. They're auctioning replicas of Princess Di's dresses to raise money. But the dresses will be modeled by *guys!*"

"Club Chaos? I've been there. Watered down, overpriced drinks. Not enough seats. One of those decaying firetraps."

"*You've* been there?" she asked, finally lifting her eyes to me. "Oh. *Oh!* You've *been* there."

If she and Andy could produce offspring, their entire lives would be italicized.

"Yes, I have. I don't think you'd like it."

I returned her message pad and walked away, rolling my eyes as I heard her say, "Cathy? Guess what. You were right about Daniel."

Good thing Blaine doesn't care if *I'm* out at work, I thought.

Blaine had a morning full of meetings and hadn't returned by eleven-thirty, so I forwarded the phones again and left. I'd decided I was being paranoid about his mysterious phone call. I refused to get worked up about anything. I had enough on my mind already.

I breezed into the restaurant with a spring in my step. It had been so long since I had the chance to spend any time with Gretchen. I walked directly to the table where she was sitting, as if I knew ahead of time which one it would be. Gretchen greeted me with a smile as I approached. She stood up, always the gentleman, and came around the table to give me a hug.

Then she took me firmly by the shoulders, and said, "Daniel, you look great. The corporate world agrees with you."

I rolled my eyes in response.

"Don't you roll your eyes at me, mister. Now spill. Who is Mr. Personality-of-a-Doorknob-Body-of-Death? And what, pray tell," she added with a slight leer, "did you do to get this job for which you have, might I mention, absolutely no experience?"

"Thank you," I replied to the original compliment. I gave a slightly audible sigh before answering her next question. "His name is Blaine Dunhill. He's my boss. What else is there to know?"

I shrugged my shoulders, hoping my question would get me off the hook.

"How about the part where you tell me how you landed the job?"

Boy, does she know me, I thought, staring at her.

She stared back, waiting for me to answer.

"It kind of started when I moved into the place I'm in right now," I began.

"The one you have yet to invite me to?" she inquired with a meaningful smile.

"The very same," I responded curtly. "May I go on?"

"Please do."

"Thank you."

I told her about my initial Blaine sighting. How intrigued I was from the first time I saw him. How I made a point to be doing something, anything, nothing, in the garden every afternoon at five-thirty. I spoke of Sheila and how Sheila led me to Blaine, and all about the first phone calls that made me tingle with a certain excitement that I had not felt in a long time. I told her about the "date," which from a dating perspective was completely disastrous, but from the standpoint of starting a new career had done wonders for me. When I dove into details about my job, she interrupted with one of her famous, abrupt subject changes.

"How long since you talked to Jeremy?"

"Jeremy who?"

"So this guy *is* significant."

"Jeremy?"

"Mr. Abs of Death. Blaine."

"He's just my boss."

"It's not like you to shove someone onto the back burner once you're interested. You can't tell me you suddenly *aren't* interested in him. I wouldn't believe you."

"I don't know what it is about him," I confided. In almost a hushed tone, as if Blaine himself could hear, I continued. "But there is *something*. I haven't said that to anyone. Not even myself. I really have tried to keep everything with him on the up-and-up. I never thought it was a good idea to date anyone from work. You know that's a rule I always held dear at the club, and it has to apply here as well. Not to mention that first night with him was such a disaster. It was so far from what I thought it would be."

"Uh-huh." Gretchen munched on a breadstick, never taking her eyes from mine.

"No, I didn't sleep with him. But I let him think we did. Well, I didn't say anything one way or the other, but it didn't hurt my position to let him think I had a little something to hold over his head."

"Daniel, with your looks, he'd have been blind not to have fallen for you immediately. You don't need to hold anything over anyone to get your way. You never have."

"Aren't you a dear?"

I took the hand holding the remains of the breadstick, made as if to kiss it, and instead took the next bite of the breadstick.

"Well, you may be one of the first people in the advertising industry to have gotten a job because you *didn't* sleep with someone," Gretchen wisecracked with a cocky grin.

"Precious. Simply precious," I said, reaching for her hand to take another bite of her breadstick. She smacked my hand with an audible crack.

"So, meanwhile," Gretchen continued, "how long do you think you can keep up this charade? Does he know about you? Does he know about 2Di4?"

"Oh, *god* no!" I shrieked in a manner Andy would have been proud of. "I told him I was a performer."

"That's fine," Gretchen shrugged. "I mean, it's honest."

"Yeah."

We sat quietly during the few moments it took for the waiter to position our food in front of us. Once he left, our eyes met again. We continued to maintain the comfortable silence that two close friends can enjoy, working on our meal with enthusiasm, occasionally spearing something off each other's plate. I was still assessing her new look. It seemed her appearance, like her friendship, would only get better with time.

Gretchen and I had met through Ken. She'd worked for the man Ken was living with at the time, Samuel. Samuel introduced them so that Gretchen could help Ken with his financial portfolio. Their relationship had progressed to friendship. A few years later, Ken introduced her to me for much the same reason.

She helped me manage whatever money I could afford to set aside. Usually this came from occasional gifts sent by Aunt Jen, and a couple of checks I got when two of my grandparents died. The money was never much, so I needed to invest it in something fairly secure. I knew this wouldn't net me a large return. But one thing I loved about Gretchen was that she was gutsy. She could sometimes talk even me into investing in something a little risky. Each time I followed her advice, it paid off.

I learned in a short period of time that I could count on Gretchen. If I called her, she called back. If I needed to see her, she made time for me. She never gave me advice that wasn't wise, even when it came to a matter of the heart, for which I turned to her on occasion. Not that I didn't have others I could trust, but when I wanted an assessment, and not just a chance to dish, I'd talk with Ken or Gretchen. They were my fore and aft anchors.

The three of us were inseparable. Samuel had died in 1987, not long before I met Ken. Ken brought Gretchen and me together about three years later, just before my twenty-third birthday. I was enamored with all that Gretchen and Ken did. They were, in a strange sort of way, my surrogate parents. Or at least the parents I'd chosen to adopt. We went to lunches and shopping. While Gretchen was a very out lesbian, she had a certain appreciation for feminine things that other lesbians I'd met before her didn't. If Gretchen said something didn't look good on me, I didn't buy it. Of course, I questioned her taste now and again, relative to my own, but she was remarkably well put together. She was a woman who knew what she liked and what she didn't. She was very vocal about both.

Often, our schedules didn't mix well, due to the fact that she worked regular hours and Ken and I certainly didn't. But we always seemed to find time for each other. Occasionally we'd go to a Saturday or Sunday matinee of the latest, greatest movie. On one Saturday when we'd set up a time and place to meet, I got a call from Gretchen saying that Ken wouldn't be able to make it. I replied something along the lines of, "Oh well, I guess we can do it another time."

"There's no rule that says it can't be just you and me," she said.

I thought about that.

"You're right. See you there in about half an hour."

We ended up meeting in front of the theater only to find that neither of us was really in a movie mood, so we decided to get something to eat. We had a blast. We sat and talked for hours, discovering things about each other that we'd never thought to ask before. Maybe that was because of Ken being there, and neither of us wanting to be redundant, although he probably wouldn't have cared. But for the first time, I learned that Gretchen was an only child, and her parents had taken it very hard when she came out to them. I shared a bit about my family background with her and commiserated about familial reactions to the "news." At that time, I wasn't out to my parents. My more combative friends had no patience with that, but Gretchen told me to go with my instincts, that I'd know when the time was right, or at least when I felt I could handle their reactions. I'd been flooded with gratitude. I figured it was never easy to be young in a city where life could be so intense. But especially at that time, because of AIDS and its surrounding politics, being out and visible was regarded as an aggressive and necessary act of survival. Gretchen helped me feel that it was okay to follow my own timeline in my personal life.

We found out that both of us loved vanilla bean ice cream, for all of its blandness, and that we both hated the movie versions of Stephen King novels. A certain bond was formed that day, and we both seemed to know that it would take an awfully strong force to sever it, if that were possible at all.

Through the years, Gretchen and Ken were constant, sustaining forces in my life. If Ken provided nurturing, Gretchen provided tough love. They'd been known to reverse those roles on occasion, but between them, I always found a safe haven based on respect, comfort, and honesty.

"I checked your portfolio this morning, by the way. Financially you're doing great. What happened to your arm?" she demanded with another rapid-fire change of subject.

That story had her choking on her food. When I finished with Aunt Jen's visit to Club Chaos, she nearly spewed her drink.

Just as I was congratulating myself on having successfully diverted her, she said, "So. What's next with Blaine?"

"I don't see anything happening with him. Except for work."

"Hmmm. Daniel, something else is bothering you. We've covered men and jobs. I know you have no money problems. So what is it?"

I looked at her, wondering how she did it. It wasn't as if Gretchen and I saw each other all that often. How was it possible she still seemed to know my thoughts and moods?

"Andy wants me to emcee a benefit auction at the club."

"That sounds like it would be right down your alley."

"He wants me to do it as 2Di4."

"That makes sense, too. Are you not okay with that?"

"He wants me to auction my dresses."

"Ah. The plot thickens."

"Remember, Blaine doesn't know about 2Di4."

"Back to Blaine, are we?"

"Gretchen, I have to think about this from every angle."

"You are so transparent."

"Why do you say that?" I asked, sounding more defensive than I'd intended.

"You wouldn't give him a thought if you weren't interested. Doing some function as 2Di4 after all you did to put her to rest, coupled with the idea of parting with those dresses"—she gave a mock shudder—"and I can see why that would make you hesitate. But why factor him into the equation unless you are interested in him on some level?"

I sighed. Right again, Gretchen.

"Daniel, I don't know what to tell you. You have to do what's right for you. If that means doing the auction to help Andy's charity of the week, or—"

"It's for AmFAR."

"Oh, good choice! Or if it means," she continued without missing a beat, "you do it because it'll put 2Di4 that much farther behind you, whatever the reason, you know I can't tell you what to do. This is one you have to figure out on your own. Have you talked to Ken?"

"Ken always supports me. You know that."

"Yes," she agreed. "But Ken is also generally willing to give more guidance and input than I am."

"I don't think I'll have a problem getting rid of the dresses. It's not like I'm going to wear them to the office. I guess the part I'm most worried about is the reaction to 2Di4."

"Everyone loves 2Di4, Daniel."

"While Diana was alive, yes. I haven't appeared as 2Di4 since her death. What if they drag me off the stage and beat the shit out of me?"

"Hardly likely."

"We don't know how the crowd might react, do we? Remember that crazy stalker girl who was obsessed with the princess and used to picket outside the club? Who knows how many nuts there are like her. I have to look at this from every angle," I repeated.

"Always the Virgo." Gretchen smiled. "Analyze, weigh, judge, and evaluate yourself into doing nothing."

"I don't want to talk about this anymore," I moaned. "Let's talk about you."

"I thought you'd never ask," she said.

I forced everything else out of my head as I listened, mentally revising her stories to make them better for later repetition to Ken and Martin.

But over the following days, there was no opportunity to talk about anything other than the auction. Ken, Martin, and I scripted the entire show. They did most of the work themselves, but I consulted them regarding the memories I would share with the audience about the various dresses as they were modeled. There were twenty dresses in all to be auctioned. Ten more were on hand in case the auction time ran short, or if the audience was in a particularly giving mood. Another ten had been running in a silent auction since the initial word on the event went public. This was one of Andy's ideas to publicize the auction and build it up. The silent auction would close before the event and I would announce how much it had raised as part of my opening. Exactly what else I would say was left up to me. We scripted the memories and song intros according to the outline of the evening, but my own banter was to be spontaneous.

Considering everything, I was amazingly focused and productive at Breslin Evans Fox and Dean. It was actually a relief to have nine hours each day when I wasn't worked up about Club Chaos. Blaine's habit was to leave the office around four and go to the gym, then work an additional two or three hours at home in the evenings. Sheila warmed my heart with a call thanking me because each night he seemed to have less to do. She said he attributed that to my efficient management of his time during the day.

Meanwhile, Sheila was caught up in the flurry of her own new career. She'd signed with Metropole. Though she hadn't yet been on any assignments, they were busily grooming her and building her portfolio with test shoots. She made brief, daily phone calls to me, apologizing for being so unavailable. Of course, I couldn't explain that I was too busy to see her anyway.

I turned down all invitations to Halloween parties. I'd long ago found that, because I costumed myself for a living, Halloween held little appeal for me. But about six that night I received a frantic call from Sheila.

"Are you going out tonight?" she asked. "I need help!"

"No. I want to be here for the trick or treaters." When that was met with blank silence, I said, "I'm kidding, Sheila. What's up?"

"I thought of calling Martin to help me, considering what he does for a living. But I don't know him as well as I know you. I've been invited to a party, and this photographer is going to be there. He's really gorgeous. I wouldn't mind dazzling him. But I have absolutely nothing to wear."

"Oh god, you don't want Martin. He'd come up with some weird, over-the-top thing. What else would you expect from a boy whose favorite color is mirror? What you want is glamour."

"Yes!" she agreed.

I knew this would be easy for me, considering all the clothes still crowding my closets that were not part of my 2Di4 wardrobe. But wouldn't Sheila wonder why I had them?

"Well, as you've noted before, we're about the same height, and we're both slender," I said. "Give me an hour then come over. I'll do you up right."

"Should I bring my makeup?"

As if, I mentally did my best Alicia Silverstone impression, but said, "Yes, please."

After I hung up, I pondered what to do. I thought of the first time I'd met Sheila when she was wearing Blaine's shirt and little else. If she really wanted to impress a guy—

"Sal!" I exclaimed, remembering my old boss in the East Village and his penchant for "gams." Of course. My Marilyn Monroe costume would be perfect for her. If this photographer knew Sheila, how sweet and wholesome she was, he'd totally get the Norma Jean/Marilyn dichotomy.

I dialed Sheila's number and barked, "Do you have any white heels?"

"Oh my gosh, I don't think so."

"Then you have an hour to find some. New ones or thrift store, it doesn't matter, but make them as sexy as possible. With a very high heel. White, not beige, ecru, ivory, winter white—"

"Gotcha," she said and hung up.

When she arrived, I had everything laid out on my bed and led her to the bedroom without a word. She gave an ecstatic sigh and threw her arms around me.

"You are absolutely the best, Daniel!"

"I know," I said. "I needed this outfit once for an audition."

There, that was honest enough. But Sheila couldn't have cared less. She was rubbing the faux fur against her face and pouting her lips.

"You're a natural," I said with a grin.

I fixed us both a gin and tonic while she slipped into my robe. Later, after using her makeup, which was adequate for the occasion, I turned her around to see her reflection. She gasped.

"Wow, Daniel, you're really good at this."

"Wait'll you see it with the wig," I said. "Usually you'd use a wig-cap on your hair. But just in case, oh, you have to remove this wig tonight, you don't want to look like the lunchroom lady in a hair-net. So I'm going to French-braid your hair flat, and if you do take off the wig, you can either leave it braided or undo it and kind of scrunch it with your fingers and, *voilà*, you'll be ready for pillow talk."

"Daniel!" she protested with a giggle. "I'm just trying to catch this guy's eye, not sleep with him."

"Which is another thing," I said, getting my best big brother expression. "If you and—what is his name?"

"Josh," Sheila said.

"Okay, if you and Josh are likely to fool around—"

"I know how to take care of myself," she said. "I'm not sixteen, you know."

"What I know is that the mindset is different in Wisconsin than here," I said. "I have sisters."

She gave me another hug and said, "Scram. I'm putting on the dress. Then will you help me with the wig?"

By the time I was finished, she was a complete knockout, with just the effect I'd imagined, sweet vulnerability juxtaposed with simmering sexuality. I felt a pang of jealousy that I'd never been able to carry off Marilyn quite the way Sheila could. She even had the walk. Female impersonators exaggerated everything to convey femininity. It was Sheila's subtlety that made the look work so well.

"You're done," I said, feeling like any parent. I wanted to scrub her face and tuck her in. Instead, I had to send out my lamb to some lecherous old goat named Josh.

"Done? I haven't even started," she breathed in a sex kitten voice, glancing at me over her shoulder.

I burst out laughing. Sheila would be fine. I sent her off with a tap on her now even shapelier ass, and without regret. I wanted a good night's sleep.

*   *   *

I mentally prepared all day Saturday for my part in the auction. I wanted to recapture my sense of 2Di4 as her own person, as if I had nothing to do with how she moved, spoke, or looked. I was worried I might feel the way I had the week before, when she seemed to be nothing more than a mask, someone with whom I no longer really connected. I went over Jeremy's advice for stage fright and preparation before a performance. He "became" his character and put "Jeremy's" fears and problems on a shelf. He retrieved "Jeremy" from the shelf only after the last curtain call.

He must've done that a lot the last month we lived together, I thought with a smirk.

After a Valium-induced nap, I decided I could get through one night of bringing 2Di4 back, then put the whole thing behind me. I spent my last hours at home bathing, shaving my body, and moisturizing. Then I put on a long, warm, terrycloth robe. In other days, I would accessorize with a towel wrapped around my head, or a hat and sunglasses. Tonight I chose simplicity, leaving my head bare. I would finish my transformation in my dressing room at the club.

Andy sent a car for me. As we rode downtown, my nagging fears began creeping back. What if the only reason everyone came was to protest my appearance as 2Di4? Was it in bad taste now that Diana had passed away? Was I being tacky? Was I personally offended? Apparently not; I was about to go ahead with it. Besides, why would people come to a benefit auction to burn the emcee in effigy? Everything would be okay. Furthermore, Ken wouldn't have agreed to organize and let me be part of the whole thing if it weren't okay.

Ken. When was I going to start making decisions for myself? Or at least learn how to survive my mistakes without leaning on him for guidance and support.

I had to put thoughts about life without Ken out of my mind. That was not the best way to quell my performance anxiety. Honestly, I couldn't remember the last time I was nervous about performing. Probably just after Ken and I created 2Di4, when I was terrified about doing a parody of a woman who was adored by millions. Which was how I felt about doing the auction, only this time the woman adored by millions was no longer alive. It just wasn't sitting right with me.

And dear god, what if Mitzi showed up with her friends? I had a fleeting vision of an audience filled with petty, shallow Evs and Mitzis. Would they recognize me? Wouldn't the cast on my arm give me away? Would I be the topic of Monday morning office gossip? How would that affect my position at work? What if Blaine found out?

My talk with Gretchen hadn't completely set my mind at ease. She was the only person who could read between my lines and see through my walls the way Ken did. However, she hadn't given me many sage words for tonight. I decided she was right about the audience loving 2Di4. That much was probably true. Besides, 2Di4 had withstood the harshest critics and mudslingers: the other drag queens on the circuit. There was nothing more threatening to a drag queen than another queen, much less a princess, rising to fame and stealing her thunder. I could appreciate this fear now. Who wouldn't feel afraid of being replaced and fading into obscurity?

I reminded myself I was choosing retirement, not having it thrust on me. I straightened my spine and set my shoulders. I relaxed my face, drew in a deep breath, and let it out slowly. I visualized my anxiety as a small object the size of a compact and mimed snapping it shut and placing it in an imaginary purse.

"It will not do to be a bundle of nerves tonight," I said aloud in the calm, soothing tones of a British royal. "There's a bit too much riding on this evening."

"What's that?" the driver asked.

"Nothing," I responded, smiling.

"We have arrived," he said, smiling back. "I'll be here waiting in a few hours."

"Thank you."

I gathered my robe tightly around me and exited the car. He had dropped me off at the back door. I moved quickly inside. The other performers, probably knowing the importance of my appearance, perhaps even instructed by Ken, did not speak to me when I walked to my dressing room. I received stares, supportive smiles, and even stony silence. It was hard to read the vibe backstage.

Maybe they're nervous, too, I told myself, but quickly stuffed the thought back in the imaginary purse where it belonged.

I finished my transformation at the makeup mirror. As always, a line from the *Rocky Horror Picture Show* flashed into my mind: Dr. Frank N. Furter shouting, *Okay, it's star time!*

Applying dewy, light foundation, the faintest rose tint to my cheekbones, bringing out my eyes with a little mascara and eyeliner, I looked the very picture of grace and beauty. I finished with a short blond wig that was waiting for me on a plastic head that seemed to watch the whole procedure.

I stared at my reflection in the mirror, but it didn't look like me at all. It was 2Di4, staring back at me, waiting for my cue. So I gave it to her. I laughed. She laughed back and we both covered our mouths with our hands.

There was a knock at the door and we stifled our laughter.

"Half hour!" a tech called from the other side.

"Thanks!" I called back.

I went over my notes of the outline and mentally sang my opening song to remember all the words.

I was startled by another knock.

"Yes?"

The door opened and Ken stepped in, brandishing a black satin wrap.

"Stand up," he ordered. He draped the wrap over my shoulders then around my arms. "Voilà! No visible cast."

"You don't think it's a little too, I don't know, Grace Kelly?"

"She *was* a princess," Ken said. "Do you need anything else?"

"No, I'm fine," I replied, assessing my reflection. The wrap made me more aware of maintaining a regal posture, and I adjusted my attitude accordingly. "A lot better than I thought I'd be, but I appreciate your asking."

"Oh my," Ken said. "The bitch is back!"

We both laughed and I knew I'd be okay.

"I have to make sure Peter has all the songs lined up and his cue sheet," Ken said.

"Go," I implored. "I'm fine. I'll see you backstage in a little bit."

Ken left and I got up to walk and get my blood moving.

"Fifteen!" a tech called after another knock.

"Thank you."

I slipped into my heels and walked some more. The satin wrap fell in soft folds around the black dress that was long and slit up the side to midthigh. My shoes were simple, nothing garish or fancy. I wanted 2Di4 to go out in style. A classic. A class act.

As I left the dressing room, I realized I was glad that Andy had given 2Di4 a chance to say goodbye. It seemed more suitable than simply running out and vanishing.

I entered the backstage wing of stage left and stood by Martin's station. He was acting as assistant stage manager in addition to modeling a dress and performing. Ken was in the booth calling cues on headsets to Martin as well as the various stagehands, lighting staff, and sound personnel. Judy would not be sharing the stage with 2Di4 tonight. Ken had announced to Andy that Judy had pulled a classic diva maneuver. She screamed, ranted, and raged that she would not play the ingenue to 2Di4, then promptly locked herself in her dressing room, took a fistful of pills, and got drunk.

I smoothed out my dress, made sure my cast was still concealed, and took a few deep breaths.

"Don't worry; you'll be fine," Martin said.

"I know," I whispered.

"Me, too," Martin said with a wink. "I've always looked up to you. You've been an inspiration to us all. And—"

"Don't," I interrupted. "I don't want to cry. I just—I know, okay?"

Martin smiled and kissed me on the cheek.

Andy took the stage to introduce the benefit, giving a short speech about my last performance. It was witty and incisive so I knew Ken or Martin had written it for him. When he turned over his emceeing duties to me, I couldn't believe the way the audience exploded into wild applause and jumped to their feet.

I walked into the glare of the hot lights to the X at center stage. I stood very still for a moment and nearly did a Sally Field imitation on the spot. I kept control and bowed my head in a simple gesture.

It's for Diana as much as 2Di4, I thought. For one magic moment, the People's Princess has returned.

"Thank you," I spoke in my soft British accent, repeating the nod. "I can't tell you how grateful I am to you for that wonderful noise. You don't know how much I needed to hear it. I also want to thank Andy and Club Chaos for allowing me to host this benefit for AmFAR. We're hoping to raise a lot of money this evening."

I stopped as the audience again erupted into applause.

Diana is dead, I thought. I'm 2Di4.

"You can be assured that even though I cleaned out my closet, I won't be using the money to update my wardrobe."

The entire audience laughed, and I used the noise to draw another deep, calming breath.

"The money we're raising will help AmFAR's AIDS research, their public policy programs, and their work toward finding a cure in the near future. Proceeds from our silent auction have already totaled eight thousand dollars, so let's see how much we can add tonight, okay?"

The audience responded with what I hoped was eager anticipation to part with their money. I was now caught up in the moment and was in full 2Di4 mode. All my anxiety had vanished, and I was determined to do my best to raise money for AmFAR.

"I hope you all received a catalog with pictures of tonight's gowns. We'll go in the order of the catalog. The dresses will be modeled by various entertainers from Club Chaos. You'll see that these dresses truly can make *anyone* look like a princess. Every dress has a story, as does every model. I won't tell you *every* story; I know the models will appreciate that, too, but I'll share a few with you. I'm sure you'll see why this club is a special place to me and why I consider everybody in it a member of my family."

I smiled and paused, a cue for Peter to ready the first song that I would lip-synch, then continued, "I welcome you, once again, to Club Chaos's AmFAR Auction. I hope you enjoy yourselves and won't mind as I wallow in a few of my memories."

The music to "Memory" began and I started a poignant lip-synch. I had argued with Ken that it would be too sappy and predictable, but Ken talked me into it. He had even gone so far as to allow me my choice of any song in the program if I stuck to this selection from *Cats* for the opening. Now I saw why. As I went into the second verse, everyone's eyes were glued to me. Almost no one was moving. A few people had their chins resting in their hands; some smiled. I realized Ken had understood that many people in the audience would be here because the event was AIDS-related. This song was about their memories of loved ones as well as 2Di4's tribute to Diana's memory.

Before the song ended, I quickly scanned the audience with a twinge of nervousness in case Blaine had come. I didn't see him; however, I did see Mitzi sitting near the back of the house. She was with several women with big hair piled on their heads. Mitzi was dabbing at her eyes with a wad of tissue and I threw all caution to the wind and smiled in her direction as I mouthed the last line.

After the applause died down, "Second Hand Rose" began and I was swept back in time to my first year in the drag race. I kicked my heel and began lip-synching the first verse, remembering the dance steps as if it had all happened yesterday. After the first chorus the music was turned down and Martin walked down the small catwalk that was installed onstage.

"Ladies and gentleman," I announced, "we begin our auction with my original Penny Dime costume, modeled by Martin. Everyone knew I was Second Hand Rose and I *did*, in fact, live on Second Avenue, but what wasn't known about Penny Dime was that she made this costume herself."

At this point, Martin paused next to me at the microphone.

"Which," he said, gesturing down at the dress, "I'm sure is no shock to our audience."

"Oh?" I feigned being indignant. "Do you think you could've done better?"

A backing track with no vocals was played while Martin and I sang a rowdy "Anything You Can Do, I Can Do Better." We had a lot of fun with it, and I enjoyed my time onstage with him immensely. We'd altered the last verse to fit the auction theme.

"Any bid you can draw, I can draw higher," he sang to me. "I can draw any bid higher than you."

"No you can't!"

"Yes I can!"

"No you can't!"

"Oh, you think so, do you?" he laughed and turned to the enrapt audience. "The bidding begins on the Penny Dime dress. You heard the story; you heard the song. The opening bid is two hundred for this one-of-a-kind dress handcrafted by our own Princess 2Di4. Bidding's at two, bidding's at two, who'll say higher?"

"Two thirty!" a woman at the back called out.

"Two thirty! Two thirty! Do I hear higher?"

"Two fifty!"

"Two sixty!"

"Now folks," Martin said, suddenly going all Ellie Mae Clampett, "this here's a benefit auction. Surely we can do better?"

"Three hundred!" a man shouted.

"Four!"

"Four fifty!"

Soon Martin banged the gavel and my Penny Dime costume was

sold for nine hundred and seventy dollars. He bowed, turned to me, and the music resumed as he walked offstage singing, "Yes I *can!*"

The rest of the auction proceeded similarly. I told stories as my memories were paraded and bid on. As I talked, it occurred to me that these were my stories, not 2Di4's. I had created them; she only told them. It made letting go so much easier. I was thrilled that my dresses, my memories, my creations, were able to benefit a worthwhile cause.

My Elizabethan costume fetched one thousand two hundred dollars, the purple gown went for six hundred, and most notably, the wedding dress was sold for two thousand three hundred to a woman who announced joyously that she would wear it for her wedding in six months. I promised to have it dry-cleaned, as it had a few stains from my Madonna crawl during the "Like a Virgin" number.

I performed "Hey Big Spender," "Money Changes Everything," "If I Could Turn Back Time," and "Dress You Up" at various times in the program. Each song seemed to revive the audience. They would cheer, clap, and even sing along.

"You probably think the wedding dress is the last one. Oh wait, it *is* the last one in the catalog, isn't it? Huh. You hoped we were finished, didn't you?"

The audience laughed and protested, their enthusiasm filling the club, and me, with energy. They didn't want it to end; I wasn't ready for that either. I looked beyond the lights above the crowd's heads and saw Ken slide open the window to the booth. He leaned out and glared at me, not having any cues or clues as to what I had planned.

I laughed as Andy stepped forward and handed me a card, gave me a peck on the cheek, and walked out stage right.

"Ladies and gentleman and those who are both," I paused until the crowd settled down, "it's been brought to my attention that, combined with the silent auction, we have raised an amazing twenty thousand dollars tonight! What a great gift for AmFAR and the tremendous effort they make on behalf of AIDS research."

The crowd clapped and cheered and I tried not to cry. I was suddenly very emotional, thinking about my friends who had died, those who'd never had assistance or support groups, and those who might still be lost.

"Yes, it's wonderful. You should all be very pleased, as I certainly am, by your generosity and kindness. But as I said, I'm not quite finished with this auction. I hope you will allow me to present one more dress for your bidding tonight."

There was no music, no special lighting from Ken. He'd had no idea I was going to spring another dress after the wedding gown. I had asked Martin to locate one of my dresses for me without any-one knowing, and he walked onto the stage wearing it. He paused, gave me a hug, and whispered the name *Felicia* in my ear. I tried not to laugh as he continued down the runway.

"This is a very special dress to me. I wanted to relate its story with you tonight more than any other. I've had a lot of fun sharing the memories and emotions these ensembles represent. This dress is, by far, the one that embodies Princess 2Di4.

"Felicia is wearing an imitation Catherine Walker halter-neck evening dress. Diana wore hers to Versailles in 1994. I wore mine here as I performed 'Picture Perfect,' a song Ken and I wrote about Diana being photographed everywhere she went and how trying that must have been for her. I also performed to 'Picture This,' by Blondie, but that's just silly and I won't get into it."

I paused and took a breath as Martin stopped and turned a few times at the end of the runway. Pictures were taken and a few peo-ple clapped. He looked quite stunning in the dress, especially with the tall, black wig and minimal makeup. He turned toward me and I went on with my story.

"This dress is very significant to me because I was wearing it when I heard that Diana, Princess of Wales, had died in a car acci-dent. I was devastated and ran out of here swearing I would never perform again. It took courage for me to come back to emcee this auction tonight, but you've all made me feel welcome and at ease. I thought the dress Felicia is modeling would be the last dress I'd ever wear as 2Di4. The bidding starts at six hundred."

Martin stood beside me and the audience sat in silence. I was afraid they were all tapped out. Or maybe that I had hit them with too much emotion. Or even worse, I had reminded them that I was a sham, a fake Diana, and they would think I was making fun of her in some way.

Then the bidding started.

"Seven hundred!"

"Seven fifty!"

"Eight hundred!"

Martin stayed to help me keep track of the bidding. I was shaking too hard to do it alone. I started crying when the bidding reached two thousand. I wondered how Andy had found people with such deep pockets.

There are good people in this world, I reminded myself, standing in awe as Martin closed the auction on my last dress at three thousand four hundred dollars.

I stood all alone after Martin hugged me and walked offstage. I knew I had to wrap up the benefit, but wasn't sure how to do it, or what to say.

"I'm not sure what to say right now, so please give me a moment."

I stumbled and held the microphone for support.

"Do a song!" a woman in the back yelled and the audience laughed. Was it Mitzi?

"Yeah, sing us a song!"

"You're 2Di4!"

"Do a number, 2Di4!"

Soon they were all chanting *Sing!* and clapping together. I looked at Ken, who was smiling at me and nodding. He held up a tape, and mouthed *Everytime* to me. I nodded to him and watched as he disappeared into the booth.

"All right, I'll do a song for you," I surrendered. The audience cheered and I gathered courage from them. "This is my last night performing at Club Chaos. Tonight Andy told me that I'm always welcome to return, but I'm no longer under contract. I'm very grateful to him, honored that he'd want me back, but we had a long talk about it and he understands. Andy is one of many people who were quite instrumental in my becoming who I am. I'll always loathe—I mean, love—him for understanding why I can't perform anymore. I hope you will, too."

Behind me, I heard the sound of the old, upright piano being rolled onstage, but I continued talking to the audience.

"An old friend of mine, Wanda, once told me that a performer needs to know two basic things. Number one is never go onstage unless you know your character. Number two is know when to exit. I thought I knew when to exit. In fact, someone just paid a huge amount of money for my last exit. But tonight is the real deal and, no, *this* dress is on loan, so you can just forget about it."

I made a quick turn to be sure Ken had made it to the piano as the crowd laughed at my joke. He had and was smiling, then nodded to show he was ready whenever I was.

"I want to keep talking so it won't end, but I know you've all got places to go. Homes to get home to. Loved ones who are waiting. Saying goodbye is always hard. Wanda told me the best way to say goodbye is from the heart. I'm still saying goodbye to Diana, Princess of Wales. I think we all are. Now I must say goodbye to Princess 2Di4."

Ken began a soft introduction to Cole Porter's "Ev'rytime We Say Goodbye," and I joined him in a subdued, slow tenor. The lights gradually faded. I walked to the piano and leaned against it, facing Ken, singing to him through the first verse. As he played a middle instrumental, I beckoned to the drag queens backstage and they came out and stood around me. They still wore the auctioned dresses, surrounding me with my memories and with people who loved me. It was a wonderful feeling and I hoped an amazing visual. I finished the second verse, singing to the audience with my family standing behind me, then gave a royal wave goodbye as Ken struck the final chord.

"Good night, everyone, and thank you. Thank you for your generosity, your kindness, and for making tonight a special evening."

The audience was still clapping and rose to a standing ovation as I walked offstage for the last time. Andy was waiting backstage with a bouquet of roses for me.

"For me? Isn't this a little sappy? I mean, I thought that song was over the top but this, I mean, this is—"

"Oh, stop it," Andy interrupted. "Would you just let down the wall for a second?"

He held me by my shoulders, leaned over, and gave me a kiss. He didn't let go.

"They're still applauding," he said.

"I'm not going back out there. I said goodbye and I meant it."

"Just go out and accept their kindness. Just for a minute," he urged.

I wanted to leave, but I realized I should take my cue from Diana. Always hungry for love, she could never turn away from offering it with an open heart. I turned toward the stage, but Andy stopped me.

"Wait. I need to say something first. Thank you. Not just for tonight, but for what you said about me. You've meant a lot to me over the years, so thank you. A lot of people would've let success go to their heads and left someone like me in the dust, but you never did. You're a class act. You're a wonderful person. Thank you for giving us your best."

"You don't fool me, Andy. I know it's the money I brought in that you loved," I laughed.

"No! It was never—"

"Andy"—I put my fingertips over his mouth—"I know." Once again I made sure my cast was covered by the black satin wrap, then as I turned to go back onstage, I looked over my shoulder at him. "I know," I repeated, and he grinned at me.

I went back out and thanked the audience one last time. I waved as the curtain closed on me and sealed 2Di4 off from any further performances.

Then I was surrounded by a swarm of drag queens. They hugged me with endless compliments and offers of undying friendship and love while ripping off wigs and costume jewelry. They were tender as they returned the dresses to the garment bags. I knew it was only the gowns being zipped away until they could be cleaned and given to their new owners. I would always have my memories. I also knew I would see my real friends again. But I ached for 2Di4. I felt like a piece of me had just been surgically removed and I wasn't being allowed time to recuperate.

Somehow Ken and Martin managed to move me away from the others. They didn't wrap themselves around me. I knew they understood what I was feeling.

"I had no idea you'd talked to Andy about your contract," Ken said.

"Did you see him?" Martin asked. "I can't find him anywhere."

"We said goodbye. I imagine he's busy rounding up the VIPs and major contributors for the big 'thank-you' party. Ken, let me find my robe and I'll return your dress and wrap," I said.

"Don't worry about it," Ken laughed. "I haven't worn either in years! I used to do a Greta Garbo thing in that dress. I doubt I can fit into it anymore. Do you want it?"

"I don't think I'll be wearing any gowns for a while," I mused. "Do you want to get a bite somewhere? I'm just not up to doing the after-hours party."

"I'm skipping it, too. I'm really tired," Ken said. "I don't think so. I'll see you at brunch tomorrow, okay?"

We kissed each other on the cheek and Martin gave me another hug.

"You were great," he said.

"I know," I cracked, but as they walked away laughing, I went back to my dressing room with a leaden heart. I stood in front of my makeup table for the last time. Only now I heard Dr. Frank N. Furter saying, *Whatever happened to Faye Wray?*

Perhaps the same will be asked about me, I thought. I turned out the lights and closed the door. Always know when to exit.

I thought about what lay ahead as I was driven home. I was afraid. I felt as if I'd been thrown out of a plane without a parachute. What if my job didn't work out? I had no skills for the "real world." I had no college education. My "degrees" were in extensive show-tune knowledge, advanced lip-synch, and how to cover up a five o'clock shadow. If I suddenly lost my job, would I try again to be an actor? That seemed like such a faraway dream. What if I failed again? What would I do then?

As soon as I was inside my apartment, I leaned against the door, staring aimlessly into space. I still felt disembodied, as if I were me, yet not me.

My thoughts fell into some black hole as I realized I had a more immediate concern. Something, I wasn't sure what, was off about my apartment. Or rather, something was on. There was an unusual glow coming through my back windows from the garden. My first thought was that the police might be chasing someone through the alley. But the light was too steady and still for that.

Maybe it's an angel announcing a blessed event, my inner voice jeered. Or better yet, the spirits of Diana and Mother Teresa coming to tell you how many jewels you earned for your heavenly tiara tonight.

It wasn't the first time I'd wished I could stifle this inner voice. Sometimes it was such a nuisance.

I walked into the living room then stopped dead in my tracks, unsure whether to be scared or thrilled. Someone had gone to a lot of trouble in my garden. I peered outside, but the gate seemed to be locked and there was not even a shadow to indicate a visitor. As quietly as possible, I unlocked and opened the back door and stepped out.

Tiny white lights had been painstakingly interwoven through my vines and plants. A lot of the pruning I'd done on the shrubs left the tops full but the bottoms bare. My attempt to make this look deliberate worked well now that the lights wound their way around the trunks and into the leaves. I had always wished my garden could be as appealing at night as it was in the day. Someone had made that possible.

It was enchanting, but I was dumbfounded. I glanced toward Blaine's window, which was dimly lit. I couldn't imagine Blaine doing anything like this, and neither he nor Sheila would have known I'd be out tonight. Even if they knew, they couldn't be sure I wouldn't come home before they'd finished. This had to be the work of someone who knew where I was and how long I'd be gone.

But most of my other friends had been at Club Chaos. So who . . .

Just as I stepped back inside, my buzzer sounded and I shivered. Could someone be watching me? That was an unnerving thought.

I pressed the "talk" button.

"Yes?"

"It's the good fairy. May I come in?"

"Who says you're good?" I asked, but buzzed him in and opened my door.

Our eyes locked as he walked down the hall toward me. When he made it to the door, he held out a bottle of Moët & Chandon.

"You probably don't feel like celebrating," Jeremy said, "but at the very least I thought we could drink a belated toast to Halloween and your new life. I see you're still in costume."

"So are you," I said.

He was wearing a black suit. His crisp, white, mock-tuxedo shirt had a regular pointed collar, and his slim, silk tie was tied with a smart knot. It was common for Manhattanites to wear black, but Jeremy loathed it. He felt there was too great a contrast between dark clothing and his fair features. However, it was the very contrast that had made my heart pound whenever he relented to my requests that he wear a black suit on special occasions.

I'd always loved men in suits because I could imagine the body underneath the layers of clothing. Not to mention the prolonged foreplay of removing the layers to get to the body beneath. Jeremy never failed to disappoint in this area. I knew his body well and it didn't take much imagination to mentally undress him down to his finely toned physique. He was never in the rippling mass of virile manhood category. His body was more like a dancer's or a swimmer's. I could even picture his bare toes inside his black wingtips.

He smiled at me, knowing I appreciated him in his black suit. His smile pushed his smooth skin over his sharp cheekbones.

He looked so good. I could feel my defenses crumbling.

"I'm not sure this is a good idea," I said. "Shouldn't you be just getting home from the theater?"

"I didn't work tonight," he said. "I wanted to see your show. Your last show."

"You were there?"

"Of course."

He seemed subdued, as if he'd come here from a funeral. I took the champagne and gestured for him to follow me inside. I still hadn't turned on any lights so we were bathed in the glow from the garden.

"Did you come here before you went to the club?"

"Huh?"

I'd know that fake innocent look anywhere.

"The garden. You did that, didn't you?" I asked.

"Yeah." He shrugged. "I thought you might be feeling a little let down. I wanted to surprise you with something that would cheer you up. I hope you don't feel like I invaded your space. You should have seen me climbing the fence with the boxes of lights. Little monkey boy."

A long pause followed my laugh. I knew I had to make a choice. I could either continue the sparring from our last few meetings or bring all of this to a fitting conclusion. Suddenly I recalled Sheila's wisdom regarding this dilemma. If she could forgive, forget, and make friends with her ex-boyfriends, maybe I should try.

"It was nice of you," I said. "I like it. Thanks."

"If memory serves me, you can never sleep right after a gig. Andy told me I was welcome to join the party at the club, but then I saw you leave alone. So I took a chance on finding you here."

He followed me to the kitchen. Seeing my wrap slip as I reached for the champagne flutes reminded me I was still dressed as 2Di4. I handed him the bottle.

"Why don't you open and pour this while I take a quick shower," I suggested.

He nodded. I left him and was out of my clothes and in the shower in record time, protecting my cast in its plastic wrapper.

If this was to be a serious talk, it needed to come from Daniel, not 2Di4. She was officially retired. The weak feeling returned to my stomach and knees. I leaned against the tile wall for a minute, taking deep breaths. I heard the rustle of the shower curtain and looked over with wide eyes. All I saw was a hand holding a glass.

"Thought you might want a little bracer," I heard him say.

I pulled back the curtain and stared at him for a few seconds then said, "I've only got one good arm."

"Want some help?"

I nodded then closed the curtain. A couple of minutes later he joined me, taking the soap and working up a lather. Even as my mind began to clamor *Don't take backward steps,* I leaned back. He wrapped his arms around me, his hands running over my chest. So familiar . . .

I let him wash me then towel me dry, delivering myself into his care. Then we took our glasses into the bedroom and sat on the bed, staring at each other.

"To better beginnings," he said, holding up his champagne.

"Or better endings," I answered, tapping his glass with mine. I took a deep breath. "Jeremy."

"I know," he said. "If your answer had been any different, you'd have called. I'm not here to plead my case."

"Why are you here?"

"Remember how the biggest events always left us with a sad feeling when they were over?"

"When we were an *us,* yeah," I said.

"You were there for my opening night. I had these big ideas about how that would go. You shot me down."

"So what is this, Jeremy? You want to see me cry after my closing night? Are you getting some kind of perverse satisfaction out of knowing me so well?"

"When did you get cynical, Daniel?"

"Oh, I don't know. Maybe when you dumped me for Robert?"

"That's the story that makes me the bad guy," he said, setting down his drink.

"It's the truth."

"The part our friends know about," he agreed. "But we know the rest of it, don't we?"

"What's your version?"

"You left me emotionally long before Robert came into our lives." He raised his palms to stop me before I could answer. "I'm not saying what I did was your fault. I made a choice. A bad choice. But you don't know how good it felt to get some attention. To feel like I mattered to somebody. To be with a man who talked to me. Who heard me when I talked. You made me feel like a ghost. You were so fucking scared of what you might lose that you shut everybody out. The rest of them couldn't see it. But I lived with you. I had to see it."

"What I might lose," I repeated tonelessly.

"See? Even now we're supposed to pretend it's not real. I don't have to pretend anymore. I don't have anything else to lose. From the day, Daniel, the *day*, that Ken told us he has AIDS, you were gone. Not from him. But from me, from Martin, from everybody else. I understood that it was hard for you to be around all your mutual friends and pretend your insides weren't screaming. I understood what it took to keep his secret so he didn't have to endure some of the shit we've seen other friends go through. But he told *us*, Daniel. He told *us* so we could lean on each other. Don't you think I'm hurt, too? Don't you think I'm scared for him and for you? I know what he means to you. But instead of taking your lead from Ken, who hasn't slowed down one bit, you went out of business. Emotionally. The only thing that stayed the same was 2Di4. Because she's make-believe."

"I don't want to—"

"Back then, I didn't get it," he interrupted. "But over the past month, while I was waiting for the call that never came, I got it. Every time I go onstage and become Billy, I can forget everything else. It's an escape the same way 2Di4 is an escape for you. But it's different because I know Billy will end. I'll play other parts, do other shows. I guess what I'm trying to say is, I understand how your alter ego could stop being an escape and become a prison. No matter what anyone else says, I think you're brave to let it go. To start over. And to know that just trading one character for another isn't the right answer for you."

I stared at my glass until he took it from me and set it next to his on the bedside table.

"You don't have the market on suffering, Daniel. You're not the only person who may lose Ken. Ken may not be the last person you lose. You can live in the past or run away from it. You can bury 2Di4 or vanish into her. But you can't change things that are out of your control."

"I don't want to talk about this."

"No shit. Look at me, damn it," Jeremy said. When I did, he shook his head. "You may think I've been an insensitive, shallow bastard, but there's more to me than that and you know it. So I'm here. Tomorrow you can go back to whatever it is you're doing. It's what you have to do, and you'll probably do it without me. Tomorrow I'll leave you alone. But I know you the way nobody else does, not even Ken. Tonight I just want—"

He broke off, enfolding me in his arms as I fell against him. When my sobs finally subsided into an occasional gulp of air, he brought me a warm washcloth so I could wipe my face.

"Moisturize," he teased, trading my Prescriptives Comfort Lotion for the washcloth. "Made you laugh."

"God, we're so fucked up," I muttered.

"I know, baby. It'll take a while before we figure out what to be to each other. We'll get there."

It felt so good to slide between the cool sheets and settle back into his arms. Our old spooning position.

"Jer?"

"Mmhmm?"

"Thanks. For the lights. For being here."

"You're welcome. Thanks for letting me in."

I understood what he meant and smiled, letting myself relax for the first time in a long while. I had bound myself in a rope made of fear, anxiety, and grief. Over the past couple of months the rope had been cut a strand at a time by Ken, Martin, Aunt Jen, Blaine, Sheila, and Gretchen. I never dreamed Jeremy would be the one who could untangle it all and let me step clear of it.

He was right. Tomorrow officially began my new, princess-free life. I could hold on to what was best about the old life and still move forward. I could explore possibilities with Blaine in the wonderful world of advertising. Or the bedroom.

I could also relent and turn over. If I did, Jeremy would be there to face that new life with me.

I heard Gretchen's voice again: *Always the Virgo. Analyze, weigh, judge, and evaluate yourself into doing nothing.*

I closed my burning eyes to all possibilities but sleep.

TEN

I awoke the next morning to find myself wrapped around Jeremy and staring into his open eyes. I blinked away sleepiness and confusion, trying to remember why I was in bed with him. The memories of our conversation the night before replayed in my head like a fast-forward movie. Jeremy sat up and started smoothing down my bed-head.

"Good morning," he said.

I sat up, too, rubbed my eyes, and yawned.

"It's alive!" Jeremy exclaimed in his Dr. Frankenstein imitation.

"Iuhnnghhuh."

"It speaks. Albeit in a foreign tongue."

It was a bit much for me, so I gave him my scariest frown.

"I forgot what a beast you are in the morning," he said, more subdued now, cautious of angering me.

"And I forgot what a morning person you are," I grumbled, but tried my best not to provoke him. This was the cause of many of our arguments when we lived together. Eventually we resorted to not talking, walking on tiptoe for the first few hours of the day, until he moved out.

"Do you want breakfast?" I asked. "I'm not sure what I have."

"Don't you do brunch today with Ken?"

"Oh yeah, thanks for reminding me. I forgot a few weeks ago and Ken almost disowned me. I'm not going through that again."

"Yeah, I heard about that one," Jeremy laughed.

"You did?"

"Daniel, just because we stopped our relationship doesn't mean . . ." He trailed off, but I knew what he meant. "Don't forget that Ken introduced us."

"I know," I murmured. "Hold on."

I hopped out of bed and went into the living room. I found one of my scrapbooks in the chest and took it into the bedroom. Jeremy looked a bit puzzled as I slipped back into bed with it and snuggled up next to him. I opened it on our laps and showed him the picture of us outside of Nell's.

"Oh, I remember that!" Jeremy laughed. "Geez, I was so nervous about meeting you. Ken had built you up so much. I was a wreck that night."

"I know; so was I," I giggled. "Look at us, hardly touching each other, like a couple of nervous teenagers. Ken kept saying, 'Move closer together. Closer. Closer!' before he took the picture."

I propped my chin on Jeremy's shoulder as he continued looking through the scrapbook.

"The Unnatural Blonde Party!" we exclaimed in unison as he turned a page.

"The one time I got you in drag," I added. "My sexy little Loni Anderson."

"Nuh-uh, *you* were the sex kitten, Barbarella," he argued.

We cracked up at the picture of Ken, whose costume made him appear headless.

"Miss Jayne Mansfield," Jeremy intoned.

"For such a nice guy, Ken's jokes could be heartless," I said. "Remember how he used to—"

I broke off, realizing I kept speaking of Ken in the past tense. It gave me a scary, unnerving feeling. Jeremy picked up on it, too.

"It's all right," he said, putting his arm around my shoulders.

"He's just been everything to me, you know?" was all I could say.

"I know," Jeremy assured me, "he means a lot to me, too. I realize he's always been your friend, but—"

"Oh no, he's always liked you a lot, Jer. He's your friend, too. Our friend. I never tried to pit our friends against you," I said. I tried to lighten the mood. "Although we never did finalize the divorce. How about I keep Ken? You can have Martin."

Jeremy started laughing, grabbed a pillow, and swatted me with it. The photo album slid off our laps and plummeted to the floor.

"Now *he's* all yours," Jeremy laughed. He and Martin never got along too well. Martin would often tell me I could do better than Jeremy, sometimes even in Jeremy's presence.

"Speaking of Martin, I should call him," I said absently, thinking aloud. "Like you said last night, I've really cut myself off from him."

We both got quiet. I didn't want to call Martin with Jeremy there and he picked up on it.

"I should go," he said. "Robert's probably wondering where I am."

"Yeah, he probably is. And you can have *him*," I snorted.

"Daniel—"

"No," I interrupted. "No explanations, please. This has been nice, really nice. Honestly. But I don't want to lead you on. I can't go forward with you as a lover, and I think you know that."

"I do," he said, resigned to the fact. He didn't seem sad or angry. Just accepting, which was exactly what I needed.

"I may have shut you out, but you still went to Robert. You gave up on me and I can't take a chance that will happen again. It hurt me."

"I'm sorry I hurt you," Jeremy offered.

"Thank you," I accepted, looking into his eyes. I could see that he meant it. But I couldn't forget how his betrayal had come at me out of nowhere. I hadn't deserved that. No one did. That thought prompted me to say, "Jer, Robert kissed me a while back, the day you were both here with Andy."

Jeremy got quiet and I was afraid I shouldn't have told him. Yet if I was to be friends with him, I wanted to move forward with complete honesty. It seemed necessary to tell him. Besides, I didn't want Robert to hurt him.

"When I left you for Robert," Jeremy said slowly, "I knew he was attracted to you. He was flirting with me to make you jealous and get your attention. I was doing the same with him. It went completely out of control, and in all honesty, you seemed almost relieved. Hurt, yes, but it was like an easy way out for both of us. I know my relationship with Robert is nothing solid. I guess we both have some moving on to do, huh?"

"Yeah," I said, wondering what to do next.

Jeremy picked up his cue and got out of bed.

"I should go," he repeated and started dressing. I sat in bed watching him for a minute, then retrieved my robe from the bathroom.

When I emerged, he was completely dressed in his suit. Though it was slightly rumpled, he still looked dashing. I moved to him and straightened his tie.

"I've always loved you in this suit," I said.

"I've always loved you," he said.

He drew me forward and wrapped his arms around me. I returned his hug and felt my hurt drain away. It finally seemed over to me; I resisted the tears that brimmed in my eyes.

We parted and I walked him to the door. He stepped outside, then paused.

"I'll see you soon, okay?"

"Yeah, I hope so," I said, and I did. "Give me a call, or I'll call you?"

"We'll leave it at that," he laughed. "We'll call. I know we will."

He waved and left. I closed the door and heaved a huge sigh, already worn out before my day even really started. I had a while before meeting Ken for brunch. I decided to give Martin a call and invite him along. I knew Ken wouldn't mind. I prepared some witty little speech as I dialed, knowing Martin would either be sleeping or screening. I was startled when Ken answered and for a moment wondered if I'd called the right number. I hesitated, then stumbled over my greeting. Ken cut me off.

"You haven't listened to your messages, have you?"

My stomach sank. I knew this tone of voice; it meant trouble.

"My ringer's off and I haven't checked for messages," I said. "Why? What's wrong? Where's Martin?"

"He collapsed this morning, Daniel," Ken said solemnly.

"Oh my god! Why? What happened? Is he all right?" I demanded in some hyper tone, giving him no time to answer between questions.

"Um, sorry, I guess fainted is a better word," Ken said. I could tell from his voice that he was smiling, enjoying my reaction to the drama of the situation. "Daniel, I told him."

I stared blankly through the window at my garden until the impact of what he said reached me.

"You what? I thought you said you didn't want anyone but me and Jeremy to know."

"That was before. This is now."

"Ken, you've never been mysterious. I've always enjoyed your straightforwardness. Bentforwardness? Sorry. But you know what I mean. What are you telling me here? Has something changed? Are you sick?"

The awkward silence on his end foreshadowed a situation for which I might prefer to sit. I fell on the couch, wondering if it would be rude to ask Ken to hold on while I switched to the cordless so I could go outside. It might be easier to face his words in the solitude and serenity of my garden. Then again, the sight of waning beauty might make things worse. Already the majority of the blooms had fallen from their stems.

"Remember that I knew I was positive for a long time before I talked to you and Jeremy. I only did that when I got my AIDS diagnosis. I needed your support and thought you might need Jeremy's. Plus I don't like keeping things from you. But a lot has changed since then. I no longer see you every day, and sometimes I need somebody to talk to. Furthermore, you're no longer with Jeremy, which means *you* have no one to talk to. So I thought it was time to be honest with Martin. For everybody's sake."

I still had the sense there was something he wasn't telling me.

"Are you sure you're okay?" I asked. "Why now, Ken? Why today?"

"Probably just emotional fallout from last night," Ken said. "You seemed to handle all of that better than the rest of us."

Do I have some news for him at brunch, I thought.

"Anyway, it's done now. I told him," Ken continued.

"And he fainted?" I tried to suppress a nervous giggle.

"Yeah." Ken didn't bother to hold back his laugh. "It was actually pretty hysterical. Right out of some Southern belle movie. He all but threw his wrist over his forehead, clutched his chest with his other hand, and fell sideways after exclaiming, 'Why, I do declayuh!' "

We both laughed hysterically over this image, in an effort to release the tension as much as anything else. I heard a noise in the background and Ken suddenly exclaimed, "Ow!"

"What happened?" I asked, still giggling.

"He must've revived when the phone rang. I was just assaulted by five tacky throw pillows," Ken said, and again we broke into peals of laughter.

"Ken," I finally said, trying to get serious.

"Daniel, listen," Ken ordered. "I told Martin my T-cell count has dropped again. But I'm fine. I feel tired a lot more, but I'm okay. Really. I just panicked after my last checkup and needed someone to talk to."

"Okay," I said. And it was. "I'm okay with this. As long as you're all right."

"I am," he promised. "Guess what? I've decided to begin the cocktails. A month from now I'm sure my counts will be much better. Which is enough of that subject."

I crossed my fingers and remembered why I had called Martin in the first place.

"Speaking of cock tales, I'm feeling the need for a Bloody Mary. Are we still meeting for brunch, or are you wiped out after last night?" I asked.

"No, I'm looking forward to it. If I can revive Scarlett, can I bring him along?"

"That's why I called him," I laughed. "Yeah. I'll see you in a bit."

After we hung up, I showered and dressed. As I took my wallet from the dresser, I paused to stare at my unmade bed. I almost wished something more than cuddling had happened between Jeremy and me. I quickly dismissed the thought, wiping it away like spilled coffee on a countertop.

It just means you're ready to move on, I thought, and immediately Blaine popped into my head.

I went into the living room to find my keys and debated checking to see if he was near his window.

Am I ready to move on to Blaine, I wondered, resisting the urge to go outside.

"If you are," Martin said later, after I posed the question to them at the Screening Room, "he's got to be better than Jeremy."

Ken put down his fork with an audible clang and glared at Martin as he chewed his bite of Spanish omelet.

"All right, all right," Martin appeased with a huge eyeroll, "don't get all *Mommie Dearest* on me. I'll behave. Besides, I have to go to the powder room. You can talk about Jeremy all you want."

"Well?" Ken asked, with his eyebrows raised.

"Well, what?"

"Jeremy," Ken explained. "What aren't you telling me?"

"Are you sure you don't work for the CIA? Or Dionne Warwick, for that matter."

Ken chuckled but kept eating, waiting for me to talk. I told him about the prior evening's events, in haste, before Martin returned. Ken stayed quiet until I finished.

"I'm thinking you don't want Martin to know, so it doesn't get back to Robert?"

"Right. I don't want to get back into that triangle thing with them. Knowing Martin, Robert would be the first person he'd call," I predicted with a derisive snort.

"Don't underestimate Martin," Ken softly said, looking around to make sure he wasn't back yet. "He's a good friend and he's done a lot of growing up. Especially in the past few months."

"You mean since I've withdrawn?"

Ken bit his lip, stopped eating, then looked at me admiringly. "You've been a good influence on him," he told me.

"You're the good influence," I protested, deflecting the praise back to him. "If anything, he's just learning from my mistakes. Still, Martin has stayed in contact with Robert. I'm not sure what that means."

"You know, I've had about enough of your martyr routine," Ken said rather sternly. Martin had been returning to the table but, upon hearing this, turned right around again.

"What?"

"It's over, Daniel, so move on," Ken said. "You used to be so giving, so caring, and always looking out for others. Lately, it's been all about you. *You you you.* Jeremy was right, you heard about me being sick and that was it. You cut yourself off."

"No," I mumbled, even though when Jeremy had said it the night before, I knew it was true. "Not entirely."

"You were still around, but emotionally you've been distant. You might consider taking some responsibility for the way Jeremy and Martin came to depend on Robert for the easygoing approval you used to provide." Ken let this sink in and took another bite of omelet. He grimaced, as if it no longer tasted good. "I'm not hungry anymore. And no, it's not because of *you.* I haven't had much of an appetite lately."

"Are you okay?" I asked again.

"No, Daniel, I'm dying."

"Ken, please stop," I begged. "I can't take it when you're angry with me."

"I'm not angry. I'm sad. Maybe I'm even jealous that you get to move on. I never got to move on to the 'real world.' Things were different when I was your age. I felt like to be me, to be gay, I had to remain within certain boundaries. You don't have to accept those limits. You get to live in an expanding world."

"You live in the same world I do," I pointed out.

"It's not the world that is at issue," Ken said. "It's living. Don't argue. I'm not giving up or being the voice of doom. I don't have the energy to start over. My goal is to enjoy what I have while I'm here. I live in the present. You can take the future for granted and make the most of your new life."

"I'm kind of nervous about it," I whispered, desperate to talk about anything except the possibility of Ken dying. "Scared, even. It's not like starting over was really my choice."

"Life throws us some ugly curves, Daniel." Ken spoke like the wise man in a tribal village.

The Elder of Greenwich Village, I mused, wondering why his words seemed familiar. Then I remembered the deli man. He, too, had spoken of life's curves. He'd also said to love is to stop resisting. Maybe he was right; maybe opening myself to Jeremy was a surrender to love, a bigger love than sex or romance.

"Life is rarely fair," Ken was saying. "Just go with it. I need you to be strong for me. For Martin. He needs you."

"I know," I said and smiled at Ken. "I've come to realize how much my friends mean to me. People sometimes only realize that when somebody's gone. At least it was only 2Di4, in my case, who had to go. But you can count on me. I'm always here."

"That's funny," Martin said, returning to his chair, "I just read that about you on the bathroom wall. 'Daniel is always here, you can count on him.' "

I smirked at Martin and he continued chattering.

"Well, I trust you two got Jeremy out of your systems? I always did say that you could do—" He stopped as Ken stabbed at the air around him with his fork. "Okay! Tell us something about Gretchen."

Ken said, "She called Friday to say she couldn't make the auction because she was going upstate to the lake. She mentioned that you two had lunch a few days ago."

"Yeah, it was nice." I was relieved to drop Jeremy as a topic. "She's got a new girlfriend."

"Anyone we know?" Ken asked, happy to hear new gossip.

"Remember that dyke we used to tease at Uncle Charlie's?"

"The one we called Stan the Man? Always sat at the end of the bar?"

"The one who wore suits and smoked cigars," Martin dryly said, inciting more giggle fits.

"Oh my god, is it her? I mean, him? It?" Ken snickered.

"Yeah," I said. I was suddenly finding it hard to breathe and was afraid of wetting my pants in the middle of the Screening Room. "But get this—"

"What?" Ken was gasping for air.

"It turns out she's an investment broker named Cindy and likes Gretchen to scream out, 'Oh Stan!' during sex!"

"Oh my *god!*" Martin squealed, choking on his French toast. A few people turned to stare, but we didn't care.

"All this time we thought she was just going along with our teasing her," Ken said through a gale of laughter.

"I know!" I crowed.

"But," Ken said, composing himself, "Gretchen actually does it?"

"Well, she said she finds it a bit on the bizarre side," I explained. "But no more than that last woman who wanted Gretchen to lead her around on a dog leash."

"Where does she find these women, anyway?" Ken marveled.

"Hanging around with us!" I said and we all started laughing again.

"You know, Gretchen will be at the lake all week," Ken finally said. "I wonder if Cindy—or Stan?—will be there, too. Gretchen invited me and I told her I'd consider it. Now I think I might *have* to go. Why don't you come with us? Could you leave early on Friday?"

"I might," I said. "Let me see how everything goes this week. If I still have a job."

"Why wouldn't you?" Ken asked.

"One of my coworkers was at the auction last night," I said. "If she recognized me, she might disrupt my new kingdom. Blaine is the crown prince of Breslin Evans Fox and Dean. He may not tolerate a royal rival."

"You know how we royals take care of people like her. Off with her head!" Martin advised with a dramatic wave of his hand.

After recovering one more time, Ken mumbled something about the bathroom and stepped away from the table.

"Hey you," Martin said. "How could you not tell me something as major as Ken being positive? I can't believe you."

"Martin—"

"I know, he didn't want you to tell me. He wanted to tell me himself when the time was right. I *can* believe you. But still, I was in shock."

"Martin, you know Ken loves you and wouldn't have told you unless he considered you a valued friend. He needs you. I need you, too."

"What do you mean?" Martin asked.

"I haven't been around you guys as much as I'd like to be. Ken's right about that. Last night at the auction was great. It was like the old days, but I have to move on now. My job takes a lot of my time and energy. I want to make it work. I need you to be there for Ken and to let me know if anything goes wrong. Can you do that?"

"Daniel"—Martin's voice went down a notch—"you know I love Ken as much as you do and would never do anything to hurt either of you. I realize I'm the shallow one of our little Ronette girl group, but I'll always be here for Ken. For you, too. We don't all have the luxury of a family who loves and believes in everything we do and every decision we make. You guys are my family; I'll do anything I can." I widened my eyes to let him know Ken was returning, and he continued in a louder voice, "I'll have to tell Gretchen she can borrow that strap-on of mine if Stan the Man needs something with a little more oomph."

"The movie is about to start," Ken said with a childlike grin.

One of the reasons we always went to the Screening Room for brunch was because they showed *Breakfast at Tiffany's* on Sundays. It was Ken's favorite movie. He loved Audrey Hepburn and joked that he identified with her character. He often said that he was a lot like Holly Golightly when he was young.

"Hey," Ken said to Martin, "maybe your new character could be a spoof on Holly Golightly."

"What? New character?" I prodded for more information.

"Well, 2Di4's gone down in history," Martin slowly said, probably testing my reaction. As I nodded, he went on, "Every drag performer in the city is vying for her spot. Andy's pretty much said he's not going to let anyone fill your pumps again. Marc suggested he join my Duchess of Windsor act as the Duchess of York. Playing off Fergie might be fun, but I'm ready to be a solo. I want to do something great so I can get the closing spot, which Ken has already declined. Miss Garland is cutting back her performances."

My head snapped in Ken's direction.

"Judy's become such a wreck," Ken said with a disapproving shake of his head. "Totally out of control. Andy agrees it would be a good idea if she takes it easy for a while, until she gets better. We're looking into a room at Betty Ford."

"Anyway," Martin said, "I'm thinking the whole royalty thing is pretty much over. My duchess act is kind of moot now. Especially with the way 2Di4 went out. That was amazing last night, by the way. You really pulled it off. So Ken and I are trying to come up with a new character. Which will be great now that I have his creative mind all to myself."

I smiled and thought about how everything seemed to be coming full circle, with Martin taking my place as Ken's protégé. I silently wished Martin all the luck in the world and hoped he would become as successful as I had. If, of course, that was what he wanted.

"If you need any help just let me know, and I'll do what I can," I offered.

"You'd better," Martin threatened.

"Hush up, now," Ken demanded, like a mother to her unruly children, "the movie is starting."

I was still humming "Moon River" the following morning as I entered the reception area at work.

"BreslinEvansFoxandDeeeean?" Mitzi, with one hand on the switchboard, answered the front desk phone as if the company name were one word, letting the "Dean" drag into a long question to be answered by the caller.

She glanced at me as I entered, then returned her gaze to the switchboard. As if suddenly recognizing me, she held up one finger to stop me. I waited.

"I'll transfer you, ma'am," she told the caller, cracking her gum into the headset she wore.

Always the professional, I thought.

"*Daniel!* Oh my *gawd!*" she bellowed.

"Mitzi, dear. I think a little less enthusiasm on a Monday morning at eight-fifty would be appropriate. I'm sure it's exciting to see me, but you—"

"Aren't you going to ask me about my weekend?" she demanded.

Hmm, here we go, I thought. The cat is out of the proverbial bag. Let's get this over with and decide, once and for all, if Blaine's ignorance about my drag life is worth a little extortion from "Ditsy."

"Okay, I'll play along," I said dryly. Then, in mock enthusiasm, *"Mitiz!* How was your *weekend?"* I clasped my hands in front of my chest.

She giggled without comprehending the satirical tone I had used at her expense.

"It was *fabulous!"*

She *is* Andy, I thought, squinting at her to see if she were in drag.

"I went with some friends to that auction! Remember? We were talking about it last week? The one with the dresses that were modeled by *guys?* The one you said I wouldn't like? *Well,* we actually *went!"* She switched her gum from the right side to the left with one big, overdramatic, lower jaw sweep. "Not only were the dresses *modeled* by guys, but there was even one who dressed up *just like Diana!* Oh my *gawd!"*

She threw her head back during the last three words, inhaling deeply, Brenda Vacarro style, before shouting them out, her eyes rolling back for punctuation. I wondered if anyone in the office knew the Heimlich maneuver, for when the gum would inevitably lodge itself down her windpipe.

"So you all had a nice time, huh? That's great, Mitzi," I said, closing the conversation and picking up my laptop to head toward my desk.

"Nice? It wasn't just an *auction,* Daniel, it was a whole *show!* We just about died! And *every*one was *so nice!* Do you know we even had a round of drinks bought for us? Can you *imagine?* In a bar like *that?* A bunch of *girls?* Like, I mean, *real* girls?"

I didn't have the heart to tell her that Andy made sure everyone who attended got at least one free round of drinks. A smart businessman, Andy certainly was aware that a room full of liquored-up people would spend more. It seemed to have worked, too, judging by the amount of money the whole thing brought in.

"Well, that does sound like you had a fabu—"

"*And,*" she continued, "the one who dressed up like Diana could have been *you!* I mean, I don't know what that one looks like without the makeup, but *I'm* thinkin' you two could be *twins!*"

"Well, you know," I began in a hushed tone, "you've never seen us in the same place at the same time. It could be like the whole Michael Jackson/Janet Jackson thing. We might actually be the same person."

I quickly backed away as I let that sink in.

Mitzi's mouth fell open, her gum falling to the switchboard. Then, with a knowing grin, she said, "Nuh-uhhhhh," and giggled.

She popped the wad of neon green gum back into her mouth, almost making me throw up.

"Daniel, you really *are* too much sometimes!" I heard her call after me as I disappeared around the corner.

You, too, Mitzi, I thought.

I started to put on my headset after getting a cup of coffee when I noticed Blaine's voice from behind the closed door of his office. I punched up his calendar on the computer, letting the headset fall around my neck for the moment. His schedule showed that he was on a conference call with a representative from DKNY, his latest prey in the hunt for new Breslin Evans Fox and Dean clients.

I noticed the light on my own phone blinking, plugged in my headset, and said, "Good morning, Mr. Dunhill's office."

"Is he in?" The question came from a condescending voice.

Why did I know this voice? I thought about it with a furrowed brow.

Coming up with nothing, I answered, "I'm sorry, Mr. Dunhill is unavailable at the moment. May I take a message, please? Or would you prefer to leave a message on his voice mail?"

"No. I've already been to your version of voice mail hell, thank you," the caller quipped without a trace of warmth or humor.

It suddenly came to me. This was the same voice that was screeching at me the day Gretchen showed up.

"Whom shall I say is calling, then?" I asked with so much sweetness that she should be requiring insulin soon.

"Mrs. Blaine Dunhill."

After regaining the use of my lungs, I asked, "Is there any message, Mrs. Dunhill?"

"No. He's well aware what this is about."

"I'll tell him you called," I answered, my head spinning.

"See that you do," she replied with an audible sneer.

I pictured her looking like Cruella De Vil sitting on a chaise covered in dalmatian fur.

As I wrote down her message, I noticed the light for Blaine's private line go out, signifying he was done with his conference call.

The intercom buzzed in my ear, followed by Blaine's voice.

"Daniel, could you come here for a moment, please?"

"Uh. Yes. Right away."

My head was still whirling. Mrs. Blaine Dunhill? Was Blaine a "Junior?" Was the caller his mother? Of course; that must be it. Certainly Blaine wasn't married.

I slipped out of my headset and picked up a pad and pen, taking with me the pink WHILE YOU WERE OUT slip that announced Mrs. Dunhill's call. I knocked, though Blaine was expecting no one else.

"Come," came the response.

I opened the door and debated making a clever comment, deciding against it after seeing the look on his face.

"Shut the door, Daniel," Blaine said as I entered the office.

I shut the door behind me and turned to face him. The windows behind him showed off Manhattan in all of its cosmopolitan brilliance. Blaine looked stunningly handsome in his Brooks Brothers navy suit as the centerpiece of the skyline.

"Yes, Mr. Dunhill?" I smiled sweetly.

He looked a little confused and said, "Daniel, I told you, call me Blaine."

I smiled with more sincerity and said, "Okay, Blaine. What can I do for you?"

"I wanted to say thank you. I know it's only been a short time since you came here, but the way you handled the situation with Mr. Harrison last week was extraordinary. Above and beyond the call of duty."

"That is why you hired me, is it not?" I reminded him with a grin. "Oh, I almost forgot. This call came while you were on your other line." I handed him the pink slip and continued, "Your mother sounds so young, albeit not one of the warmest phone personalities I've ever . . ."

My voice trailed off as I handed him the phone message. Blaine looked at the message, drew a breath, and sank into his high-backed leather desk chair, running his hand through his hair as he released a big sigh.

"Not my mother. My wife."

I felt the wind get knocked out of me for the second time that morning. This was exactly what I wanted to avoid knowing. Didn't he realize that I was trying to give him an out?

He stared at me. I stared back.

"I have a wife."

"So you said."

I knew the jealousy I felt was irrational. Blaine's night of drunkenness had turned me off the idea of myself one day being Mrs. Dunhill. Still, as Gretchen had pointed out, I wasn't entirely over the attraction. But Blaine was an enigma to me. I found him so attractive, yet every time I began to warm up to him, either he or someone associated with him threw me for a loop.

A dozen emotions clouded his face while I stood in front of him: desperation, fear, confusion, helplessness. He reminded me of a cornered animal. I seemed to be grappling with many of the same feelings. I didn't know what to do. Part of me was angry, yet I felt there had to be an explanation. We'd grown too close for him to have any malicious intent in keeping this from me. Maybe it was just none of my business.

I relented, saying, "You don't owe me an explanation, but . . . I guess what I'm trying to say is that if you need to vent, or just talk . . ."

I drifted off without finishing.

Blaine took a deep breath. His eyes were so miserable that I sat down to signal that I was here as his friend, not his employee.

"Remember when I told you the secretaries here have been a problem for me? How they get crushes?"

"Uh-huh," I answered, not getting his point.

"It's always been this way. High school, college. You're a handsome guy. You must have the same problem. Always girls with expectations."

"Like Sheila," I said.

"Huh?"

"I think she has a bit of a crush on you. Does *she* know about your wife?"

"Sydney *stole* me from Sheila," Blaine said. "I mean, Sheila was gracious about it. She was in our wedding. I think that was for me more than for Sydney. They don't really get along. As a matter of fact, the reason Sydney has been calling me is because she found out Sheila's staying here with me. She's not happy."

"I guess I understand," I said, though I didn't.

Blaine must have heard the doubt in my voice and said, "Let me start at the beginning. When I went to college, Sheila was my girl-friend. She was younger and our families are friends. Everyone expected me to be the perfect gentleman with her. Which worked out fine for me. She was a great excuse for not dating. You know, because I had a girlfriend back home."

"Doesn't really sound fair to Sheila," I said.

"Sheila was just a kid. It didn't hurt her popularity any to be dating a college guy."

"Mmmm."

"Sydney's from Eau Claire, too. She's my age so she was at school with Jake and me."

"Jake."

"Sheila's brother. My best friend. Anyway, one weekend we were hanging out drinking, and—"

"Jake seduced you?"

"Do you want to hear this or not?"

"Sorry."

"No, Jake didn't. Sydney and I—well, she was—let's just say the equipment worked. After being confused for so long, I thought that meant I was normal."

I bristled and he held up one hand, saying, "I'm just telling you how I felt then. Will you relax? Anyway, we ended up married. Big mistake. It was a five-year nightmare that ended when I accepted the position here and Sydney left for art school in Chicago."

"Why aren't you divorced?" I interrupted.

Blaine's intercom beeped and Mitzi's nasally voice said, "Mr. Dunhill, Eric Raines from Clairol is here."

"Okay, Mitzi, send him back." Blaine looked relieved. "Can we continue this later? Maybe over a drink after work or something?"

I stood and moved toward the door, still facing him.

"You got it, boss. Just no repeats of our first dinner, huh?" I playfully joked while reaching for the doorknob.

"No, I wouldn't do that to you. I hope you know that," Blaine said in a serious tone.

"No, I don't think you would either."

The air was charged. It wasn't romance, but it definitely was charged with something. I left the office, holding the door open for Eric Raines.

The remainder of the day was mostly uneventful. I had to commend myself on only losing one phone call, a new record for me. Now that I was getting better at my job, I found the corporate whirlwind exciting.

Blaine emerged from his office promptly at five o'clock.

"How 'bout that drink? I'm buying."

He shrugged into a gray and black herringbone topcoat. My breath quickened. Blaine getting dressed was even sexier than Jeremy getting undressed. I had to stop myself from fantasizing about taking him out of the coat and suit later.

"Sounds good to me," I responded in a dazed, Mitzi kind of way.

I slipped my scarf around my neck and handed my coat to Blaine, holding up my broken arm as my excuse. He helped me into it without missing a beat.

The evening air was crisp and cool. We walked without talking to Buck Wild and entered, Blaine holding the door for me.

We could get used to this, eh, Daniel? my inner voice asked. I elected not to acknowledge that thought, leading Blaine to a table so we could have more privacy than at the bar.

"About Sydney," he began, looking down after we ordered our drinks. "We've both talked to lawyers about starting divorce proceedings. There are a lot of financial things to work out, and now she's all stirred up about Sheila being here. I'm trying to placate her and protect Sheila. I feel all this pressure in my personal life and at work and I'm trying to hold everything together."

"Blaine, I meant what I said. You don't owe me an explanation. What's done is done, right? I mean you are my boss, and I don't think—"

He cut me off as I was trying to redraw the line that I had blurred earlier.

"I know that. But is that all I can hope to be? I mean, we can be friends, too, right?"

"It's all very confusing. There's been a lot going on with me lately, too. Most of it is just stuff that I have to deal with on my own. But to be honest, some of it is about you. You are incredibly handsome. I'd be kidding myself if I didn't admit at least that much, and I do like you. I just don't know if it would be wise for us to get involved, you know, on that level, especially while I'm working for you."

"I guess there's no easy way to solve this, Daniel. I feel very much the same way. It is confusing. But I suppose you're right. I just wish . . ."

I looked into those emerald eyes.

"You wish what?"

"I wish I had done things differently. I wish that about so many things."

I could sense his mind drifting off to face whatever problems Sydney was throwing his way.

"Well, hey," I said in as upbeat a tone as I could, attempting to change the mood, "if nothing else, we have a great opportunity ahead of us, right? I mean, you can never have too many friends." I thought about those I'd left behind, wondering if Blaine was yet another step in the healing process. "Besides," I continued, "who knows what could happen?"

My words slipped out before I had a chance to stop them and hung in the air like a rain cloud.

Blaine looked at me and I was sure I detected a sparkle in his eyes. He smiled and raised his glass.

"Well, then. To whatever may happen."

Geez, Daniel, I thought as I picked up my glass, from Club Chaos to Life Chaos, huh? Someday you might consider keeping your mouth shut.

Our glasses clinked in the air.

Just as he had during lunch on my first day of work, Blaine slipped from would-be suitor to boss with apparent ease, talking about the meetings that would take him out of town the remainder of the week and all of the following week. I struggled against asking him if any of those meetings involved Sydney, not wanting to make the conversation personal again.

Afterward, in the cab, I had a sudden thought.

"Would it be a problem if I left early on Friday?"

"Why?" he asked. "No, strike that. It's none of my business."

"Some friends have invited me to go out of town for the weekend," I volunteered.

He seemed to brood as he stared from the window, but merely said, "Sure. Take the whole day off. You've earned it."

"If you feel like I'm taking advantage of you—"

He gave a little laugh and said, "No. Not at all."

I let it go and we finished the ride in silence. When the cab stopped at my building, my voice was meek as I said, "See you in a week, then."

"We'll be talking on the phone," he reminded me.

"Enjoy your trip," I said, somewhat at a loss.

"You, too," he answered.

As I trudged up the stairs to my building, I felt uncertain about making the trip to the lake. Was it only two days before when being rid of 2Di4 had made my life seem uncomplicated? I suddenly felt as confused as ever.

ELEVEN

With Blaine out of the office, the week dragged its feet until Friday. I thought about Sydney while I packed for my trip upstate. I wondered if Blaine had been able to pacify her into not confronting Sheila. I decided to call Sheila, though I knew I couldn't bring up the subject of Sydney. However, if anything had happened, she might appreciate someone to talk to. After the third ring, I decided I wanted to get Sheila out of town, too. We could both leave the city behind and share solace in rolling hills and majestic lakes.

"Hello?" Sheila picked up almost out of breath.

"Sheila? Did I interrupt something?"

"Nothing important, just me and Jane Fonda doing our daily exercise." I could hear her taking big gulps and breathing hard. I certainly hadn't caught her in the cool-down period.

"Do you have any plans for this weekend?"

"As a matter of fact, I don't. Did you have something in mind?"

"Oh good, I was hoping you could come along."

"We're going away?" Sheila began to sound excited, getting that girlish tone that I loved.

"Yep. Me, Ken, and Martin are all going up to my friend Gretchen's resort. It hasn't officially opened yet, so it won't be crowded with tourists. She's only inviting personal friends at this point, to get our opinions. I think each of us might even get our own room and bathroom."

"Sounds fancy."

"Actually, I'm not expecting fancy. It's in a renovated hotel from the twenties. It's huge, but I think her plans for it are simple. Gretchen is this communal-eco-geopolitical-left-wing-ultraliberal lesbian, so I'm kind of expecting bean sprouts for dinner and a grass mat to sleep on."

"Hmmm. Maybe I'll take a rain check," Sheila chuckled.

"Okay, I'm exaggerating a bit. Gretchen is actually very tasteful, so I'm sure that the grass mats will have padding and the bean sprouts will be gourmet. Anyway, get ready because Ken said he was picking me up in about two hours."

"Geez, Daniel, you don't give a girl much time . . ."

Later, the tension slid off my shoulders when the city disappeared behind us as we drove up the highway. Martin bopped along to "I Need a Hero" on the radio while Sheila flipped through *Outdoor Living*, preparing for the weekend in the country. Ken drove silently with a pensive and preoccupied look on his face. I sat back and enjoyed the last of the red and yellow leaves on the trees. We took a route that followed the Hudson River toward the Catskill Mountains. The river looked orange as it reflected the leaves and caught the last rays of the day's autumnal light. The cool air snuck into the car through minuscule cracks and made me drowsy. I fell asleep as the peaks of the Catskill Mountain Range came into view.

I was jostled awake as the car bounced up and down on a dirt path. It was completely dark as the trees closed in above us. The dirt road became asphalt as the trees ended and we drove into a clearing. Under the feeble moonlight I could see the silhouettes of five small structures and one enormous building. We headed toward the largest. The ten windows on the lowest level of the house were illuminated with soft lighting. A figure appeared at one of the windows. A few seconds later a door opened and the light spilled onto a wooden porch. As we got closer, I realized that the building before us was the renovated Victorian-style hotel. When I had last seen it, the walls were complete only to above the first story. Since then, the workers had added a second and third story. Now it was huge. I hadn't expected anything so grandiose.

"Welcome!" I heard Gretchen call out as we stopped in front of the house and got out of the car. Gretchen ran up to Martin and gave him a huge hug. Just then lights came on along the edge of the roof on the first level of the house.

"This is the main compound," said Gretchen as she released Martin from her strong grip, "where all of you will be staying. There's a room for each of you."

"Compound?" Martin whispered to me. "How David Koresh."

"Shh," I commanded.

I introduced Sheila and Gretchen as we all walked into the foyer.

"Gretchen, I wasn't expecting the renovations to be so extensive. I thought it would still be little huts around the pond."

"This used to be a hotel in the early twenties," Gretchen explained to Sheila, pointedly ignoring my sarcasm. "Most of it burned in 1930. Before there was a road, a cable car came up from the bottom of the mountain, which is how everyone got up here when this place was in full operation. You can't see it now, but in the day you will; there's a steep drop about fifty feet from the pond. The road will be paved by the time this place opens next summer. Right now I'm open by special arrangement and for friends who just need to get away."

The ceilings on the first floor were high and arched. It didn't seem like there was another level above this one, but a staircase curled gently up toward a balcony that split off into two hallways going in either direction. The foyer led into a large dining room that had floor-to-ceiling windows all the way around, with an adjacent ballroom that had a stage and orchestra pit.

"Okay, stop gawking and follow me," Gretchen said as she took my hand to tug me toward the stairs.

Gretchen showed us to our rooms and we unpacked. Then we met her downstairs for sandwiches in the kitchen. I was glad that I'd brought Sheila with me to meet Gretchen. I was pleased that my New York family was coming together and a little disappointed when Ken went to bed early. He said he was tired from the drive, but I had a sneaking suspicion that he didn't want us to worry that there was something else going on with him. It was typical of Ken to internalize all that he was feeling in order to protect us from the truth of his condition. In a way, I resented it. I wished he would just open up and let us know that he needed us. Especially after all of the times that I had needed him. I wanted him to allow me to give back some of what he'd given me.

Not long after Ken went to bed, Martin and I followed suit. Sheila and I were rooming next to one another on the third floor. Both rooms had skylights but the night was too cloudy for stars. I could just barely make out the shadows of the mountains as I gazed from my window, which overlooked the valley. I heard a knock on the door and opened it to Sheila carrying a tray with two mugs and a steaming pot. She set it down on the table by the windows. I moved from the edge of the bed to one of the overstuffed chairs by the table.

"Where did you find that?"

"While I was chatting with Gretchen in the kitchen, I noticed this great tea service and wanted to take advantage of it. Classy, huh? Apparently, Jane Gorman, the television producer, is one of the investors in this place. Gretchen says it's going to be a retreat for businesswomen during the spring and part of the summer. During the second half of the summer, it will be a family resort. I think it's a great idea."

"Gretchen has the Midas touch. As soon as she started handling Ken's money—" I cut myself off, feeling like I was about to overstep boundaries.

"What is Ken's story?" Sheila asked in a way that made me remember that she was probably the least harmful person to share his background with. In fact, it might be a good thing for her to know, considering her limited engagement with the gay community.

"Oh god, where should I begin?"

"The beginning?"

"A very good place to start," I chuckled, ready to break into a rendition of "Do Re Mi."

Sheila poured a cup of tea for me then one for herself. I sank back into the chair and stared out the window as if the view would make the story of Ken more clear to me. I began slowly, wanting everything to come out right.

"Ken came of age in the Stonewall era—do you know what that is?"

She nodded and curled up in the chair, looking like a little girl getting ready for a bedtime story.

"He worked at various jobs in the city and performed in off-Broadway theater after graduating from high school. He had a lot of affairs with wealthy, closeted men who were more than happy to part with money or surprise him with gifts to keep Ken from exposing them as homosexuals to the press, their business partners, or their wives.

"In the late seventies, Ken found love with the owner of a presti-gious bank in Manhattan that had branches all over the tri-state area. This guy had a penthouse apartment in Manhattan, a home in Connecticut, and a brownstone on the Upper West Side where he housed Ken and spent every other weeknight with him. His name was Samuel. He had a wife and two young children who went to private school on the East Side, where the penthouse was. Sam-uel would 'work late' nights, spending his evenings with Ken at the brownstone, then go home to the wife and kids and live his farcical heterosexual existence with the picture-perfect family.

"Ken could endure living this way if it meant he would receive Samuel's love. And he did. Samuel loved him with all his heart, but he believed if he left his family to be with Ken, everything in his life would crumble down around him. As much as he loved Ken, he couldn't give up the world he'd created for himself before Ken had arrived in it. He also felt a certain responsibility to his wife and chil-dren. Maybe when the kids grew up and he was nearer to retire-ment, the time would be right to think about leaving that life behind for Ken.

"Ken didn't want that responsibility and was usually content to be the 'other woman,' building his whole life around Samuel and the time they shared, cutting himself off from old friends who were celebrating the freedom of what was then called 'gay liberation.' Samuel got him work in his bank's television ads portraying a teller who explained to viewers why they should open accounts *today*. Samuel taught Ken about opening retirement accounts, high-inter-est yields, the stock market, how to buy low and sell high. He even gave him money to invest with.

"In 1987, Samuel had a heart attack and died without saying goodbye to Ken. Ken found out when he saw the report on the news that night about the sudden death of one of Manhattan's wealthiest men. He saw Samuel's wife and children sobbing and shielding their faces as they were led by the police from Beth Israel Hospital to their car. Big local news. No one had known to break it to Ken gently.

"He was in shock, but felt jealous that they were there and not him. They got to publicly mourn their loss and he would have to hide his, because Samuel was a well-respected man in the straight world. The heroic efforts of the drag queens of Stonewall weren't enough to change Samuel's life, or Ken's, for that matter. Ken was forced to take a hard look at his life as it was played for him by the evening news. He realized he needed help. He'd abandoned his friends for love and wasn't sure if he could turn to them.

"Ken knew he only had a short while before Samuel's lawyers discovered the brownstone and the secrets it held. I would have donned Jackie Kennedy widow's weeds and shown up at the funeral. Not Ken. With no time to mourn his loss, he called several of his old friends, who were more than happy to help. They set to work 'straightening up' the brownstone and removing evidence of Samuel's homosexual life. When it was done, Ken settled into an apartment on the West Side, allowing his depression to finally take over.

"Everything changed in that moment when Samuel died, and Ken began to feel as if their life had never happened, even as if he had meant nothing to Samuel. Then, after several weeks, he received a letter from one of Samuel's attorneys. Samuel had left a mysterious bequest in his will, a gift of five hundred thousand dollars to a stranger named Ken Bruckner.

"This all happened around the time I met Ken. He was mourning Samuel by day and masking it as Judy by night. He told me later that meeting me saved him from giving up. I reminded him of himself when he was all alone in the city. He had no idea how to survive after Samuel, just as I had no idea how to survive after my failing acting career and shattered dreams. He taught me everything the drag queens and Samuel had taught him. I benefited from his knowledge and took it all a step further.

"I owe a lot to Ken. He helped create Princess 2Di4 and the person I am today. He's such a huge part of my life. He deserves a lot more than I'm giving him."

I felt my eyes widen as the realization of what I'd just said to Sheila hit me. She didn't know about 2Di4. I turned my head slowly, expecting to see her wearing a vexed look. When my eyes met hers, I could tell she knew. She had a slight smile on her face and her eyes darted away for a second, then she said, "I know about 2Di4."

"Martin?" I queried.

"He slipped the night we went to the theater. We all were a little tipsy and worried about you." She reached over and lightly tapped my cast. "I feel like you're upset about something, Daniel. What is it you think you're doing wrong? Giving up drag? Working for Blaine?"

I stared at her with an uncomfortable realization.

"I think living a lie is wrong," I finally said. "I think what Ken really deserved was the chance to openly enjoy his life with Samuel. I don't mean Samuel shouldn't have taken care of his wife and children. That goes without saying. But why does a person have to be cheated out of the one thing most people take for granted? Time. Time to be who you are. Time to be with the people you love. All Samuel's money couldn't buy them more than that half-life they lived together. And nothing can buy Ken time now. It's just so fucking unfair."

I stopped, afraid I'd said too much. It was not my place to tell Sheila that Ken had AIDS.

"I don't think Ken would say he has regrets, Daniel. I think he'd protect Samuel even now, even from you. That's not a story about lost love. It's a story about love. That may be the part of it Ken would rather you learn from."

"I just don't feel like lying anymore, Sheila. I really don't feel like helping anyone else lie. You know what? Sometimes I think you're the only person in my life who's comfortable inside her own skin."

"What do you mean?"

"The rest of us spend our lives being someone else. Everyone I know is either a drag queen or an actor—of one type or another."

Sheila's eyes fell to her tea as she stirred cream into it.

"Blaine's gay, isn't he?" she finally asked. When I said nothing, she looked at me. "You don't have to tell me. I saw the two of you in your garden the night you had dinner with him. You tried to gloss it over later, but if that's one of the lies that has you so unhappy, forget it. It's better that I know. Remember the story I told you about the woman who stole my man?"

"Sydney?" I asked.

"You know about her?" she gasped, amazed.

"I just found out this week when she called the office. Blaine told me a little bit about their relationship."

"*Relationship,*" she scoffed. "Blaine was more like a trophy. She went after him and didn't care who or what was in her way. Looks like she didn't win much after all, doesn't it?"

"Blaine's not so bad," I said. "He's just confused, I guess. I was honest about one thing—nothing happened between us that night. Nothing has ever happened between Blaine and me."

"That makes two of us," she said with a little grin.

"Well, at least you know it isn't because of you," I said. "After all, a man would have to be gay not to want the next top Metropole model."

That earned me another grin.

"I don't know," she said. "Look at some of the former Metro models. Bulimia, heroin, messy divorces from rock stars."

"You'll be fine," I said. "You're grounded, Sheila, which is one reason why I enjoy my time with you. I always feel so calm when we're together."

"What do you want to be when you grow up, Daniel Stephenson? What would make you comfortable inside your skin?"

"My god, if you knew how much I wish I could answer that question."

"I think we should make a pact," Sheila said. "You help me keep my feet on the ground while I dazzle the world with my *Vogue* covers, and I'll help you keep your head in the clouds."

"How so?"

"Once there was a boy with a dream. The big, bad world wouldn't let him be the prince of Broadway so he became the princess of Downtown. But you still dream, don't you? Your face the night we saw *Anything Goes* told that story. I can't make your dreams come true. But if you never try, neither can you."

"You know, I'm really not unhappy with what I'm doing now. I mean, it may not be glamorous like modeling, or fun like drag, or fulfilling like acting, but I do wake up with a sense of purpose. I feel like my life as 2Di4 kept me wrapped in some kind of gay cocoon. It's a part of the world I don't want to lose, but it's not the whole world. More than anything else, what I want to be right now is a good friend."

"Can you make a career of that?" she asked.

"Depends on how good I am," I quipped.

"Okay, you joke. But one thing is not going to happen. You are not going to play Ken to Blaine's Samuel."

"You don't think Blaine could fall in love with me?" I asked.

"I don't think Blaine can perpetuate the myth of being straight the way Samuel did," she said. "I wonder why Sydney's calling him, what she wants? Not that it matters. I may as well just face it—I am not going to be the next Mrs. Blaine Dunhill."

"That makes two of us," I echoed her earlier comment and we smiled together like old friends. "Since we're being honest, I invited you this weekend for a reason. Blaine said Sydney was upset when she found out you're living with him. He thought she might confront you. I figured if she had, you might be upset and need to get away."

She thought that over and finally said, "She probably could upset me. She has no scruples when she's on a mission. I haven't seen her for years. I tried really hard to be friends with both of them after she took my place. Remember, I told you how I try to stay friends with my ex-boyfriends? After a while, it was easy to stay friends with him. He's been part of my family my whole life. He's my brother's best friend. I don't think Jake knows Blaine is gay."

"Would it bother him?"

"I have no idea," she shrugged. "I'd like to think not. Jake's a pretty good guy. Anyway, after Blaine married Sydney, I felt sorry for him. He seemed so lonely to me. I figured that probably happened to everyone who got married. You know, they couldn't hang out with their friends anymore. They had to be mature and serious and plan for the future. Blaine became this total workaholic, and no one saw very much of him, not even Jake.

"Then Blaine took the job in New York. Since Sydney left at the same time, we all assumed she was with him. I had no idea, until I got here, that she wasn't. He told me she'd had this opportunity to go to some art school in Chicago, so they commuted to see each other. It didn't take me long to see through that. I mean, she never called, he never talked about her, and the only trips he took were business trips. I didn't feel it was my place to ask questions. I didn't want anyone back home to think I was filling her shoes, though. Or more accurately, her place in his bed, so I sort of went along with his charade. But Blaine seemed as lonely as ever, and I began to wonder why he didn't at least try to rekindle our relationship . . . until I saw him in the garden that night with you. Everything clicked into place. Their breakup, his silence about it, the way he never showed the slightest interest in seducing me." She grinned, then became serious again. "All those years of pretending to be something he wasn't. It makes me feel really sad for him. If he could just tell the truth—"

"Coming out doesn't ensure happiness," I reminded her. "I haven't done so hot in the romance department myself. At least Blaine has a very successful career."

"Martin told me you were quite the sensation."

"That was 2Di4, not me," I answered. "Sometimes drag seems like just another closet."

She shook her head and asked, "What one thing in your life makes you happy now?"

"My garden," I answered. "And even it's about to die."

"Not die, Daniel. Rest. So it can bloom again for you in the spring."

"Is that what you think I'm doing? Resting?"

"There's nothing wrong with taking a break, is there?" she asked.

"No, I guess there isn't," I said as I yawned, feeling the soothing herbal tea settle into my veins, calming me. I shut my eyes for a second and the chair seemed to envelop me.

I opened my eyes, feeling light beating against my eyelids. I was confronted by the most beautiful sunrise over the mountains. They were red and orange and sprawling across the sky. I looked to my right and saw that Sheila, too, had been captured by the chair. Her blond hair fell around her shoulders like a blanket. She was beautiful in the early sunlight and looked posed, as if someone were painting her portrait. She took in a big breath and squinted as her eyes cracked open.

"We slept together?" She let out a soft chuckle.

"What will the neighbors think?" I responded, standing and stretching. I heard footsteps pass outside the door then head down the stairs. "Should we see what the boys are doing today? I would love to go on a hike."

"Sounds fabulous!"

Sheila stood and stretched like a cat. After we took turns in the bathroom, she picked up the tea service and headed for the door. I followed her down the stairs. We went from the foyer into the kitchen, where Gretchen was buzzing around, already showered and ready to start her day.

"Good morning! Welcome to the Happy Hollow Resort! Would

you like coffee or tea?" Gretchen smiled as she flicked on the blender. "I'm making a soy milk, banana, and wheat germ smoothie. Any takers?"

I wrinkled my nose and went to one of the huge refrigerators with stainless steel doors.

"You just sit back and let me serve my favorite guests," Gretchen commanded. "I have eggs, vegetarian bacon, and sausage . . . whatever you want, I've probably got it somewhere. What'll it be?"

Following a tomato, feta, and basil omelet washed down with one of Gretchen's total Vitamin C smoothies, I felt ready for a long day of hiking. After parting to shower and dress, Sheila and I met in the foyer and headed outside into the brisk fall air. My eyes were met with dazzling sun and clean air. My lungs felt light after being stuck in the stuffy air of the city for so long. I had almost forgotten what it was like not to have a constant influx of air pollution. I was sure that after a while the body became dependent on the smog, that people who lived in big cities physically evolved into another species because of the air. I was convinced it gave us tougher insides, even though, as of late, I hadn't been feeling all that tough.

At least, my newly reemerging positive inner voice urged, you are beginning to move forward with your life.

I felt lighter because of a dawning realization. I was beginning to feel like a whole person, rather than a shadow hiding behind a stronger persona that I had created in order to impress, seduce, and fool everyone I knew.

Ken emerged from the compound with his car keys in hand, followed a few moments later by Martin. Ken looked well rested and well dressed. He obviously had not planned on a day of hiking.

"Where are you two off to?" I asked.

"Martin and I are going into town to look for antiques. I'm having my spare room redone and Martin insists on having the last word on what he calls 'style.' "

Martin playfully smacked Ken on the back of the head.

"I have to keep those tacky throw pillows from sneaking their way into every room of my home," Ken teased.

"Then what will I throw at you?"

"Words," Ken replied. "They've always been your best weapons." He glanced from Sheila to me. "You two look like you're going to engage in some serious mountain climbing."

We were wearing our tough hiking boots. Amazingly, we'd both brought the same Nike headbands to keep our blond locks from getting matted to our faces.

"Sisters, sisters," Martin sang.

"You joke, but they do look alike," Ken said, waving goodbye as he went to the car. Sheila and I waved back and blew kisses as Ken and Martin got in and turned down the road toward the bottom of the mountain.

"Which trail should we take?" I asked. "The one with the blue markers is easiest, yellow is intermediate, and red has some actual rock climbing."

"I feel rugged today," Sheila said as she tossed back her blond hair and flashed the smile that I knew would soon be on the cover of *Mademoiselle*. "Let's take the blue trail."

"Rugged, huh?"

We walked behind the hotel to where the trails led up and away. It was easy going up a path that was worn down from use. During the summer many tourists and locals hiked up the trails to the lookout tower, which closed at the beginning of October.

Sheila and I trekked in silence. We both had many things to contemplate. I kept picturing my night with Jeremy, allowing the *what if's?* to climb into my thoughts. I knew I couldn't let them have too much power, though. Romantically, Jeremy and I were dead, but we'd been through so much that we couldn't just stop. The natural result was friendship, but as with all friendships that evolved from a romantic relationship, the lines between us were blurry.

I emerged from my thoughts, realizing that the end of the trail was nearing. It turned into gravel as the small ranger's cabin came into view. The trees were all evergreen and let out their sweet scent. The air was also cooler and seemed even cleaner.

I turned around to look at Sheila. She had stopped on the path and was looking out at something. I turned and went back down to her to see what had her so enrapt. She was staring over the Hudson Valley in the direction of Manhattan. It wasn't visible, but from this height, I could see the highway that led there and the reservoir that gave the city its water. It was beautiful. It was where the Catskills began; flat earth was suddenly interrupted by glorious hills.

"What do you see?" I asked her.

"You know what, Daniel? When I look for the city and don't see it, I can still feel it. I feel it calling me back. I am happy here, yes, but I finally found where I belong. At first I wasn't sure. I think it was because of how things were going with me and Blaine. Now that I definitely know it would never work, I still want to stay in New York. I belong, Daniel. Do you know I've never felt that before?"

"I think with your charm, you'd belong anywhere."

I smiled at her. After the discussion the night before I felt totally comfortable hearing about all of the details that made Sheila who she was. I knew at that moment we had something solid.

"I've always felt like everything around me was right, but for someone else. Eau Claire, not that anyone feels like they belong there, college, everywhere I've been, I've felt out of sync."

"Let me tell you, I think you're just what New York City needs."

"Maybe," she said. "Let's go to the lookout and see what the rest of the world looks like."

We made our way past the ranger's cabin to the lookout. We climbed the metal stairs to the top. I opened the hatch and climbed through. Once up there, I could see for miles in all directions. I looked deep into the heart of the mountains and turned around to face the wide belly of the Hudson Valley. I felt small, but more importantly, I felt like a part of it all.

We turned to exchange a delighted look, and she voiced my thoughts, as she seemed to do so effortlessly.

"It's almost like a moment happens when you feel right inside your skin, and then wherever you are seems right, too."

I nodded and she reached for me. We stood that way for a long time, hands clasped, staring out at the world.

The magic of that moment cast its spell over the rest of the weekend. I continued to sense that Ken was preoccupied. But it was impossible to fret too much when I was enjoying the easy companionship that developed among him, Martin, Sheila, Gretchen, and me.

Even after returning to the city and resuming my routine, I felt as if that magic cushioned me. No work crisis flustered me. With Blaine still out of the office, I was able to focus entire days on the research he wanted. In the evenings I was surprised when people began shrugging into coats and saying their goodnights.

Friday night I thought about going to Club Chaos to see if Martin had a new act yet, but apparently my body had other ideas. I fell asleep on the couch, oblivious to the sound of my book hitting the floor. Saturday morning nudged me awake like an amorous lover, demanding that I fulfill all urgent needs. I whimpered, remembering that this was my day to sleep as late as I wanted. But my internal clock had officially readjusted. Now I was an early riser whether or not I liked it.

It was a beautiful day. After puttering a while in the garden, I showered and took a walk, breathing in the sights and smells of the reviving city. I still felt rejuvenated by my weekend and decided to walk down to the Village. Though the terrain was less rugged than the mountains, I remembered how clearheaded I'd felt when Sheila and I had returned from hiking and our ravenous appetites afterward. My reward along the way to the Village would be donuts from Krispy Kreme.

My progress down Broadway was slowed by two girls in Times Square as they stopped to gaze at the shows listed at the Tkts booth. They had the look of Kennedy grandchildren, healthy and toothsome. They could have been mistaken for sisters except that one had her hand tucked into the back pocket of the other. Their romance seemed to cast them in a shimmering glow and I felt envious as I stepped around them.

As I scanned the groups of other early-morning risers for eye tag candidates, it seemed all I saw were couples. Two beautiful boys who couldn't have been more than twenty were passing a single Starbucks cup between them. Outside a souvenir shop, the proprietor and his wife were bickering amiably about how to most attractively arrange figurines of characters from *Cats*. As I passed a florist's kiosk, a man in the previous night's leather regalia was sentimentally tucking a rosebud into the T-shirt pocket of his companion.

My need to feel like part of something was sudden and sharp. It was too early to call any of my friends, so I bought a cup of coffee when I got to Krispy Kreme and tried to recapture my moment of well-being from the ranger's station. But as I began to relax into it, two men came through the door. They were typical Chelsea clones—shaved heads, blue jeans, white T-shirts under leather bomber jackets—except for one odd detail. They had a baby. The ease with which they handled the baby and all her paraphernalia bespoke routine. They were obviously a family and I couldn't stop staring at them, trying to figure out their story.

When one of them caught me, he grinned and said, "Amazing what modern medicine can do, huh?"

"Evidently," was all I could say.

"I'm Greg. He's Dean. And this"—here he rumpled the hair of the contentedly chattering toddler—"is Tish."

"Daniel," I said.

Dean nodded briefly at me before hiding behind his newspaper.

"We met her mom through GMHC," Greg said. "She was pretty sick, didn't have any family, and Tish's father was long gone. Dean helped take care of her. Finally we just moved her and Tish in with us. It's easier."

"But her mother isn't—"

"Oh no, she's much better. Dean and I are Tish's legal guardians, you know, just in case. But mostly, the four of us are a family now."

My throat got tight as I experienced, again, the pride of being a gay man at the turn of the century in New York. I felt a momentary yearning that Blaine would allow himself to connect with all this. That feeling was followed by another wave of loneliness. I said goodbye to Greg and Dean and bought a mix of donuts before heading outside. I felt a pressing need for someone familiar, someone who knew me and would understand, without explanations, how I was feeling.

The doorman recognized me from earlier visits and didn't stop me from going inside and taking the elevator to the fifth floor. I inhaled deeply, preparing myself for anything. It was too early on a Saturday morning to arrive without warning, but until I actually knocked, I hadn't been sure I wouldn't lose my nerve.

Robert opened the door with a surprised expression.

"Daniel?"

"Robert. I brought donuts. Coffee made yet?"

"I've been up for hours," Robert said, leading me inside. "But if you came to see Jeremy, he isn't here."

"I guess I should have called, huh?" I asked.

"It's unusual for him to be out and about so early," Robert said. "He met his parents for breakfast. Then they're doing a museum or something before they take in *Anything Goes* tonight."

While Robert went to pour our coffee and put the donuts on a plate, I looked around. The apartment was as immaculate as ever. Robert's decorating was almost spartan; even so, the few personal touches and subdued lighting made everything look very welcoming. It was odd how nothing had changed, as if Jeremy had never come to live with him.

"Where's Jeremy's stuff?" I asked Robert when he returned.

Robert smiled and said, "Follow me."

I trailed behind him down the narrow hallway, feeling a bit as if I were intruding. He opened a door and said, "I gave him the bigger room."

I laughed. Jeremy's bed was unmade, covers piled in the middle as always. Every surface in the room was hidden by *Playbills*, publicity photos, accumulated junk that bore mute testimony to Jeremy's various hobbies and interests. A bulletin board was crammed full of snapshots, many of them taken on our trip to Oregon. The faded tapestry of Mama Caprellian's Victorian loveseat was hidden by a pile of clothes. I remembered going with him to haul it from his grandmother's attic over the protests of a dozen Caprellians of various ages. It hadn't mattered; Jeremy was always his grandmother's favorite and she would refuse him nothing.

We returned to the living room and I settled myself on one end of the couch as Robert pressed a switch on the stereo, filling the apartment with the softness of Chopin, before he sat on the opposite end of the couch. He nervously grabbed a small pillow and picked at nonexistent lint.

"I guess Jeremy was telling me the truth," I said after taking a swallow of coffee, which had some delicate flavor I couldn't identify. "I mean, the separate rooms."

"You jump right in, don't you?" Robert commented. When I remained silent, he said, "We do. We aren't lovers, Daniel. We had a fling. If you'd been a little more understanding and waited it out, I doubt Jeremy would ever have moved in with me."

"Jeremy and I did not have an open relationship," I said. "Infidelity was hardly some little thing I could overlook."

"Then you both lost," Robert said. "Unless your unexpected appearance means you've had a change of heart?"

"No. I have not had a change of heart, at least not where Jeremy's concerned. I mean, I'd like to stay friends with him. But that's all."

"Ah," Robert replied, taking a sip of coffee.

Except for the music, we sat in silence for a time. I had no intention of elaborating on my feelings about Jeremy to Robert.

"Robert, I suppose I owe you an apology."

Robert looked at me with one eyebrow raised. I couldn't tell if the look on his face meant, *Well? Where is it?* or *What on earth are you talking about?*

"I was pretty awful to you the last time we saw each other," I continued. "I need for you to know I really am sorry. At one time, our friendship was valuable to me, and I suppose on a certain level it still is."

"You don't have to apologize to me. I understand. You were having a rough time with all that was going on. Believe me, I was not in favor of going to your apartment that day, but Andy insisted. I must admit that I wanted to see you, but I didn't feel the time was right. I didn't think it was a good idea for all of us to descend on you at once. I guess I was correct, judging by your reaction."

"Nonetheless, I never should've said what I did, and for that I am sorry."

"Consider the topic closed," he said with a wave of his hand.

Again, Chopin provided the only relief from awkward silence.

"Would you like more coffee?"

"Please," I answered.

"To tell you the truth, I've felt like an idiot since that day. I avoided you like the plague on the opening night of the show," Robert called from the kitchen.

"Yeah, well, there was plenty going on that night, as well," I muttered.

"I beg your pardon?" Robert asked.

"Nothing," I called back.

Robert returned with two steaming cups of coffee. The Chopin was beginning to make me nervous because it only seemed to amplify our silence. Robert reclaimed his space on the end of the sofa, and I recrossed my legs in the other direction.

"Robert, I think—"

"Daniel, I couldn't control it. I didn't mean to force myself on you that way, but I had to tell you, show you, do something, to let you know I wished you were more than a friend. Truth be told, I still do wish that. I can't help it. As for Jeremy, I made a mistake."

"Honestly, I've been avoiding you, too. I overreacted that day. I behaved badly. But the timing was all wrong." Deep breath. "And maybe I acted that way because there was a little something in me that liked it."

There. I'd said it. Robert looked up from the pillow he was holding. His soft, brown eyes were childlike in their surprise.

"You—"

"Yeah," I cut him off.

We looked at each other and I shrugged my shoulders.

"Well," Robert finally said, "that was the last thing I expected to hear you say this morning."

"At least we have a flavored coffee to celebrate this moment in our lives," I wisecracked.

Tension wrapped itself around every corner of the room as we stared at each other. Robert shifted on the end of the sofa as if he had to pee, and I tried to keep my composure as I lifted the coffee cup to my lips. I wasn't sure whether this moment was a sincere desire to explore something with Robert or a reaction to the barrage of couples from my morning walk.

Chopin paused and there was a clicking from the CD player and the opening notes from *Anything Goes* began to play. Robert leapt up and dashed to the stereo.

"Anything but that!"

I laughed and watched Robert from behind as he scanned his CDs for something else to play. His every move was graceful and I remembered dance had been part of his training. Time seemed frozen as my eyes devoured him. The scrubbed look of his pink-tipped ears, the sharp cut of his hair, his well-shaped head, his neck, the nice squaring of his shoulders . . .

He turned and we stared at each other as I measured the distance between us.

"Daniel?"

"I can't," I gasped. "I don't know why. I just—I can't."

"Is it Jeremy?"

"I don't know," I said honestly. "God, I'm confused."

"Just tell me how you feel."

"I was attracted to you from the beginning. If you and Jeremy hadn't—I really did want you," I finished helplessly.

"Past tense," was all Robert said.

His eyes were so beautiful when they were full of tears. Seeing them took me right back to that day in my garden. All I had to do was cross the room and we could replay that scene a different way with a happier outcome.

So why am I frozen to this couch, I wondered.

"I don't want to make another mistake," I said miserably.

Robert gave a hurt laugh and said, "Maybe you should leave. I care about you too much to be an experiment, Daniel."

"Whether you believe it or not, I care about *you* too much to make you an experiment," I answered.

He didn't move as I walked to the door. I turned to take one last look at him.

"Don't," he whispered.

I left the apartment without insulting him by saying any of the stupid, inadequate words that were all I could seem to think of.

Now what, my inner voice demanded.

"I have no idea," I said out loud.

TWELVE

I walked in a daze to Christopher Street, where I saw the Wormhole, which had replaced one of my favorite pre-performance bars, Mama's. I laughed at the implications of its new name. I'd heard it was full of cyber-geeks and trekkies. It was not even noon, but I needed something to take the edge off my nerves. I paused in front of the door then stepped inside to face a garish sight.

It resembled the bridge of the *Starship Enterprise*. There were computers in two corners of the bar. The screens displayed starscape screensavers. The place was empty except for the bartender, who leaned against the bar watching a rerun of an old "Star Trek" episode. Above, written on three chalkboards, were the names of drinks for geeks. The first board was titled "Original Cast," the second, "The Next Generation," and the third was titled "Deep Space."

I surveyed the drinks and decided I needed to be propelled into the farthest reaches of the galaxy. I ordered a Warp Speed from the Deep Space board. I took my drink to a section of the bar that looked like Guinan's domain in "The Next Generation," half expecting Whoopi Goldberg herself to appear.

My eyes were fixed on a television screen showing *Star Trek II: The Wrath of Khan,* when I felt hot breath on my neck. I closed my eyes and couldn't decide whether to be carried away or to turn around and slap whoever had decided I was going to help him explore the final frontier. Then I felt soft lips on the back of my neck and a shiver ran through me.

Why did he have to follow me, I wondered. My mind knows getting involved with him is a bad idea. But my body says resistance is futile.

The gentle kisses continued and gave way to light brushes of lips on the nape of my neck. It was unfortunate that this started before I was halfway into my first drink. After the second or third, I might have succumbed and gone with the moment. Sadly, it was barely noon on a Saturday, and I was still quite sober.

"You know," I began, took a big swallow of the drink, winced at the impact of cold alcohol on an empty stomach (Whoa! What the hell was in this thing?), and continued, "you really shouldn't follow people, Robert. It could be taken as an act of desperation."

The kisses stopped.

"It could, maybe, but I'm not Robert," a strong, deep voice intoned from behind me.

I winced again, feeling the blood drain from my face, and slowly turned around to look into Blaine's green eyes. I couldn't believe how off my instincts were on this one. I decided the Deep Space drink was stronger than I'd realized. I also knew I'd better stop this in a hurry; my morning had left me feeling defenseless.

"Shouldn't you be meeting with divorce attorneys or something?" I asked, my voice dripping with sarcasm and also what I thought might be Jack Daniels in my mystery drink.

"Not even a welcome home? I saw you come in and couldn't resist your neck," Blaine said with that pearly smile.

"Caps."

Oh god, did I say that out loud, I wondered with panic.

"What?"

Damn, I did.

"Nothing. What do you want, Blaine? I thought we agreed this was not going to happen," I rattled like a recurring character on a Fox prime-time drama.

"I missed you. We're not at the office. I'm sober this time. And it's just a short cab ride to my apartment."

My mouth fell open. I was caught off guard by the blatant invitation for sex with a man who . . . well, sex with a man. It had been a long time since I'd had sex. Except for my one indiscretion at Pride, the last time had been with Jeremy. That had been like watching *The Wizard of Oz* for the millionth time. It piqued my interest, but I knew how it would turn out.

My mind raced with the options that lay before me. I could go home with Blaine and have what might be the most incredible sex I'd ever had. Or I could stay here on the bridge of the *Enterprise,* get drunk, and create my own version of the Holodeck.

"Beam me up," I said.

"I'm sorry?" Blaine looked confused.

"That means yes," I explained.

Blaine wasted no time beaming us into a cab uptown. The whole way up Eighth Avenue I berated myself for giving in to lust and temptation. I'd decided against pursuing a personal relationship with Blaine. My hormones reminded me it wasn't a relationship I was pursuing at the moment. It was exploring the regions of Blaine's hard body. To seek out excitement and ecstasy. To boldly go where no man—

"Blaine, have you ever *had* sex with a man?" I asked.

"Um, no." Blaine glanced uncomfortably at the driver in the front seat and whispered to me, with a little wink, "Actually, you'll be the first."

Where no man has gone before!

We reached his apartment building and frantically paid the driver. Blaine nearly broke his key in the lock of the front door trying to get us inside. Once in the front hall, he grabbed me by the shoulders and kissed me hard on the mouth. I was in the mood to be manhandled, so I gave in and kissed him back.

"Good lord, what were you drinking in that bar?" Blaine asked when we came up for air.

"Why, is it really terrible?" I asked, horrified that I might have offending cotton-mouth.

"No, it's really refreshing," Blaine said in amazement and kissed me again.

I had to admit that a sober Blaine was a sexually gratifying Blaine. He did things with his tongue that seemed next to impossible, and I couldn't wait to feel it somewhere other than inside my mouth. His hands roamed my entire body, under my striped DKNY shirt and inside the loose waist of my Helmut Lang jeans. I pushed the sound of a cash register out of my mind as I contemplated projectile buttons, broken zippers, ripped seams.

My next thought was not so easily dismissed.

"What about Sheila?" I gasped as we fumbled with each other up the stairs.

"She's at a test shoot," Blaine answered, removing his shirt on the second landing.

I was treated to the sight of his washboard abs. I remembered my quest to run my tongue over them, realizing there was no time like the present. I grabbed his waist, fell to my knees, and began licking around his navel.

I took his *Mmmmmm* as a compliment and continued covering his stomach with kisses, nips, and flicks of my tongue. I unbuckled his belt and considered lashing him to the banister with it.

"Come on," Blaine urged, practically dragging me up the next flight of stairs.

Once within the confines of his apartment, we began shucking our clothes. I was happy that Blaine made no attempt to shut his curtains or draw any blinds. I was never shy at performing for an audience, and the thought that a neighbor might be watching us with binoculars only heightened my arousal. After kicking off my Prada lace-ups—clothes, I thought, am I thinking of fashion to avoid facing how much I want this?—I bypassed the couch and lay down on the carpeted floor in front of the open window. I wanted to give any potential witnesses full viewing pleasure.

Blaine covered me with his large frame and began kissing me all over. It was just like the night at my place, only this time he knew what he was doing and would remember it the next day. And what he didn't know, I would be more than happy to teach him.

"Do you have—"

"Condoms?" Blaine interrupted and began nuzzling my ear with his lips. "Yes."

"That's good, but I was wondering if you have to put—"

Just then Blaine tensed all over, the muscles in his thighs and abs getting hard as a rock. Dexter, having jumped on Blaine's back, poked his head over Blaine's shoulder, looking at me and twitching his ears.

"—Dexter up," I finished.

Blaine placed his knee between mine for leverage and reached around and plucked Dexter off his back, bringing the cat between us. He placed him on my chest and began stroking his neck, just as he'd stroked me minutes ago.

"Someone is awfully curious to know what's going on," Blaine observed with a wicked grin.

"Now, now," I pretended to scold, "we must think of the children. What would Social Services say?"

"If they knew what we were subjecting our baby to?" Blaine spoke in a baby voice in Dexter's ear.

"Yes, if they knew the baby was the only thing separating your hot, strong, naked body from mine . . ." My voice trailed off as Blaine rose to a kneeling position, bringing Dexter with him.

The sight of the tiny cat being held against Blaine's chest in his massive arms took the words right out of my mouth. Blaine gave Dexter a tender kiss on the head and gently placed him on the floor, whereupon he ran to the kitchen.

Blaine put one arm around my shoulders, the other under my knees, and easily lifted me off the floor.

"I don't want to be disturbed again," he whispered.

Feeling like the heroine in some bodice ripper, I was carried to the bedroom, where he placed me on the bed and never broke contact from my body from that point onward. Gripping my shoulders, he kissed me hard, and I held on to him, remembering why I liked men so much. I liked being held hard, feeling the strength in his arms as we clasped each other tightly. I slid my hands up the expanse of his back and grabbed on, pressing our bodies together even more forcefully.

"Oh, yeah," I moaned, as I enjoyed the friction of our bodies rubbing together. I didn't care if I sounded like a badly scripted porn movie.

Blaine reached around my back with one hand and rolled over, pulling me with him until I was on top of him.

"What do you like?" he asked, looking deeply into my eyes from below me.

"I like this. I like being with you like this," I said.

He reached out and grabbed my head with both hands and kissed me deeply. When he broke the kiss, he began kissing the palms of my hands.

"You taste salty," he said and started laughing. "I don't know why I said that."

"It's okay," I said. "I'm nervous, too."

He smiled up at me, hugged me hard, and then surprised me by knowing exactly what he was doing.

It was that thought that made me ask later, "Are you sure you've never done that before?"

Blaine laughed shyly and gave me another kiss on my forehead. I untangled the sheets and moved myself out of the wet spot and closer to Blaine. He wrapped me in his arms again, and I found myself lying on top of him. I tried to maintain a casual feeling, but it was next to impossible as I found myself anxious about what might happen next.

I was surprised to realize how glad it made me that he wasn't the type to jump up, towel off, say something lame like "Thanks," and wait for me to take the hint and leave. I wanted this moment to linger. I wanted to watch movies in bed with him. I wanted to have sex again. But I was sure a fourth time would be asking too much of even a stud like Blaine.

"Really," Blaine said with an embarrassed smile, "that was honestly my first time. My first three times."

"Well, you don't need me to tell you how good you were," I commented, grinning in spite of myself at his blatantly smug expression.

"I don't?" Blaine slapped me lightly upside the head.

"Okay." I giggled. "I can take a hint. You were good. Oh man, were you good. I had no idea I could stay upside down that long."

"Well, it was worth breaking the lamp, that's for sure."

We both looked at the shattered remnants of what had been a bedside lamp and burst out laughing.

"Oh my god, I'm so sorry. I thought I had broken something, but wasn't sure," I said. "It's this damn cast. It makes me all clumsy."

"It's okay," Blaine said after catching his breath, "I told you it was worth it. You were worth it."

He grasped my shoulders in his large hands again and drew me up for another prolonged kiss.

What was it I had against this guy anyway, I wondered.

"About Sydney," I said, pulling back a little.

Blaine shook his head and said, "Listen, how 'bout if time starts right here and now. I don't ask you questions; you don't ask me questions. About before. We've been safe, right? So what else matters?"

"How 'bout if time started about noon today?" I amended.

"Deal," he said.

The kiss resumed. Whatever his experience, the man knew how to kiss.

"What was that?" Blaine suddenly asked, breaking away.

"Huh?"

"I thought I heard something," Blaine said in a hushed tone. We both got very quiet and listened. Nothing.

"Maybe it's the cat—" I began, but was interrupted by the sound of a cabinet door opening and banging closed.

We looked at each other with wide-eyed expressions. I fought back a sadistic, startled urge to break into nervous giggles, and Blaine put a finger to my lips. He mouthed Sheila's name to me very sternly. I shrugged my shoulders in an attempt to convey *So?* to him, but he took it to mean *What is she doing here?* and shrugged back with confusion.

We carefully and quietly got out of bed. Blaine started pulling on some clothes and I looked helplessly around me, remembering that my clothes were lying in various areas of the living room floor. Blaine realized this, too, and handed me a pair of pajama bottoms and an old sweatshirt.

"Should I hide?" I whispered.

I thought it would be absurd if I did, but if he thought the two of us together would somehow hurt Sheila, I would go along with it. He'd obviously known her better and longer than I had. Besides, only the week before, Sheila and I had commiserated over Sydney's existence and the fact that Blaine wanted neither one of us. I wouldn't blame her for thinking I'd been a little hasty about jumping into bed with him.

"I don't know," he whispered back.

"Well, what do you want me to do?" I hissed at him.

Blaine put his hand on his head, then on the back of his neck, then on his hip as he weighed his options against Sheila's personality. He bit his lip, raised his eyebrows, and signaled for me to follow him.

"Sheila?" he called, opening the door and walking down the hall toward the kitchen. "I hope that's you."

I followed hesitantly, not knowing what to expect.

"I'm in here," she answered from the kitchen.

We rounded the corner to the kitchen and found Sheila pouring Chinese take-out into bowls. Dexter was winding his way between and around Sheila's calves, obviously hoping for a bite of something. I understood; the aroma made me suddenly ravenous. Or maybe it had been all that sex.

"Is there enough for three—"

I broke off uncomfortably, uncertain how to continue.

She pointed toward the table, set with three plates, and said, "I figured you two worked up a hearty appetite."

I glanced at the clock, astonished to realize it was nearly seven. I was grateful for Sheila's thoughtfulness, her open mind, and the precious smile that spread over her fabulous face. I looked at Blaine and could tell he was, too.

"How do you stay so thin?" I asked as Sheila began munching on an egg roll, obviously feeling as ravenous as I was.

"I'm not like Princess Diana, if that's what you're wondering," Sheila said.

My heart skipped a beat as I met her eyes, but some kindness in her face let me know she had no intention of telling Blaine about my past.

I ducked out and found my clothes, dressing quickly as Blaine went to the bathroom. I was back in the kitchen before him, but Sheila busied herself with the food, giving us no opportunity to talk before Blaine rejoined us.

"Sit, relax, tell me about your day," Sheila said as she grabbed soy sauce and duck sauce from the kitchen counter and took them to the table. "Well, maybe not *all* about it, but the details that you're comfortable sharing."

She gave a little giggle as Blaine and I looked anywhere but at each other. Her giggle further reassured me that Sheila was not angry.

"All right, enough teasing," Blaine said and took a place at the table. "Besides, there's really nothing to tell."

Sheila and I both looked at Blaine with raised eyebrows. Nothing? We'd just completed several hours of marathon sex. And this, despite the recent discovery of Mrs. Blaine Dunhill, despite the fact that he was my boss, despite the fact that his ex-girlfriend had come home during said marathon and was providing dinner for us. Nothing?

"Okay, it's not nothing, but I don't want to make a big deal out of it," Blaine said. "Maybe not just yet, okay?"

"Okay," Sheila said, looking at me.

"Could you pass the rice?" was all I added.

Blaine passed the bowl and gave me a small grin. I returned it, still caught up in the day we'd shared.

"Sheila," I said, "how was your day?"

Sheila thoughtfully chewed her bite of moo shoo pork.

"Well," she said and swallowed, "it was great. Getting up at six wasn't that great, but the rest of it was. I did test shots for a new ad campaign. They'll pull the ones they like for my composite cards. The photographer kept putting me in all these ridiculous outfits, though. Including ski wear. The set was made to look like the inside of a ski lodge. Whatever. They sent a car for me and took me to the studio; spent hours doing my makeup and catering to my every need. And even though I was being treated like the glamorous woman I am, the whole time I was being pushed and prodded along like a farm animal. Very strange."

"Yes, I believe I know how that feels," I commented.

Sheila nearly spewed her tea across the table. Blaine rolled his eyes.

"Very funny," he said, and adroitly changed the subject. "Wouldn't it be strange if you ended up modeling for one of my clients someday? We could all work together."

I appreciated the way Blaine made us sound like a team instead of treating me like a subordinate. It seemed to level things between us.

The conversation took a comfortable turn as we talked about growing up in Eau Claire and what it was like for each of us. Sheila was like me, restless and always longing for something else, never feeling like she quite belonged. Blaine always knew he'd leave as soon as he got the chance to go to college. His father wanted him to go into the family business (he was an electrician), but Blaine had no interest in it.

After dinner, Blaine and I helped Sheila clear the table and insisted on doing the dishes. Blaine washed and I dried. Sheila sat on the counter and directed me to the various cabinets and drawers in which the dishes and utensils belonged. While we washed, dried, and put away, she sipped wine and talked to us. Finally she reached for the fortune cookies lying on the counter.

"We're forgetting something," she said, tossing one in the air and catching it.

Blaine wiped his hands on the dishtowel that I handed to him and took one from her cupped hands. He broke it open and read it silently to himself, then a devilish grin crossed his face as he took a breath to read it aloud.

"A happy event will take place shortly in your home."

Sheila and I said in unison, "In bed!"

Blaine frowned and rolled his eyes again, but finally laughed with us.

"You are perceptive and considerate when dealing with others," Sheila read her fortune.

Blaine and I looked puzzled at each other, but said together, "In bed?"

I opened my cookie and ate half of it while I read my fortune, nearly choking.

"If you wish good advice, consult your mother."

"Uh—" said Blaine.

"I don't know your mother," Sheila said, "so I'm leaving that alone. However, there is a fourth cookie."

"Oh good," I said, and took it from her hand.

"Two small jumps are sometimes better than one leap."

"In bed!" we all exclaimed together.

"Although," Blaine said slyly, with no intention of finishing. We looked at each other and grinned.

"Okay you two, break it up," Sheila said, coming between us and putting her arms around our waists. "Kiss me good night, because I'm beat and going to bed."

I realized Blaine and Sheila could probably use some time alone to talk about what had happened and sort out their feelings. I decided to follow Sheila's lead and announced that I was fading fast and had some things I needed to attend to at home.

"I believe the phrase is *calling it a night*," I said, kissing Sheila's cheek. "Sheila, thanks for a fabulous dinner. I can't remember the last time I ate so much."

"I hope it was when I made that beef Stroganoff for you," Sheila said. "I'm glad you enjoyed it. Maybe we can do this again real soon."

I moved in for a big hug from her and she whispered in my ear, "If we don't talk soon, I'll never forgive you."

"Count on it, then," I whispered back. We separated and grinned conspiratorially at each other.

"Sheila, I'm gonna escort our guest home," Blaine said.

"Okay."

"Blaine, you don't have to," I protested.

"I'd like to," Blaine insisted. "Besides, my mother taught me to be a gentleman. Sometimes I remember; sometimes I don't. But this seems like one of those times I remember. I'd go with it, if I were you."

"I would, too," Sheila said quietly and padded off to her room.

I acquiesced and Blaine walked with me around the block. The streets were bright with light. People still raced up and down the sidewalk. Most of them seemed to be heading home, although some strayed in front of restaurants to read the menus in the windows. A few handed out flyers or murmured code words for the various vials of crack they were selling. New York never failed to display all walks of life. The loneliness I'd felt on my morning walk had vanished; I felt like part of my city again.

At my stoop, Blaine paused, and I could tell this was the end of the line for him. I wondered to myself if this might be the end of the line for our sexual relationship as well. Would he go back to the role of typical male and forget this ever happened? Would I become a role in his sexual folklore? *Oh yeah, there was this one guy in Manhattan who was really good. Really scored big with him. What was his name? David? Denny?* Followed by big laughs, back slaps, and belching.

"Daniel, thanks," Blaine said.

"Oh, geez," I said, "I was hoping you wouldn't say that. I'm sorry, but it's true. It makes it sound like I did you a favor or performed a big chore. Something cheap like that. I don't want this to be something cheap. I don't know what I want it to be, but I know it wasn't cheap. I'm not saying I want a relationship with you. I might, maybe. But I just don't want this to be the type of thing that gets trivialized by a thank-you and a handshake. Do you know what I mean?"

Blaine looked at me like my hair was on fire.

"It's okay," I said. "You can speak now. I think I'm done ranting."

"Oh, good," Blaine said, recovering from shock. "I was just going to thank you for having dinner with Sheila and me. But I have a lot more to thank you for. Thanks for not talking about what happened with us to Sheila. I'm glad you gave us some time to work it out later instead of making it a dinnertime topic. I'd like for you and me to talk about what happened sometime, though. Would that be okay?"

"Yeah," I said in a zombielike trance.

"Also, I'd like to thank you for being so patient with me," Blaine continued. "This afternoon, I mean. During sex. I'm glad you were my first. And my second. And my third."

We both laughed and looked into each other's eyes. He stepped forward and wrapped his thick arms around me. His hug meant more to me than the hours of fantastic sex we'd had earlier.

Who am I kidding, I wondered. But still, it felt good to be safe in his arms.

"I'll call you tomorrow," Blaine promised.

"Wait," I said as I was released from the embrace. "This might be the 'guy' thing brewing. You say you'll call and you don't? I don't think so. Can we just say, 'See ya,' and take it from there?"

Blaine grinned.

"See ya," he said.

"I'll call you tomorrow," I said with a laugh and ran up the stairs.

As I put my key in the lock, I glanced back at Blaine. He was laughing and shaking his head as he walked up the block.

I'd thought I would lie awake for hours reliving the day, but before I knew it, the sun was streaming in on me and the clock said ten. I lay there a while, remembering the gratifying sex with Blaine. I'd be energizing myself with those memories for a long time.

I toyed with fantasies of long lunches and quickies in the supply closet with Blaine as I showered and donned appropriate brunch attire. It was Sunday and time for my routine date with Ken.

I wanted to look sexy, I wanted to look gay, I wanted to look well fucked. I put on my deep black Levi's and my black Dolce and Gabana pullover with the white stripe across it. I finally donned my Armani sunglasses and was off.

It was getting too cool to dine outside, and among Ken's reasons to brunch at the Screening Room was being indoors. He was careful about our fair complexions and didn't want us freckling in the midday sun. He also had a personal theory about the preserving effects of air-conditioning, the details of which escaped me.

The host greeted me with a warm reception. He could never remember my name, nor could I his, but each time I arrived, he treated me like an old friend. I liked that. It disproved the old notion of the mean New Yorker. I was graciously seated and promptly served coffee.

An hour passed and Ken hadn't shown up. As much as I shifted, it still felt as if the chair had become part of my posterior. I got up and used the phone to call Ken's town house for the third time. No answer. I was beginning to wonder if I were being repaid for standing him up that one time. But that wasn't Ken's style. I started to worry and dialed Martin's number.

"Talk dirty to me," Martin said upon picking up the phone.

"Martin, it's me," I said.

"Hey, you," Martin chirped. "What's up? Why aren't you at brunch?"

"I am; that's what's up," I said grimly. "Ken hasn't shown. Do you know where he is?"

"I'd have assumed he was with you, but apparently that theory has been blown," Martin said in his most blasé tone. "Speaking of being blown, what's new with you, child?"

Did he know something about my day yesterday? Where *did* he get his information? I shook my head vigorously. No, he couldn't possibly know.

"Martin, look, I'm worried," I said firmly. "What was Ken doing last night? Did you talk to him?"

"Yeah, he helped me with my new act. Oh my god, you won't believe—"

"Did he say anything about going out afterward?" I asked, cutting him off.

"Daniel," Martin sighed, "this is Ken we're discussing. No, he said nothing about going out afterward. Ken hasn't gone out after we've performed in a long time. I'd say five years. Maybe because I've only known him for five years. But in my memory, Ken's never pulled an all-nighter. Unless he has some secret life we don't know about, I'm putting all my money on the square that says Ken went home, drew a hot bath, and was in bed before Club Chaos even closed."

I knew Martin was probably right. Ken never went out with the other performers, most of whom had second gigs elsewhere, though a few went clubbing all night. Ken had given up all that a long time ago. He was too dignified. And he had no lover. So, if he wasn't oversleeping in some man's bed and he wasn't with me . . . where was he?

"I'm going to his place," I said uneasily.

"Should I meet you there?"

I considered it and shook my head, then realized Martin couldn't see me.

"No. I'll call you if anything's up."

I took care of my bill for the coffee and caught a cab to Ken's Jane Street address, making sure I still had his key on my ring as I fought my feeling of foreboding. I didn't even consider knocking when I reached his door.

The town house was dark and quiet and I hesitated, considering and rejecting one scenario after another. Ken with a guest. Ken waking up in someone's bed in another apartment. Ken sleeping soundly, maybe having taken a sleeping pill. Ken maybe being depressed and taking a lot of sleeping pills.

I practically ran into his bedroom. The bed was unmade but Ken wasn't in it and I panicked.

"Ken? *Ken?*"

"Oh, Daniel, shit, you scared me," Ken said, coming from the bathroom.

My relief at seeing him was quickly replaced with concern.

"What's wrong?"

"Horrible night," Ken said, crawling into bed. "Night sweats, nightmares, you name it. And I'm having a reaction to the medication." He exposed his arms to me and I saw he was covered with a rash. "This itching and nausea."

"Have you talked to your doctor?"

"Yeah. They're gonna cut back on the dosage and call in a prescription for something to help with the itching."

I exhaled and said, "You scared me, too."

"Damn, I forgot brunch," Ken said. "I'm sorry."

"Oh god, who cares. You should have called somebody though. Me, Martin—"

"What could you do?"

"The first thing I'm doing is having Martin pick up your drugs. Then you're getting into a nice, soothing oatmeal bath, the kind you used to make me take when I was all stressed out. You still buy our favorite blend, don't you?" When he nodded, I continued, "While you're soaking, I'll change these sheets."

"I'm not an invalid—"

"You're my best friend in the world," I said. "Period."

I left to call Martin then drew Ken's bath, making small talk from the bedroom as I took care of his linens. Finally I went into the bathroom and sat on the edge of the tub, gently sponging his back. In spite of his age and illness, Ken still looked good and I told him so.

"Big liar," he said comfortably.

"I am a big liar, and I'll tell you all about it when Martin gets here. You know how he loves a good story."

Martin's eyes when he arrived had a bruised, helpless look. He solemnly handed me Ken's prescriptions and some Benadryl.

"Fix your face," I hissed at him. "If you look at him like that, he's gonna be buying his cemetery plot."

I went back to help Ken from the tub, giving him his favorite extra-thick, white, terrycloth robe. After he took the Benadryl, Martin and I followed him to the bedroom, settling on either side of him in his massive bed. I told them everything about Robert and Blaine, even filling in some of the details about Jeremy for Martin, no longer caring what he told Robert. Somehow I managed to make it all sound funny, but Ken finally ruffled my hair.

"Now tell Judy and Wally, hon, you like this Blaine, don't you?"

"I like him a lot," I admitted. "I didn't mean to, but yeah. I do."

Martin sighed and asked, "Are you sure you're not just punishing Jeremy?"

"What do you mean?" I asked.

"Isn't there the tiniest little part of you that wants to go back—"

"Nope," I said. "I'm a lot more interested in thinking about a future with Blaine than my past with Jeremy. I know this seems like a bad idea because he's my boss. But all joking aside, I think I can handle it. I think he can, too."

"Danny, if you bring Blaine into your world, he's going to find out about 2Di4," Martin said sensibly. "How do you think he'll feel about that?"

I shrugged, knowing if I talked about how bizarre Blaine found drag, it would damage their opinion of him.

"He said the past doesn't matter," I reminded Martin.

"Oh, it never does at first. But sooner or later—"

"Leave him alone," Ken said. "Let him enjoy it, Martin. He can deal with all that when he has to."

It surprised me when Martin surrendered so easily, then I noticed the way he was looking at Ken. It occurred to me maybe I was the one who was out of place in this scene.

"Uh, maybe I should take off," I said abruptly.

Ken laughed and said, "No, Martin has to perform tonight. You can keep me company."

"I'd love to," I said. "Tell me about the new act, Martin."

"Well," he began, drawing a breath for dramatic pause. A look passed between us and I remembered he had tried to tell me about the new act earlier, but I had cut him off in my panic about Ken. He saw that I remembered and gave me one of his covert winks to let me know it was okay. "I think it's a brilliant idea, if I do say so myself."

"And he does," Ken sighed, with a roll of his eyes, "over and over and over and—"

"Anyway," Martin loudly interrupted, "you know how I practically grew up in Catholic schools?"

"Oh yeah," I groaned. Martin's stories about his years of incarceration in various Connecticut Catholic schools made him sound like a cross between Christina Crawford and Mother Teresa.

"I decided to use all the guilt and emotional scarring from my formative years and turn it into a brilliant act."

Martin's use of the word "formative" reminded me of how Jeremy's improved vocabulary had shocked me. I looked at Ken, who was coughing behind his hand to hide his giggles. Martin ignored us and continued his explanation.

"I'm going to perform as Sister Mary Amanda Prophet. Get it?" I repeated the name mentally a couple of times.

"Sister Mary Amanda Prophet? Oh. Sister, marry a man to profit! I get it. How very *Sister Act* of you," I said.

"More like *Sound of Music*," Ken said.

"But it will be better than that," Martin protested. "I mean, a drag nun. It's the next step after 2Di4. You took on the royal family; I'll continue with the Catholic Church. It's new. I mean, sure, there's that group of drag nuns in San Francisco who does charity benefits."

"The Sisters of Perpetual Indulgence," Ken offered.

"Yeah, them," Martin dismissed. "Boys always dress up as nuns for Halloween, too, but I've never seen a nun-themed drag performance around here."

"You've never seen *Nunsense?*" I asked.

"Oh god," an exasperated Martin exclaimed, throwing his hands in the air and falling back on the bed.

"You know how Martin has to be dragged to the theater," Ken said.

"Martin, it sounds good. If anyone can pull this off, it'll be you,"

I said kindly. I didn't want to shatter his vision and was genuinely interested in what he would create. "Are you doing her tonight?"

"Yup," Martin grinned. "Last night I joined a couple of the other acts as a nun, just to test the reaction. Everybody loved her. So Sister Mary Amanda Prophet will debut tonight."

"You helped create this?" I asked Ken.

"Yes," Ken said happily.

"I'll bet it's great. Andy doesn't deserve it."

"Andy doesn't, but the audience does. There'll be no demands for Judy."

"But this is all just for now, right?" I asked anxiously. "I mean, until Judy gets out of rehab and returns to Club Chaos in triumph?"

"I'm not going back, sweetie," Ken said. "The hours, the drama . . . It's time for a change. You made one. Now you have to let me do the same."

"But what will you do if you're not Judy," I wailed in spite of myself.

"Well maybe," Ken grinned, "I can get a nice cushy job as an assistant for some hunky virgin who wants my body. Martin, you run along. You have a show to do. I expect to hear all about it tomorrow."

"I think," Martin said slowly, "if you don't mind, maybe I'd like to come back and tell you about it tonight."

They stared at each other, and again I felt as if I shouldn't be in the room.

"I think," Ken said as slowly, "maybe that would be a good idea. You still have your key, right?"

"I do," Martin said.

His lips lightly brushed Ken's, then he winked at me. He picked up a large, wooden rosary from the dresser and twirled it around as he exited the room.

"Well," I said, somewhat at a loss.

"I love you, Daniel, but you can be a little—"

"Dense?"

"Self-absorbed. Things happen."

"Evidently."

"And they always happen for a reason, right?"

"And exactly how long has this been going on?" I teased.

Ken smiled and said, "Let's just say you didn't make things easy for us at Happy Hollow."

"Oh my god, Ken, why didn't you two just tell me to get lost?"

"Because we knew you'd ask a lot of nosy questions and we were just sort of, uh, checking things out."

"Uh-huh. And, uh, how were *things?*"

His grin could only be described as smug as he answered, "Things were fantastic. Now settle down next to me and tell me how on earth an antique like you manages to keep up with a young stud like Blaine. I could use some tips."

"I'm beginning to see you are perfectly capable of orchestrating your love life without any direction from me," I said primly.

"Hello, Diana," Ken laughed.

"I don't think we're in Kansas anymore, Dorothy," I shot back.

"Wisconsin!" Ken cracked and we both burst out laughing.

THIRTEEN

I breezed into the office about fifteen minutes late, dropping my Coach attaché next to my desk. I glanced at my "in" box and the pile of chores to be done as I picked up my coffee cup and headed to the copy room. As I passed the desks of the other drones, I singsonged, "Good morning," to each person, most not acknowledging or merely glancing up stone-faced as I walked by. It was definitely another Monday morning.

Unlike my coworkers, however, I had every reason to be in a good mood after a great weekend. I'd made peace with Robert. I'd left Ken sleeping peacefully after his medicine kicked in. But the best part of the weekend had been my incredible afternoon and evening with Blaine. I was tingling with the anticipation of seeing him this morning.

I poured a cup of coffee and started back to my desk. As I turned through the doorway, bad timing resulted in a surreal sense of déjà vu. I bumped into Evelyn, sloshing hot coffee all over her white silk blouse. She squealed and tottered on her high heels, pinwheeling with one hand and using the middle finger and thumb on the other hand to hold the hot, wet blouse away from her skin. The papers she was carrying to the high-speed Xerox fluttered to the floor in no particular order. She landed on her backside in the hallway with an audible thud.

"Oh my god, Evelyn, are you okay?" I asked, suppressing a laugh as best I could.

"You . . . you did that on purpose!" she accused.

"On purpose? I was just coming around the corner. How could I know you were there?"

"Don't think for one second I don't have your number. I don't know how you got this job, but I've had my eye on you. And this is not the first time you've done this to me."

"Evelyn," I began, "I honestly don't have it out for you any more than you do for me." I paused while I considered the idea that she might have it out for me more than I thought. "Anyway," I confided to her in a hushed tone, "if I really had it out for you, do you think I'd be satisfied with scattering a few papers?"

Her brow furrowed slightly, then, ignoring my outstretched hand, she countered, "Something isn't right here. You're not qualified to be Mr. Dunhill's assistant. You and I both know that. I'll find out what's behind all of this, you can be assured of that."

I was beginning to tire of her.

"Ev, you really know how to endear yourself, don't you?" I said as I walked away without helping her up.

Instead of returning to my desk, I took the elevator down to see Bernie in purchasing. Bernie had played pro hockey in his younger years. Though this illustrious career seemed to have left his dental work intact, it also left him with a unique style of managing his department. He was the goalie who regarded all requisitions for office supplies or equipment as pucks flying at him from hostile opponents. He swatted forms back with force and speed if he found the most minor flaw in how they were filled out.

Most of my coworkers tried to get around Bernie with hearty conversation about hockey games. Since I knew very little about the sport, I'd quickly figured out a different approach. Bernie was one of those bulldog kind of guys whose gruff exterior hid a secret. I quickly noticed how his eyes never followed any of the women who passed by him, but he knew my name by my second trip to his department. A few days later when I had to submit a supply requisition, I included a couple of magazines in the interoffice envelope. Though ostensibly for sports lovers, they primarily featured photographs of sweating, muscular men working out, wrestling, or assuming other manly poses. I got my supply order in record time. From then on, I always made sure to include a little gift in all my mail to Bernie.

As I approached his desk, he gave me a wink.

"Are we late filling an order for you, Daniel?"

"Hi, Bernie. No, I just thought I'd ask you a question. Do you think it would be possible for Mr. Dunhill to have his own coffeemaker? In his office?"

Before I could summon up justification for this, or promise to submit the correct form, Bernie nodded and said, "I'm sure that would be more convenient for his clients. As it happens, we have a couple in stock now."

He gestured for me to follow him and I picked the sleeker of the two then grinned a goodbye to him. He winked again, knowing that I understood his largesse was to remain our little secret.

I got back to my desk and noticed that Blaine's office door was open. I poked my head in with a smile.

"Good morning."

"Good morning to you, too. Hey, do you have a minute? I need to coordinate some dates with you to make sure everything's on the main calendar. Shut the door and have a seat."

"I come bearing gifts from Bernie," I said, lightly kicking the door so it would shut behind me as I marched into the room to set the coffeemaker next to his wet bar.

"You're joking," Blaine said, wide-eyed. "I once scored him tickets to a Rangers game and it still took me six weeks to get my Montblanc pen."

"Next time, get him tickets to a dive meet. Or gymnastics. Men's gymnastics."

Blaine's green eyes got big as he said, "Bernie? Are you joking?"

"Do you now have your own coffeemaker?" I asked.

"So what'd you do to get it?" he teased.

"Forget it. He likes you big, jock-looking guys."

"His loss," Blaine shrugged, giving me an up-and-down look that left no doubt in my mind about whether or not he would pretend Saturday hadn't happened. I knew that once we settled down to work, his flirtatiousness would end, but it was a great way to start a new week.

I sat down, and he handed me his Palm Pilot, taking another electronic gadget out of his shirt pocket. I glanced down at the minicomputer, surprised at how comfortable I'd become with this gizmo.

You've come a long way, baby, I thought to myself.

"Actually, the first date I wanted to confirm you won't find on

there. I wanted to know what you're doing after work tonight." He
grinned at me.

"What did you have in mind?"

"Oh, I don't know. I thought we could get together and play
Yahtzee," he said, still smiling and walking around his desk to get
closer to me.

"Is that what it's called now?" I responded.

"Call it whatever you like," he said, leaning over me from behind, his hands on the arms of the chair I sat in. He kissed my
neck, his hot breath tickling me. I responded by turning my head
toward him, kissing him full on the lips. I felt his tongue push its
way into my mouth, and mine responded in kind. He broke the kiss
to swivel my chair to face him, dropping to his knees so that he
could be level with me.

"Why, Mr. Dunhill!" I exclaimed. "Don't you have a pressing appointment?"

"The only thing I want to press is my body against yours."

"Here? Now?" I feigned shock.

"Mmhmm," he answered, kissing me again.

"Well, I just saw him not ten minutes ago," Evelyn's voice said
from outside the door.

Our eyes flew open at the same time. Blaine pushed himself to a
standing position, using my shoulders for assistance. Without
knocking, Evelyn opened the door to Blaine's office to find him
resting nonchalantly on the corner of his desk, holding a folder in
front of his tenting crotch, and me sitting in the chair, fiddling pur-
posefully with the Palm Pilot. We both turned our gazes to her. I
hoped it wasn't apparent that our hearts were pounding.

"May I help you?" I asked sweetly, noticing how the coffee stain
on her blouse looked roughly like the shape of Florida.

Blaine suddenly changed gears from Romeo to Superexec, snapping, "Why are you coming in here without knocking?"

His tone, so different from the one he'd used before, surprised
even me. I shot him a bewildered glance as Evelyn gaped at him.

"I'm sorry, Mr. Dunhill. I didn't realize you'd come in yet."

"And that gives you carte blanche to make yourself at home in
my office?"

"No, sir. But Daniel—"

"Daniel has every right to be in here, with or without me, and he doesn't need to fill out one of your requisitions to do so. You still haven't said why you're here."

Evelyn's eyes fluttered, and she stammered, "I just wanted to—"

"Mr. Dunhill," I said calmly, "what Evelyn means to say is that I told her I would get some club soda from your office bar. I spilled my coffee on her and didn't want her blouse to stain. I'm sure she was just making sure I hadn't forgotten. And I had, Ev, which was very thoughtless of me. I'm sorry."

Evelyn and I exchanged a look of understanding. As much as she might regret it, she now owed me one. I was sure Blaine's icy behavior was due partially to the adrenaline rush of almost being caught with me, but also because he was truly very territorial about his office space. With good reason. It hadn't taken me long to realize that his extremely competitive peers were always trying to get information on him. I had no doubt their assistants helped them in any way they could, just as I helped Blaine. But as far as I knew, the officious Evelyn played no favorites, disdaining everyone equally. If Blaine chose to, he could make her position very unpleasant, as she had no real allies.

"Please get your soda and get out. We're trying to get some work done here."

"Yes, Mr. Dunhill," she said as she made her way to the bar. She retrieved the soda and half jogged to the door. She glanced at me with a mixture of appreciation and suspicion just before she went out, gently shutting the door behind her.

Blaine's and my shoulders dropped when we exhaled deeply, as if we'd both been holding our breath until she left.

"That was close," he said.

"You got that right," I answered.

We sat for a moment looking at each other. A small smile crossed both of our lips at the same time.

"Kind of exciting, huh?" I asked.

"Almost getting caught, you mean?"

"Yeah."

He smiled and said, "Well, I don't know how soon I'd want to do it again, but it was a rush."

We both broke into laughter.

"By the way, tonight sounds like fun, in answer to your previous question."

"Yahtzee!" we said together, still laughing.

That evening we shared a cab, dropping Blaine at the gym while I went on to my apartment to make sure it was presentable and princess-free. I turned on Jeremy's lights in the garden. I briefly considered lighting some candles, but settled for a single lamp in the living room, leaving the bedroom in darkness. I didn't want to seem too eager, as if Blaine hadn't been able to tell in the cab how wired I was. Of course, I could always blame that on too much coffee, now that it was more accessible. At least saving Ev today meant she would be unable to find a way to chastise me for getting my boss a new perk—so to speak.

I opened the door later to a sweaty Blaine.

"I guess I should have showered at the gym, but I just wanted to get here," he said.

So much for not seeming too eager, I thought, wrapping myself around him to make it clear that a hot, sweaty Blaine was more than welcome. I nuzzled my lips into the crook of his neck to give him a tender kiss.

"Apparently you don't mind," Blaine said, giving in and dropping his gym bag to the floor.

"Not at all," I murmured into his ear and gave it a lick.

He laughed and took my head in his hands, giving me a long kiss on the mouth.

"You may not mind, but I'd like nothing more than a hot shower right now," he said.

"Nothing more?"

"Well"—he stopped and pretended to ponder—"perhaps some dinner afterward."

"Whatever you wish, Mr. Dun—"

"Oh stop it," Blaine laughed and grabbed my hand.

He helped me cover my cast later so we could shower together. When we finished, we ordered take-out and ate in the garden after I found a robe that would fit him.

"Is this yours?" Blaine asked, belting the robe.

"As opposed to . . ."

"A former boyfriend's. No, don't answer. I said we don't owe each other explanations."

"My life is an open book," I lied. "Yes, it's mine. I do have an ex, Jeremy. We broke up last spring."

"How long were you together?"

"A couple of years. It ended because there wasn't enough room in our bed for another guy."

"I beg your pardon?"

"We broke up when he got involved with someone else."

"Huh," Blaine said. "Last spring. That's about the time I got my call from Breslin Evans and moved here."

It was obvious he wasn't going to talk about Sydney, and I tried to find a safer topic.

"What I can't figure out is how you could have been here all those months without hooking up with somebody. I mean, you must have gotten offers. At the gym?"

He shook his head.

"The market? The subway? Anywhere?"

"I wasn't looking for any offers," he said.

"Manhattan is like a feast. Weren't you hungry?"

"Not until Labor Day," he said, glancing around the garden with a little smile.

I felt a strange glow deep in my stomach. I was pretty sure it wasn't the spinach lasagna.

"If you were watching me while I was watching you," I said, "how come when we finally met, you were so aloof?"

"Because the object of my fantasies had just brought flowers to Sheila," he said. "How was I to know you had ulterior motives?"

"Me? Ulterior motives?"

He laughed and pulled me up, leading me back to bed so we could work off a few calories. I kept chastising myself for dreading the moment when he would dress and go home. I knew better than to move too fast too soon.

"I was wondering," Blaine finally said, then stopped himself.

I felt a tremor of anxiety, unsure what he'd decide to ask me next.

"What?"

"If I could stay here tonight. I've never . . ."

"Slept with a guy?"

"Right."

"I'd like that," I said.

He settled more deeply under the covers, his head next to mine on the pillow.

"It's hard for me to believe someone would leave you for another guy," he finally said.

"I'm sure Jeremy could give you a list of my faults."

He reached across me and turned on the lamp, then stayed propped on one arm so he could look at me.

"I'd rather find out about you on my own. And I don't mind talking about me if there's something you want to know. I don't want to get into the whole Sydney thing, but other than that, you know, whatever."

"Okay, let's talk about work."

"Work," he repeated, sounding surprised.

"I understand why it wouldn't be good for anyone, like Evelyn, to catch us in the office. But do you really think they'd care if they knew you were gay?"

"It's not them," he said slowly, as if trying to work it out as he talked. "It's me. I've spent most of twenty-five years hiding things I didn't like about myself. No, maybe more like things I didn't want to face about myself. I don't know how your family is, but mine will never accept this."

"Your family isn't here," I reminded him. "I know where you came from and how people are there. I came to New York so I could be myself. I'd be the first to admit I was pretty wild when I got to the city. I felt like my life began then, and I couldn't wait to experience everything."

"I was too busy, Daniel," Blaine said with a laugh. "You see how competitive things are at work. I started with several strikes against me. People thought I was too young and inexperienced to have the position I have. I put all of my energy into proving myself. Most of the summer I was working twelve- and fourteen-hour days. When Sheila came at the end of August, I worried about leaving her alone too much, so I cut back my hours. My first real appreciation of Manhattan came from starting to explore it with her. Then you moved in. When I began watching you from my window, that's when I became aware that I had no life other than work."

"You are such a hot guy," I grinned. "Why me?"

"You don't think you're a hot guy?" he asked with a laugh. "There you were, digging in the dirt, looking so, I don't know, so sure of what you were doing. You'd move around with such grace, then sprawl out on a chair and survey your work. I guess I don't know how to make that sound as sexy as it was."

"You're doing okay," I argued. "Go on."

He laughed and said, "Trust me. You were really sexy. I kept trying to figure out how to get your attention. I couldn't stay away from my window."

"All that time, I was watching you, too," I said. "Standing there with your shirt unbuttoned, looking like a *GQ* ad."

"Posing," he assured me. "I'm just a boy from Eau Claire."

"Me, too," I reminded him.

"That was another thing I liked. When I would look at men here, they intimidated me. Like they knew everything, and I knew nothing. I didn't know how to start anything, how to connect. I was scared. Maybe I waited because . . . it had to be you. Someone who'd understand where I came from, who I am."

His green eyes looked entirely too vulnerable. I stifled my inner voice as it started some lecture about first boyfriends and transitional boyfriends and people in the closet and bosses . . .

"Come here, you," I said, and we settled into each other's arms.

I loved his kisses, the way he seemed to hold nothing back physically. Maybe in time we'd both be comfortable enough to share more about our pasts. Maybe not. I was determined simply to accept this for what it was right now and not try to figure out what would happen next.

Sometime in the night I got up and cleared our dishes from the patio. Sheila's windows were dark. I wondered if she had any idea Blaine was with me. I had promised to call her so we could talk about it all. I needed to do that soon. Though I'd initially intended to use her to get to Blaine, even if things cooled between the two of us, I knew Sheila was someone I wanted to keep in my life. And there could be worse things than having Blaine as a friend, as well.

It was cold outside and I hurried to get back under the covers. He didn't wake as I slid next to him, but seemed to sense that I was shivering and wrapped himself more tightly around me. We woke up that way, and I discovered that, in spite of what Jeremy might think, I was quite capable of being more than civil in the morning.

"I'm going to be late," Blaine finally moaned.

"I'm not. And I'm the one who knows you had a meeting out of the office this morning."

"With whom?" Blaine asked.

"With your gardener," I said, and he laughed. "Now get dressed and get out of here. I have a very demanding boss who doesn't like it if I'm not on time."

If my morning at the office was Blaine-free, it was also blessedly

Ev-free. I found myself humming while I worked, answering the phone with abnormal cheer.

"You've been getting laid," Martin said when I took a call.

"A gentleman never tells," I said.

"Are you married yet?"

"La la la," I said. "Why are you up so early?"

"It was a mistake, but I figured I'd make the most of it. You're coming to the club Friday night. Sister Mary Amanda demands it. You don't want to piss off the church."

"Never," I said. "I'll be glad to see you pray to statues or whatever it is you do."

"You're welcome to bring your future ex-husband with you."

"You're such a cynic. He'll be out of town on business."

"See? Business trips without you. That's what happens when you take advice on love from the deli lama. Gretchen's coming. Bring Sheila along if you think she can handle high mass with the drag queen."

"Good idea. I'll ask her."

After we hung up, I searched for Sheila's new pager number. When she returned my call, I told her about Martin's invitation.

"I'd love to," she said. "Can I bring someone?"

"Blaine's going to Baltimore," I reminded her. "And I don't think he's ready for this yet."

"Oh, not Blaine, silly. Your secrets are still safe with me. I want to ask Josh."

"Ah-ha," I said. "You get to know all about my private life, but you've been awfully quiet about your own."

"He asked if I wanted to do something this weekend, but we haven't made definite plans yet. This sounds like an interesting way to get to know him better."

"Well, don't surprise him. Believe me, that would not be a good idea."

She sighed and said, "You know, you can be a bit heterophobic, Daniel. Straight people are everywhere. Probably some of your best friends are straight!"

"Really? How can you tell when they're straight?"

"Hmm," she said. "They *do* cry when they watch 'ER,' but it's not because they think Nurse Hathaway needs to tame her hair or because George Clooney seems so emotionally unavailable."

"You're brilliant," I said and heard her laughing as she hung up.

The following days were busy. Blaine and I remained very circumspect at work, contenting ourselves with eye contact. He spent Tuesday night with me. On Wednesday night, we went out to dinner, then I put him in a cab so he could catch his flight to Baltimore. My apartment seemed empty without him, but I was glad I'd decided to stay in when he called me later to let me know he was safely in his hotel room. I didn't expect to hear from him Thursday, as I knew he had several client meetings that would stretch into late evening. Friday I talked to him from the office, but that was all business, until he asked if I'd keep Sunday open for him.

Moving too fast! my inner voice warned. To no avail, as I assured Blaine my Sunday was all his. I'd have to remember to cancel brunch with Ken, but I hoped he'd understand.

I felt like I was floating by the time I met Sheila and Josh outside Club Chaos on Friday night.

"Daniel Stephenson, Josh Clinton," Sheila said.

"Oh," I said, returning his firm handshake, "just like the . . . city in Iowa."

He laughed and I liked him immediately, as much for the way his brown eyes crinkled when he was amused as because he got my little joke.

"So you're a photographer," I said.

"I am. And you're Sheila's best friend in New York."

"It is a full-time job," I agreed.

"Why do people always act like I'm high maintenance?" Sheila asked, tossing her hair.

I watched Josh as we went inside, liking the way he seemed to view everything with good-natured interest. I wondered what he would think of tonight's show.

We joined Ken and Gretchen, already seated, and ordered drinks. I sat back and listened to the small talk, trying not to be too obvious with my scrutiny of Josh. He had the kind of features that at first seemed merely cute but, as he talked, became more handsome. His brown hair was a little curly, a bit longer than was stylish, and his tan looked as if it came from playing some outdoor sport rather than a tanning booth. He was about my height, with a good body, and looked comfortable in his black jeans and black sweater. His leather jacket looked expensive with just the right amount of wear. I could find no fault with him and gave Sheila an approving look, which she acknowledged with slightly raised eyebrows before she, like Josh, became engrossed by something Gretchen was saying.

"Can you tell me if he has a birthmark and what he had for lunch?" Ken asked softly.

"Oops, was I staring too much?" I asked.

"Yeah," Ken said and laughed at me. "I think she'll be fine with him. Stop worrying."

"I'm a Virgo," I said, then turned my attention to the stage as the house lights went down.

The opening acts were all well known to me. Some were old favorites. Others had been in their infancy just before I stopped performing. In any case, they were all familiar enough to allow me to watch our table rather than the show.

Sheila's expression was full of delight as she watched "A Rainbow of Divas." This was always a crowd pleaser because the performers were not lip-synching, but actually singing in the style of the women they impersonated. The show began with a crimson-clad Bette Midler doing "Friends," gradually joined by Cher in orange leather and Diana Ross in yellow chiffon. After the song they exchanged banter, one-upping each other until, as a group, they traded baffled and somewhat horrified glances when they were interrupted by the twangy strains of a banjo.

Dolly Parton, overabundant in green polyester and sequins, appeared, pushing the rail-thin Cher and Miss Ross onto a now squashed Bette until they looked like a human cornucopia. Dolly urged the crowd to join her in a rousing rendition of "Two Doors Down."

Josh was now laughing as hysterically as Sheila as the divas tried to regain their composure and out-sing Dolly while avoiding her pendulous breasts. They all stopped dead in their tracks when the music died and a drum rolled. Spotlights swept the stage as, from the sound booth, Andy boomed in his best announcer voice, "Ladies and gentlemen, now appearing in a show produced by, directed by, written by, staged by, casted by, scored by, choreographed by, lighted by, costumed by, catered by, *reviewed* by, *Miss Barbra Streisand!*"

By the time Barbra stepped out, resplendent in blue velvet, Sheila was weeping and holding her stomach. Josh was mesmerized by Barbra's six-inch nails, dripping red polish, as she shoved the previous performers aside on her way to the front of the stage to wail out "The Main Event." Bette's red curls went flat, as did Dolly's breasts. The feathers on Cher's and Diana's boas fluttered to the floor, leaving them with pathetic strings around their necks. Even Ken, who'd written this show, laughed as Barbra gave the audience a slightly cross-eyed look of victory, secure that she'd won this round of dueling divas.

Until, from the back of the crowd, emerged a familiar battle cry: R-E-S-P-E-C-T. The room exploded with applause as Aretha, in majestic purple satin, made her way through the patrons and took the stage. Barbra's nails joined the fallen feathers as she bowed before the Queen of Soul. In a final, ultimate tribute, Bette, Cher, Diana, Dolly, and Barbra became backup singers as Aretha brought her performance to a triumphant conclusion.

"Oh my god, I love them, I love them," Sheila said as the curtain came down. "I want to be a drag queen!"

All eyes turned to Josh, who laughed and said, "Don't look at me!"

"If you did do drag," Sheila said, "who would you be?"

"I'm partial to Marilyn Monroe," he answered with a grin.

Gretchen's expression was a little puzzled, and I explained, "I dressed Sheila as Marilyn on Halloween."

"Ah," Gretchen and Ken said together.

My curiosity about how Josh would react to a drag show was now satisfied. Some straight men could handle straight-appearing gay men. Others were more comfortable with gay men who were markedly different, as if that meant there were no danger that homosexuality might be contagious. Josh seemed to be one of those guys who was secure enough about himself to be casually friendly or entertained, whatever was called for. I relaxed into a comfortable sense that Sheila had a good instinct for picking men. Should their relationship get serious, at this point I definitely considered Josh a keeper.

And Blaine, I wondered, how would he react to all of this?

The night I'd brought Aunt Jen to Club Chaos, I was still confused about my future. More than that, I'd felt like drag was a past as snugly tucked away as my scrapbooks. Even at the auction that had marked the end of 2Di4, I'd felt slightly disconnected from it all. But tonight, though I was as committed as ever to putting my drag career behind me, I realized that the feelings of joy, competition, fun, drama, and camaraderie would always remain a part of me. I wanted them to.

I looked at Ken, thinking again about his history. All those years ago, when he'd met Samuel, he'd turned his back on this life. But when Samuel had died, his old friends had rallied around, helping him and encouraging him to come back home.

Had I really worried that this family I'd made would desert me? Of course they wouldn't. I needed to learn from Ken's mistake and not abandon them. Though Blaine had said there would be no need for explanations about the past, if he wanted to be in my life, he had to understand how this huge part of it had gone into making me the man I was.

I realized Gretchen was watching me, and I smiled at her. The look she gave me was a little curious but mostly kind.

"Missing it?" she asked.

"Appreciating it," I answered, turning my attention back to the stage.

Between each of the musical numbers were comedy routines by legends such as Bette Davis, Joan Crawford, and Tallulah Bankhead, whose act consisted of redirecting a frazzled Meg Ryan in her *When Harry Met Sally* fake orgasm scene. The crowd loved Rita Hayworth as Gilda singing "Put the Blame on Mame" to a group of shirtless hunks. I had to fight back a sense of sadness. Rita was in Judy's old spot, the last number before the closing act. I might have found the strength to put 2Di4 behind me, but I'd never stop missing Judy.

"It's a good audience," Ken said. "I think they're ready for Martin."

I fervently hoped for Martin's success in the show closer that had once been mine. The curtain had barely gone down before the music swelled into the opening notes of "The Sound of Music" then segued into funereal organ chords. A lone light pierced the stage, and a black figure unfolded until we realized we were looking at a most pious, if heavily made up, nun. Andy's voice intoned, "Dearly beloved, Sister Mary . . . Amanda . . . Prophet."

Sister Mary Amanda's hands embraced her crucifix as she began her song. The music was a hypnotically slow version of "How Do You Solve a Problem Like Maria," with words rewritten by Ken. Martin's voice was soft and angelic.

How do I find a husband for my Susan
How do I find a man who'll let her be
The free spirit that she is
A girl with a lot of fizz
Who must be allowed to have her headstrong way
Oh, how do I find a husband for my Susan
Who can afford to buy her lingerie

The singing nun was joined by Tommy in schoolgirl uniform, face and hair like Madonna's in *Desperately Seeking Susan*. As Susan danced up, Sister Mary Amanda removed a ruler hidden in her robes and gave her a little smack across her back end, then continued her song.

How do I find a husband for Evita
How do I find a man who'll let her be
The power crazed lady luck
Who everyone wants to . . . tuck
Away in a madhouse or a nunnery
Oh, how do I find a husband for Evita
Who can afford to buy her a country

They'd been joined by Marc in a matching uniform, daintily tucking blond hair into his Madonna as Evita bun. He gave Susan a little shove and received a tap on the head from Sister Mary Amanda's ruler.

Martin—or Sister Mary Amanda—now gave a deep sigh and looked heavenward.

How do I find a husband for Madonna
How do I find a man who'll let her be
A glamour girl and a queen
A harlot on magazines
A star with the power of celebrity
Oh, how do I find rich husbands for my schoolgirls
They must not give themselves away for free

The audience clapped wildly as another schoolgirl, a newcomer whose name I didn't know, emerged from backstage as Blonde Ambition Madonna, with breast cones placed over the outside of her school uniform.

Sister Mary Amanda Prophet watched in dismay as a tape of "Diamonds Are a Girl's Best Friend" allowed the others to break into a provocative dance. Martin began lip-synching the words as he thrust himself into the audience to consider men for his schoolgirls. Susan dashed behind a screen and emerged completely in character, all black lace, leggings, and necklaces. By the time she reached the edge of the stage, Martin had found a victim, a mortified straight man in his fifties who allowed himself to be dragged to the stage so Susan could dance around him. The table of matronly women with him raised their glasses with boisterous yells.

Marc darted behind the screen then reappeared in Evita's balcony suit, grabbing the gorgeous Chelsea boy Martin selected for him. Still lip-synching, Martin glided through the audience until he turned toward our table. He gave me a quick wink and I glanced at the stage where Blonde Ambition Madonna was waiting for her man. Martin certainly couldn't be heading my way.

He was definitely coming out of his habit, though, and by the time he uncovered his wig, he was in full Material Girl as Marilyn drag. The song ended and I saw him surreptitiously turn on his remote microphone as he swept around me to put his hands on Josh's shoulders. Josh wore a huge grin and Sheila was screaming with laughter.

"Ooooh," Martin cooed, "who do we have here? What's your name, handsome?"

"Josh."

Martin ran his palms down Josh's arms and held up his hands so the audience could see them.

"Look at this, such *big* hands!"

He produced his ruler and dramatically measured Josh's hand from wrist to fingertips.

"Really big hands. You know what they say about big hands, don't you?"

Josh shook his head, mesmerized by Martin.

"Big hands . . . *deep pockets!*"

Martin broke into "Material Girl" as he led Josh to the stage, shoving Blonde Ambition out of the way. Josh was an excellent sport, a willing and adoring dance partner for Martin as he finished the song. The other guys got into the act with their Madonnas, Chelsea Boy doing much better than Straight Guy, while Blonde Ambition pouted on the sidelines, lower lip thrust out like her cones.

"Don't forget," Martin trilled just before he and his gyrating schoolgirls disappeared behind the curtain, "sister, marry a man to profit!"

The applause was great and I reached over and nudged Ken.

"You finally succumbed to the lure of Madonna, huh?"

"What can I say," Ken sighed. "The woman somehow became an icon. Doesn't Martin do her well?"

We all nodded, and Sheila gave Josh a big hug as he returned to our table.

"Thanks for going along with that," Ken said.

"I loved it," Josh protested, his arm around Sheila.

They really were a striking couple and I felt myself warm toward him even more.

"I never thought Martin could be so beautiful as a woman," Sheila said. "I mean, he's a great-looking guy, but still."

"You should have seen this one," Gretchen commented and pointed at me.

For one second I flashed my demure Diana look at her, and Ken grinned appreciatively then said, "I promised Martin I'd hang around, but if you—"

"I'm not going anywhere," Sheila said. "This has been so much fun."

"I think she really does want to be a drag queen," Josh said.

"Yeah, well, you didn't exactly flee from the spotlight," Sheila commented as she sat down.

"Some night when I'm with Blaine, I'll let you two play in my closet," I promised.

As we ordered another round of drinks, I tried again to picture Blaine here. Maybe if he could see how relaxed Josh was, he'd loosen up a little.

Now that the entertainment was finished for the night, the dance floor filled. Ken was absorbed by a conversation with our waiter. When Sheila and Josh left to dance, Gretchen scooted next to me.

"I was thinking," she said. "I'm not going to Pennsylvania for Thanksgiving. Had you planned to go to Wisconsin?"

"No. I may end up going for Christmas, but I already told my mother I won't be there Thanksgiving."

"Cindy and I talked about going to Happy Hollow. Even though Cindy's not in the picture anymore," she grimaced, "I wouldn't mind going there with friends and doing the whole turkey or tofu routine. If you're interested, maybe we could put together a group? Ken, Martin, anyone else you feel like asking, some of my friends."

I thought it over, wondering if Blaine or Sheila had plans. I knew if Sheila wasn't planning to go to Eau Claire, she'd jump at the chance for another weekend out of town. She might even want to ask Josh. Was it asking too much of Blaine to strand him for a long weekend in a house full of strangers? Were he and I comfortable enough together to put ourselves in that situation?

For a split second I longed for Jeremy. If being part of a couple sometimes got boring, one did have the advantage of knowing exactly what the other would and would not put up with. Blaine remained an enigma, and whatever was happening between us was still a mystery. Was he my boss and an occasional bed buddy? Were we a couple? Did we want to be a couple? Or would we just stay coworkers and friends, each of us moving on to other sex partners and potential husbands? Was I merely Blaine's escort into a new world where he could be himself? Would he find it easier to inch his way out of that intense need to guard his private life if he were around other gay people?

"It's just an idea," Gretchen said, watching my thoughts chase each other across my face. "Think about it and we'll talk."

After Martin had the chance to join us and receive our congratulations on his show, I shared a cab home with Sheila and Josh. Whereas I wanted to take advantage of the close quarters and interrogate Josh, Sheila immediately began pressing me for stories about my days at Club Chaos. I told them what it was like to work with Martin ("Very spontaneous. He rarely sticks to the script."), how we came up with the sketches ("It's amazing what can come from a good case of late-night zanies."), and the story about how Ken and I created 2Di4.

Josh reaffirmed my faith in Sheila's good taste by joining the conversation, laughing along with us and asking questions of his own.

"It sounds like you really enjoyed performing at Club Chaos, Daniel," he said. "I can't believe you gave it up."

"I really didn't have a choice," I reminded him. "Plus I needed a change. I did enjoy performing and loved all my characters, but I was beginning to feel a little . . ." I trailed off, not knowing how to put it in words.

"Tired of it?" Josh offered.

"Schizophrenic?" Sheila guessed.

"In a way, both," I nodded. "I loved performing. I probably still would, but after a decade of drag, I'm enjoying the change of scenery Blaine's office is providing."

"He's enjoying it, too, I believe," Sheila said.

"Oh?"

"Yes, and that's all you're getting out of me," Sheila insisted. "I really don't want to get in the middle of you two."

"I'd think most women would jump at that opportunity," Josh said, and we all laughed.

We exited the cab together, since Sheila lived only a block away and Josh wanted to see her to her door. We said our goodbyes, and I meant it when I told Josh it was a pleasure to meet him. Sheila and I promised to talk the next day.

As I walked home, I decided to accept Gretchen's offer to spend Thanksgiving at Happy Hollow. But I still wasn't sure about inviting Blaine. If he was enjoying our time together the way I was, it would be nice to share a holiday in the country and get to know each other on a more intimate level. But if we went to Happy Hollow, Ken and Martin would be there. And of course, I'd want Sheila to come, since she didn't have many close friends in the city and my friends were her friends, too. It would be nice if she brought Josh, but surely with everyone together someone was bound to spill the beans about 2Di4. I wanted to be honest with Blaine, but I still wasn't sure if he'd be comfortable with my past.

I went into my apartment and filled my watering can to give my late-season plants a quick drink. I gazed up at Blaine and Sheila's apartment; there was a light on, but no movement inside. I wondered if Sheila was alone then chided myself for thinking like a big brother. Sheila had said she didn't want to get in the middle of my relationship with Blaine. Though we still hadn't had a chance to talk about it, I understood she was letting me know that she didn't want to be a part of another relationship triangle. I decided to return the favor and stay out of her relationship with Josh, although that didn't mean I couldn't enjoy their friendship over a holiday weekend.

After watering the plants, I climbed into bed. Whether or not

Blaine would enjoy my 2Di4 stories as Sheila and Josh had, I finally resolved that I would invite him for Thanksgiving. I was tired of thinking in circles about it all. If someone said something that sparked his curiosity, I'd deal with it then. At the very least, I owed him the chance to decide for himself whether or not my past was a problem.

Or, I thought, as I buried my face in the other pillow, hoping to find some lingering scent of him, maybe we'll just spend all our time in bed.

FOURTEEN

I ate spaghetti only when I was eating alone. I always managed to get half of the sauce on my shirt or face, so I never ate it when dining out with friends. It was far too embarrassing, and I felt like a slob midway into the meal. However, I loved spaghetti and enjoyed twirling the pasta around on my fork after spending an hour or more perfecting my homemade sauce.

I finished sopping up the leftover sauce with a piece of garlic bread then stacked my dishes, taking them to the kitchen to be washed. I thought about planting my own herbs next spring in my garden. Perhaps fresh basil and oregano would bring out a new flavor in my sauce.

I filled the sink with hot water and began setting the cutting board, silverware, saucepans, and plates in. I hated washing dishes and found it funny how something so calming as slicing, dicing, and stirring could end in annoyance. Both activities allowed time for thought and reflection. However, washing dishes was dull and boring and not creative at all.

Most of all, I felt lonely; washing dishes only intensified the feeling. The idea of cleaning up after a turkey dinner for one on the upcoming holiday certainly didn't seem festive. I shook the suds off my hands and reached for the phone.

"Gretchen? Did I wake you?"

"No, I was just looking over a client's portfolio and having a glass of wine before bed," she said.

"Whatever turns you on, babe," I joked.

"It's all I have. What's up?"

"I decided to accept your invitation for turkey day."

"Fantastic! I'm so glad to hear it. I was worried I'd be bored out of my mind."

"What do you mean?" I asked as I continued washing dishes.

"Well"—I heard her shuffling papers together on her end of the phone and shutting a file drawer—"although it's supposed to be a holiday getaway weekend, I've also invited a few clients to share dinner with us."

"Is it too late for me to back out?" I joked.

"No! I mean, yes, it is," she laughed. "It's not like that. They're cool. You'll like them. Not only are they clients, but also investors in Happy Hollow. Who are you bringing? And what's all that racket?"

"I'm washing dishes. It's amazing how many dishes get dirtied just making spaghetti for one."

"For one? Where's Mr. Man?"

"Still out of town on business, but he'll be back tomorrow," I sighed.

"Did you invite him to Happy Hollow?" Gretchen asked.

"Don't worry; I'm going to ask him," I said and dried my hands on a dish towel. "Are Ken and Martin coming?"

"Of course. It wouldn't be the same without them," Gretchen said. I heard her sip at her wine as I poured a gin and tonic for myself and went to the living room to sit down. "Hey, Daniel? Please invite Sheila and Josh, too. She's a nice girl. I enjoyed having her up here last time."

"She's straight, you know," I giggled.

"Oh please," Gretchen groaned in my ear. "I know. Besides, even if she did ride our bus, I'd probably break her in half. I like my women a little more—"

"Able to fell trees with a single chop of an axe?" I interrupted.

I could hear Gretchen hold the phone away from her and bellow with laughter.

"No, not trees, my boy," she said, "the kind of women I like tend to chop other types of wood."

"Touché!" we said simultaneously.

"Yes, I'd love to invite Sheila and Josh. In fact, I thought of asking them on our way home last night from Club Chaos. I had a good time with all of you."

"But you had to think about asking Blaine?" Gretchen queried.

"Yeah, I did. I was worried that instead of turkey we'd have, 'Hey, did you know Daniel used to perform in drag?' as a main course."

"You're not still stuck on that, are you? You haven't told him?"

"I did a lot of thinking about it last night and have decided that if I'm going to have a meaningful relationship with Blaine, I have to tell him," I said emphatically.

"Good for you," praised Gretchen.

"And then I spent all day today weeding my garden and convincing myself not to back out of that decision."

"Don't worry," Gretchen said. "If it's meant to be, it'll work out. And the only dish I plan on serving will be soy-based. I hate to be a stick-in-the-mud, but I'm wiped out, hon. I need to get to bed."

"Tough week?"

"Yeah," she sighed. "I had a good time last night, too, but I brought work home with me this weekend because the holiday week will be short. Plus the wine is doing its magic and I'm getting sleepy."

"Okay. I'll talk to you soon to let you know what's going on. Good night."

"G'night."

I hung up and took my empty glass into the kitchen. I was feeling tired, too. It was only eleven in the evening, and I felt like it was sunrise. The phone started ringing the minute I finished brushing my teeth. I ran to pick up the extension in the bedroom.

"Hello?"

"What are you wearing?" Blaine growled.

"A Christian Dior ball gown, Manolo Blahnik satin heels, and a tiara. How about you?"

While Blaine laughed, I realized I'd opened a window of opportunity to tell him about my past. It was a perfect moment to start the conversation, but it stuck in my throat.

"How are you?" was what came out instead. I didn't want to talk about it on the phone. I wanted to talk about it in person.

"Tired. Worn out. Wiped. Frazzled. Weary. Oh, did I mention that I'm tired?"

I laughed and started taking off my clothes.

"Working hard, are we?"

"I have single-handedly convinced Lillith of Lillith Parker Designs to let us handle her advertising," Blaine said.

"That's fantastic," I cheered and crawled into bed. "I knew you could do it."

"I wasn't sure. Lillith turned out to be a tough nut to crack. Nut being the key word. We could only meet either at exactly six twenty-eight in the morning, or ten forty-nine at night, because those were the moments chosen by her astrologer as being the best times for her to conduct advertising meetings. Her assistant was practically barring the door to her office with a Swiss timepiece."

"What's next?" I asked.

"I want to come home," Blaine sighed.

"I meant with Lillith Parker Designs, but we can talk about that some other time," I giggled.

"It's late and you're off the clock anyway," Blaine said.

"Are you still coming home tomorrow?"

"Yes. Am I still going to see you tomorrow?"

"Yes," I promised. I couldn't help but smile. I realized how much I'd missed him while he was gone. Most of all, I missed being held in his strong arms. "When does your flight get in?"

"Eight A.M. and you're the first person I want to see other than the driver picking me up. Is that okay with you?"

"It is. I'll see you when I wake up then," I confirmed, surprised at how happy I felt.

"Good night," he said and hung up the phone.

I fell asleep quickly, despite being excited to see Blaine again and nervous about Thanksgiving at Happy Hollow and potential revelations about my reign as Princess 2Di4. I was awakened by the piercing ring of my intercom, alerting me that Blaine must be at my front door. I looked bleary-eyed at the clock on my bedside table. It was eight-forty. I stumbled out of bed, went down the hall, and pressed the "talk" button on the intercom.

"Wha—huh?"

"Avon calling," Blaine's voice crackled through the archaic intercom.

"Don't you mean Lillith Parker?"

"I left her in Baltimore with her crystal ball. Let me in."

I pressed the button to open the lock on the front doors of the building, opened my apartment door, and peeked into the hall.

Blaine was coming toward me in boots, blue jeans, and a peacoat, with a carry-on bag slung over his shoulder.

"Hey, sailor," I mumbled, "wanna dock in my port?"

Blaine rolled his green eyes as I let him in.

"I've missed you," he said and dropped his bag so he could enfold me in his arms.

"I know the feeling," I agreed and kissed him.

Blaine broke the kiss and said, "We can do this later. I've really missed *you*. Talking with you like we did the first night I slept over. Let's go for a walk. Get dressed."

I stood and stared at him in shock for a minute. I really liked this guy.

"I'm sorry," he said. "Please get dressed."

"No, it's not that. I . . . you . . . Never mind. I'll be right back," I stuttered and dashed into the bedroom to dress, not knowing what Blaine had in mind for our day.

Fifteen minutes later we were walking up Eighth Avenue in the brisk autumn air. We ducked into a bakery for large cups of coffee and donuts to take with us as we walked.

"I can't believe it's getting cold already," I said.

"It is November," Blaine reminded me. "Besides, this is nothing compared to back home."

"I know."

We crossed Columbus Circle and Blaine guided us through the southwest entrance to Central Park. I hadn't been in the park in a long time and was pleased to see that the first few cold days of autumn had left their mark on the trees. Red, brown, orange, and yellow leaves were being carried by the breeze through the air and across the ground. We crossed the road that looped around the center of the park and headed north. Even though it was still early for a Sunday, the park was alive with people jogging, biking, roller blading, and walking.

"Oh, thank you, Blaine. This was a really good idea."

"I needed a good dose of nature," Blaine explained. "It's been a while."

"When was the last time you were home?" I asked. "In Eau Claire, I mean."

"Well, gee. When did I move here? May?"

"Long time, no nature, huh?" I asked, trying to keep it light. I thought there might be a reason for him not to go home. Sydney, perhaps, but he'd said he didn't want to talk about her, so I didn't intend to bring her up.

"I'm still new to the company," he reminded me. "I want to go home for Christmas, but I feel funny about taking time off. Though I already have a week's vacation coming to me."

"That reminds me, I have a proposition," I announced. "We've been invited to spend Thanksgiving at my friend's place upstate. There'll be more nature than this and all the tofu you can eat."

"Daniel, promise me you'll never write ad copy, okay?"

"I'm serious," I said and playfully swatted him with the bag of donuts. "My friend Gretchen is a great cook, and the place we'll be staying is beautiful. It'll be really relaxing, and I think you'll enjoy my friends."

"Is this the place you went to with Sheila?" he asked. We walked by Tavern on the Green and Sheep's Meadow, where people were tossing Frisbees and footballs. There were even a couple of die-hard sunbathers.

"Yes. The very place," I answered.

"She said it was amazing," Blaine confessed. "And I'd like to meet your friends."

"You should definitely meet my friend Ken. I gave up Sunday services with him to be with you today."

"Is he someone you go to church with?"

"No. Brunch." I laughed. "We go to brunch every Sunday at the Screening Room. We used to call it Sunday services a long time ago when we met, because we'd be out really late on Saturday. We'd meet on Sunday to worship the healing power of pancakes and Bloody Mary."

"Ah," Blaine mused. "Hangover pancakes. I know them well."

"After a few years we gave up the late nights, but still continue meeting for brunch. Plus Ken's hair would curl if he missed his weekly dose of *Breakfast at Tiffany's.*"

Blaine stopped still and looked at me wide-eyed.

"I love that movie!" he yelled.

"Well," I said, somewhat surprised. I thought it was a bit out of character, but I remembered that I was still getting to know him.

"I know," he began as we resumed walking along the road through the park, "how gay of me."

"No, not at all. I like it, too. Oh yeah. I'm gay."

"I love Audrey Hepburn," Blaine explained. "Especially in that movie. I just want to—I don't know—take care of her when I watch it."

Let me be his Holly Golightly, I thought to myself.

"Hey, let me show you what I like," I said and pulled him off the sidewalk. We had reached Bethesda Terrace, one of my favorite spots in the park. We stood at the top of the stone stairs that led down to the terrace, which overlooked the lake. We could see the shores of the Ramble and the Boathouse in the distance.

"Wow, this is beautiful," Blaine agreed.

We walked down the many steps to the terrace.

"You've never been here?" I asked.

"I've walked outside of it, but I'm ashamed to say this is my first time in the park," Blaine admitted. "But this place looks really familiar."

"It's been in a few movies. The drug scene in *Hair* for one."

"That's where I saw it," Blaine said. "Another movie I love."

"Boy. You're just full of surprises," I laughed. "I would've thought you'd be into movies like *Wall Street* or *The Usual Suspects*. Instead you give me a musical and a gay icon."

We tossed our empty coffee cups into a trash can at the bottom of the stairs. Blaine took the donut bag from me and peered inside.

"There's one left," he observed.

"What kind?"

"Uh, looks like chocolate."

"It's yours," I offered.

He took it out of the bag, tossed the bag into the trash, and led me to the wide rim of Bethesda Fountain. We sat down, and Blaine thoughtfully munched away on the donut.

"You know," he began after swallowing, "one of the best things about new relationships is getting to know the other person."

"It never stops," I said with a smile.

"No, it doesn't. You'll always learn stuff about them that may, or may not, surprise you. Sometimes you might like what you learn and sometimes you might not. But if you're lucky, you're right, you never stop getting to know them."

I found myself with another opportunity to tell Blaine about 2Di4. This time we were in person and the window was wide open. Blaine was revealing himself to be a very rational man, but I was still afraid that he wouldn't be able to handle it. The night he'd drunkenly told me about seeing my act, he hadn't sounded so open and rational. I was afraid I'd lose him. But how long could I avoid the subject?

"Listen," he said.

There were a lot of people wandering about the terrace, some sitting on the edge of the fountain like we were, most staring across the lake. There were many conversations floating past us, and I didn't know if that's what he meant.

"What?" I asked.

"It's so quiet here. It's hard to tell you're in the heart of Manhattan."

"That's one of the reasons I like it here. We're near one of the roads through the park, but when the roads are closed, it's like you're in another world," I said. "Also, what I really wanted to show you was the angel sculpture in this fountain. I think it's one of the most beautiful things in this city."

We both looked at the sculpture. The large stone angel loomed above us with her wings outstretched as if she were in midflight.

"I always feel like she's protecting me. I come here when I need to feel safe," I said.

I looked back at Blaine and he was staring at me with a smile. I felt surprised and touched when he leaned over and kissed me gently on my lips. This was progress for someone who guarded his privacy so zealously.

"I'd like to protect you," he said.

"I'd like to let you," I answered.

"Come on," he said, standing up, "let's keep going. Rest time is over. Think there's a coffee vendor in here somewhere?"

"There should be. Let's find one."

We kept walking, and I played tour guide for Blaine. I took him to Strawberry Fields, where we found a vendor and savored the hot coffee he offered. We walked through the Ramble to Belvedere's Castle, and through Shakespeare Garden, another of my favorite spots. Blaine made me promise that we'd return when it was in full bloom so he could get a lesson in flora.

We continued walking north and talked more about movies, our favorite songs, and books. I found out that Blaine loved mythology, especially Greek and Russian legends. We kept the conversation light, telling each other about things we enjoyed, what made us happy, rather than reciting our autobiographies to each other. It seemed like time had stopped, but then I realized we were dodging an obscene number of joggers.

"Blaine," I said, looking around and realizing where we were, "we've almost completely circled the Reservoir."

"Yeah, I guess we have," he agreed with a broad grin. "I hadn't realized it, either."

"You must be exhausted. What time is it?"

"Oh, who cares?" Blaine asked, throwing his head back and arms out, nearly decapitating a passing jogger as he embraced the sky. "It's beautiful out and I feel so alive. The air actually seems clean today. We need to do this again very soon. When is Thanksgiving, anyway?"

"This Thursday."

"Can we leave Wednesday night?" he asked.

"Yes," I replied and Blaine grabbed me in a fierce bear hug that lifted me off the ground.

He adds to my happiness, I mentally told Ken.

I suddenly realized that during all this time in the park, I hadn't once thought of Jeremy or the times we'd spent here. It was as if Blaine made it all new for me, as if he made *me* new.

Hello, I spoke to my inner voice. Here's your chance to warn me about moving too fast. To remind me that I'm still dealing with the end of one relationship and shouldn't jump into another. To say whatever it takes to keep me from falling in—

Whoa! it shrieked. That *is* going too far.

"What are you thinking?" Blaine asked when he saw me smile.

"That you give great hugs. Let's go home and fight over the remote."

My Monday at the office was a long day, with me making Thanksgiving arrangements in addition to my other work. I called Gretchen at her office to confirm the plans for Happy Hollow. Blaine, Sheila, Josh, and I would all have rooms at the inn and places at the table, along with Ken, Martin, and Gretchen's friends.

"I spoke with Ken about your situation," Gretchen said.

"My what?"

"You know perfectly well what I'm getting at," Gretchen said, obviously not alone in her office and reluctant to go into detail. "Hang on a second. Mary, would you go copy these forms for me?" After a count of ten, she returned to our conversation. "Sorry. Mary was in here with me."

"Who's Mary?" I asked. Another call came through on my phone, and I let it go to voice mail without answering.

"She's my assistant. She used to see you regularly at Club Chaos. Mary had the biggest crush on 2Di4. Anyway, Ken shares my opinions regarding you and Blaine, but agrees that you have to decide for yourself when the time is right to talk about that stuff. As for Martin, we can't promise anything other than we'll be on guard for any outbursts from him."

"That's like trying to divert the path of a tornado. Thanks, Gretchen."

"Don't mention it," she chuckled. "I hate to do this, Daniel, but I've got tons of crap on my desk to get through if I'm going to get to the Hollow tomorrow."

"I thought you were going up on Wednesday."

"I've got nearly a dozen guests coming now. I'm psyched, but I'm too much of a perfectionist not to get up there early and make sure everything is in order. Besides, I have tofu pies to make. I'll see you Wednesday night."

I laughed when I hung up, hoping the tofu pie was a joke, then retrieved my calls from voice mail. Two of them were appointments for Blaine regarding Lillith Parker. Apparently Ms. Parker's astrological calendar did not take into consideration busy holiday seasons.

By Wednesday afternoon, I was sure Blaine was as tired of work as I was. I waited in the building lobby for him to join me after a meeting with Mr. Fox.

"Did you remember to turn off my coffeemaker?" Blaine asked as we climbed into a cab.

"Fifty-fifth and Seventh Avenue," I directed the driver, who lurched into the traffic heading uptown. "Of course I turned off the coffeemaker. You know how efficient I am."

"Mmhmm," Blaine said.

"Anyway, relax. This is our time now. I don't want to talk about work."

"Okay," Blaine agreed and settled into the backseat with me.

The cab let us out in front of Hertz, where Sheila and Josh were waiting on the sidewalk.

"Hey!" Sheila greeted us and gave us each a big hug.

"Do you have our bags?" I asked. I had dropped my weekend bag off at Blaine and Sheila's apartment before I left for work. Sheila had promised to meet us at the rental car agency with our bags and Josh so we could get an early start.

"The bags are all here," she reassured me, gesturing at the luggage at Josh's feet. Josh gave a small wave, moved forward, and shook our hands. "Now you boys go get our cars. We'll watch the bags."

I'd made reservations for two cars, one in Blaine's name and one in Josh's name. Sheila and Josh had kept their schedules for the following week open, which allowed them a full week to stay at Happy Hollow. Although Gretchen would be returning to the city on Monday, she had encouraged them to stay at the resort as long as they wanted, since there was now a full-time caretaker at the main house.

Once Blaine and Josh were out of earshot, Sheila pulled me toward her and linked her arm in mine.

"It's cold," she complained. "Are you nervous about this weekend?"

"A little," I admitted.

"Me, too," Sheila said and exhaled as if she had been holding her breath for a week. "Josh and I haven't had much time alone. I'm worried that spending a week together so soon might make or break us."

"Ditto," I said.

"By the way, Josh is under strict orders not to say anything about our visit to Club Chaos or anything regarding 2Di4."

Before I could comment on that, the boys each drove up in shiny new Fords and got out to help Sheila and me load the bags into the cars.

"Not so fast," Sheila said to Blaine and Josh, who each stood next to a car waiting for us to get in. "You two are taking one car, and Daniel and I are in the other."

"I just assumed—" Blaine began.

"So did I," Josh said.

"Nope," Sheila said, shaking her head. "Josh, we'll have a whole week together. I haven't seen much of Daniel lately. I'd like to take advantage of the drive and have him all to myself."

"Aw," I gushed as Sheila wrapped her arms around me. "This will give you guys time to get to know each other."

"Come on, Josh, get in," Blaine said, opening a car door for him. "It'll make your week a lot easier if she gets her way."

Sheila stamped a foot on the concrete and shouted, "I am *not* difficult, damn it!"

"Here," I said, handing Blaine a piece of paper. "Gretchen faxed me a map and directions to the resort. I already know the way, so you can use it if we get separated."

We set off for the highway, me driving with Sheila as my copilot, Blaine and Josh following us. I was careful not to lose them in rush-hour traffic, as commuters made a mass exodus from Manhattan to their homes in the tri-state area. I was mindful of Sheila's position of neutrality regarding my relationship with Blaine and waited for her to bring up the topic of relationships. I only had to wait until we reached the "on" ramp to the highway.

"How are the boys doing?" she asked.

I checked the rearview mirror and could see Blaine laughing at something Josh was saying.

"They look fine. Does Josh always talk with his hands?"

"Yes," Sheila giggled. "He was telling me a story about some photo shoot the other day and nearly wiped Dexter off the back of the couch. Poor kitty."

"Have he and Blaine talked much since you started dating?" I asked.

"Not really. Either I'm at Josh's, or Blaine's at your place, or Blaine's at the gym, or we're all at work. Blaine's apartment has been like a—" She broke off, not sure how to describe it.

"Rest stop?" I offered.

"No, I went before we left," Sheila said. "I have to say, though, I haven't seen Blaine this happy in a long time."

I saw the brass ring and went for it.

"He's happy?"

"Oh yeah!" Sheila exclaimed. "Are you kidding? You and I haven't talked much lately, but it's okay because he always has something wonderful to tell me about you. He's very impressed with you at work and as a person. And I can tell you're rubbing off on him in a really positive way. He's definitely not as stiff as he used to be."

"Actually, I rather like his stiffness," I commented.

Sheila gasped and swatted my shoulder then dissolved into a giggle fit.

We spent the rest of the drive discussing our new jobs, new boyfriends, and new lives. I had forgotten how much we had in common. Not only did we share a link regarding Blaine, but we were both coming out of an awkward transitional period in our lives.

Sheila was now getting small jobs through Metropole. She was hired as a fit model for a local fashion house, which bored her, as it involved many hours of standing in place in a body stocking as people fit various dress patterns to her body. She'd also landed her first magazine ad, which featured a close-up of her face as she held a tube of toothpaste in her mouth.

We never lost Josh and Blaine on the drive. Occasionally they drove alongside our car in the passing lane when there was no traffic, to make faces and wave at us. They seemed to be having as much fun as we were, which quelled my nervousness about the impending weekend.

Gretchen and her friends were sitting with Ken and Martin on the porch of the main lodge when Blaine, Sheila, Josh, and I arrived. We leapt from our cars and stretched before walking up to the porch. Gretchen stood and spread her arms wide.

"Welcome, one and all."

The sun had just set, leaving only a little natural light. There were introductions and handshakes all around. Everyone walked inside to the large sitting room, where a fire was already burning in the gigantic fireplace. Gretchen excused herself as she went into the kitchen to prepare a light dinner.

"I want you all to be starving for tomorrow's feast. It will be a Thanksgiving to end all!"

At first it seemed that the room was divided into cliques. The lesbian contingent sat closest to the fire in a small circle. The three investors—Cathy, Millicent, and Veronica—sat on the edge of a plush maroon sofa. Cathy was the CEO of a small software company developing programs for the Internet. Millicent owned a chain of gay bookstores and coffee shops. Veronica was a litigator. She had the same aggressive air as Gretchen but, unlike Gretchen, lacked that undercurrent of warmth. On the floor, legs tucked neatly under her, sat Jane Gorman, a television show producer and close friend of Gretchen's.

Ken, Martin, Blaine, and I sat opposite the power lesbian sofa. I nervously watched Martin suck down his fourth glass of wine. I hoped he wouldn't start reminiscing about the good old days. As much as I loved him, I knew that Martin's tongue and alcohol very rarely mixed well. At least for anyone who had anything to hide. Though I'd prepared myself for Blaine learning about 2Di4, I had no intention of letting it happen during the first hour of our holiday.

Sheila and Josh had mysteriously disappeared without anyone noticing. I speculated about what they might be doing. Just as my imagination began to create stories, they walked in from the porch.

Josh came in first, carrying a large bottle of vodka and a bottle of vermouth. He held them above his head as if he'd had to go into the woods to hunt for them. Martin looked up at the bottle and clapped his hands excitedly.

"Martinis!" He leapt up, yelling, "Gretchen? Do you have any olives?"

A muffled Gretchen responded from the kitchen, "Sure do!"

Gretchen appeared in her Martha Stewart apron and set the olives on the bar at the opposite end of the room. She quickly returned to the kitchen. Sheila followed her to offer help. Martin hopped over the bar and gathered up a shaker, ice, and martini glasses.

"All my years at the club taught me more than just dancing and singing," Martin bragged as he tossed the shaker into the air and spun underneath it like Tom Cruise in *Cocktail.*

Minutes later he rejoined us with four perfectly prepared martinis. I sat back and sipped his magic mixture, picking out an olive and letting the salt and vodka mix together on my tongue.

"So did you and Daniel ever appear on stage together?" Blaine asked.

"Oh yeah, almost every night for years."

My stomach twitched nervously, and I shot Martin a look that missed him completely. Luckily Ken intercepted.

"All three of us were in a show together, actually."

"Really? What was it called?"

"Making Mr. Right," I blurted before Martin could respond. "It was years and years ago."

Josh suddenly became very preoccupied with his cameras, obviously intent on dodging this discussion. Martin twirled his olive around in the glass. Ken eyed him strangely, then looked at me with an almost apologetic smile.

"So you're a big fan of *Breakfast at Tiffany's,*" Blaine said.

"Oh yes. Daniel told you that we rarely miss it on Sundays?"

"He did. I would love to see it in the theater sometime."

"I think that can be arranged," I said, slipping my arm around Blaine's shoulder.

I could tell when I touched him that he felt at ease here. I realized this was probably one of the first times he'd been surrounded by people from whom he didn't have anything to hide. It made me very happy to know that I was providing him with something he'd been missing and, from what I could tell, wanted very badly.

"You know, Daniel was one of the best performers," Martin said, looking up from his olive.

"Really?" Blaine replied as he looked at me, smiling almost proudly.

I, on the other hand, tried not to visibly squirm in my seat.

"Yes, and he can sing like nobody else. Whenever he took the stage at the club as—"

I jumped from my seat, realizing Ken wouldn't save me this time. Before I knew what I was doing, I took the olive out of my mouth and plopped it into Martin's. His eyes were nearly crossed when he looked up at me. He fell back against the chair.

"Geez, Danny, if you didn't want the olive, you could've just told me."

"Who's the actor?"

Our heads whipped around, realizing that our two cliques were about to join. Jane Gorman addressed our group over her shoulder.

"Sorry, I couldn't help but overhear."

Before anyone could answer, Gretchen appeared from the kitchen ringing a tiny silver bell.

"Dinner is served," she said in her best Jeeves voice.

"What the hell is wrong with him?" I muttered to Ken as Gretchen began giving directions to everyone about where they could wash up and replace or refresh their drinks.

"He's nervous," Ken answered softly. "He wants to make a good impression on Blaine."

"Blaine is fine," I said. "*I* feel like Olivia de Havilland in *The Snake Pit.*"

Blaine emerged from the small washroom by the sitting room and slipped his arm through mine. I looked over my shoulder to see Martin swaying by Ken's side. Ken whispered into Martin's ear. Martin looked at me, eyes widening. A hand flew over his mouth.

He then mouthed the word *sorry* to me as Blaine and I disappeared around the corner into the dining room.

We sat around a large oak table and dug into Gretchen's light dinner. She'd prepared soy-based chick-none and broccoli, spring rolls, and basmati rice. Gretchen never ceased to amaze me with her varied talents. As we all munched quietly, Blaine leaned over and whispered in my ear.

"We are going to be eating real turkey tomorrow, aren't we?"

"Oh no," I joked. "It will be tofu molded into the shape of a turkey."

A worried look passed over Blaine's face, then he realized I wasn't serious.

After we had finished eating, we all helped Gretchen clear the table and prepare for the next day's big feast. Jane Gorman insisted on helping me take the dishes to the industrial-sized dishwasher.

"Have you ever thought about television?" Jane asked as she loaded plates onto my good arm.

"Well, I watch it occasionally."

"No, I mean acting for television."

"I did move to New York to establish an acting career. Lately, though, I seem to have moved on."

"Just from watching you this evening, I really think you'd be perfect for a part in a television pilot I'm developing. The thing is, it requires a few months in Los Angeles."

"Wow," was all I could muster as it sank in. "I don't know. That's a big step."

"You don't have to answer me now, obviously. Take some time to think about it."

She slipped her business card into my back pocket. I smiled at her as she helped me set down my large stack of plates. I didn't want to think about this opportunity just yet.

Whatever happened to that dream? my inner voice asked, against my wishes that it remain silent about the subject. I had just met a great man, one who made me want to stay in New York indefinitely.

It's just a few months in Los Angeles, the voice reminded me, and I demanded that it not be mentioned again until we returned to the city. I wanted simply to enjoy the holiday without complications. Other than Martin, of course, though he was subdued, at least for the moment.

"Ready to retire for the evening?" Blaine asked with a mischievous gleam in his eye.

"Definitely," I said swinging around in his arms.

We awoke the next morning naked and wrapped around one another in the soft sheets on the large Victorian bed. I looked at Blaine's smooth skin and hard body as the morning sun danced across him. The smell of roasting turkey crept under the door. I rolled over and looked at the clock. I turned back to Blaine and ran my tongue up the length of his spine.

"Mmmmorning." he mumbled, just waking.

He turned to me, the sun bringing out the yellow flecks in his green eyes, almost like cat eyes. I loved that. I lifted a hand to touch his face, making him smile. He pulled me against him and kissed the back of my neck. I could have stayed like that for the rest of the day, but knew we had to get moving.

"Come on, lazy, time to get ready for the feast."

"I think I need to work up an appetite."

I couldn't resist the look on his face, like Rock Hudson in *Pillow Talk*. He had a slight smirk and a glint in his eye. I kissed him without insisting that we brush our teeth first. It was dirty but romantic, just the way I liked it.

After sharing a long, hot shower, we got ready to join our Thanksgiving family. When we entered the foyer from the staircase, it was obvious everyone had been downstairs for hours, except Sheila and Josh, who came down the stairs just after us. I gave Sheila a knowing look which she returned with a satisfied smile.

When Martin and Ken came inside from a walk in the woods, we were ready to eat. Everyone filed into the kitchen to grab a plate. It was quite a spread, reminding me of big family dinners in Eau Claire. The fattest turkey I'd ever seen shared the center of the dining room table with lasagna, which I assumed was Gretchen's vegetarian main course. Both were surrounded by apple slices and kale, homemade cranberry sauce, salads, breads, and several vegetables, including the traditional green bean casserole with breaded onions on top. Gretchen beamed as she presided over the table.

"Gretchen, this is fabulous," Ken said as he helped himself to some yams.

Everyone agreed, filling their plates then taking their places at the table. I looked around and realized that I had never felt so at ease at a Thanksgiving gathering, either those in Wisconsin or the ones I'd shared with friends in New York. I knew there would be no fighting, no veiled comments of disapproval from family members, no political disagreements, and no one throwing their drink in anyone's face.

Gretchen took her glass and stood to address us.

"Thank you all for coming and making this one of my best Thanksgivings ever. I'm sure you all have family traditions. When I was growing up, we all had to say what had made us happiest during the year. If you don't mind, I'd like to begin."

Gretchen held her glass high in the air and looked around the table, smiling equally at everyone. We all took our glasses and raised them to her as she began.

"I'm not sure you all know about my relationship with my father. It wasn't very good after I told him that my boyfriend wasn't a guy named Michael, but a girlfriend named Michelle. That was right after college, nearly twenty years ago. Since then, we've barely spoken. This past April, he called me out of the blue and simply said, 'I'm sorry.' That day, that phone call, was the happiest moment of my past year."

I choked up, thinking of my own strained relationship with my parents. I was happy for her and clapped my hands.

I was so intent on listening to everyone else that I hadn't thought about what I wanted to say. Suddenly Sheila was talking, and I would be next.

What has made me happiest this past year, I wondered. It had seemed like such a bleak year until I met Blaine. Was that the happiest moment? Could I say that in front of everyone? Did he feel the same? Would I scare him away?

There's only one way to find out, urged my inner voice.

I waited a few moments after Sheila had finished telling us that her happiest moment was the day she set foot on the island of Manhattan, finally feeling like she had opportunities that she wouldn't have had if she'd stayed in Eau Claire.

When Sheila sat down, I stood and held my glass high, realizing that my hand was trembling. I took a deep breath and glanced around at everyone, pausing when I looked down at Blaine, who was looking up at me. I felt sappy but true to my emotions as I began.

"It's been a trying year for me. As most of you know, a lot happened. But there is one moment I will never forget."

My eyes locked with Blaine's.

"I'll never forget looking up from my garden at five thirty-three and seeing the most stunning man in the window of the building across the alley. He never called the cops on his stalker, and I thank you for that, Blaine. Ever since I met you, my days have gotten better and better. Not only does that have to do with you, but how I feel when I'm with you. Each day is a pleasure, and I'm having the best time learning about you. And I've gone on way too much and this is way too schmaltzy," I finished, then did a little curtsy and started to sit down.

Blaine rose and kept me standing by grabbing my arm.

"That was the most—" He stopped, at a loss for words. "Thank you."

Sheila and Ken both started tapping their forks against their wineglasses, as if they were at a wedding, signaling for us to kiss. We both shrugged and kissed. I felt a little like a trained seal, but it was still enjoyable.

"I guess I'm next," Blaine said, addressing the table. "And I think you stole my line," he added, looking at me. "I don't know if I can say this is the happiest day of the past year, but it is one of the highlights. I've realized, being here with all of you and seeing how comfortable you are with yourselves, that I haven't been honest with myself. You'd think after being in New York for seven months that I might have made one or two other gay friends, but I haven't. I've stayed careful about not saying it out loud; admitting it, really. Being here has made me want to change that. Daniel, you have made me the happiest and most honest."

I didn't need the clinking of glasses to encourage me to kiss Blaine this time; I did it voluntarily. We sat down, and he held my hand as Veronica and Millicent recounted their happiest moments.

"Thank you, everyone. And finally, dig in!" Gretchen commanded.

We all munched, making only occasional grunts of contentment. We finished off the meal with pumpkin pie and coffee. Gretchen and her friends sat by the fire to play a cutthroat game of Monopoly. Blaine and I excused ourselves to take a walk through the woods.

I led him toward the pond. As we neared, I stopped him.

"Look," I said, pointing.

Just by the pond were two deer, bowing their heads to drink.

One was a buck and one a doe. Blaine took me in his arms as we watched them.

"Daniel, I'm having a wonderful time. Your friends are really great. Martin's a regular comedian."

"He has never failed to either aggravate me or make me burst into laughter. He's the most unpredictable of the whole group. I must say that you fit in nicely."

"I feel like I do."

"I'm glad. Now kiss me."

"Wait," Blaine said. "There's something I want to talk about."

His tone was serious, which made me nervous again, wondering if someone had finally said something that made Blaine curious about my past.

"Okay," I said.

"I meant what I said about wanting to live more openly. Feeling at ease in public with you, or with friends like this, means a lot to me. I'm not exactly ready to be out at work, and you know what my situation with my family is. But there is one thing I have to do by the end of this year. Sydney and I have finally stopped fighting about the terms of our divorce. It's time for me to break the news to my family. I think I should do that in person. Christmas is probably not the best time, but it's when I can get back to Eau Claire, and I don't intend to keep lying about my marriage to my family. I'm really scared, because I know they're going to react badly."

He paused, and I waited.

"I don't know exactly what will happen, but I do know one thing. I don't want to spend Christmas a thousand miles away from you. I don't know if you've already made plans, but I'd like to buy your ticket if you'll go to Eau Claire when I do. Even though we'll be staying with our families, just knowing you're nearby would mean everything to me."

I thought it over as Blaine watched me anxiously, then said, "Of course I'll go. But you don't have to buy my ticket."

"I want to," he said, relief flooding his face. "Just consider it your Christmas gift to me."

"You want to buy your own present?" I asked.

"The gift is that you'll be there when I need you. It's all I want."

"Believe it or not, knowing you're in Eau Claire will make my visit home easier, too," I assured him.

"You're sure you don't mind? You don't already have plans with your friends?"

"I don't. But even if I did, I'd change my plans for you," I answered, realizing it was true. There was nowhere I'd rather be at Christmas than where Blaine was. And though he was unable to tell his family about me, maybe I'd find the opportunity to tell my family about him.

I considered the implications of all that. To choose Blaine's comfort over time with my friends, to want to talk about him to my parents in a way I'd never talked about Jeremy . . . I was obviously now entering relationship territory.

Instead of making me edgy, the idea filled me with contentment. It was turning out to be a great year after all. I really did have a lot to be thankful for: Blaine as my potential boyfriend, Sheila as a friend, a new job I was handling more than capably, Ken's continuing good health, and, I grinned to myself as Blaine put his arms around me again, the joy of watching Martin struggle against revealing my secret. Maybe in Eau Claire I'd tell Blaine about my glamorous history. In the meantime, it was rather entertaining to see Martin on his best behavior, even if it would last only a few days.

FIFTEEN

As soon as I walked into Breslin Evans on Monday morning, I could sense tension in the air. Mitzi held up a hand to stop me from grabbing Blaine's mail and heading for my desk.

"Blaine's in a meeting," she said when she got a break from the switchboard. "Upstairs. Said to let you know all his appointments for the day have been rerouted to someone else. Did you have a nice Thanksgiving?"

"Uh-huh," I answered vaguely, wondering what was up.

There was nothing on my desk, or Blaine's, to give any clues. But "upstairs" meant he was meeting with the partners. There was no reason for that to make me nervous. No one at the agency could possibly know about Blaine and me and the fact that we'd just spent Thanksgiving together. But evidently Blaine's desire for secrecy was beginning to have an effect on me. I felt doom creeping in and wondered if he would blame me if his career went south.

It's not always about you, my inner voice reminded me.

Two hours and several cups of coffee later, I was like a sixth grader who'd missed his Ritalin dose. My phone had been uncharacteristically quiet, so when it rang, I nearly came unglued.

"He's on his way," Mitzi hissed and hung up.

I could hear him talking to someone as he came down the hall. By the time he rounded the corner, he was alone.

"My office," he said, hurrying past me.

When I followed him in, he pushed the door shut, locked it, then grabbed me and startled me with a kiss.

"What the heck is going on?" I demanded.

"Remember how Allure Cosmetics brought me to New York when they moved their advertising to Breslin Evans?"

"Yeah."

"And all the research I've been making you do on Lillith Parker Designs and how I met with the wacky Ms. Parker in Baltimore?"

"Uh-huh."

"What I couldn't tell you was that Lillith Parker and Allure were planning a merger. The deal went down over the weekend. Frank Allen remains head of the Allure Division. One of his requirements was that Lillith Parker keep us as their agency and give me more responsibility. I guess it was in the stars because Lillith agreed. I just got promoted to Account Planner. From now on, I'm the single point person for packaging, promotion, product development, acquisition, anything to do with Lillith Allure Cosmetics. It's my only account, but it's all mine."

"Congratulations," I said. Even if I didn't understand it all, I could see that he was thrilled. "How does this change things for you here?"

"I won't be run ragged trying to satisfy a lot of clients," Blaine said. "And I don't have to put up with so much of the competitive bullshit around here. As long as the bottom line stays good and that's tied to the advertising—which, of course, it will be—I'm set. Plus I report directly to Mr. Fox now. I'll be working as hard, but I'll be a lot happier. And you and I are moving up a couple of floors. You'll have your own office and no Evelyn to torment you."

"It's sounding better every minute," I said with a laugh.

"One other thing. I'm pretty sure Frank Allen knows I'm gay, and it's obviously not an issue for him. If the partners find out, even if they have a problem with it, they'll want to keep our client happy. I feel like I can breathe, Daniel. I never expected things to come together for me so soon. I have to tell you, lately I've been feeling a little unfocused. I knew I wasn't working as hard as I did when I came here. I just didn't feel excited. This has given me a whole new perspective. I think you brought me good luck. You and the planets, of course."

"Should I read up on what it means when Mercury is in retrograde and Jupiter aligns with Mars?" I asked, giving him a hug.

"All you have to do right now, babe, is work your magic with Bernie and furnish our new offices. But prepare yourself. These next few weeks of transition will be busy. Plus you can expect some hard feelings from a lot of people around here. Don't take it personally. It's the nature of the business."

Though I liked the way he made me feel like part of his career, I felt a quiver of apprehension. The more visible Blaine became, the more damaging any public awareness of our relationship could be to him. Seeing his excitement now reminded me that I never wanted to be a professional liability to him. At least I wouldn't have Evelyn watching over my shoulder all the time.

"Will this change our plans to go to Wisconsin?" I asked.

"Nope. They know we're both taking a few days off before Christmas," he reassured me.

Blaine had been right when he said we'd be busy. The days were a blur. But one thing I could be sure of was that three times a week, no matter what, Blaine kept his date with himself at the gym. His commitment to that made me conscious of myself. When I was performing, I usually stayed in shape by stretching and dancing. Lately I hadn't been doing much of anything physical, other than between the sheets with Blaine. On nights he was at the gym, I looped the Reservoir a couple of times, if not with the same stamina as when I'd run with Bill as a teenager, at least with enthusiasm. It made me happy that Blaine had rekindled my appreciation of Central Park.

The other constant part of the weeks before Christmas was Sunday brunch with Ken. Blaine even went with me once. Martin wasn't there, and Ken was so delighted to share it with another *Breakfast at Tiffany's* fan that I might as well not have been there either. It actually made me happy to be ignored as I watched Ken and Blaine bond over the movie.

Somehow we even managed to get some Christmas shopping done, usually with Sheila along. More and more I felt myself settling happily into these new relationships and patterns. It was hard to believe that only four months earlier, I'd felt like my life was falling apart.

The night before Sheila left for Eau Claire, the three of us ate by the fireplace at the Renaissance Diner to say goodbye and celebrate the fact that I was finally out of my cast. It had stayed on two weeks longer than they'd expected; I'd been anxious that it wouldn't be off before I went to Eau Claire. Proof that I kept such things from her would only cause my mother to worry even more. Of course, my arm looked all pathetic, but long sleeves would conceal that.

Blaine was thrilled that the cast was gone, as he'd been its victim on more than one occasion. He promised to badger me into rebuilding my arm muscles.

Sheila sighed as she watched us and said, "I wish you two were leaving tomorrow, also. It's going to be so boring in Eau Claire."

I wrote my parents' number and address down on the envelope she'd brought with some of Josh's photos from the Happy Hollow trip.

"We look like an Eddie Bauer ad," Blaine said, flipping through pictures.

"We look happy," Sheila said.

"We are happy," I added. "We'll all be available to save each other in Wisconsin, I promise."

Blaine looked a little apprehensive. I knew he was dreading the confrontation with Sydney and his family about the divorce.

"Are you sure Dexter will be okay being boarded?" Sheila asked, giving me a quick look to show she was reading Blaine, too. "I feel guilty."

"He was fine during Thanksgiving," Blaine reminded her. "It's a resort. Catnip appetizers, pigeon under glass—"

"He did *not* eat that pigeon," Sheila interrupted.

"I'm just saying, feathers on the floor, wicked gleam in his eye, the evidence adds up."

"It's the circle of life," I added.

"You're both beasts."

"I never ate raw pigeon," I disagreed.

That night Blaine went home with Sheila to keep her company and help her with her luggage the next morning. I missed him, but I was excited to think of the few days we'd have all to ourselves before we had to split up in Eau Claire. I found myself dreading that more than I'd expected. Part of it was the idea of separation, but I knew some of it was just outright jealousy. I had no idea what arrangements he and Sydney had made. I wanted to think they intended to tell their families immediately. But for all I knew, they'd stay together at one family's house until they worked out their story. And this was assuming Sydney planned to cooperate. Blaine had told me on the day I found out about Sydney that they were having difficulties agreeing on the terms of their divorce, though apparently those issues were now resolved.

It was also apparent that Sydney didn't know Blaine was gay, as she'd been furious when she found out Sheila was living with him. I hoped she didn't assume they were a couple and cause problems for Sheila with the Meyers family. But since Blaine didn't want his family to know he was gay, it would probably be a lot worse if she found out about me.

It was too confusing to think about without all the facts. I knew the reason I didn't push Blaine to talk was because I had my own secrets. When I was away from him, it all seemed ridiculous and I'd make up my mind to force conversations about Sydney and 2Di4. But when I was with him, I'd lose my nerve and let one opening after another slip by.

When we were finally in the air—first class, which I hadn't experienced since my tenth birthday with Aunt Jen—I steeled myself to at least try.

"Will you be staying at your parents' house?" I asked casually.

"Not the first couple of nights," he said. "I'll be at the Ramada Inn."

"Alone?"

He looked at me and shook his head, saying, "She'll be there. We're meeting—"

"At the airport?" I asked.

"No, I told you I'm renting a car and driving you from the Twin Cities to Eau Claire. It would hardly be wise to have her along. We're meeting at the hotel."

"So I can't call you."

"Are we going to have our first fight over"—Blaine rose above me to look out the window—"Ohio?"

"No, we're going to have it over Sydney." I laughed, realizing how stupid that sounded. "I'm just jealous at the thought of you being with her."

"As flattering as that may be, I assure you it's unwarranted. We're going to talk strategy, make sure our divorce papers have everything we agreed on, then take her to her parents' house so she can give them the news. Then I'm going home to have that same pleasure with my family. Of course you can call me. And we're definitely seeing each other Christmas Eve, right?"

I nodded, wondering why three days seemed like such an expanse of time that I had to nag him about it. Furthermore, I could hardly expect Blaine to do more than I was willing to do. It wasn't like I was rushing home to tell my parents about him, after all.

I let out a deep sigh, and he shook his head.

"Stop worrying. I've reserved my room at the Ramada for the duration of my stay. Depending on how things go, I may be using it. Which means if you're available, we can have all the privacy we want."

I wasn't entirely mollified, but I let it drop. He obviously really did not like talking about Sydney.

He reached over to clasp my hand, tossing a nice smile at the woman across the aisle who gave us an odd look. I was tempted to give him a big kiss and was glad I resisted the urge when her face softened into a return smile. I had to stop seeing everyone outside Manhattan as the enemy, but it was my usual mood whenever I returned to the Midwest.

"I hope you get a chance to meet my sisters while we're here," I said. "They'll like you."

"Did Jeremy ever meet your family?"

"Nope."

"Maybe when I drop you off, you could introduce me."

"That might not be such a good idea." His eyes looked a little hurt, and I explained. "I didn't tell them I was coming, so I'm not sure who's there or what's going on."

"I understand."

"No, really," I assured him. "It's not you."

He stared at me a moment before saying, "You don't deal with this parent thing any better than I do, do you?"

"You're right. We don't talk about it because that would make it real. The next time I hand out advice, you are free to remind me of that."

"Hey, Daniel?"

"Yes, Blaine?"

"We're on the same side."

"I know."

Time seemed to move at warp speed. We were at my parents' old farmhouse too soon. I couldn't force myself out of the car.

"It's nice out here," Blaine commented. "Isn't it great the way they used stained glass in these houses when they built them? And they last forever. I could see—"

He broke off.

"What?"

"I could see myself living in a place like this. Just not here. Sort of like what Gretchen has on a smaller scale."

"When it's Dunhill Breslin yada yada, you'll have your country home upstate," I promised.

"You think?" he asked.

"Absolutely. I guess this is it. You've got my number. I've got the number at the hotel. We'll talk?"

"We'll talk."

We stared at each other until I said, "Oh, the hell with it," and leaned over to kiss him, trying not to look forlorn. He had enough on his agenda without pressure from me, too.

When he pulled away, I trudged to the front door. I pushed, but it didn't budge.

Odd, I thought, they never lock the door.

I rang the doorbell and no one came. I ran to the back of the house. All of the lights were off.

I dropped my bag on the back porch, turned, and sat on the steps, unsure what to do next.

"Fuck!" I shouted and felt a lot better. I laughed and propelled myself off the steps. Ten feet in front of me was my mother's garden. She had expanded it and included a latticed arch at its entrance, which was covered with grape vines. It looked like the cold had killed them, adding a nice Gothic effect to the garden.

I felt a little less disoriented when I saw that the link between my two homes was a garden, even if my mother's had died and so would mine.

Not die, Daniel. Rest. So it can bloom again for you in the spring. I could hear Sheila's voice.

I turned back to the house, thinking of Blaine's words of admiration. It was a rather stately old home that had once stood alone among hundreds of acres of farmland. Now it was in Eau Claire's version of the suburbs. The nearest house was a few hundred feet away, but still within viewing distance. On the south side of the property, adjacent to Mom's flower garden and separated by a row of small elm trees, was Dad's vegetable garden. It was quite large and produced my family's winter feast of potatoes, tomatoes, peas, beans, squash, and corn.

I walked back up to the house and around to the front. I finally remembered the hook inside the garage where my parents kept an extra key. I found it, returning to the front door to unlock it. As the key turned in the lock, a voice from behind startled me.

"Now hold it right there, and don't move," the voice commanded with such authority that I did as I was told. "I've got a deer rifle and you're a lot smaller than a deer, so I suspect it'll do some damage if you make any funny moves."

"Last I heard, Mr. Gunderson, you haven't hit a deer in ten years," I said loudly to the front door after recognizing our neighbor's voice. "I could probably get away before you adjusted your eyes to the sight, which leans to the left, not that you even know that."

"Daniel Stephenson, is that you?" he asked, laughing. "Holy buckets, son, turn around and let me look at you."

I did just that and met him in the drive for a firm handshake, followed by a slap on the shoulder that nearly sent me sprawling to the dirt.

"Having a gun pulled on me makes me feel right at home, but thanks for lowering it. I appreciate that," I said good-naturedly.

"Heck, son, you should be used to that living in that city of yours."

"Well, it's the city so they're a bit more advanced. They've upgraded to handguns now."

Not getting my sarcasm, he just nodded, perhaps pondering picking up a pistol for his collection. Mr. Gunderson had been our neighbor across the street for years and always looked after our property as if it were his own. He explained that my parents had gone to pick up Lydia from Stevens Point. They wouldn't be returning until the next day.

"Sure you don't want to come over for dinner tonight, son?"

"No, sir, but thanks for the offer," I replied. "I'm awfully tired after my flight and I'm sure Mom has leftovers in the fridge. I'm here for several days, so I'll be seeing you."

He gave me another firm handshake and turned to cross the road after tossing me a hearty wave. I let myself into the house and pocketed the key to replace later in the garage. Everything was quiet. As I walked through the entry hall to the family room in the back, I began to imagine living in it myself sometime in the future. Would I want to retire here? It was really too big for one person. Perhaps Blaine and I could—what, raise a family?

It dawned on me that I had never thought about raising a family with anyone before. Much less in the house where I'd grown up. I disappeared into a fantasy of having a young child on my lap in the rocking chair in front of my parents' fireplace. We'd look through a photo album, turning the pages together, each photo evoking a story to tell my child.

"What's this picture of?" the child would ask, pointing to the album.

"That is me, your father, singing in drag at Club Chaos in New York City. I was quite a brilliant performer, if I do say so myself, and could've continued my career if—"

"What's 'drag,' Daddy?"

I shuddered away the vision and went into the kitchen to forage for food.

Later, after giving up the relentless pursuit of something interesting to watch on a television that only broadcast four channels, I took my bag upstairs to my old room. It still amazed me that my parents had never changed it into a second guest room or a study. Except for Gwendy's addition of the photo of me dressed as 2Di4 on the dartboard on back of the door, everything was exactly as I had left it when I was eighteen and went to New York. Whenever I came home to visit, I felt as if I had stepped into an episode of "The Twilight Zone."

The single bed was still pressed against the corner of the room near the window. The drama award I had won in my senior year of high school still hung next to a framed photo of Bill and me costumed for *Rebel Without A Cause*.

I opened a dresser drawer and changed into a pair of flannel pajamas. It was a bit chilly upstairs, and I knew I'd appreciate any extra warmth they'd give me. I crawled into bed and fell into a deep sleep.

I awoke with a start and felt shooting pains in my stomach. Wincing, I took some deep breaths and clutched my aching stomach with both hands. Something wasn't right; my stomach was huge.

"Blaine! Blaine!" I screamed, but he didn't answer. I remembered that I was at my parents' house and tried to calm down.

"Mom! Dad! Is anyone home yet?"

My mom sailed into the room in a gauzy pink dressing gown which flowed behind her.

"Oh, Daniel, it must be time," she said with glee as she sat down beside me on the bed. "This is so exciting. I know you must be feeling some discomfort right now, but soon it'll all be over."

"Discomfort! It feels like I've been poisoned. What did I eat?" I gasped.

Mom laughed.

"Where's Dad?" I groaned. Mom continued to laugh. "Mom? Where's Dad? Mom!"

She kept laughing as she got up and left the room.

"Okay. Okay. Just keep calm," I said to myself and got out of bed, ignoring the searing pain in my stomach. I went into the hall and nearly screamed. The hallway was circular and turning like something in a funhouse. I tried to make my way to the stairs at the other end but kept slipping on the spinning hallway.

"This is ridiculous!" I exclaimed. I crawled back to my bedroom and sat panting in the doorway. The shooting pains started again.

"Help!" I yelled and crawled onto my bed, which rolled slightly, as it had been replaced with a hospital bed. "Oh, how tacky."

"Daniel," Ken said as he walked briskly into my room. "Here's the latest change to the show. I know, I know, it's really short notice, but you've only got ten pages to memorize. I know, I know, you've only got a few hours."

I screamed as another searing burst of pain soared through my body.

"Okay, maybe we've got less time than I thought. I'll break it down for you. Your contractions go on for another three pages—"

"Contractions?" I interrupted.

"—then you have about five pages of birthing; the rest is the finale. You should really focus on that part. I don't think ad libbing will cut it."

"Daniel," Martin exclaimed as he burst into the room in a nun's habit, "Sister Mary is here. Dominae Christae what-the-hey."

"I don't believe this," I groaned, moving into a semisitting position.

"Nurse, I want ten cc's of gin and tonic standing by."

"Sheila!" I shrieked, relieved to see a sane face.

"Daniel, sit back and try to remain calm," Sheila commanded as a team of nurses tied sterile scrubs behind her back. "Just go through your breathing exercises, and this baby will be delivered in no time."

"Baby? Baby?" I was feeling hysterical. "I don't know nothin' 'bout birthin' no babies."

The room erupted with laughter. Martin blessed himself and tried to look pious.

"Daniel, I'm serious," Sheila said. "Where's your coach?"

"My what?"

"Here I am," Ev said and entered the room in gray shorts, a gray sweatshirt, socks pulled to the knees, and sneakers, accessorized with a silver whistle and a hat that said COACH.

I shrieked as she walked boldly up to me and slapped me across the face.

"All right. Enough chatter. Now breathe! Breathe!" Ev said and blew on her whistle.

I started huffing and puffing as my feet were placed in stirrups. Martin sat back in a corner with an enormous tub of popcorn. Sheila was slowly getting plastered as she placed herself between my legs to receive my baby. I noticed that the team of nurses were the ad agency's Mitzi, Lisa, and Teresa in supporting roles.

"Where's my script?" I moaned.

"Too late," Ken said from the old typewriter at my desk in the corner. "We have some last-minute changes. You're gonna have to wing it."

"*Nooooooo!*" I screamed.

"Daniel!" I heard Lydia yell from downstairs.

"Lydia!" I answered, but Sheila was moving into position.

"Here it comes," she slurred, and everyone moved around her to see.

I started yelling as I felt my stomach turn inside out.

"Keep pushing, Daniel. Keep pushing," Sheila calmly said, as another gin and tonic was given to her with a bendy-straw.

I pushed, despite my bewilderment at giving birth. How was it biologically possible?

No, don't think about that, I told myself.

"We're almost there," Sheila cheered.

"Push, you damn bastard!" Ev yelled in my ear.

"This is going in my act for sure," Martin said.

"Aieeeeeee!" I squealed and felt the pain subside to a dull throbbing.

"It's a ball!" Sheila exclaimed and tossed a red rubber ball into the air.

Everyone applauded and started to pass it around the room with a series of taps.

"Daniel!" Lydia yelled, bursting into the room.

I awoke with a start, feeling my stomach to make sure I was awake. It was normal sized. I slapped myself just to make sure I was fully conscious.

"My god, I just had the most bizarre dream," I moaned. "Stop yelling at me!"

Lydia jumped on my bed, as she had for as long as I could remember, bouncing me up and down until my teeth felt loose. I easily flipped her over and pinned her. She was the only petite person in our family; everyone else was tall, and Gwendy was the first to admit she was built like a fullback.

"You think your *dream* was bizarre?" Lydia leered at me. "That's only the beginning. Why didn't you tell someone you were coming?"

"I wanted to surprise you. I couldn't believe no one was here when I got home."

"Blame Creed," Lydia said cryptically.

"Creed? What?"

"Creed is the guy our parents think I'm dating. They met him when they picked me up. He's so outrageous that you can only look good by comparison."

"Gee, thanks," I said.

"I'm a giver." Her expression was angelic. "Anyway, they didn't bring me straight home from Stevens Point. We went to the Twin Cities. Creed was doing a poetry reading, plus"—she paused for maximum effect—"we all went to an exhibit yesterday."

"You got Mom and Dad into a museum?" I asked, too stunned about that to even broach the whole poetry reading thing.

"Nope. It was an exhibit of panels from the Names Quilt."

"Okay, obviously I'm still dreaming. Go away and let me sleep."

"You shouldn't be so judgmental," Lydia said.

"*I* shouldn't?"

"You don't know your parents half as well as you think you do," Lydia insisted.

"What's next? PFLAG?"

"I wouldn't be surprised," Lydia said. Her face became serious as she added, "Really, Daniel, be a little gentle with them, would you? They don't disapprove of you nearly as much as you think. They were so disappointed when you didn't come home for Thanksgiving. It was really hard for them to see the Quilt and worry about you. I think it's time the three of you had a talk."

"They haven't wanted to talk about my life in the twelve years since I left," I muttered.

"How do you know what they want? You make as many assumptions about them as they make about you. Oh, I'm not saying they understand everything. And no, I doubt they'll be calling the local chapter of PFLAG. But they do love you."

"Yeah, so much that when I do come home, they don't even come upstairs."

She gave me an exasperated look and said, "You're *so* pleasant when you wake up. How pissed would you have been if they'd come charging in here, Mom hugging you and Daddy asking a bunch of questions?"

"All right, all right," I said. "Let me take a shower, then I can face them."

When I finally made it to the kitchen, Lydia was conspicuously absent. My father was on a ladder doing something to the tile trivets that were just one of the things my mother collected. He waved his hammer at me while my mother hugged me before pushing me into a chair. She had rarely waited on me while I was living at home, but now I seemed to make her nervous in the kitchen.

"We're so happy you decided to come home, Daniel," she trilled. "Though you should have let us know. I feel terrible that no one was here to welcome you."

"Sure there was," I disagreed. "Mr. Gunderson met me with his deer rifle."

"He couldn't hit the broad side of a barn," my dad pronounced.

"I've already called your grandma and told her you're here," my mother went on. "But if you don't want to go to the nursing home, she'll be with us on Christmas Day."

"No, I'll go see her before," I insisted.

I never minded going to see my grandmother. Her nursing home was like a little soap opera, and she and her group of friends loved to regale me with stories that, innocent as they were, would have scandalized my mother. I was their best audience. On more than one occasion, their dead-on commentaries about life and people had found their way into my act.

As I drank my coffee and started in on my eggs and bacon, I got an update on Mary Kate's pregnancy. I was expected to go see her as soon as possible. That was fine. I got along with Mary Kate and Ray, and I always liked seeing my nephews, Troy and Danny. I felt a little guilty because I hadn't found Christmas presents for them yet. Then I remembered the collection of Marvel comics under my bed. Both boys had always gravitated to them, but I wondered if they were old enough now to take care of them. Just because I was ready to give them up didn't mean I wanted them trashed.

I posed that question to my mother and she said, "Oh, they'd love them. You don't have to worry about that. Whenever they're here, they treat them like the Holy Scriptures."

I did a double take. Had my mother just made a joke?

She grabbed my plate as I finished, and my father came down from the ladder, clearing his throat.

"Your aunt tells us you have a different job," he said.

I felt my mother get tense at the sink.

"Yes, I stopped working as a female impersonator," I boldly said. "I work in an office now. At an ad agency. In fact, my boss is from here. Blaine Dunhill."

I felt a secret thrill of pleasure just saying his name.

"Dunhill? Like Dunhill Electrical?" my father inquired.

"Yes."

"That name seems familiar," my mother said. "Oh, is that the one who married the Kepler gal?"

This was not going the way I'd planned, and I said a little glumly, "Yes. How do you know that?"

"Oh, the Keplers are Dr. Noble's patients. I've cleaned their teeth for years," my mother replied, then with a quick change of subject added, "You probably have good benefits at the agency, don't you? Like health insurance?"

All right, I thought. I can deal with this one right now and get it out of the way.

I took a deep breath and said, "Mom, I'm not sick. I'm not going to get sick. I've been tested for HIV. I don't have it, and I don't have AIDS."

She almost seemed to shrink under my gaze, and I suddenly

wondered when my parents had gotten old. I felt guilty at the way I'd thrown those words at her. We'd been fine dancing around these issues in the years since I'd dropped my bomb on them about being gay.

You have not been fine, my inner voice finally piped up. You've felt like an outcast, and they let you feel that way. This is your chance to tell them how it felt to grow up with your terrible secret, about all the loneliness and fear you felt. They should know that the last twelve years haven't been all glorious as you found a re-placement family. They should know what it feels like to hear your sisters constantly praised while you've been invisible to them, just someone who comes home for an occasional holiday visit and has to hide everything that's important to you so they can be comfort-able.

I opened my mouth and heard myself saying, "So. How're the Packers doing this year?"

"Hey, Daniel?" Lydia yelled from the front of the house. "You have company!"

Blaine, I thought, and immediately my mind went through a dozen scenarios. He'd already told his family about Sydney. Or maybe about me, and they'd kicked him out. Or maybe he just re-alized how wrong it was for us to be staying apart, and he'd come to get me. How would my parents react to that?

I realized I didn't care. Just like with my drag persona, I was tired of living a dual existence and ready to put a stop to it.

I hurried to the living room to find Sheila.

"Oh my god," she said, hurling herself into my arms. "I know it's rude that I didn't call first, but I had to get out of my house. I for-got to bring your number but I retained a general sense of where you lived. Please forgive me for barging in on you this way, but I swear, if I have to endure another minute—"

"Slow down!" I said. "What's wrong?"

"I'd like to kill Blaine and Sydney for the position they've put me in. It's just one question after another about living with them in New York. How can I tell my parents the truth when I don't know what *their* parents know yet? Plus when I told them I'm dating someone, it turned into the Inquisition. I feel like I'm sixteen again!"

When she finally stopped to take a breath, still clinging to me, I realized my mother was standing in the doorway watching us with a bemused expression. She smiled knowingly, waiting for an introduction.

"Mom, this is Sheila Meyers. Sheila, this is my mom."

"Nice to meet you, Mrs. Stephenson."

"Please, call me Joyce."

"Thank you Mrs. . . . . oh," she caught herself, "Joyce."

"What can I get you, dear? Would you like something to drink? How about a nice cup of hot chocolate?"

"Oh, no," Sheila blushed. "Thank you very much. I really am sorry to have barged in. You must think I'm some kind of nut. But oh, my parents are making me insane."

"Come into the kitchen and tell us about it, dear," my mother said, and I knew Sheila was about to be absorbed into the family. All important happenings took place in the kitchen. "Daniel, bring your friend into the kitchen so she can have a seat."

The emphasis on *your friend* wasn't lost on me.

Hope springs eternal, eh Daniel, the inner voice groaned.

I looked at Sheila and rolled my eyes, guiding her to the kitchen and whispering, "Speaking of feeling sixteen."

In spite of the fact that Sheila had declined any refreshments, my mother instantly presented her with a cup of Ovaltine and a small plate of shortbread cookies that contained about two sticks of butter per cookie.

"Now, dear," my mother began without hesitation, "you must understand that parents are entitled to be overprotective. They invest too many years in caring for you and loving you to let you run off to . . ." She glanced at me. "Well, they just love you is all. They don't mean you any harm and want to make sure you're taking care of yourself since it's difficult for them to do from so far away."

"I know. It's just hard sometimes, you know?"

"Have you and Daniel been friends long?"

Something in the way she said *friends* made me want to grind my teeth.

"It really hasn't been that long, but it sure feels like it's been forever, doesn't it, Daniel?" Sheila asked and hugged my arm, completely oblivious to any inferences my mother might be making, then ran her hand through my hair.

"Sometimes things are just meant to be," my mother added with her usual finality.

This translated that it was meant to be as far as she was concerned, so the rest of the details of our relationship, like the fact that I was gay and that Sheila and I were just friends, were immaterial.

My father returned to the kitchen, hammer in hand.

"Hello, who have we here?"

"Louis, this is Daniel's new friend, Sheila."

"Uh, I—" Sheila began, finally starting to get my mother.

"It's good to meet you," my father said, giving me an odd look in reaction to the tone of my mother's comment.

I rolled my eyes again and shook my head. What an amazing day.

"It's nice to meet you, Mr. Stephenson."

"Oh, call me Louis. All of Daniel's friends do."

I shot him a startled glance, wondering to whom he was referring. Then I remembered that he worked with a lot of my old classmates. In his view of the world, they probably were my friends. I ran through my mental Rolodex, appallingly gleeful at the idea of either of my parents meeting some of my real friends.

I sighed, knowing that wasn't likely. However . . .

"Mom? Dad? I've been seeing someone," I blurted.

Sheila's eyes widened.

"We know, dear," my mother beamed, with a glance at Sheila.

"I should go," Sheila said.

"Who are you seeing?" my father asked.

"Sheila," my mother said.

"What?" Sheila answered.

"A man in New York. He's actually my boss," I responded to my father.

"No, dear, I was talking to Louis," my mother addressed Sheila.

"What?" my father asked.

"I've been seeing my boss," I repeated, thinking my father hadn't heard me.

"Oh? You two are working together?" my mother asked.

"Who's working together?" My father was getting more and more confused.

"Louis," my mother had an exasperated tone, "aren't you listening to any of this?"

I put my head down on the table. I heard Sheila's chair scrape across the linoleum floor.

"I really ought to go," she said again.

I sat up and said, "No. I think I'm going to need you here for this."

She sat back down.

"Daniel, didn't you just say your boss is married to that Kepler gal?"

"Yeah, Dad. He's married."

"You're seeing someone who's married?" my father asked.

"They're separated. He intends to divorce her. That all happened before I met him. Blaine is really a nice guy, and I would have told you about him but . . . well, you never wanted to hear about that part of my life before."

Sheila put her arm around me, sensing that I could use the support.

My mother was very quiet as my father considered my words. Everything seemed to hang in the balance, and I held my breath.

"If he's important to you, Daniel, you should be able to talk about him," my father finally said.

This was more surreal than my dream. I watched my father as he poured himself a cup of coffee and topped mine off.

"He's a special guy, Dad. In fact, when Sheila got here, I thought it was him. I was really excited that you'd get the chance to meet him. I guess maybe you still will; I hope you do. I want to share more about my life, the things that are important to me, with you. I feel like we only talk about safe topics; sometimes that gets hard for me. It's like you don't want to know anything about me, so we end up talking about everyone else. A little of that is okay, but sometimes when you ask, 'How's everything going,' I wish I could really answer you and tell you the truth. Does that make sense?"

My father nodded and my mother looked down.

"I know this isn't easy for you. It's not exactly what I signed up for, either."

"I've always been sure this is your aunt's fault," my mother said.

"Mom, the only thing Aunt Jen ever did was insist that I live with a sense of self-worth and dignity. In order for it to be anyone's fault, someone would have had to do something wrong, and no one did. This isn't anyone's fault, and it's not a choice I made at some point, either. I've always thought I was born this way. It's like having blue eyes. I just have them. But the other thing you need to know is that while this may not have been my choice, it's not something I regret.

I wouldn't change being gay even if I could. I love who I am, and I'm proud of who I've become. I guess I wish you could be proud of me, too. Even if you don't understand everything I do, if you could just trust that I'm doing my best."

"Of course we're proud of you, son," my father said.

"It's not easy being a parent," my mother said slowly, as if searching for words. "You can't help but have hopes and expectations for your children. It's part of the reason you have children. You raise this person who can share your hopes and dreams, that you can give all the best to. What they don't tell you is that the person you're raising is going to have hopes and dreams of his own, and they may not be the same as yours. It would be too much to say that's a disappointment, because it's not. You haven't disappointed us. But the realization that things won't be the way you thought can be a bitter pill to swallow."

My father broke in, "But make no mistake, Daniel Stephenson, you've never given us any reason to be anything but proud. Do you know," he continued, turning to Sheila, "Daniel was always taking care of things. Stray or hurt animals, anything or anyone who needed help. His best friend in high school moved here in the tenth grade. You know how kids can exclude someone new. But Daniel befriended him right away so the other kids did, too."

I couldn't help but laugh, thinking of how bizarrely different our perspectives of my adolescence were.

"That's exactly what he did for me," Sheila said, her eyes dancing. "There I was, new in the city, and Daniel brought me flowers—"

"Shut up," I said with a smile, knowing full well that she'd long ago figured out that lust for Blaine was my motivation for worming my way into her apartment and her life.

"Maybe we didn't say it enough. But son, there's a difference between always telling you how proud we are, and telling you we've always been proud."

As my father talked, my mother grabbed Sheila's cup to give her more Ovaltine. It was obvious that the conversation was making her uncomfortable, and Sheila, always tactful, allowed herself to be waited on to give my mother a distraction.

"I'm sure your parents are the same," my mother finally commented, determined to direct the conversation back to Sheila. "Even though we make a lot of mistakes, and sometimes we drive you crazy."

"Thanks," Sheila said with a smile. "I know you're right."

"Our two younger girls are both away at school," my mother went on, placing Sheila's cup in front of her. "I worry about everything. Whether they are eating and sleeping properly, who their friends are. I can't imagine my girls living as far away as you. What do you do in the city?"

"I'm a model," Sheila said. "And I'm well taken care of because I have Blaine and Daniel to look after me. Even though I can take care of myself, it does mean a lot to me that I can count on Daniel. He's a wonderful friend. And he's introduced me to many of his other friends, who are also great. I feel like I have a whole family in New York, thanks to Daniel."

"When you are in Eau Claire, you're always welcome to visit us, too."

I gave an inward sigh, wondering how long my mother and Sheila would talk at cross-purposes, with Sheila standing up for my real life and my mother clinging to her vision of what my life should be.

"So you say Blaine is visiting Eau Claire, too?" my father asked.

"Yes, sir."

"I would like to meet him," my father pronounced.

"Louis, you know how busy the holidays can be," my mother said, shooting him a meaningful glance.

I could have kissed Lydia when she chose that moment to join us, asking, "Sheila, what size shoe do you wear?"

We all blinked at her, then Sheila gamely said, "Eight and a half, or nine."

"I was thinking it would be fun to go ice skating. Mary Kate's skates are a size nine, if you're interested."

"That sounds like fun," I said, relieved.

Sheila took her cue from me and said, "Sure. Where do you skate?"

"The Gundersons have a pond," Lydia said. "Come upstairs with me and we'll dig the skates out of the closet."

The girls left, and as I stood to go find my own skates, I said, "I don't know if Blaine has any free time or not, but I wouldn't ask him over unless I knew he'd be welcome. Anyway, I didn't mean to start an argument about it."

Lydia and Sheila were giggling together like old friends by the time they joined me downstairs. I was determined to fake a good mood as we trudged through snow to the pond. I backed up Sheila's assertion that the ice rink in Central Park left something to be desired after growing up skating in the pristine beauty of the Wisconsin countryside. When both girls discovered they'd been in skating competitions as children, their bond was complete. I skated away as they tried to remember old routines amid much laughter and a few falls. I felt like being alone to consider the conversation with my parents.

If my father had proven to be an unexpected ally, I knew my mother would have the last word on Blaine. A few years before, I would probably have packed and left to make a point to her. But I didn't want to be excluded from Christmas. I didn't even care if Blaine was part of it. I just wanted some acknowledgment that I was who I was and would not change.

I heard someone skating up behind me and turned, expecting Sheila or Lydia. But it was Gwendy, who stuck out her tongue at me and yelled, "Race!"

By the time we'd circled the pond a few times, I was winded and gave up, leaning on Sheila. Gwendy laughed at me, confident as always of being the superior athlete. Since I couldn't breathe, Lydia introduced the two of them.

"Uh-huh, I heard about Daniel's friend who is *not* a girlfriend but a friend of his boyfriend's," Gwendy said. "And I hear you have a new job."

"You got a lot of information in a short time," I commented as we skated to a fallen tree to sit down.

I told them about the ad agency, making them laugh at the office politics I was subjected to. Then Sheila recounted for them how shamelessly I'd used her to meet Blaine and get my job in the first place.

By the time we'd walked back to the house, my good mood was genuine and Sheila appeared ready to face her own family again. We said goodbye and I followed the girls inside so we could get ready to visit Mary Kate, Ray, and the boys. It felt good to know that whatever happened during the remainder of my time in Wisconsin, at least my sisters would make it more bearable because, with them, I could always be myself.

SIXTEEN

The next morning I woke up because I thought I heard Blaine say, "Where there's smoke, there's fire."

I looked around, trying to orient myself, then I realized where I was and that I did smell smoke. It must be getting colder if my father had built a fire this early in the day.

I took my time in the shower, hoping that when I finally went downstairs, everyone would be busy somewhere else. Nothing further had been said about the conversation in the kitchen the day before. We'd gone back to our old routine of pretending nothing was amiss. After we'd visited Mary Kate, I went alone to see my grandmother, who was in good spirits and looking forward to spending Christmas Day with us. Even though I never considered telling her the complete truth about my life, she was one of the few relatives other than my sisters with whom I relaxed. She never asked awkward questions about girlfriends or anything else. In fact, usually our conversations were about her, which I didn't mind at all.

I had no idea how many of my other relatives would be in and out of our house over Christmas. I just knew it would be an ordeal.

I wondered if things were going any better for Blaine than for me. I decided I couldn't wait until tomorrow night to see him and would call him this morning to see if Sydney was finally out of his hotel room and his life.

I went downstairs to stand in front of the fire while my hair dried, but the hearth was cold. Now the smoke seemed to be coming from the kitchen. Maybe someone had burned breakfast.

I pushed open the swinging door between the dining room and kitchen and dodged the lit end of Aunt Jen's cigarette as she swung her arm to make a point to my mother.

"Oh my god!" I said, following my impulse to grab her and hug her.

"Happy to see me, are you?" Jen asked with one eyebrow arched. She lightly tapped her perfectly manicured nails down my arm to show that she noticed my cast was gone, then, continuing her conversation with my mother, said, "I spent three hours with Lucinda listening to that drivel. As far as I'm concerned, this country is going to hell."

After a moment, I remembered that Lucinda was my aunt's hairdresser and perhaps the only person on the planet who possessed the secret of Jen's real hair color.

"What drivel?" I asked, as my mother, lips tight, handed me a bagel and pointed to the cream cheese on the table then went back to chopping onions.

"Oh, these talk shows," Aunt Jen said. "I don't know where they find people willing to spill their innermost secrets to all of America. It's disgusting. As I told Lucinda, a few more good manners and a lot less true confessions would certainly improve our quality of life. Not to mention afternoon television."

"For once, I agree with you," my mother said. "Some things should remain private."

I could tell my aunt was slightly discomfited, but she quickly said, "For example, when I was last in New York, I met some of Daniel's friends. Delightful. Perfect gentlemen. It was quite refreshing."

"They liked you, too," I said, smearing a bagel with cream cheese.

"Of course they did," Jen said, her eyes darting around the room. "Joyce, what *did* you do with that ashtray?"

"I emptied it. It's right behind you," my mother said.

Aunt Jen was the only person allowed to smoke in our house. We all knew my mother hated it. Jen usually kept one lit, even if she didn't smoke it, just to demonstrate her right to do so.

"Yesterday," Jen said, "one show was on men who dress as women and the wives who shop with them and give them makeup tips. It was all rather disheartening."

"You don't approve of men dressing as women?" my mother asked, looking up from the onions.

"Heavens, it's nothing to me if they do or they don't. But they looked simply dreadful. Let it be done with taste or not at all."

"Like my friends?" I brazenly asked.

"Oh, their impersonations were flawless," Jen said. "I could see why their performances are so popular. Do you miss it, dear?"

"Not really," I said. "Being an alluring woman is a lot of hard work."

Up went the eyebrow again as Jen said, "You're telling me. Another of the shows was about men demanding paternity tests before they'd acknowledge their children. They were giving the test results right there with an audience of millions. Deplorable."

My mother nodded, and Jen's icy blue eyes narrowed. It was obvious she was in no mood to find herself on the same side as my mother.

"Of course," she said, "privacy has its limits. Take that Hoover fellow. If he really did like to dress in women's lingerie and take male lovers, it was his business. But that he headed an organization that specifically banned the hiring of homosexuals negated his right to privacy. As you know, I believe hypocrisy is far worse than bad taste. Still, I see no necessity for private citizens to invite us all into their bedrooms."

"Or their kitchens," my mother said so softly that only I could hear her.

"Where are the girls?" I asked, taking pity on her.

"They've taken your father to do his last-minute Christmas shopping," my mother said. "He's a day early this year, since Christmas Eve is not until tomorrow."

"He tells me that you're dating your boss," Jen said, stubbing out her cigarette and carefully placing another one in the holder. "You know that never works out. I say scrap the job and keep the man, if he's worth it."

"He is," I said.

"Good. You deserve some happiness. I hear he is in Eau Claire, too. When do I get to meet him?"

Inspect him is more like it, I thought.

"Blaine's with his family," I said. "They don't know he's gay, so of course I can't go near there. He and I are having dinner out tomorrow night. It's my only chance to see him while we're here."

"In other words, I'm not invited," Jen said with a sigh. "Well, I suppose I understand. It's a shame about his family. Secrecy cheats everyone out of so much. Not that being open always works, either. Did you hear about your cousins?"

"Which cousins?"

"Your cousin Linda had to get married. To a man from Pakistan, and her parents are out of their minds because their first grandchild is going to be dark-skinned. The man is a doctor and they live in a mansion in Milwaukee, but you'd think they were homeless the way your uncle and aunt carry on. They're not speaking to her. Let's see," Jen continued, "your Uncle Harlan's oldest boy, I can never remember his name, has moved to Omaha and is living with a woman and a man. They're not sure which one he's sleeping with. Your cousin Mark has become a Buddhist and shaved his head and won't let anyone eat meat around him. Which makes things hard, because his sister Joanna has a safety pin in her ear and won't eat anything but meat. No one's sure yet exactly what religion that is. In any case, Christmas should be pretty lively this year, with no one knowing who's invited where or who's speaking to whom."

"Maybe they should all get together for turkey and stuffing with Maury Povich and let America share the joy," my mother interjected.

Jen and I both turned to stare at her. After a slight pause, I laughed.

"Don't sound so surprised, Daniel," my mother said. "Even I can make a joke now and then. You're right, Jen, secrecy does cheat us."

Her tone was angry. My aunt and I continued to watch her as she seemed to struggle with her thoughts.

"I can't imagine treating any of my children the way Ralph and Crystal are treating Linda. She's a lovely girl. Gwendy met her husband and says he's absolutely smitten with Linda. To think of Ralph and Crystal not being part of their grandchild's life because of some silly prejudice. It's cruel and wrong. And this young man— Blaine," she amended, "being forced to act as if he's ashamed of Daniel. My son!"

I held my breath, waiting, while Jen lit her cigarette with a satisfied smile.

"I baked a ham for Christmas," my mother said, and I felt disappointed that she was retreating back to some safe, irrelevant topic. "I see no reason why we shouldn't have it tonight. Jen, of course you're welcome to join us for dinner. And you," she turned to me, "should invite Blaine."

I tried not to gape at her, wondering if I'd heard her correctly.

"Unless," she said anxiously, then stopped.

"What?" I asked, dreading to hear what conditions might be placed on the invitation.

"He's not a vegetarian like Mark, is he? I suppose we could have something other than ham."

"Mom, he'll love your ham," I assured her.

"Don't you have a call to make?" Jen asked, as if afraid my mother would change her mind.

I nodded. As I left the kitchen, I heard my mother say to my aunt, "Don't look so pleased with yourself. Louis and I had already discussed this last night."

I grabbed the cordless and hurried up the stairs to my bedroom. Blaine was still at the Ramada and answered on the second ring.

"How are things going?" I asked.

"I miss you so much," he said. "Sydney's gone to her parents' house. My family knows. They're furious with me. They think all of this has something to do with Sheila. I'm such a coward for not telling them the whole truth. I'm sorry."

"Blaine, I already told you that's something you can do only when you're ready. You don't have to do it for me. I know what you're going through, believe me."

"I feel like I'm in exile here. I can't wait to see you tomorrow night."

"That's why I'm calling," I said. "We don't have to wait that long. If you think you can endure it, my parents would like for you to come to our house for dinner tonight. It's a big step for them, so I can't promise it won't be without tension. My sisters will be here, and they're fun. And my aunt, who's quite a character. But if you'd rather not take on my family while you're trying to deal with yours, I'll understand."

"I told you when we got to Eau Claire that I wanted to meet your family," Blaine reminded me. "I'd love to have dinner there. I promise not to shock your parents or anything."

"Just be yourself, Blaine, and they'll understand why I, uh, what I see in you," I amended, startled at what I'd been about to say.

"What time?" Blaine asked.

"I don't know when dinner is," I said, feeling a bit dazed. "Why don't you just come over around four, if that's okay, and we'll have time for everyone to get acquainted before we eat."

"That sounds good. I'll see you at four. Thanks, Daniel, for letting me be around one functional family."

"That I can't promise," I said with a little laugh.

After we'd hung up, I stared at the phone, thinking of what I hadn't said.

I love him, I thought. I'm not in danger of falling in love; I'm already in love. How ridiculous that I had to come back to Wisconsin to figure that out.

But I don't *need* to be in love with him, I reminded myself. It's too complicated. He's my boss. And he's so closeted at work. Not to mention with his family.

Besides, I'm his first guy. He's too young and inexperienced. He's just getting out of a bad marriage. He needs to enjoy life as a single, gay man. The timing is wrong. And if he hurts me, the way Jeremy hurt me . . .

I stared at the picture of 2Di4 on the back of my bedroom door. She looked so poised, so sure of herself, so unlike me.

Certainly so unlike the me Blaine knew. I could always greet Blaine at the door dressed as my former alter ego and earn his contempt before I got into this any deeper. But now that I'd admitted my feelings to myself, the idea of not being with him made my heart hurt. Why hadn't I leveled with him long ago?

I was the coward, not Blaine. He was juggling so many new things. But I was old enough, and certainly had enough experience with men, to know better than to deceive one.

I remembered telling Sheila not to surprise Josh with a drag show. And I'd decided to take whatever came at Thanksgiving, then allowed everyone, even forced Martin, to keep my secret from Blaine.

For years I'd expected the people who loved me to accept who I was and what I did. Then I'd treated it all as something shameful so Blaine wouldn't reject me. And now I was in love, so losing his respect, losing *him*, would be much worse.

One thing was certain. I could not ask my family to conceal the very thing I'd tried for years to make them acknowledge. If tonight was the beginning and the ending of Blaine and me, so be it. I was through hiding.

But how was I going to tell him?

Another slice of ham, Blaine? And speaking of ham, did I ever tell you that I used to parade through the streets of Manhattan dressed as the Princess of Wales?

Or how about, *Does your family serve dressing with turkey? And speaking of dressing . . .*

I fell against my pillows, staring at 2Di4 as if she'd step out of the picture and give me a place to hide.

"Are you done talking to your paramour?" asked Aunt Jen as she breezed into my room with an ashtray in one hand and a lit cigarette in the other. She deposited the ashtray on my nightstand and sat on the edge of the bed.

"Yes," I told her. "Blaine will arrive around four."

I thought about cracking a window to air out my room but remembered how cold it was outside. I actually didn't mind the smell and wondered if I'd return to my pack-a-day habit if I took a drag of Aunt Jen's cigarette.

"Do you want a drag?" asked Aunt Jen, reading my mind. "No pun intended."

"No," I laughed, but changed my mind instantly. "Yes. I do."

She handed it over and I inhaled the smoke into my lungs and held it for a minute, then exhaled it slowly. My head felt like it expanded and retracted in a subtle second as a little tension eased from between my shoulders. Then I realized I was left with a slightly icky aftertaste on my tongue.

"Menthol?" I asked, screwing up my face like a child who was just served Brussels sprouts.

"Yes," Aunt Jen said, inhaling and exhaling an indignant plume of smoke to the ceiling. "Nobody held a gun to your head."

"I never could stand menthol," I confessed. "Why aren't you downstairs antagonizing my mother?"

"I'm tired of that," she said, waving her hand in the air as if sweeping the topic behind her. "Besides, I wanted to see how you're doing."

"I'm fine," I proclaimed.

"Just fine?" she asked. "Daniel, that's an answer for those who are hiding or avoiding a topic."

"I'm not," I laughed. "Really. Everything is going great."

I told her how I was enjoying my new job. The transition from drag diva to personal assistant had gone smoothly. I wasn't discovering new elements or ancient remains, but I felt gratified at the end of the day.

"How was your Thanksgiving?" she asked.

"I spent it at Lesbian Lake," I said with a chuckle.

"Where?" Aunt Jen asked, her eyebrow nearly flying off her forehead and bouncing off the ceiling.

I told her about the trip to Gretchen's Happy Hollow retreat in upstate New York, Sheila and Josh, Martin and Ken, the fantastic dinner, the long walks in the woods, and how relaxing it all was for everyone who attended.

"It was a wonderful way to spend the holiday with my Manhattan family. I was afraid that when I said goodbye to Princess 2Di4, I'd somehow lose my friends in the process. I'm so glad that didn't happen."

Aunt Jen stubbed out her cigarette and asked, "You know that saying about one door closing and another opening?"

"Yes."

"That may be true. However, elevators are better for that saying. Always think of elevators."

"What on earth are you talking about, Aunt Jen?"

"Elevator doors have sensors on them and won't close if someone is walking into or out of them. That way, whenever an elevator door is opening and closing for you, your friends can follow," she explained and sat back, a look of satisfaction on her face.

I pondered what she said for a moment, as if hearing a lesson from the Dalai Lama.

"Are you saying that if the friendship is true, my friends will follow no matter what I do?" I interpreted.

"In simplistic terms, yes," she confirmed. "You have to make your own choices in life. Get in the elevator and press the buttons. Just try to go to a higher floor, dear."

"I get scared sometimes," I admitted.

"Change is never easy. Not for you or for your friends. I lost a lot of friends when I left the judge. My fourth husband."

"I thought he was your second husband."

"Don't question me," Aunt Jen said. "I think I would know my own husbands. He was my second as well as my fourth, if you must know. Speaking of husbands, is Wayne—"

"Blaine," I corrected. "And yes, he's divorcing his wife."

"I've heard all about that, my dear. I was going to ask if you love him."

You don't *need* to love him, my inner voice reminded me.

"I think I do," I said. "Oh damn. I know I do."

Aunt Jen patted my hands and got up from the bed. She picked up the ashtray and took it with her to my bedroom door.

"Love is more frightening than change," she declared.

"Oh thanks," I said, falling back against my pillows again. "What am I supposed to do with that?"

"I loved every one of my husbands. Just because a couple of those relationships didn't work out doesn't mean I don't still love them. People are complex. Not love. Love is the simplest thing in the world, Daniel, as long as you stop resisting it. Now, I'm off to my hotel to change for dinner."

She soared out the door and left me alone, her words ringing in my ears. Where had I heard them before? I remembered the words of the deli man after Jeremy had told me he still loved me.

Blaine was *not* Jeremy. I closed my eyes and thought about my day in the park with him. When we sat on the edge of the fountain beneath the angel sculpture, I knew I loved him even if I hadn't admitted it to myself. I hadn't needed the angel to watch over me and make me feel secure that day. I had all the security I needed right by my side in Blaine.

"I love Blaine Dunhill," I whispered with my eyes closed and lay perfectly still.

After what seemed like five minutes, I opened my eyes and realized I was now on my stomach and hugging a drool-stained pillow to my chest.

"Oh no," I said and sat up with a start. A quick glance at the clock confirmed my fear that I had fallen asleep. It was now four-thirty.

"Let him be late. Let him be late," I chanted and ran to the window in the hallway.

Blaine's rental car was parked in the driveway, letting me know that he was being subjected to my family on his own. I went to the kitchen at lightning speed. My mother was carrying a large ham to the oven to reheat.

"Oh, Daniel, honey, just in time. Open the oven for me."

"Mom," I said, opening the oven door, "why didn't you wake me? Is Blaine here?"

"Yes, dear. Get me the baster from that drawer."

"Where is he?"

"He's in the—no, not that drawer. The other drawer. He's in the living room with your father, the girls, and your aunt."

My mind reeled with fear as my inner voice shrieked, he's going to find out from them and not you!

I found the baster and passed it off to my mother like a baton in a track and field event as I raced out of the kitchen.

I found Blaine in the living room, seated on the couch between Lydia and Gwendy. Aunt Jen and my father were in the high-backed easy chairs flanking either side of the couch. A spread of appetizers lay before them on the coffee table. Aunt Jen was closely examining a tiny sweet pickle she held between her thumb and index finger.

"What on earth is this?" she asked.

"Sweet pickles," Lydia answered. "Mom grows and pickles them herself."

"I see," Aunt Jen said, and daintily bit the end off of the pickle. "Daniel! There you are. Do enjoy one of these wonderful pickles. You can start with this one."

I laughed and took the pickle from her. As I ate it, I stared at Blaine, trying to assess how the visit had been going without me. He grinned at me, obviously happy to see me and none the worse for wear.

"Hi," I said.

"Hi," he replied.

"Oh, how romantic. I may faint," Lydia said and pretended to swoon.

"Did you have a nice nap?" Blaine teased.

"I'm sorry about that. I guess I fell asleep," I lamely apologized.

"It's no matter, son," my father assured me. "We've been getting to know Blaine in the meantime and hearing all about the advertising business."

"I'm sorry. I didn't mean to ramble on about work," Blaine said.

"No dear," Aunt Jen cut in. "A handsome man like you should never apologize for making advertising seem so fascinating. I smell a delicious ham cooking. Dinnertime must be drawing near. Daniel, why don't you change for dinner?"

"And comb your hair," Gwendy added.

I reached up to feel my hair sticking out in several directions. In my haste to get downstairs, I hadn't even thought about my appearance. I must have looked appalled because Lydia started snorting and laughing.

"Young lady," Aunt Jen said, swinging her head in Lydia's direction, "you'd do well to get out of those overalls and put on something respectable for dinner with our guest."

"Try all you want, Jen," my father urged. "We've been hoping to get her out of those things for months."

"Dad. Please. It's not like I only have one pair," Lydia whined, obviously embarrassed.

"Go," Aunt Jen commanded. "And take Blaine with you. Give him a little tour of the house. He's been bored with us long enough."

"My room's a mess," Gwendy warned.

"You know," we heard Jen say as Lydia led Blaine and me out of the room, "a cluttered room is indicative of a cluttered mind. Louis, make me a Brandy Manhattan and see if Gwendy needs to help Joyce in the kitchen."

"She's like a sergeant in the army," Blaine said as we went upstairs.

"Don't let her hear you say that," Lydia warned. "She'd accept nothing less than general."

"She'd rather be Mata Hari," I disagreed. "Lydia, do you even own a dress?"

"Yes, and she didn't say anything about a dress, mister," Lydia huffed and went into her room to change.

I led Blaine down the hall to my bedroom, showing him my sisters' old bedrooms, my parents' room, the guest room, and the upstairs bath along the way. Each room had been wallpapered by my mother and decorated with the antiques she loved. Except for my sisters' rooms, of course, which remained as they had been when each of them moved out, just like my room.

Blaine stood in the center of my bedroom and looked around at my memorabilia from my days in high school. He picked up the picture of Bill and me.

"What's this?" he asked.

"A picture from a play I did in high school. *Rebel Without a Cause,*" I answered.

"Were you the rebel?" he laughed.

"No. I was never a rebel. I was always the boy out of place, looking for someone to watch over me," I said, realizing I was wandering into new territory.

"I've told you I want to watch over you," he said, returning the picture to its place. He walked to me and placed his hands on my arms. "I want to protect you."

"I know," I said.

Blaine wrapped his arms tightly around me. I felt that warm, safe feeling wash over me.

"I've never had a boy in my room before," I said.

"Oh?"

Blaine smiled and pulled me onto my bed. We laughed, and Blaine rolled on top of me, pinning my shoulders with his hands.

"Say uncle," he teased.

"No!"

"Say it," he insisted.

I strained upward to kiss him. He looked down at me with affection and rolled over to lie on his side next to me.

"That wasn't uncle, but it'll do," Blaine said.

We stared into each other's eyes with wordless contentment, and I realized how much I wanted to tell him that I loved him.

"Ew! Gross! Boy cooties!" Lydia shrieked as she raced into my bedroom, slammed the door, and jumped on my bed. We bounced up and down with her as she laughed.

"She's adopted, I swear," I said to Blaine, who held on to me to keep from falling off the bed.

"If you're done wooing your boyfriend, instead of changing, Mom said dinner will be ready in ten minutes," Lydia announced. She stopped bouncing and rested her head on Blaine's lap. "What'cha doing?"

"Nothing. Go," I demanded, going to the dresser to find something that would meet Aunt Jen's approval.

"Noooo," Lydia said. "I want to play with Blaine, too."

"Why are you acting like an eight-year-old?" I asked, pulling a black sweater over my head.

"Why are you acting like a nervous nelly?" Lydia retorted.

Blaine laughed and lifted Lydia's head off his lap so he could stand up.

"I like this," he said. "So much more fun than my family."

Lydia lay on my bed, pushing back the cuticles on her fingers, obviously not wanting to make any of this easy on me. Blaine continued to wander around my room, waiting for me to finish changing.

"What's this?" he asked.

"That's my brother's most fabulous creation ever," said Lydia, and I realized with horror which picture she was referring to. "Princess 2Di4."

Blaine removed the picture from the dartboard and kept looking from it to me. I could see confusion turn to realization as he finally rested his gaze on me.

Lydia was still looking at me with pride as she rambled on, "2Di4 was legendary in Manhattan. Daniel did her for years, performing at benefits, Pride events, and at Club Chaos. He was the best."

"Really?" Blaine asked. "Yes, our Daniel is quite a good actor."

"The best," Lydia repeated, totally unaware of the tension in the room.

"Lydia, I need a minute with Blaine alone," I whispered.

"I don't—"

"Now, Lydia!" I shouted, interrupting her. She ducked her head and crept out of the room, knowing the tone in my voice all too well.

"Blaine, I don't know what to—"

"I don't know what to say either, Daniel," Blaine interrupted. "She's right, though, you're an excellent actor. You sure had me fooled."

"I never—I didn't—"

"Lie? You didn't lie to me?"

I sank to the bed, defeated.

"I didn't realize you remembered that night. You were so drunk. I did lie to you. I told you I wasn't the Diana impersonator you saw. I was. The way you were talking about her wasn't respectful. It didn't sound to me like you understood what she was. What I was. It made me scared," I said, wanting to cry.

"Scared of what?" Blaine asked.

"I worked hard for years to be proud of myself," I started slowly. Blaine sat next to me as I continued. "I never felt like I belonged.

Not when I was growing up here in this house and certainly not when I first arrived in Manhattan. I wanted to be an actor, but I was too afraid of rejection. I wasn't comfortable with myself as a person. To face casting directors screaming, *Next!* day after day was more than I could bear. Then I discovered drag. Drag was something else entirely. It wasn't me trying to get work in clubs and bars, it was my creations. My characters. I could be anything. Anyone. I could be Marilyn and know, as Marilyn, that nobody was going to say no and tell me *Next!* It was the first time I felt like I was in control."

Blaine's face was too empty for me to discern if he understood, so I went on.

"I made friends who not only understood but embraced what I was doing with open arms. It was Ken who helped me come up with 2Di4. I know it may sound silly, but as 2Di4, I realized I could use drag to benefit the gay community and society. It wasn't only gay people who came to Club Chaos, but straight people, too. And they loved 2Di4. I used my act to show people that, gay or straight, we are all human, with the same needs. The same weaknesses and strengths. They got it. They loved it. They loved her, and I loved that I could be someone to inspire people. It's not like I was Mother Teresa or anything, but I did what I could with my act. And yes, I loved the small bit of fame I had. Well, that 2Di4 had. We were quite famous around town. I felt like what I was doing mattered to people, and I was proud of that. I still am."

Blaine still didn't speak.

"That night when we had dinner and you got drunk, you were speaking very derisively about the drag performers you saw. It seemed like you were judging me without knowing me. Since I wanted to get to know you before I made the same kind of judgment about you, I decided to dodge the situation until we knew each other better."

Blaine still said nothing, and I was starting to feel defensive.

"Yes, I did lie. I wish I hadn't. I wish I'd handled the moment differently. More honestly, anyway. I'm sorry I lied, but I won't apologize for my past. It's all part of who I am."

The silence stretched between us until I wanted to scream. But I refused to keep explaining, and finally Blaine started talking.

"I was tired, upset, and drunk that night. To be honest, I don't really remember a lot of what happened. I probably was boorish and offensive, but that was because of my ignorance. Plus I was terrified. I hadn't been with a guy before. I wanted you so much, but I felt stupid and awkward. You know how inexperienced I was. I admit, I don't understand drag queens so the idea makes me uncomfortable. Now that you've talked about it, I understand a little better." He held up the picture of 2Di4. "I'm not repulsed by this. It's a pretty good picture, actually. You're quite beautiful in it." He placed the picture on the bed behind him and took my hands. "I wish you'd been able to trust me enough to tell me before. I'd like to think you know me better now and that you intended to tell me."

"I wanted to," I said. "The right time never came along. This morning, when my mother told me to invite you for dinner, I knew I needed to stop acting ashamed of my past, even if it was something you couldn't accept. I just . . . I didn't want to lose you."

He smiled and said, "I'm still here. You're obviously a complex person, Daniel, and I want to keep getting to know you."

I suddenly felt a desperate need to tell him that I loved him. But now it might seem like a test, as if he had to say it back to prove he really wasn't upset about my past.

Tomorrow night would be better. We could be alone in his hotel room after eating a relaxing dinner out—

"Oh, hey," I suddenly remembered. "There's a group of people waiting uncomfortably for us downstairs. I bet my mom's wringing her hands, wanting to tell us dinner's getting cold but afraid of what she might see if she comes upstairs."

"Then she should send Lydia," Blaine laughed and kissed me lightly before we left to join my family for dinner.

It was an amazingly laid-back evening. I could tell my family was pleasantly surprised by Blaine, which was only a little annoying, as if they'd thought I'd date someone like Lydia's friend Creed, with his multicolored hair and piercings. Of course, I had in fact dated one or two guys that fit that description, but I'd never invited them home.

I felt a moment's remorse about Jeremy. My parents would probably have liked him, too, if I'd ever had the guts to let them meet him. But we'd always had his family, and that was enough. Maybe mine would be enough for Blaine, too, for a while. It sure didn't sound like his own family would be part of our lives anytime soon.

Of course, it was to our benefit that Jen was present as the focus for my mother's disapproval. Although both women seemed pretty mellow and dinner was peaceful.

Shortly after Jen had left for her hotel, Blaine and I did the dishes, endearing him to my sisters, and my parents settled in front of the television. After the kitchen was clean, Gwendy dove into the hall closet and emerged with, "Yahtzee, anyone?"

Blaine and I looked at each other and laughed, remembering our code word in the office.

"I'd love to play Yahtzee," Blaine said with a gleam in his eye.

"You'll get your chance tomorrow night," I murmured, then said to Gwendy, "You never get tired of losing, do you?"

"Sure she does," Lydia said. "That's why she won't play Scrabble with you."

"I used to play killer Scrabble. But I was even better at Boggle," Blaine said, and my eyes widened. He was certainly no Jeremy.

"Just never play poker with Daniel," Gwendy warned, handing us each a score card and a pencil.

"Yes, my acting skills give me the perfect poker face," I said smugly.

"No, because you cheat," Lydia countered.

"We play what we call full-sheet Yahtzee," Gwendy explained to Blaine. "All six games at once. So it takes a while."

"I've got all night to beat you," Blaine promised.

"Oh, a cocky one. My favorite kind to take down," Gwendy said.

"Mine, too," I said, and Lydia giggled.

Blaine and Gwendy were equally competitive. Lydia and I encouraged them and occasionally switched loyalties to keep things lively. They were both horrified when they realized that Lydia had quietly managed to accumulate the most points. They demanded another full set of six games, which Blaine won.

By that time my parents had long been in bed. Blaine said good night to my sisters and promised Gwendy a rematch. When I walked him to his car, I felt more at ease than I would ever have thought possible.

"This was good," Blaine said. "You don't know how miserable I've been. Your family is great."

"They are pretty great," I agreed. "Believe me, it hasn't always been this way. Maybe one day yours will surprise you, too. It's cold; you should go."

"Sit in my car with me while it warms up," Blaine begged.

We sat in the car, both of us shivering, and I said, "I wish you could just stay here."

"Me, too. Or that you could go with me."

"Tomorrow night," I promised. "Hey, what about Christmas Day? Is it going to be okay with your family?"

"I'll get through it. And then we fly home."

"I can't wait," I said.

"You can't be as eager as I am to get out of Wisconsin," Blaine said fervently.

"I'm just eager to be alone with you."

"Tomorrow night," Blaine mocked me.

I laughed and kissed him good night then got out of the car, shivering as he drove away.

"Tomorrow night," I whispered again, warmed by the idea of a dinner with no tension and time alone with Blaine afterward, when I could tell him and show him all the things I was feeling. It was great to know there would be no more secrets between us.

The next morning I woke up to my mother tapping on the door and coming into my bedroom. When I saw her old green velour robe and the little curlers in her hair, I had to smile. This was nothing like my dream of a few days before, which featured her wafting in and out of my room in a pink dressing gown. This was real, familiar, and comfortable.

"Just bringing in your clean laundry," she said when she saw that I was awake.

"I was going to do that," I said.

"Now you don't have to." She turned to leave the room then turned back. "Danny, I know you're flying back to New York tomorrow night. I don't know about Blaine, but I did want to tell you that if things are uncomfortable for him at his family's, he's welcome to come here."

"Thanks, Mom. I'll tell him," I said, not making a big deal of it. I knew this was my mother's way of apologizing for being reluctant to meet him, as well as her way of showing approval of him. It was turning out to be a great Christmas.

I spent the day helping my sisters bake some of our traditional family desserts and other Christmas goodies. Mary Kate joined us in the afternoon. We were all a few years older than the last time we'd done this, but we easily slipped into old patterns. Only this time, I was the one who had to leave our group because a date was coming to pick me up.

I heard Blaine's car pull into the driveway at seven-thirty. I started down the stairs when I heard Lydia throw open the door and call out, "Daniel! Your date is here."

When I reached the foot of the stairs, I saw Blaine walking onto the front porch with a bottle of wine in his hands. I smiled at him, excited that I would finally get to spend some time alone with him. It would be a night without pressure or a reason to hide any feelings.

"I want to give this to your parents," he explained, holding up the bottle of wine. "To thank them for their hospitality and warmth. Neither of which I've gotten at my own house."

I walked him into the kitchen where my parents were having their evening coffee before heading to the candlelight service at their church. It was one of the occasions they never missed. My mother loved the singing and the Christmas decorations. I was pretty sure my father went only to appease my mother.

They both looked up as Blaine held the bottle in front of him.

"This is a token of appreciation for your hospitality yesterday."

"Blaine, you shouldn't have. This is so wonderful," said my mother, her eyes sparkling.

"Very thoughtful of you," my father added, concise as ever.

"We'd better go before they give our table to someone else," I prompted, afraid that my parents would invite Blaine to church and he'd accept to please them.

We said our goodbyes and walked out to the car. As I got in and slid the seatbelt over my shoulder, Blaine reached behind his seat.

"This is for you."

I turned to see him smiling and holding out a small box wrapped in green paper.

"What is it?" I asked excitedly.

"Open it and find out," he said with a sexy smirk.

He started the car and began driving while I fumbled with the tape. It wasn't giving, so I reverted to my childhood instincts and tore off the paper with greedy zeal. I opened the velvet box inside.

"This is too much, Blaine."

"Nothing is too much for you, Daniel. Put it on."

I slipped the Bvlgari watch onto my wrist.

"It's perfect on you," he said, leaning over to kiss me as we stopped at a traffic light across from the restaurant.

"You don't get your present until tomorrow night," I taunted him.

"I'll get my present tonight, believe me," he said with a satisfied smile.

We parked in the lot next to the restaurant. As Blaine reached to open his door, I caught his arm.

"Wait," I said. "There's something I didn't get a chance to say last night."

"What?"

"I wanted to say thanks for not getting all weird about my past. I really worried about that. It caused me almost as much anxiety as coming out to somebody."

"At the risk of sounding politically incorrect, I'll be totally honest with you," he said. "I don't think I could handle being with a guy who liked to dress as a woman because it turned him on or something. To me, what you did was a job, no different from any acting job. Does that make me a bad person?"

I laughed and said, "No. I appreciate your honesty. We've all got preferences, and I was never turned on by guys who liked me *only* because of my drag persona. But you understand that I have friends who still perform in drag, as well as friends who cross-dress just because they like it. They'll always be part of my life."

"Then maybe one day they'll be part of my life, too," Blaine said. "I've done okay with your friends so far, haven't I?"

"You've done great," I said and gave him another quick kiss, grateful for times when I was pleasantly surprised.

We went inside the busy restaurant and were seated at a table close to the fireplace. It was just how I wanted my Christmas Eve to be. Dozens of poinsettias and wreaths hung throughout the restaurant.

After we ordered, I glanced around. I felt a little disconcerted when I recognized people from my past in Eau Claire. A few of the waiters had been in school with me. At the opposite end of the restaurant was my gym teacher, which made me shudder as I remembered how tortured I'd been almost every day for four years.

A large woman wearing a full-length, faux fur coat was bearing down on our table. She looked like a bear. It took a second for me to recognize who she was. I stood up to greet Bill Hamilton's mother.

"Is that Daniel Stephenson?"

"Hi, Mrs. Hamilton."

Before I knew it, my head was buried in thick fur and a suffocating hug. She shook with laughter, and I struggled slightly to turn my head to the side to heave in a gulp of air. Luckily she gently pushed me away to get a good look at me.

"You are so handsome. Bill asked if I'd seen you recently. Now I can tell him yes. He wants to contact you again. You know where he's living?"

"It's been a while since we were in touch."

"He's back in San Jose, but he does a lot of traveling. He works in casting at Fox. And who is this handsome gentleman?"

"Blaine Dunhill."

I introduced them as Blaine stood with hand outstretched, but she enveloped him in a hug, too. His look of surprise mingled with panic nearly made me lose control. Fortunately the waiter chose that moment to deliver our entrées.

"Well, I must get going and leave you two to your dinner. Here, take Bill's card. He'd be tickled if you gave him a surprise call. Blaine, lovely to meet you."

Mrs. Hamilton hobbled toward the door where Mr. Hamilton was waiting. The sight of them always made me chuckle, as he was as thin as a rail and she was not quite lean.

When Blaine and I sat down, I talked a little about my friendship with Bill while Mrs. Hamilton's words rang in my ears.

"He always thought I should act," I said. "Now he's the one in the business."

"In casting," Blaine said. He watched me a moment then asked, "What are you thinking about?"

"Coincidence. First Jane Gorman told me I should consider a television part. Then my aunt told me it's not a good idea for me to work for my boss. Now Betty Hamilton shows up and tells me my best friend from high school is a casting agent."

"So what are you suggesting?"

"Maybe the time has come for me to pursue an old dream. As long as you and I work together, we'll have to hide our relationship. Even if the agency is okay with you being gay, you know they wouldn't be okay with you dating your assistant."

"I like having you there," Blaine protested.

"I like being there. I love working for you."

"With me," Blaine corrected.

"See? That's part of the problem. You always treat me as an equal, but at Breslin Evans, I'm not your equal. If people find out about us, especially the ones who are jealous of you, that could cause you a lot of trouble."

"I see your point," Blaine said.

"When we go back, let's focus on finding and training the ideal assistant for you."

"Like one who can type?" Blaine asked, laughing.

"That might help," I admitted.

"Can you afford not to work while you're looking for acting jobs?"

"I've got savings. If money gets tight, that'll just push me to try harder."

"Okay," he said reluctantly. "You sure you're not just getting tired of seeing so much of me?"

"Never," I assured him, and he smiled.

A shadow fell over the table. I looked up to see a pale, round face with blue eyes and tight little lips looking down at us. A shower of red hair fell to the shoulders of an elegant young woman who looked less than pleased to see Blaine. It suddenly clicked who this must be.

"Well, Mr. Dunhill, I'm surprised you aren't here with a fresh New York socialite."

I held my tongue as Blaine stood and faced Sydney. My peaceful dinner plans were turning into something quite different.

"This is a surprise." Blaine smiled nervously, briefly glancing my way.

"How sad. Out on Christmas Eve with a man. Probably commiserating over the evils of women."

Sydney didn't even look at me as she tossed her hair over her shoulder. I recognized this as a sign of aggression used by many a drag queen.

"Sydney, I'm in the middle of a meal."

"You ruined our marriage, so forgive me if I ruin your meal. I suppose you're happy now. Do you know how embarrassed I was? To tell my parents, right before Christmas, that I'm getting divorced? To have half the town thinking you left me for Sheila?"

I felt the nerves along my spine twinge with resentment at the way she spit Sheila's name at Blaine.

"Can we talk about this at the bar? Daniel doesn't need to hear it."

"I don't know Daniel. I don't care what he hears. Don't worry; I won't torture you much longer. My friends are waiting by the door."

I looked over my shoulder to see three frosty-looking women shooting eye daggers across the restaurant at Blaine. His ears were turning red. I wished there were something I could do. But I knew my own natural reaction to this kind 'of behavior, honed by years of dealing with much more daunting opponents than these provincial princesses, would not play well in Eau Claire. I had no desire to make things worse for Blaine.

"Here, I don't need this anymore," Sydney snapped as she set a diamond ring on our table next to Blaine's plate. "Soon our marriage will be just a bad memory."

"Sydney, I don't want it to be like this. There's a lot you don't understand."

"I understand that I'm leaving now. Hopefully this will be the last time I see you."

Sydney turned, not waiting for Blaine's response. He sat down with a slightly bewildered look on his face.

"That was bizarre," Blaine said. "Up until now, she's been mostly civil."

"She was showing off for her friends," I explained. "Her pride is probably making her a little bitter. In time, she'll come around."

"You don't know Sydney. Once she cuts someone out of her life, it's for good." He paused to pick at his dinner, which was starting to get cold. Finally he shrugged and said, "Look, I'm happy just being here with you tonight. Let's forget that this happened."

"Fine with me," I said, smiling and stretching my hand across the table.

Blaine misunderstood my gesture and handed me Sydney's ring. My impulse was to drop it. Instead I tucked it into my pocket.

"In case you're wondering if that has any sentimental value, it doesn't. I actually gave Sydney my grandmother's engagement ring, but it didn't suit her. She bought that one later. I'm surprised she gave it to me."

"Just another display for her friends," I said. "You can mail it to her from New York."

Blaine's green eyes were even more intense when they filled with unshed tears. I wanted to be alone with him, to hold him and make him feel better. Now that I'd experienced Sydney in person, I had nothing but compassion for him.

"I know it's not easy," I said. "Even a bad relationship—"

"That's not why I'm upset," Blaine said. "I should have told her who you are. To me, I mean. I shouldn't be afraid to take your hand in public when you hold it out to me. I shouldn't be afraid to look at you and say—"

"I love you," I interrupted.

"Right. Because I do. And I should tell you," Blaine said.

"Wrong. I mean *I* love *you*. It's my nature to plan everything or to wait for the perfect time to say what I want to say. Just like telling you the truth about 2Di4. The perfect time is when I feel it. I feel it now. You don't have to make public announcements or displays. You don't have to explain me or us to anybody. None of that matters. What matters is that I love you. And that—"

"I love you," he said, only now his eyes were bright with happiness.

"Right."

"Let's get out of here," he said. "If you're still hungry, we can have food delivered to my hotel room later."

"You're not getting your Christmas present early," I reminded him.

"I already got it," he answered.

He dropped some money on the table, and we walked outside. The packed snow crunched under our feet. As I started toward our parked car, Blaine caught my sleeve. A flatbed truck had rounded the corner too fast and something fell into the street.

"Wait," Blaine urged, and darted into the street to bring it back to me. "What is it?"

I looked at the small sapling in the black pot and said, "I think it's probably a variety of spruce."

"Our first Christmas tree," Blaine said. "If we can get it back to New York, do you think you can grow it in your garden?"

His hopeful expression made me smile, and I answered, "I think I can grow almost anything in that garden."

I held tightly to the potted spruce as we walked to the car. My mind felt as clear and clean as the Wisconsin air. I finally understood what I'd been looking for. Home wasn't what I'd left in Eau Claire or what I'd created in Manhattan. It wasn't what I'd failed to keep with Jeremy or lost with 2Di4. Home was believing in myself enough to fully experience life's losses as well as its celebrations. And it was the strength to trust this man beside me, who draped his arm over my shoulders to warm me in the winter night.

	DATE DUE	
NOV 2 6 2007		
MAR 1 5 2008		
AUG 1 2 2008		
NOV 2 0 2008		